FORSAKEN FATE

RUTHLESS GODS: WOLF GOD, BOOK 3

VERONICA DOUGLAS

For Carol and Mark

DREAMSPIRE
ORACLE'S TEMPLE
THE FORT
REALM OF THE UNDYING COURT
SACRED GLADE
SARION'S PORTAL
RIVERBEND
DEAD FOREST
FROSTFALL
DEAD FOREST
MIST SEAS
SHADOWSTONE
THE 3 PYLONS
MISTVEIL MOUNTAINS
MISTWIND HARBOR
SOUTHERN ROAD TO AUREN'S DOMAIN
THE WOLF GOD'S REALM IN THE DREAMLANDS

<h1 style="text-align:center">OUR STORY SO FAR...</h1>

In case you need a refresher...

Book I: Wolf God

When the **Dark Wolf God** broke free of his prison in the **Dreamlands** and invaded the city of **Magic Side, Chicago**, our heroine **Samantha Bennet** stood against him with her pack. The **Mood Goddess** gave them three **moonstones** filled with her power to recharge the spells of his prison. The Dark God tried to stop them, but Sam saved her friends by cursing him with one of the moonstones. In a rage, he forced Sam's best friend **Savannah** to kill her.

Although Samantha died, the **Three Fates** weren't done with her yet. With the help of the Moon's magic, they brought her back for a purpose they didn't reveal.

While the Dark Wolf God was stopped, he wasn't defeated. Samantha was approached by **Sarion**, an emissary of **Ayanna, Queen of the Fae** who wanted Sam's help to destroy him once and for all.

Unfortunately, the Dark Wolf God got to Samantha first and

imprisoned her in his fortress at **Shadowstone**. He believed that she could heal the curse she'd caused. To his frustration, she didn't have magic of her own—or so she thought.

Sam quickly learned all was not as it seemed in the Dreamlands. The fae weren't innocent victims but were attacking shifter villages and had infested the Wolf God's realm with vines that leeched the life and magic from his land. They fought together to protect the werefox village of **Frostfall**, where he saved her life. She began to see him as a ruthless protector of his people and to think of him as *Cadean*. She also learned she was half-fae.

When Sam witnessed Cadean use an artifact called the moonshard to temporarily escape his prison and destroy a fae village, she vowed to stop him and protect the innocent people on both sides of the border. Sam drugged him and stole the moonshard, then fled with the help of **his brother, Auren**. The Dark God pursued, but she stabbed him with the moonshard and turned the barrier solid with her newfound magic.

Book 2: Hunter's Kiss

Samantha was just as trapped in Auren's realm as Cadean's, and worse, Auren was messing with her mind. Desperate to get Samantha back, Cadean realized that he needed to earn her trust. Although he couldn't leave his prison he could **shadow-cast** to her. He offered a truce and trained her to resist Auren's influence.

Auren arranged a surprise meeting with the Queen Ayanna, who still wanted Sam's help to kill the Dark Wolf God. Ayanna revealed she had taken Sam's mother hostage, giving her no choice but to return with her to **Dreamspire**, her palace. Sam learned that the fae were suffering from a withering curse which caused them to die young. Ayanna and her inner court, however, could prolong their lives indefinitely by eating the fruit of the vines.

Samantha began training with a group of fae, making an enemy of the most powerful girl in her cohort, **Asta**. She also made an enemy of **General Slaine**, who suspected her motives and began to stalk her. Using his power to shadow-cast, Cadean helped her survive the queen's trials and uncover the sinister underbelly of Dreamspire. Sam realized that the queen was stealing her power and planned to kill her. She also discovered a secret chamber—the Well of Life—where the roots of the vines converged. She watched in horror as the queen sacrificed Asta to the vines and fed them her blood. Before she could escape, she was attacked by General Slaine, who she killed using Cadean's **black axe**. He wanted her to destroy the vines, but she refused, as doing so would also destroy the entire fae city.

The queen tried to stop Sam from escaping and murdered Sam's mother. Sam and Sarion made it across the border with Cadean's help, but Sam knew the queen would not stop hunting her. To stop the vines and the queen's army, Sam used her control over the barrier to transform it into a solid crystal wall. The process burned her alive, but Cadean fought through the magic of the **pylons** to heal her. Now fully aligned with the Dark Wolf God, she vowed to find a way to protect the people of the Dreamlands and kill the queen once and for all.

And that is where our story begins...

1

———

The Dark Wolf God's Realm, one week after Samantha's escape from Dreamspire

Cadean

Soft bands of shadows and moonlight stretched across Samantha's sleeping form, illuminating her bare skin and golden hair. She'd cast the heavy comforter aside, leaving it twisted and rumpled, as if she were searching for something in her dreams.

With one arm draped above her head and the other folded across her chest, she was agonizingly beautiful. When she'd first arrived in my lands, watching her sleep had been my secret pleasure. Now, it made my heart ache. I couldn't savor her peaceful beauty without also seeing the woman I'd nearly lost.

She'd been consumed by magic after transforming the Moon's barrier, and even now, she had no idea how close she'd come to death. It had taken all my power and Mel's craft to heal her savage burns and wake her from the coma.

My throat tightened at the bitter truth. She'd nearly died protecting my people *because I couldn't*. The Moon and the Fates had tied my hands behind my back and left me powerless to defend them or the woman I loved.

And yet, she slept as if there were nothing to fear. As if the Queen of the Fae weren't circling us like a rabid dog. As if she hadn't nearly died escaping the fae the week before.

Her chest rose and fell in hypnotic motion, drawing me closer, bidding me to nestle against the soft curves of her body. But I couldn't rest, not while she was in danger, not until Ayanna's head was on a spike.

I tore myself away and grabbed the pack I'd prepared, then strode to the balcony. Without daring to look back, I stepped up on the railing and flung myself over the edge and into the night sky.

Shadows burst around me as I took the form of a great horned owl. With keen eyes and quiet wings, it gave me a perspective I didn't have as a wolf or a man—a chance to see my realm in full and to be reminded of everything that was at stake.

I softly beat my wings as I soared over my kingdom. High above me, the Moon's barrier glistened, a glass dome dividing my realm from that of the fae.

Not the Moon's, Samantha's.

My little wolf had claimed it when she'd taken control.

For now, the shimmering wall prevented the queen's vines and soldiers from penetrating my lands, but I knew the peace wouldn't last. Ayanna would strike again soon.

As the night stretched into the darkest hours of the morning, the forested slopes of the red mountains beneath me gave way to a wide plain spotted with dark shapes: the sod-covered homes of Frostfall. Once a peaceful village with smoke rising from the squat stone chimneys, it was deserted now. The werefoxes had moved on to Mistwind Harbor and other havens in my realm, away from the queen's bloody raids and the agonizing memories they'd left in their wake.

Yet one light remained, flickering at the edge of the forest—one soul who feared neither the queen nor me.

I tipped my wings and circled the abandoned town, descending toward the source of the light. Flying deftly between the trees, I landed in front of a small cabin and transformed back into the shape of a man.

The front door stood ajar, with golden-orange firelight streaming through the gap.

Apparently, Sigrun had been expecting me.

I gently pushed the door open, ducking my head to fit within her tiny abode. The old werefox stirred the embers in her hearth with a long iron prod, then turned to measure me with a predatory gaze. "I thought you would've come to me weeks ago, Lord Wolf. But then again, I cannot see the future."

"I've been busy dealing with the Queen of the Fae."

She returned her iron poker to its rack. "I assume you actually mean that you've been busy with Samantha. Frankly, I'm surprised you managed to leave your bedroom. Men are awfully weak when it comes to that kind of thing."

My neck heated. Samantha was a siren. When she was awake, I couldn't resist her, and when she slept, I could barely bring myself to leave her side. We'd clung to the sanctuary of each other for as long as we could, but I couldn't hide from my duty any longer, or the questions that plagued me.

Sigrun's single eye twinkled as she gestured for me to sit on one of the small stools by the fire. The table beside it had been set with a clay bowl filled with herbs and two mugs of golden mead—one for her and one for me.

I hesitated a fraction of a second, and she revealed a toothy smile. "Afraid I'll nip?"

My jaw ticked with annoyance. "I'm always wary of those the Fates have touched."

Sigrun took a long drink from her mug and chuckled. "If

you're this afraid of a little old woman, then it's no surprise your kingdom is falling apart."

"You're no little old woman."

Her grin widened. "No. I'm not. Now, are you going to sit, or are you going to stand there until Queen Ayanna tears your balls off?"

Sigrun drained her mug as I laid my pack down and took a seat on the ornately carved chair. "I have questions."

"Questions are free, but answers have a cost. I assume you know the price."

I pulled two bottles of Selene's mead from my pack, and Sigrun greedily plucked them from my hands. "Fates, I miss that girl. Your gift is well accepted, but of course, I assume you're prepared to pay the true cost, Lord Wolf?"

My fists knotted, and the hair on my neck bristled. "I am."

Sigrun was no werefox. What she was, I was uncertain, but I knew she fed on knowledge like it was venison and on secrets as greedily as she drank her mead.

The true cost was to be *seen*, to allow Sigrun to strip bare my soul and peer inside. She would see past the thousands of lies and delusions I'd woven around myself and find the sin and shame and doubt that I'd buried. In exchange, she gave answers the Three Fates did not want others to know. The secrets of a god would be a meal beyond all others. I hoped the answers would measure up.

Sigrun uncorked one of the bottles and refilled her mug, a greedy glint of anticipation in her eye. "Let us begin."

Moving like a viper, she seized the little bowl of herbs from the table and hurled it into the fire. The clay shattered, and the contents sizzled and hissed. Plumes of white mist twisted upward, and the scents of salt, angelica, moss, and birchwood whirled about us. I breathed in the damp air, and fire filled my lungs.

For a moment, there was nothing. Then, the shadows of the room changed—no longer leaning away from the fire, but each in the direction of its own choosing. The colors of the house began to run like paint bleeding down canvas.

Sigrun covered the scarred socket of her missing eye with her palm, then slowly pulled her fingers away from her face as if removing an invisible mask. A sapphire light blazed where her missing right eye had been. Her magic ripped through me like wildfire, devouring me from within and tearing truths from my soul. My ribs became iron, each breath a struggle.

"So many secrets and so many lies," she said in a raspy voice. "What is it you wish to know from me Lord Wolf? Because I know more than I ever imagined I could about you."

"Who is Samantha Bennet?" I demanded. "Why did the Fates bring her back?"

Sigrun's eyes dilated, and as the shadows danced around us, her voice flowed in and out like the ocean. "Both shifter and fae, she is a tool of the Fates and a child of two worlds—both the waking world and dreaming. But all this, you already know, Lord Wolf. What is your true question?"

It was the one that haunted me relentlessly—the one I asked every time I looked at her, every time she moved or spoke or breathed. My mouth turned dry, but I forced the words out anyway. "Is Samantha Bennet my mate?"

Sigrun revealed her sharp teeth. "Yes. But you must both accept the bond."

My ribs felt as if they were caving in against my heart. "Why would the Fates pair a mortal with a god? Why create a bond that can only end with both souls broken?"

"I cannot tell you, only that the Fates brought her back for a purpose."

The words tore a low growl from my throat. The Fates had been fucking with the world for millennia. They were callous and cruel, and they had no qualms about sacrificing mortals to achieve their aims.

I wouldn't let Samantha be their pawn.

Shadows of the room swirled around me as my fury rose. "The queen's oracle claimed she was a coin spinning on edge with the power to free me or bring me to my knees. Are the Fates trying to use Samantha to destroy me? To break my soul through her death?"

Both gods and demigods had been broken by love before.

"Arrogant beast!" Sigrun spat, her sapphire eye blazing with reproach. "Why must all men think the universe revolves around them?"

Frustration simmered under my skin. "I'm worried that the Fates will destroy *her* to get to me. If for a moment I thought that was true, I'd banish her from my kingdom and bear the grief of not seeing her ever again."

"How noble." Sigrun sneered. "Are you truly so self-absorbed? Her fate isn't about you or your heart, but about what *she* is to achieve in this world. And yet here you stand, trying to make it about *you*."

Heat seared my jaw as my stomach churned. It was not my fate I cared for, but hers.

"Then tell me what her purpose is," I demanded roughly. "Is it to protect my people? To defeat the queen? To save the fae? Tell me, old woman."

Sigrun shook her head. "No one knows the true motives of the Fates, not even I."

I flexed my fist, my impatience seething. "Then can you see what will become of her?"

Sigrun's fierce expression softened, and her mouth turned down. "Samantha will die. She was returned for one task, and when that task is complete, the thread of her life will unwind."

A suffocating hollowness settled over me. At last, I whispered, "How can I stop it?"

The old fox shook her head. "Samantha is mortal. You may be a god, but you cannot fight death, Cadean. You cannot stop it."

"What if she never completes her task?" I asked in desperation. "Would it stop her from dying? Would she..."

Sigrun's blue eye snapped back to me with an accusatory glare. "And what would you do, greedy wolf? Keep her for yourself? Lock her in your tower to die of old age?"

"If I had to," I snarled. "To keep her safe from the Fates."

"You are a fool, Lord Wolf," Sigrun said pityingly. "If you try to keep Samantha from her purpose, it will break her heart, *and you know it*. Anyone can see that her purpose is her spark. Without it, she will wither into nothing."

The landslide of helplessness consumed me. "And if I cannot save her or stop her, then what am I to do?"

She stirred the fire with iron poker, then sat. "I cannot tell you that."

A wretched silence drifted between us, and finally, I scrubbed a hand across my face. "What would *you* do, old fox? Because I have no answers."

She opened her mouth to speak, but I held up my hand to silence her. "I'm not asking Sigrun the mystic—or whatever the hell you are. I know *her* answer: nothing. I'm asking Sigrun, *my friend*. The old woman I've shared wine and mead and whiskey with, the one I've sheltered in my realm for centuries without asking anything in return."

The glowing blue light faded from her absent eye, and Sigrun gently laid her hand on my arm. "Death comes to all mortals, Cadean. But if I had a mate, I would stand by them against the world. Whatever the cost. Whatever their fate."

2

———————

Samantha

I stalked through the deserted halls deep beneath Ayanna's palace, following the thick purple vines that led toward the Well of Life, the heart of the fae kingdom. I could almost feel the heartbeat pulsing through the vines as they drained the lifeforce from Cadean's realm.

The world stretched and twisted with each step, and the shadows moved in unnatural ways. I knew it was a dream, but my heart was pounding all the same. The danger was real.

In the waking world, dreams were nothing. Harmless visions. Illusions of a restless mind idly shifting through old memories and the remains of the day. But I no longer lived in Magic Side or the waking world—I was part of the Dreamlands now, and here, dreams could be deadly. The boundaries between what was real and imagined were blurred. If you were wounded in a dream, you might wake up bleeding, and if you died, you might never wake at all.

Torches lit the walls with dim, flickering light, and I froze as Queen Ayanna's shadow slipped through the corridor ahead of me. Footsteps sounded from behind, and as I turned back, her shadow drifted across the other end of the corridor.

I sniffed the air, trying to separate the illusion from what was real.

It felt like I had been stalking the queen for hours, though time had little meaning in dreams. Whenever I drew near, she slipped away into the darkness as if playing an idle game of keep-away.

I hurried down the corridor toward the dying echoes of footsteps even as doubt tore at me. Was I dreaming of the queen, or was she dreaming of me? Could she be toying with me in her sleep? If so, she doubtless knew how to navigate dreams far better than I did.

Evil bitch.

I refused to relent. She'd twisted my mother's mind and murdered her before my very eyes. Nothing in the waking world or the Dreamlands would keep me from my vengeance.

I paused and listened, stilling my breath and heart. I wouldn't be her prey any longer. In this dream, *I* would be the hunter. Perhaps if I could catch her here, I could hurt her for real.

A shadow moved ahead, and I reached for my magic. A tingle of power skated across my skin, then faded, like water slipping through my fingers. I reached for it again, but in its place, I found only exhaustion.

My lip curled. Fuck it. I'd gotten by my whole life without my magic, and I could get by now. I extended my claws. Magic or not, they could still tear out a throat.

I followed the queen's scent until I emerged into the Well of Life. The deep pit descended hundreds of feet below me, with columned sides that hid a spiraling staircase. It led down to the grate where Ayanna had sacrificed Astra right in front of me.

The woman had made my life miserable while I was in Dreamspire, but she didn't deserve to die.

Everything was exactly as I remembered it, even the shattered throne and fresh blood. Almost everything. Here, in the dream, the vines were different. I hadn't noticed at first, but some had tips spiked with thorns.

No, not thorns—fangs. My mouth soured. Of course they did. They fed on blood, after all.

As if woken by the thought, two of the vines ripped themselves from the wall and slithered forward over the stones, fangs bared like vipers. I dodged back as one lashed out, but the other struck my calf. I twisted and tore it free, severing the end with my claws. Blood soaked my palm and ran down my leg from the open wounds.

All across the walls, the vines began to writhe, stirred by the scent of blood. Dozens of serpent-like tendrils coiled into the air, and I backed away.

This dream was rapidly getting out of hand.

I turned and ducked deeper into the tunnels, trying to wake myself by pinching my skin.

The queen laughed from somewhere in the darkness. "Run, little wolf! You cannot hide forever."

I drove my feet against the stones and sprinted forward, trying to find some way to force myself awake. Suddenly, my ankle jerked, and I slammed onto my knees. Ignoring the pain, I tried to rise, but the vines were on me in seconds, some coiling around my arms, others tearing at me with their fangs. Tendrils like little tongues forced their way into the wounds and began to lap up the blood.

My magic flowed into them along with my life.

"Cadean!" I shouted in desperation, but my cry was choked off as the vines twisted around my throat. Fighting for air, I clawed and tore at them, but where one snapped, two grew back in its place. They wound around my arms and chest. Tears forced themselves into the corners of my ·eyes as my vision began to blur. My lungs burned, and darkness pressed in.

And then I gasped as the pressure on my throat released. The vines disintegrated into fine ash beneath my fingers and sloughed off me in silken clouds as I clambered to my feet.

What had happened? I still felt the distorted reality of the dream.

My skin prickled as the tunnel grew cold and the air turned stale. A suffocating power radiated from the shadows, pounding against me like a rainstorm and carrying with it the scent of incense and the desert at night—a signature I didn't recognize.

"Who's there?" I rasped through bruised vocal cords.

"You do not belong to the queen," a voice growled from the darkness. The words were cold and distant and reminded me of the sound of stones crumbling and of wind whipping through sand.

Slowly, the darkness morphed into the towering form of a giant jackal, almost as large as Cadean in his wolf form. But where the Dark God's wolf was muscled, the creature before me was sleek and lean—though just as deadly. His teeth were tinged with blood, and I had no doubt he could have effortlessly bitten me in two. It wasn't his bite that I feared, however, but rather the deathly power that emanated from him in waves. This was a god, and not one I knew.

"Cadean!" I shouted.

"You don't belong to the Wolf God, either." The voice chuckled. "Your soul is mine, Samantha Bennett, and mine alone."

I backed away from his golden gaze. "Like hell it is."

The jackal prowled forward, his fur shifting from obsidian to ash and back again.

My back bumped against the wall, and I sucked in a sharp breath as my jaw clenched.

"You escaped me once before," the black jackal growled in warning. "Never again. I will never let you go."

Something in the tone of his words filled me with a terror like I'd never known. I spun and fled. Whatever powers I possessed, I couldn't stand against this god.

The corridor shook behind me as I ran, shuddering as the beast drew closer with every stride. I skidded to a stop as I burst back into the Well of Life, and then without hesitation, I hurled myself over the railing.

I plunged down, two dozen feet, a hundred. The world slowed as the floor raced toward me, and I twisted back to look up. Those haunting golden eyes stared down from above, and I could hear the jackal laughing.

My body slammed back against the mattress, and I gasped for air, my spine arching in pain.

I thrust my hands to my sides, searching the rumpled comforter beside me.

"Cadean? Are you there?" I croaked.

But the bed was empty, and I was alone in his chambers.

Dizziness clouded my vision as my heart hammered against my chest. I sat up and rubbed my throat. It was sore and felt bruised from the vines in my dream. I dropped my gaze to the red spatters of blood that stained the sheets.

No wonder Cadean rarely slept.

Who the fuck was *that*?

I was surrounded by gods and monsters—Cadean, Auren, the Moon, the queen, and now this new god. They all thought they had a claim on me.

"To hell with them." I shoved myself up off the mattress. My legs ached as if I'd been running for hours, and I felt drained in a way I'd never felt before—at least, not since Ayanna had tried to steal my magic.

Where was Cadean? Each night, I'd fall asleep in his arms,

but he was never there when I woke. He always had an excuse—he'd been stalking the border or hunting assassins or looking for some way to protect me when all I needed was to be in his arms. They were the only place in the Dreamlands that I would ever find comfort.

I pulled on my shirt from the day before and a pair of breeches, then checked the bathroom and the balcony. No sign of him.

I headed out into the hall. Four wolf shifters were standing guard, intently monitoring the cold stone hall. The sergeant dipped his head. "My lady."

"Where's the Wolf God gone now?" I asked.

"Not sure," the sergeant said. "He didn't leave by this passage."

That meant little. Cadean could fly and teleport through the shadows.

I shook my head. "Take me to the throne room."

The shifters followed me through the dark corridors of Shadowstone and down the spiraling staircase. Auren and Queen Ayanna had used bodyguards to spy on me and control my movements. Not Cadean's guards. He had given them all a single, unwavering order: *protect her with your life.*

The truth was that if the queen's assassins were skilled enough to breach Shadowstone's defenses, the guards would be of little use, which was why I was with Fang or Melanthe or Wulfric most times. I didn't chafe at their presence. I sensed Cadean's desperation for some way to protect me when he was gone, and if having them at my side gave his soul a little rest, then so be it. He had enough on his mind.

So did I.

By transforming the Moon's barrier into a wall, I had found a way to protect Cadean's people—but not the fae. They were still in Ayanna's grasp. Their withering curse made them die young, so they served her, desperately hoping she would let them eat the fruit of her vines.

Did I have the withering curse, too, because I was part fae? Would *I* die young? Was that why death was in my dreams?

Or perhaps it was the path fate had put me on.

We reached the heavy oak door that led to the back of the great hall, and I placed my hand against the carvings of wolves and stags. I pushed through, stepping into the room, though I knew Cadean wasn't inside. I would've sensed his presence long before, lapping over my skin like waves and pulling me forward like a riptide.

Enormous trees lit by torches towered above me, living pillars that supported a roof of stars. Cadean's throne of antler and bone sat on the wide dais at the end of the great hall. I found him there often, brooding in the dim light. Empty now, it was simply a reminder of everything that was at stake. Not just my life, but an entire kingdom—all of us depending on the strength of a god who I feared was growing weaker every day, trapped within the prison of his own realm.

Somehow, I would find a way to help him, to save both his realm and the lands beyond from the fates-damned Queen of the Fae.

3

———

Mistwind Harbor, Cadean's Realm
Samantha

Cadean was brooding and distant when he returned to Shadowstone, so I kept my distance and didn't mention the dream. But like a festering wound, it preyed on my mind and mood, so I was relieved when I had an excuse to head into town two days later—a distraction to take my mind off the dream, the queen, and *him.*

Unfortunately, letting go was easier said than done.

I'd spent nearly three months in the Dreamlands, and most of that time, I'd been imprisoned or fighting for my life. Even now that I'd escaped and there was a solid wall between us and the fae, I couldn't relax.

"Everything okay?" Mel asked as we strolled through the streets of Mistwind Harbor.

Although the port town was quaint by Chicago standards, it was the largest city in Cadean's realm. The streets hummed with noise and activity, and a mélange of scents swirled in the chill air: crackling hearth fires pushing away the cold, sweet peddlers and bakers, and shifters of all breeds—werewolves, foxes, bears, even some I suspected were birds or seals.

I shrugged and shifted my new leather jacket around my shoulders. "Just Ayanna on my mind."

She gave me a stern look. "For the first time in centuries, the people of this realm are safe, and you're safe, too. You can permit yourself a moment to breathe. You nearly burned yourself to death trying to wield the Moon's magic, and you need to rest."

My palms itched with suspicion. "Are those *your* thoughts or Cadean's marching orders?"

The Wolf God had grown more and more agitated over the last week, and now he was on guard like never before. Every time I suggested experimenting with the barrier or trying to cross it, he killed the conversation and slipped into agitated brooding.

"They're Cadean's thoughts *and* mine," Mel said, her tone putting an end to the conversation.

We headed toward the blacksmith's shop, taking the harbor front road. My senses filled with the taste of salt, the moist scent of the surf, and the roar of the waves crashing against the breakers. Heavy mist shrouded the far horizon, and somewhere in the distance, I knew that the barrier cut through the sea itself. I'd heard tales of ships that had come upon the wall while navigating the mists and had to abruptly change course to keep from colliding.

"How far does the sea go?" I asked Mel. "What's on the other side?"

"It's endless," she replied. "Eventually, the water becomes mist itself. There are islands of dreams floating out there, like the ones Cadean used to build this realm, but they're always moving and shifting. You might run your ship aground, and after the mist cleared away, find yourself stranded high and dry in the middle of a desert or jungle."

I shook my head in astonishment. There was so much I didn't know about the Dreamlands, and yet somehow, it had become my home.

The ringing of hammers and the scent of hot iron greeted us as we reached the forge. Half a dozen brawny shifters hammered away beneath the roof of the enormous smithy. Shirtless and soaked with sweat, they were enough to make a girl go a little weak in the knees.

The master smith was deftly turning a red-hot blade back and forth, working the glowing edges. He looked up as we entered and nodded in acknowledgement. A burly bear shifter returned the blade to the coals, then retrieved a sword in a polished leather scabbard from the rack. The pommel was the head of a snarling wolf, and the sapphire-inlaid cross guard ended in a pair of vicious, claw-like spikes that seemed just as deadly as the blade itself.

General Slaine's sword.

Not Slaine's. Mine. I'd claimed the blade when I vowed vengeance for my mother, and it would be the blade that I rammed through Queen Ayanna's neck one day, even if it killed me.

"It's a magnificent weapon," the master smith said as he handed the heavy sword over with a look of expectant pride. "I simply sharpened it and cleaned the steel, but does the new scabbard meet your approval?"

"It's beautiful," I said as I lovingly traced my fingers over the intricate leatherwork. It was dark brown, polished to a shine, and decorated with an interwoven pattern of severed vines—a reminder of the job I had yet to do.

His hearty grin broadened. "Well, the wife will be pleased. She normally works the iron with me, but she's even better with leather. And she has an artistic eye that I never acquired. She does our etching as well, should you ever need a design in steel."

I hung the scabbard at my side and adjusted the position so that it rode comfortably. The blade was longer than I remembered. Wearing it would take some getting used to, but I had to admit, it looked pretty badass.

The smith helped me reposition it slightly. "Now, like I mentioned before, it's a rather large blade for...er...such a slight individual as yourself."

I glared. He meant that it was too big for a woman to wield. We'd been through this dance before.

His heat-flushed cheeks turned a deeper red beneath my withering stare, and he cleared his throat. "Of course, I know this one has a special meaning for you, my lady, and it will look right fine—but I have others that might be a bit more practical as an armament."

In a practiced motion, I stepped back and smoothly unsheathed the blade, pointing it in his direction. The tip didn't waver. "I've killed plenty with this one already, but thanks so much for your considerate offer."

He swallowed. "Certainly."

Slaine had called the blade Wolfeater. But I'd killed him, and it needed a new name now.

"Wolf's Vengeance," I said as I sank into cobra stance. "That is what this sword will be called."

The name felt right. The weapon would know its purpose, just as I knew mine.

The smith bowed slightly. "May it honor its name and bearer."

"The new grip feels good," I said, testing the blade. I'd had him replace the leather wrapping on the hilt in an attempt to remove the memory of Slaine's greasy hands.

Shifting my feet, I tried two of the stances Kassian had taught me. Iron tower first, and then I dropped into scorpion. Yes, it felt *very good*.

"Wrong." A familiar voice tsked from behind me.

My heart jumped, and I glanced back, still holding the form. Fang. The damn vampire had stolen up behind us and was shaking his head with a mildly perturbed expression. Sometimes, I felt like just thinking of the prick would summon him.

"Where the hell did you come from, Fang?" I asked, holding my stance for Kassian's inspection out of habit. He'd been working with me every day, and the routine was drummed into my skull by now.

Kass circled, then gently nudged my rear foot with his. I stumbled a little, and he scoffed. "It's like you're inviting someone to knock you over. Forget about the sword— the only thing you need to master is the footwork."

"I was just testing how the new grip felt."

"You were showing off and being lazy—a bad combination." He kicked my forward foot, but this time, I held my ground.

"Better," he muttered. "But tomorrow, we need to talk about your knees."

I eyed the vampire suspiciously. "Did you want something, or does the sound of shoddy footwork summon you like a genie?"

"I found the werefox woman you asked about."

My mood brightened, and I instantly forgave him for his incessant nagging. "Selene? She's here?"

"Working in a local brewery. It's not far."

My heart felt lighter than it had in ages. She was safe. We all were.

We paid the smith, and then Kass led us to a tall wooden building with overhanging balconies. Despite the cold, locals were clustered on long outdoor benches in sets of two and three, drinking ale and laughing. I pushed through the front door and instantly spotted Selene. She was head down, energetically mopping the floor on the far side of the room.

"Selene!" I shouted over the midafternoon din and made my way around the surprisingly packed tables.

The pretty werefox looked up in surprise, her expression as pale as if she'd seen a ghost. Then a broad grin cut her face, and she dropped her mop against the wall. "Sam!"

Her arms wrapped around me in a forceful embrace as we came together. "Fates, it's good to see you. I've heard so many things—that you'd run off with Auren, that you'd been captured by the queen of the fae, that..." She hesitated, studying my face. "That you control the wall now."

"All true." I grinned, stepping back out of her arms. "But what about you? I heard that everyone abandoned the village."

"What you see is what you get," she said, curtseying playfully. But then her smile faded slightly. "We all moved on when the fae attacks got worse. At least I found a job in a brewery. It's not the same as making mead, but it's a start."

Mopping floors was a long way from running her own meadery. Losing it had to be a gut punch.

"Why don't you return to Frostfall? The queen can't cross the barrier anymore."

Selene shrugged. "The cold months are hard enough there as it is, and we lost a lot of winter stores in the raids before the wall went up. A lot of people, too. I think for many the memory is a little raw, so we'll see what spring brings."

Meaning that she and her people would wait and see if the wall would truly keep the queen and her army at bay. I couldn't blame them. Reports were that she was massing an army on the other side, and it was likely rumors had spread.

Selene pulled me toward the bar. "Come, let's grab a drink and speak of happier things."

She motioned for two mugs of cask ale, then pulled up a seat. I checked over my shoulder. Kass and Mel were in a back booth arguing—his posture suggested he was being an ass, and Mel was upbraiding him for the sport of it. It amazed me how accustomed I'd grown to their company...and their friendship.

The bartender thumped two briming mugs of beer down in front of us, sloshing the head over the rim. Selene drank deeply and then gave me a wicked smile. "So, you're shacking up with the Wolf God. That has to be spicy."

I nearly choked on my beer. The little vixen went straight for the jugular, didn't she? Wiping the foam from my lips, I glanced around. "Um...we're in a bar full of shifters with excellent hearing. Maybe we should save that kind of talk for another day."

"You can't fault a girl for being curious, love." Selene leaned in. "You owe me details, anyway—it was my dress that helped you first catch him at our feast."

That was somewhat of a revisionist history, but I could tell by the twinkle in her eye she wouldn't be dissuaded. "I still owe you a new one."

"Never mind that. It was freely given, though I'll gladly take all the gory details of your lovemaking in exchange."

But I'd stopped listening. Something was wrong. The bartender was staring past me with a wary expression I knew too well: trouble.

I looked over my shoulder. For one instant, I caught a glimpse of two werewolves in the doorway with weapons out—and then I saw the truth. They were fae disguised by a glamour.

Fucking hell. Assassins.

4

Samantha

I leapt to my feet and shouted as one of the fae assassins held his hands up, releasing a blast of crackling light that slammed me against the oaken bar. I dropped to the ground, gasping for breath, my skin screaming in pain.

Pandemonium erupted as horrified patrons leapt from their seats. I could see through the glamour because I was half fae, but to them, it would seem like a pair of werewolves had started slinging spells.

Disentangling my new scabbard from the rungs of the stool, I thrust myself up off the ground.

A ball of light flared in the second assassin's hand, and as swiftly as an adder's strike, he hurled a searing blast of magic straight at us.

I summoned my shield of moonlight, blocking the blast. Unfortunately, strong stances weren't just the domain of sword-play, and the impact knocked me back against the bar again. I gasped as my spine rammed into the counter, but at least my shield absorbed the crackling burst of magic.

One of the fae drew a blade, but the other yanked him backward and out the door as Kass vaulted over a table, sword out and fangs bared. They fled with the bloodthirsty vampire on their heels.

You're fucked now, boys. I dismissed my shield and threw myself forward in pursuit. How the hell did the queen's assassins get through the barrier?

I burst out the doors and slowed for a moment as my eyes adjusted to the light of day. The bastards had split up. Kass raced toward the waterfront in pursuit of one, but the other was already halfway up the street, running as fast as he could in the opposite direction.

Feet pounding against the cobblestones, I sprinted along the street, dodging frightened onlookers as I ran. The assassin was fast, but I was faster—that was, as long as the prick didn't unleash his wings and take to the air.

My assailant glanced over his shoulder, then darted left into an alley. I swung around the corner at top speed, spotting my quarry at the far end of the narrow street. Two strides in, a dark shape exploded from a shadowed doorway and rammed me against the wall. I grunted as the bite of a blade raked across my ribs.

I stumbled backward and reached for my blade, but the blast of magic from the far end of the alley lifted me up off my feet and into the air. My back slammed into the cobblestones, and the breath exploded from my lungs, leaving me gasping in pain.

My head rolled to the side as a dark shape started running down the alley toward me, magic still crackling around his hand. Apparently, the assassin had a friend.

The bastard that had knocked into me drew a knife and lunged for my throat, but I summoned my shield in a blaze of light, blocking his strike. As he pressed his blade against the magic barrier, I released the spell's energy in a shockwave, and the blast hurled him backward into the wall. His head ricocheted with a sickening crunch that should have knocked him out cold, but by his moaning, I could tell he was still conscious.

I leapt to my feet and drew my sword, then rammed it through his gut without remorse.

Before I could finish him off, his partner bellowed in anger and hurled another blast of magic at me. It exploded against the wall, sending chunks of stone raining down. I summoned my moonlight shield as he hurled bolt after bolt of lightning at me. My heart was hammering a hundred miles an hour, and I could feel my reserves of adrenaline and magic running dry.

Suddenly, a falcon's cry split the air.

I glanced up as a winged shape flashed over my head and landed behind the second assassin. It wasn't a bird, but rather an absence of light—a nexus of shadows that twisted and grew as soon as its feet touched stone. The darkness rose behind the assassin like a black tidal wave, and in a quake of power, the shadows took the form of a god.

Cadean.

He swung his black axe, and before I could draw a breath, the assassin's head flew from his shoulders, and a ribbon of warm blood sprayed across my face. The headless body teetered there for a second, but Cadean slammed it out of the way and strode toward the other assailant. He grabbed the prone and bleeding fae by his face and heaved him to his feet. The assassin lashed out with his dagger again and again in futile defense, but the Dark Wolf God ignored the blows and pressed the man's head into the wall. One second, the assassin was standing, and the next, his skull exploded like a ripe tomato.

I fought back vomit as I looked on in horror.

Two breaths.

In two breaths, I'd gone from being outnumbered and on my own to being covered in the blood of two men. It was awe inspiring and sickening and terrifying beyond words.

The stones of the street vibrated with Cadean's rage as he turned toward me. He was death given form by the shadows, and in spite of myself, I took a stuttering step away from him.

"Are you hurt?" he growled, his voice almost animalistic.

I shook my head. "No."

He shoved my hand out of the way and examined my side. "You're bleeding."

I looked down. My clothes were soaked in the blood gushing from a gash just below my left breast.

"Oh, fuck..." I slurred, suddenly lightheaded. "This was a brand-new outfit."

Something was wrong. My gut was reeling, and my veins felt like they were on fire. The world spun as my muscles began to convulse. Poison.

My knees buckled, but Cadean caught me and roughly pressed his hand against the open gash. I gasped as the flames of his healing magic blazed through me. It was agony and delight and anything but gentle, but my body still arched against his touch. My muscles clenched, and I bit down on my lip as the torn flesh knit. I could feel his power burning the assassin's poison from my veins.

And then, just as quickly as it started, it was gone. I pitched forward into his arms, dizzy with the lingering pain and the fading glow of his power.

He looked around. "Where the fuck are Kass and Mel?"

"There was another assassin. Kass chased—"

"Fucking fools," Cadean growled. "Protecting *you* is what matters. They should have stuck to your side. How is it that I cannot leave you alone for a moment?"

Untangling myself from his gasp, I glared. "I didn't need Kass or you. I could have taken them both."

He gave a bitter laugh. "I don't doubt it, but that's not the point. Had that dagger struck a vein or your heart—" His voice broke off.

I opened my mouth in retort, but Mel swung around the corner. Her eyes widened at the scene of carnage. "Fates, are you okay?"

"Why weren't you with her?" Cadean snapped with a such ferocity that Mel took a step back. "I told you not to take your eyes off of her!"

I seized his arm and sank my claws deep into the skin, drawing blood. "Stop it! I outran her. I'm a wolf, and she's not. I'm twice as fast."

Cade snarled and yanked his arm away, but I fixed him with a defiant glare, willing him to calm *the fuck* down. His jaw worked in irritation, and eventually, he stifled his temper. "What the hell happened?"

Still breathing hard, Mel nodded back toward the street. "Two assassins attacked Sam back at the brewery. We were watching the door, but they were disguised with a glamour, which I failed to discern."

While Cadean, Kass, and I were resistant to fae illusions, Mel was not, and I could tell from her expression that she was unfairly chiding herself for missing the signs.

Shadows rising from his shoulders like black smoke, Cadean slammed his fist into the wall of the building. "Fucking Ayanna!"

Shards of stone and mortar rained down around us in a fine mist as Kass strode into the alleyway, sword out and slicked with red. "Hell, and here I thought I was having all the fun."

"Is that what you think it is? You were supposed to guard Samantha, not chase fucking assassins on your own."

Fang shrugged. "I left her in the bar. She should have stayed put."

I considered digging my claws into Cadean's arm again if he flew off the handle, but after a long stare-down with his right-hand man, he simply sighed and ran his fingers through his hair, closing his eyes. "Kass. When has Samantha ever stayed put?"

I prickled. "I'm standing right here, you know."

He gave me a pointed look. "I'm well aware. Next time, don't play the hero."

Baring my teeth, I stepped into his space. "If someone attacks me, Cadean, I am going to fucking hunt them down and kill them."

"Attagirl." Fang grinned, then shut his trap as Cadean glared back at him.

"Double your training with her, Kass. Triple it until she can take your fucking smart-assed head off with that sword."

Mel knelt by the first assassin's body, and I had to look away. The wall was streaked with blood, and there was little left to the man's skull but ruby-red chunks of cranium.

"Fates, Cade. You could have left one of them alive," Fang muttered. "Now I don't have anyone to interrogate."

"You could have left *yours* alive," the Dark Wolf God grumbled.

Mel pulled a vial out of the assassin's belt pouch, then popped the top and sniffed it. She looked at me. "That blade was sheathed in poison. How are you feeling?"

I examined my side. "Tender. Cadean healed me, but I don't think I'll be able to salvage the clothes—which I think may break my heart. At least the jacket is mostly intact."

Mel tore the gash in my shirt wider and examined the cut. "I don't know what your healing magic does or does not cure, but the scar is inflamed. I want to look at this again as soon as we get back to Shadowstone."

"Is Selene okay?" I asked Mel.

"I had to stop her from running after me."

"Good." My mouth soured with guilt. This wasn't the first time she'd been in danger because of me.

Mel's lips pursed. "What I want to know is how the assassin got through the barrier."

Cadean's jaw tensed, and he flexed his hand. "They probably slipped through the town portal disguised as shifters."

Kass examined the second body down the alley. "That, or they were here already—sleeper agents, perhaps still lurking in town from the attempt on Samantha's life ten weeks ago."

Fates, had it been that long?

Cadean dismissed his axe and looked around. "In either case, we need to act fast. If there are three, there're probably more. I'll close the portal. No one goes in or out until we've worked out an inspection protocol. Kass, turn this town upside down. It's full of shifters, so find some loyal wolves and sniff out any remaining fae."

Kass cracked his knuckles as he rose. "With pleasure."

"What about me?" Mel asked.

"Seeing as we don't have anyone to interrogate, can you learn anything from their blood?"

She pursed her lips. "Probably little we don't already know. I'll see what I can do, and then I'll incinerate the bodies."

"Good." Cadean lifted his hands, and curtains of shadow walled off the area around us. "That should keep prying eyes away while you work."

I knelt and cleaned my blade on the clothes of the nearest assassin before sliding it back into my new scabbard. "What about me? I'm not going to go hide in my chambers."

The Dark God turned, jaw set and eyes burning with protectiveness. "You're coming with me. I'm not letting you out of my sight again, little wolf."

$$5$$

Samantha

Cadean stalked down the alleyway, and I followed beside him. The walls behind us were scorched by magic and splattered with blood. It looked like we were leaving a war zone, and the panicked voices of bystanders echoed from the street beyond. Kass and Mel would have their hands full putting things right.

"You attract trouble like a cat in heat," Cadean grumbled.

I raised my eyebrows. "I assume that's why you showed up so quickly."

He paused and looked back, but instead of smiling at the quip, the lines of his face drew taut. "No. I showed up because I can feel when you are afraid or hurt. I was in a meeting with the city elders, and the sensations lanced through me like a knife. *That's* how I knew to come for you."

I nodded. We'd never openly discussed it, but I'd already figured out that it was something like that. Almost every time I'd been in trouble in Auren's palace or at Dreamspire, Cadean had shadow-cast to me moments later, as if pulled there by my very suffering. "Why are we connected like this?"

I had my suspicions, even if they were impossible. I just needed to hear him say it.

Cadean opened his mouth to answer, but then simply brushed away the hair clinging to my damp cheek. His touch sent a shiver down my spine, and the corner of his mouth pulled up affectionately. I thought he was about to bend his lips to mine, but he let his hand drop away.

My stomach dropped with it. More of the same, a growing rift between us. Why? What had changed?

His fleeting caress had left my skin sensitive and center wanting, but now my neck was flushed with self-conscious embarrassment. What was wrong? I looked down and caught sight of my red and tattered clothes.

I was literally covered in gore, head to toe. That might be it.

"Fates, I'm disgusting," I muttered as I touched the spray of dried blood that still coated my face. No wonder he'd broken off the kiss.

I turned away, but he gently drew my chin back to him. "No, Samantha, you're not. You're stunning."

"Covered in blood?" I stared up at the deranged man—*god*—before me.

"It just speaks the truth: you're a warrior, through and through. And it makes me want you more."

His gravelly voice and scent confirmed his words. There was desire there, fierce and savage, but it was sharply repressed. I, on the other hand, felt much less restrained. My brush with death had sent adrenaline pumping through my veins, and between his scent and the look in his eyes, I was almost ready to take him right there, despite the streaks of another man's blood on my face.

I raised my eyebrows playfully. "So that's what does it for you? Watching your lover fight for her life?"

As if I'd doused him with ice water, the smile vanished from his face, and his eyes flared with an emotion I couldn't quite place. He grasped my shoulder. "You need to be careful, little wolf, now more than ever."

"I am."

His fingers tightened almost to the point of being painful. "That's not good enough. I need you to *know it*. I need you to feel the danger in your bones. You cannot let your guard down. Ever."

Was this just about chasing the assassins? My blood heated. "I'm not going to spend the rest of my life jumping at shadows. You say I'm a warrior. Well, I'm going to fight."

I struggled against his iron grip, but he didn't let go. "Your safety comes before everything. I couldn't—"

Cadean's voice broke off, and when he continued, I was certain he'd been going to say something entirely different. "I can't protect you unless you protect yourself. Understood?"

He'd always been protective and possessive, but this was different. I scrutinized the worried lines of his face. "What's going on? Is this just about the assassins?"

Cadean let go and stepped away. "We've grown lax. The assassins are proof of it."

I was certain that wasn't what had set him off. He'd been on edge for the last few days. There was something more—something had changed between us, and he wasn't planning to tell me. Despite my frustration, I could tell I wasn't going to get any more out of him at the moment, so I simply nodded. "I'll be careful. I promise."

He studied my face for a long while, and then, without a word, headed down the alley.

~

Cadean led me to a wide square in the middle of town where five streets met. Vendors had erected garishly decorated stands around the perimeter and were selling everything from spiced nuts to mulled cider to heavy coats for winter. The center of the space was dominated by a wide-stepped dais with a towering stone archway. The portal filled the gateway like a shimmering quicksilver pool. Several members of the watch stood on guard beside it, checking the identification and purpose of all those that passed through.

The thin crowd glided away from us with looks of trepidation. With battle-torn clothes, a bloody gash in my side, and a wicked-looking blade, I was probably an unnerving sight on my own. But the Dark Wolf God—he was something else entirely.

Cadean's expression was relentlessly grim, and the shadows flowed toward him as he strode forward. Towering over even the largest of the bear shifters in the square, he was impossibly imposing with his broad frame and dark tattoos. Even with him repressing his presence, I was certain everyone in a quarter mile could feel it pressing in on them. I'd grown used to his aura, but I remembered how frightening it once had been.

How many of these people had actually ever laid eyes on the God of the Wolves?

Some just bolted for the alleys surrounding the square, but most bowed in acknowledgement before quickly backing away. This was their liege lord and god—responsible for their wellbeing, but without a doubt, terrifying to behold.

Cadean paid them no heed as he strode up the steps to the portal. The mail-clad shifters of the watch stood to attention, and I could smell their building dread. I didn't blame them—the Dark Wolf God did not look pleased.

"I'm shutting the portal," Cadean rumbled at the sentries. "Several fae assassins may have slipped through."

They looked from Cadean to me, then to my bloody

wound, and their faces went ashen. The sergeant, a wolf shifter by his scent, dropped low in submission. "My lord, I am sorry. We did not scent any fae passing through. The fault is mine alone."

"They may have arrived another way, but if there are still assassins here, we cannot allow them to leave. Send a runner to your captain and tell him to coordinate with Kassian, who's taking charge. He'll need accounts of everyone who came through but hasn't yet departed. The rest of you, check the crowds here for anyone who has a scent of fae but doesn't look it."

The sergeant cleared his throat as he rose. "Respectfully, my lord, the people will be angry when they find out the portal is shutting, especially those with family. What do we tell those trapped on this side?"

"That the portal is closed and nothing more. Anyone who needs lodging is to be put up at an inn or hostel at my expense. Anyone who complains may petition me at Shadowstone. That should silence any protests."

Cadean dismissed the sentries as I stared in awe at the portal. The slowly undulating surface was framed by a curved archway wide enough to accommodate a cart. The stone was inlaid with glowing magic sigils and decorated by carvings of entwined wolves and ships.

However, it wasn't the beauty of the stonework that held me rapt. I was three steps away from a portal out of the Dreamlands, and I didn't even feel a flicker of desire to make a run for it. I was absolutely floored.

Once, escaping had been the only thing I'd wanted. I'd dreamed of slipping out of Shadowstone unnoticed and making my way to the city to find this very portal, hoping that some connection would lead me back to Magic Side.

Now, I'd been in the city all day, and it hadn't occurred to me to even pass by and assess the situation, let alone try to get home. I shuddered as I felt the ghosts of my old life slip away.

A wry smile spread across Cadean's face as he followed my gaze. "Should I be worried you'll run off?"

"Clearly, you're not, or you wouldn't let me within a mile of here," I muttered.

Cadean laid a hand softly on my shoulder. "You're not my prisoner anymore, Samantha. You haven't been for a long time."

Had I really given up all hope of returning to Magic Side, and to my friends Savy and Jax? Maybe not completely, but I sure as fuck wasn't going back to Deerhaven. There was nothing for me there anymore. My mother was gone and—

Clenching my teeth, I thrust the thought from my mind. That life was over. There was nothing I could do to change the past. All I could do was seek vengeance.

I tightened my hand on the hilt of my sword. "You know as well as I do that I can't leave this place. I've got work to do, and it begins and ends with Ayanna."

Cadean glanced down at the blade and nodded. "We'll find a way to defeat her. I promise."

I followed his gaze. The new scabbard was already coated with blood, both mine and fae. It would probably wash off the sealed leather, but I was of half a mind to leave it stained. Despite its beauty, it wasn't for show. Like me and the blade, it had a purpose, and that purpose was all that mattered.

I stepped back. "Let's shut this thing and hunt down any remaining operatives. I want to know what the fuck Ayanna thinks she's up to."

Cadean searched my eyes for a moment, then turned and raised his arms wide. A swell of power built around him like the anticipation in the air before a rolling storm. Shadows twisted upward around his legs, and the sky darkened.

"Close," he commanded in a booming voice.

The magic sigils powering the gateway flared, and the dais shuddered. For a moment, I was afraid the stones would tear themselves apart, but the shimmering portal dissipated in a clap of thunder, leaving the archway empty. I could now see the terrified faces of onlookers on the other side staring back at us.

We were all stuck here together, for better or worse.

The sudden silence in the square surprised me. The thrum of the portal's magic had permeated the space, but I hadn't noticed it until it was gone, like the whir of a fan or an air conditioner shutting off—the sudden presence of a silence that had not been there before.

I let out a long, slow breath. My way out of here was closed, and I didn't feel a thing.

I knew that my place was in the Dreamlands now, and my old life was gone. There were assassins after me, an army lurking at the border, and a wicked queen pulling the strings. There was no time to look back. My fate lay ahead, whether I liked it or not.

6

Cadean

After escorting Mel and Samantha back to Shadowstone, I returned to Mistwind Harbor to hunt assassins and their collaborators. With Kassian and his men pounding on doors and asking questions throughout town, I hoped that any remaining agents might make a break for it under the cover of darkness rather than risk being discovered.

Wulfric and his pack had fanned out in the countryside and woods surrounding town, and I'd summoned a host of ravens to patrol the skies. If anyone tried to slip away unnoticed, we'd know.

I moved through the alleys like a shadow, grinding my teeth at the futility of it all. Most likely, Ayanna's spies were long gone. Yet if there was even a slim chance of uncovering another assassin, we had to try. Catching a single collaborator would make the effort worth it. I wanted to know how long the assassins were in my city, who the fuck was helping them, and whether there were more.

My thoughts wheeled like the birds circling above, endlessly tumbling without finding solutions. The hunt was just white noise, unable to tear me away from my deeper concern: Samantha.

I had to tell her the truth soon—I owed her that much. Yet every time I'd searched for the words, they failed me.

We were mates, and she was doomed to die. How could I tell her that?

She'd become entangled in the toxic mess that was my very existence, and she would be the one to suffer most. The Fates were treating her like a chess piece, and I swore, whatever their hand in this mess, I would find a way to pay them back in blood.

But beneath that, there was the deeper dread, one I had no idea how to explain: I cared for her, without a doubt...but I had no idea how to love her.

Every instinct I had roared at me to protect her, but if I locked her away or tried to keep her from her purpose, I knew it would kill her soul. Yet if she fulfilled that purpose, she would die.

What the fuck was I supposed to do?

Ravens cawed above an adjacent street, pulling me from my dark reverie. Someone was coming.

I heard the footsteps and heavy breathing a moment later, and soon after, a shifter appeared at the far end of the alley. Her armor glinted beneath the lights, marking her as one of the city watch.

She raised her hand in acknowledgement. "Lord Wolf!"

I shadow-stepped to the end of the alley, quickly teleporting between the patches of darkness. "What is it?"

"We've found where they were staying," she said, still breathing hard. "Kassian is there now. It's not far."

"Show me."

I followed her through the winding alleys of the harbor town. She ran, though it only took me a striding gait to keep up. We emerged onto a residential street moments later. A few doors down, golden light poured from the open door of a house with sentries posted at the entrance. I didn't wait for the runner, but shadow-stepped there in seconds.

"I don't know what you're talking about!" a man's voice protested from inside.

"Come on," Kass laughed, threat lingering in his voice. "You're a shifter—couldn't you smell the fae on them? How much did they pay you to look the other way?"

"There are plenty of fae in town. I had—"

His voice cut off as I stepped inside.

Kass had the man up against the wall, a knife at his throat. The vampire let the blade relax and shook his head pityingly. "Remember how I said there was an easy way and a hard way? The hard way just walked in."

The shadows of night followed me as I strode into the room. "This man was sheltering the assassins?"

The man's eyes widened, and he shook his head. He was in his forties, and a stoat shifter by the scent of him. That made sense, at least. A wolf would never have betrayed their pack like this.

Kass nodded. "Several townsfolk claimed he had some outsiders staying here, and they matched the descriptions of the two assassins who showed up in the bar."

The man leaned heavily against the wall, trembling as my shadow crossed his face. "I swear, I didn't know who they were!"

I breathed in, measuring the emotions trapped in his scent. Terror. Guilt. Deceit.

"And yet you harbored these strangers in your home instead of sending them to an inn? Who did you think they were?"

"Merchan—"

I unleashed my alpha presence, cutting off his words. He trembled and pissed himself as he dropped to the ground.

Putting his hands over his head, he cried, "I thought they were just spies! I didn't know they would harm anyone."

The scent of truth intermixed with the stink of urine.

"Fucking hell. I should kill him on the spot," Kass spat.

I raised my hand to quiet him and crouched in front of the cowering man. "Why would you let fae spies into my realm after what they've done to our people?"

"They have my sister," he said, sobbing. "She's a trader and was trapped on the other side when the wall went up. They threatened to..."

He didn't finish the thought, and he didn't need to. I was quite familiar with fae interrogation techniques. Perhaps I should have had sympathy for the man, but those bastards had nearly killed my mate.

I seized his shirt and hoisted him up against the wall. "You put the realm at risk, so you're going to tell us everything they said and did."

He nodded, quaking in my grip.

"When did they contact you?"

"A week ago."

Kass cursed. "That's right after the wall went up. Ayanna didn't waste any time."

"And how many were staying here?"

"Four. Three men and a woman."

My heartbeat quickened. *So there had been more.* I glanced at Kass. "Search the house."

As he headed for the back, something thumped against the ceiling. We looked up, and there was an explosion that sent dust raining down. Glass shattered.

"What the fuck was that?" Kass shouted as he headed for the stairs.

I threw the traitor into the arms of one of the sentries. "Don't let him get away, and don't let anyone kill him—they might try."

The shifter's face went white.

"There's a fire and a broken window up here!" Kass yelled.

I shadow-stepped into the back garden. There was glass on the ground, and the back gate was open.

Apparently, our luck hadn't run out. Assassin number four had been lying low and eavesdropping upstairs.

I rushed into the alley as a figure turned the corner. That glimpse was all I needed. I surged through the deep shadows of the night. She was running down a narrow shop-lined street. I could smell her scent and fear. She was mine.

I shadow-stepped past her, blocking the far end of the street. "Don't move another inch. You're going to tell me everything Ayanna ordered you to do."

"I'd rather die." She released a wave of flickering green flame.

Razors of pain raced over my skin. Shielding my eyes, I strode through the fire anyway. "I'm a god. Your death magic means nothing to me."

She bolted back the way she'd come but stopped short as Kass stepped in front of her, smirking as he drew his blade.

Trapped between a vengeful god and a vampire, the assassin bounded forward and repelled off the wall. She released her wings and soared above us, but I summoned a ferocious gust of wind, knocking her out of the sky. She crashed to the ground but quickly flipped to her feet and drew a wicked dagger, looking back and forth between Kass and me. "We all knew your little *whore* was a traitor. I should have taken her pelt when I had a chance."

"I doubt you could have managed it," Kass said, advancing with his sword out.

"Doesn't matter if I live or die. You can't stop this. Ayanna will drain the life from you and your half-breed whore before she destroys you both."

My hand yearned for my axe, but I restrained my magic. "You're not going to die. You're going to *talk*, one way or another. Who else were you working with? What were Ayanna's orders?"

The assassin laughed. "Kill the wolf bitch and don't come back. And if you can't take her pelt..."

She spun and hurled a wave of green witchfire at Kass.

No.

Instinct took over. I snapped my hand up, summoning a black wind. It roared down the alley, knocking Kass to his knees and driving the deadly flames back on her. Green flames enveloped her body, and consumed by her own death magic, the assassin dropped to the ground.

Her screams tore through my heart like a dagger, and I froze as memories flooded my mind. Suddenly I was in another time and place. It wasn't the fae assassin screaming, but Samantha, and the flames were white.

The memory was as searing and vivid as life itself. She'd laid her hands on the pylon and seized control of the wall, but it had been too much. Even as the barrier bent to her will, the Moon's power had blazed through her, burning her from the inside out.

Mortals weren't meant to channel divine magic.

I'd roared as she'd fallen backward, consumed with white flames. I'd tried to get to her, but the pylon's magic had been created to keep me at bay. It was like trying to run against a surging sea of fire. I'd dropped to my knees and crawled to her side, digging my claws into the earth, and fighting the waves of power.

Her clothes had been burned away, and her skin was charred. I'd been certain she was dead, but as I'd pulled her into my arms, I'd felt her chest rising and falling and the beat of her heart.

Driven by the terror of losing her, I'd poured my healing magic into her. I'd never called my magic in such desperation or felt it rage through me like it did in that moment—but still, it had barely been enough. Samantha hadn't woken until after I'd healed her a second time back at Shadowstone.

"Cadean!"

Kass's voice shattered the memory, and suddenly, I was back in the alley. I summoned my axe, glancing around in a daze. "Samantha..."

"Fuck, man," the vampire said. "You were in a trance."

I shook the fog from my head and rushed to where the assassin lay. "Is she dead?"

There'd been no need to ask. My stomach churned, and I looked away. It was too vivid of a reminder of what Samantha had risked.

Kass sheathed his blade. "Let's just say she won't be taking any more pelts. That was some serious death magic."

And there went our only source.

"Fuck!" I snarled, ramming my fist into the wall. The stone cracked, and I shook out my hand. I'd just reacted. I was losing my grip. I needed to get my head straight, fast.

"Well, I'm glad you decided to keep me around instead," said Kass, "though I'm afraid we're not going to get much from the assassins' lair, either. That'll be all gone in the fire."

I looked up. Orange flames billowed above the rooftops. *Fuuuuuck.*

Closing my eyes, I reached out with my power over the wilderness, summoning a storm. The wind rose and clouds above us began to darken, and soon, there would be torrential rain.

I knelt beside the corpse and pulled free a charred satchel. "See if there's anything you can salvage once the fire's out and lock that stoat in the dungeon. Find out if there's anything else he knows about the assassins or Ayanna's network."

"Gladly."

As he turned to go, I rubbed the bridge of my nose and released a frustrated sigh. "And Kass, contact your spies on the other side of the border. I want the stoat's sister found and brought back—and I want to know if Ayanna has any other hostages she's using for leverage."

He nodded and walked away, and I glanced back to the charred remains before me. It was a gruesome sight, but I didn't feel an ounce of pity for the woman. She'd been part of a plot to kill my mate and was burned alive by her own magic. I would kill her a thousand times over if I could. My only regret was that I hadn't had a chance to wrench a confession from her mouth before she'd died.

Ayanna was up to something, and I was certain that the assassins were just the tip of the iceberg.

7

———

Shadowstone, three days later.

Samantha

"Your magic is better than your swordsmanship." Fang smirked.

I glared at the vampire, but before I could set my stance, he lunged like a viper. I danced back and deflected his blade with mine, sending the sharp clang of steel resounding off the stone walls of the training room.

"And keep your eyes up," he said. "I can practically read your mind."

"Drop that sword, and I'll show you a real fight," I said with a biting smile. My eyes stung from sweat, and my muscles were beginning to feel like jelly. I knew my way around a fighting ring, but dueling with a blade was another matter, and everything he did made me feel like a rookie again.

Fang shook his head as he slowly circled. "I don't doubt it, but swords beat claws, and a certain god will have my balls if I don't teach you how to at least defend yourself with that thing."

I adjusted my grip on Wolf's Vengeance. Even with fresh strips of soft leather on the tang and gloves, blisters had blossomed along my palms, and the strong blows coming from Kass weren't helping matters. He was using a dull training blade, but it was just as heavy.

I parried another strike and grimaced as the force of it reverberated through my forearm. The general's old blade was long and heavy, but as a werewolf, I was far stronger than the fae and could wield it was ease. It was the technique that was killing me.

Fang's eyes darted to the hole in my tunic where his training blade had torn my shirt, revealing a strip of skin at my hip. His lips curled up. "You're slowing down, wolfling. Maybe you need a rest?"

Yes.

I was exhausted. Hell, I'd felt sluggish all day, and not only because of my scuffle with the assassins three days prior. It was like I'd woken up with leaden weights tied to me, and after parrying Kass's blows and subpar insults for the past few hours, every inch of me was screaming for a break.

"I'll rest when I'm dead," I said, resetting my grip on the hilt of the sword.

"If you keep fighting like that..." he said, then shrugged, as if there were no need to finish.

Cocky fucker.

I raised my blade high, luring Kass in with an opening. I blocked his attack, holding his sword against mine as I lifted my left foot and kicked him in the groin.

He grunted and stumbled backward before unleashing a slew of curses.

"If I keep fighting like *what*?" I asked.

Kass shot daggers at me with his eyes. "Like a godsdamned animal."

Hell, yes, I did.

Kass was a deadly swordsman, but he fought by the book. Every movement he made was practiced and precise. I, on the other hand, had learned to fight in the ring where anything went. We fought tooth and claw and used every dirty trick we could to win, because winning was all that had mattered. It still was.

"I'll do whatever it takes to destroy Ayanna," I said, chest heaving and vitriol dripping from my words. "I'll gouge her in the eyes and pull her hair if I have to."

Kass scoffed. "You know the queen isn't going to duel you, darling girl."

"Good. Then she won't be able to stop my blade when I ram it through her chest."

A sudden heat warmed my skin, and I tipped my gaze toward the balcony.

Cadean.

He was watching me, his face stern but with the faintest hint of approval tugging at the corner of his lips. A shiver of delight snaked down my spine.

Fates. Would I ever be immune to his presence? Just the sight of him undid me. Every. Time.

"Nice move, little wolf," he purred, resting his bare forearms on the wooden railing. "Kass gets too stuck in his ways."

His praise sent a buzz of warmth through me, and I looked away. Brushing the damp hair out of my eyes, I raised my blade to Kass. "Again? Or do you need a rest?"

Cadean chuckled, and Kass snorted in disdain as he pointed the tip of his blade at me. "I'll give you that one, Samantha. But you can't always rely on deception. You must hone your skills, and that starts with footwork."

The intense thrum of Cadean's presence drew close behind me and his words skimmed the shell of my ear. "You need to pivot and adjust your stance. Let the power come from your hips and feet."

My body responded out of instinct as he placed his hands on my hips and gently corrected my alignment. I silently cursed.

There was no chance of focusing now.

"Keep your knees soft so that you can move when he does," the Dark Wolf God instructed.

I had to fight to keep my breathing steady. This was just training. Footwork. But I couldn't quite repress the anticipation that had begun building when he gripped me from behind.

"Don't give Kass any opening or advantage," Cadean said, sliding his hand along my upper thigh. "He doesn't deserve it."

The husky tone of his voice nearly undid me again, but Kass sighed audibly, pulling me back to the task at hand.

"I know I was getting sloppy," I said, glancing up at the impossibly large god. "I'm just a bit tired today, that's all. I didn't sleep well after you left."

Cadean's brow furrowed, like he was trying to parse some unspoken meaning from my words. Then he ran his thumb along the sweep of exposed skin along my hip. "I can help with that."

His magic flowed into me, and I sucked in a short, sharp breath as the chill of his power spread inside, moving to my limbs, easing my aches, and restoring my spent muscles. It was like waking refreshed from a deep afternoon nap.

Then his hands slipped away, and the spark of connection faded. The early winter air suddenly felt a little colder as Cadean returned to the shadows at the edge of the dueling grounds.

The vampire raised an eyebrow at the Dark Wolf God. "Really, Cade? Tipping the scales? She needs to learn to fight exhausted."

"She needs to perfect her technique first, and you've got centuries in your pocket. Quit griping and get on with your lessons."

The blisters on my palm had healed, and a renewed energy pulsed through my veins. I rolled my shoulders to loosen them. "How about it, Fang? One more round. I'm feeling lucky."

Kass chuckled. "Are you, now?"

I lunged when the words were halfway out of his mouth, and he had to spin away to avoid the tip of my blade. Drawing on the reserve of energy Cadean had given me, I pressed the attack, strike after strike. Sweat dampened Kass's shirt, but he showed no signs of fatigue—yet I was slowing quickly. Where was my werewolf stamina? With Cadean's boost, I should have been able to go for hours.

I stumbled and Kass's blade swept across the top of my thigh. Although the edge was blunted, the thick fabric parted like butter, and red blossomed between the frayed edges of my trousers. Cadean hurled a warning at Kass, but I ignored it and continued fighting.

"Enough!" Cadean stepped between us and pushed Kass back.

I braced myself against the wall, breathing hard and my head spinning.

"The next time you draw her blood, I will take your heart," Cade said to his advisor, venom dripping from his words. "You have better control than that."

Sword in hand, Kass lifted his arms in submission. "Understood." Then he glanced over at me with an uncharacteristic expression of concern. "You okay, Samantha?"

"Fine," I snapped, and gave them my back as I made my way to the water ewer at the far side of the room and pulled off my light training pads.

A dull throb emanated from the wound on my leg, and I casually touched it. Warm blood coated the tips of my glove. Not only was I fatigued again, but I wasn't healing as quickly as I should. Unease twisted in my gut. Something was wrong.

I poured myself a cup of water and knocked it back. Cadean's shadow loomed over me, protective and powerful. "You don't seem fine."

I wiped the water from my lips. "I've been training with Kass all afternoon. He's tiresome to begin with, and his incessant nagging has drained me. I made a mistake."

It wasn't entirely the truth, but Cadean had enough on his plate without me adding more. A little fatigue didn't register on the scale of things to worry about.

He brushed his knuckles along my jaw as he so often did, admiration and something else in his eyes. "Mistakes happen. But you're improving more quickly than I'd hoped. Before long, you'll be giving Kass a run for his money."

"I'd say *that* is an overstatement," Kass said dryly.

I forced a smile for Cadean, though it wasn't hard. His dark, wavy hair, his perfect jawline, the way he looked at me when he thought I wasn't watching—every part of him made my chest squeeze in on itself. Made me feel like I was sixteen again and foolish.

A rush of warm air broke his spell over me, and I glanced at the door as Wulfric strode in. An unfamiliar wolf shifter followed just behind.

"Thank the fates," Kass said, sheathing his sword. "The air in here with these two was practically suffocating."

Wulfric's grim expression said 'official business,' so I withdrew to the shadows along the wall. Kass joined me as Cadean turned to his second in command. "What's happened?"

Wulfric pushed the unfamiliar wolf forward. "This is a runner from the Red Mountain pack. Tell the lord what you told me."

The shifter dropped to his knees before the Dark Wolf God, eyes lowered, and every muscle tensed in a desperate attempt to conceal his fear. His scent spoke of terror and wonder, awe, and trepidation.

It was so easy to forget what Cadean truly was and how much I'd once feared him. He was god to these people, with unlimited power. He'd made the land, and he could destroy it and all who dwelt there in an instant.

I wondered if they worshiped and prayed to him. Would they think it blasphemy that I shared his bed each night? A mortal, not even a pure shifter? I pressed myself further into the shadows, suddenly conscious of how out of place I was here, in his realm.

The messenger cleared his throat and began uneasily, though his voice was strong. "I was sent by our alpha. Vines have infested the northern reaches of the wall, just east of Red Mountain."

"What do you mean by 'infested'?" Cadean asked as he stepped closer. "Like they're searching for a way through?"

The messenger shook his head but didn't look up. "That's what we thought when the tendrils first appeared Five days ago."

"Five days?" Kass snapped. "Why didn't you report it then?"

The shifter's shoulders tensed at the vampire's voice, and I could smell his resentment. "Because if we reported everything the fae did along our border, the god would never hear an end to our burdens. We assumed the vines were simply probing for weaknesses, so we waited and watched."

"What changed to bring you down from the mountains?" Cadean asked.

"All the vines in the region have started converging on a single section."

"Like they're trying to break through?"

The shifter shrugged. "We're not sure."

"I knew Ayanna was up to something," Kass muttered. "It's been too quiet."

"Apart from the assassins?" I hissed just beneath my breath.

Kass shrugged. "Besides that."

Cadean growled low to quiet us. "Wulfric, it's a long run from Red Mountain—get this wolf some venison and beer and a place to rest. Then send scouts to the other border packs. If Ayanna is attacking one stretch of the wall, she'll be probing others."

Wulfric nodded curtly and led the messenger away.

"Grab Mel," Cadean said as he turned back to us. "We're riding north. I want to see what Ayanna is up to with my own eyes."

8

———

Samantha

I threw on the elaborately embroidered fur coat that Cadean had given me as a gift, then rousted Mel from bed. By the time we joined the others in the courtyard, the aviary master had saddled four griffstriders. The eagle-headed mounts were scraping the cobbles with their talons and stamping their hind hooves, agitated by the unanticipated activity but excited by the prospect of a brisk ride.

Dozens of birds circled the sky above, cawing and calling to each other in a deafening racket. Cadean brushed the crown of the hawk that was perched on his arm. "Scout the border and return to us. I want to know everywhere that the vines are attacking the wall."

He thrust his arm upward, and the hawk burst into the air. The other birds wheeled around it as it soared past them, and soon, the entire host was following it toward the northern horizon.

My griffstrider Elowyn clopped over and nuzzled my hand with her skull-crushing beak. I brushed the feathers of her neck, then lodged my toe in the stirrup and swung myself up into the saddle. "Good to see you, too, Ellie."

As soon as Mel had mounted up on Dawnfire, Cadean spurred Vega, and we galloped over the long, elegant causeway that spanned the gorge separating Shadowstone from the far side of the cliff. The sound of waves echoed upward, and I leaned over in the saddle to look down, but I couldn't see through the thick mist that had filled the chasm.

Our griffstriders charged along the main road, their talons and hooves pounding like gunfire against the gravel. It was impossible to hold a conversation over the noise, so I just kept my eyes on the path ahead and watched Cadean, who flowed in perfect sync with his mount. There was a relentlessness to the way he leaned forward in the saddle like a warrior eager for battle. The harsh angles of his jaw and ferocity in his eyes sent a shiver down my spine, but not out of fear—that had long since passed. Whatever else he had done, whatever destruction he was capable of, I knew he would never harm me. He would fight for me with all his strength, and I would fight for him.

Of course, it wouldn't matter in the end. I was mortal, and my life was hanging by a thread. The longer I thought on it, the more certain I became that the dark presence in my dream on the morning of the assassination attempt had been real, or at least a premonition—death itself, lurking around the corner, watching, and waiting.

Was I going to lose Cadean just as soon as I'd found him?

For all his strength, there was nothing he could do to keep me from death in the end.

I was going to have to love him while I still could.

After a few hours, we peeled off the road and into the thick stands of trees. Cadean's magic billowed out ahead of us in streams of shadow. The trees bent their branches back, creating an arching tunnel of limbs so that we barely had to slow our traveling speed.

I pulled alongside him and shouted, "Aren't we headed to Red Mountain? Why are we leaving the road?"

Cadean glanced over. "I'm following a hunch. We already know the vines are attacking Red Mountain, but that won't be the only place. The vines were thickest in the dead forest near Riverbend before the wall rose, and that's where they will be at their worst. That's where we'll see what Ayanna is truly up to and whether she can break through."

I glanced at the shimmering dome above. I'd assumed the wall was invulnerable—that the Moon's power would cut Ayanna off from Cadean's realm forever. Could she really have found a weakness in the barrier? Doubt crept along my spine, and I found myself sitting uneasily in the saddle.

As the sun passed its crest, the living trees began to fade, replaced by lifeless, blackened trunks with skeletal limbs. Rather than bend away from Cadean's magic, they simply shattered, leaving a path of splintered wood ahead. Vines wound across the forest floor beneath us and entwined around the brittle trunks, but they were as dead now as the trees that they'd strangled. When I'd transformed the barrier into a crystalline wall, it had cut the vines in two. While the portions beyond the barrier would have regenerated, those trapped on this side had turned into withered husks, no longer able to spread or kill.

But the damage was already done. I felt hollow as I looked at the desolation around me. Nothing lived, not moss or grass or even lichen. This was Ayanna's legacy: entire stretches of Cadean's realm drained of life. She claimed that it was to help her people, that the fruit of the vines would heal the withering curse.

But the people didn't get to eat the fruit of the garden. Just her court—the Undying Court. She lured them all along with promises of eternal life, but I knew the truth: she cared only for power, and she would sacrifice anyone or anything to obtain it.

The vines fed her, and her alone.

"Do you think it'll ever come back?" I asked.

Cadean's jaw was rigid with restrained fury. "My magic has never worked on it before. I can heal the forest, but I cannot bring back that which is dead."

"Perhaps it'll find a way on its own," I said without conviction.

"Perhaps," he grunted. "Nature has a fierce will to it—almost as willful as you."

I felt the heat of his gaze and forced a faint smile. Whether it took the forest decades or centuries to return, the odds were almost certain I wouldn't be around to see it sprout.

I shook my head to clear the dark thoughts. It didn't matter if I didn't see the end—just that I did what I could, while I could. That meant stopping Ayanna.

A falcon appeared in the sky above us, beating hard to keep up, probably the only animal for miles around. It keened, and with a nod, Cadean turned west to follow. "She's found something."

We fanned out as we approached the border, and as the dead forest thinned, my heart dropped.

"Holy fucking fates," Fang whispered.

The crystalline wall rose ahead of us, sparkling gold in the late afternoon light, but we couldn't see through to the other side. The vines were mounded over the surface of the wall like a nest of vipers, clinging and climbing ten to fifteen feet above my head.

"I've never seen the vines this thick," Mel murmured as we brought our striders to a halt in front of the wall. "Ayanna must be trying to force a way through."

The memory of the dream tightened around my neck, and I

could almost feel the vines strangling the life from me again. The crystalline wall seemed to ripple, and a shiver raked down my spine.

My mouth went dry as the horror of it all sank in.

"They're not trying to break through the wall," I whispered. "They're draining it." I spun Elowyn to face Cadean as rising panic pressed against my chest. "I'd thought I'd prevented her from stealing power from your land, but she can just siphon the Moon's magic straight from the wall with no one to stop her or cut the vines away."

"Fuck," Kass said, for all of us.

Cadean's gaze bored into the barrier, his jaw set.

My skin flushed as fury and frustration welled up. "I thought I'd beaten her. Instead, I've given her *exactly* what she needed— an infinite battery of the Moon's magic."

Cadean turned and fixed me with stone-cold eyes. "This is not your fault."

His voice vibrated with power and finality, but as much as he meant it, it wasn't the truth. Maybe I hadn't seen it coming, but this *was* my fault, and by gods, I was going to fix it.

I gritted my teeth and knotted the reins in my hands as my mind raced.

"How did the vines grow back so quickly?" Mel asked, her voice still disbelieving. "It's only been less than two weeks since they were cut off by the wall. Regrowing like this should have taken months."

I knew how, and the thought of it sent my stomach tumbling into an abyss. I swung off Elowyn and slowly approached the barrier. "The queen fed the vines with the blood of her people. Rivers of it."

I glanced upward as I stepped into the shadows of the vines. All I could think of was Astra's blood dripping off the grate down into the pit at the bottom of the Well of Life. I could hear the earth churning and her bones breaking as the voracious roots pulled her corpse down into the soil, devouring her flesh and magic.

How many others had the queen murdered to restore the vines severed by my wall? Had Kirin, my training partner and only friend in Dreamspire, been one of those she'd offered up in blood?

No. I fucking refused to believe that. She was too smart to get trapped in that place, wasn't she?

I fought down the vomit in my throat as I channeled my dread into rage. I wasn't going to let Ayanna steal the wall's magic, and I sure as hell wasn't going to let her sacrifice my friends. Heart pounding in my ears, I wrapped my hand around the hilt of my blade and looked back at the others. "Who's going to help me get these vines off *my wall*?"

9

———

Samantha

"What, exactly, are you proposing?" Cadean asked, stepping between me and the barrier.

"I stopped you once at the border by making a small portion of the barrier solid. I bet I can do the opposite and make a hole through it." I unsheathed my sword. "Then we cut the vines down."

"Not to burst your bubble, but every time we cut the vines, they regrow twice as thick," Kass cautioned, his expression taut and worried. "It's why Cadean seldom cut them. We could make the situation worse."

Not to mention Ayanna would simply sacrifice more people to regrow them. Yet there was something utterly wrong about seeing the wall covered with her vines. It was visceral. Sickening. I could almost feel them on my skin, draining my life along with the Moon's magic. The taste of revulsion soured my mouth.

"I am not going to stand around while *that bitch* gets stronger draining power from *my wall*." I narrowed my eyes at Kass. "Cutting them will buy time and stop Ayanna from getting any more power until we find a permanent solution."

"Like mounting her head on a spike," he muttered.

"I used to cast warding spells to prevent the vines from regrowing and penetrating further into our lands," Mel said as she dismounted and began rummaging in her saddlebags. "I still have everything I need in here. The enchantments won't be permanent, but they can hold the vines at bay for a time."

"Good." Cadean nodded. "Time is what we need."

Sword out, I strode toward the wall, trying to shove down my apprehension. I barely understood how the Moon's barrier worked, but my gut told me that I could do this. I'd stopped Cadean by instinct. This was just the opposite. Just make a hole.

The Moon's magic washed over my skin as I approached the barrier, warm and cool at the same time.

As always, ethereal whispers rose around me as I stepped close, calling '*Samantha*' hauntingly on the wind. I shivered.

Were they the voice of the wall? Or of the Dreamlands itself?

I closed my eyes and pressed my hand against the smooth surface of the wall. Electricity sparked, and the magic flowed between us, making me feel like I was part of something infinite and limitless. Somewhere in the back of my mind, I could almost see the intricate latticework of the Moon's spell—magic held under impossible tension, waiting to be set free. Forming the image of what I wanted in my mind, I gritted my teeth and forced my will into the wall. *Let me through.*

At first, there was nothing, but as I pressed harder with my will, a wave of power swelled through me, spreading down my arms and through my hands. Suddenly, the wall vanished beneath my fingers. Cadean seized me around my waist, and he hauled me back against his firm chest as a mass of vines dropped right where I'd been standing.

"Shit!" I heaved in a breath. "I should have expected that."

Without a solid surface to cling to, the vines along the section of the barrier where I'd made a hole had collapsed.

Cadean steadied me as he stepped around to inspect the opening. The corner of his mouth twisted up, and I could tell he was forcing down a cocky smile. "Perhaps—but the important part is that it worked."

I looked up. Where there had been a crystalline surface, there was simply a patch of gently wavering light—a thirty-foot-wide gateway into the queen's domain. The early winter breeze whipped through the gap, bringing with it the aromas of the forest beyond—hickory, beech, and maple, and the promise of snow in the air. Most of the trees had lost their fall leaves, though tiny patches of yellow and red still clung to a few branches. My wolf stirred in interest. The scents of animals and splashes of color were a sharp reminder of everything Ayanna had taken from Cadean's realm.

He stepped back a few paces toward Vega, and his half-smile had faded. Perhaps the others wouldn't notice, but I could see the agony hidden by the hard lines of his expression. Guilt twisted my gut. I'd forgotten how much being near the barrier hurt him.

Fang glanced at Mel. "How much space do you need us to clear for your spell?"

She pursed her lips. "The larger, the better. Maybe thirty feet across."

He whistled low. "That's going to take forever without Cadean."

It was true. I'd been nearly useless the first time we'd attacked the vines along the border. I gripped my sword but doubted it would be much more use than the little knife I'd used when I was still the Dark Wolf God's prisoner.

A lifetime ago.

I glanced at the jet-black weapon hanging loosely in Cadean's grip. "Give me your axe."

His eyebrows rose in for a split second then dropped as a

tempest crossed his face. His hand tightened around the haft. "Absolutely not."

"I've used it before."

"And I swore I'd never let you touch it again. The blade is poison."

I tightened my shoulders at the memory of how the axe had twisted my mind in the Well of Life. I'd been consumed by its hatred, and after I'd killed Slaine, the hunger for destruction had only grown. A thousand deaths wouldn't have been enough.

Yet I'd also come to understand the truth of what the axe was —not just an enchanted weapon, but a manifestation of Cadean's dark power. A sliver of his soul.

He glanced at Fang and held the weapon out. "She's right, though. You won't make any progress without this. Take it."

Before Fang could respond, I stepped forward and wrapped my fingers around the haft, just above his. "Why won't you let me wield it? Are you afraid to let me see this part of you? Because news flash: I've seen you at your worst, killing fae and laying waste to my home. I'm not afraid. I'm still here."

His jaw tightened.

"Let me do this, Cadean," I pleaded. "I can carry your burden for a time. Giving me the axe is giving me the power to defend *my* wall."

His iron expression didn't flicker, but slowly, his fingers released. My arm dipped as I took the full weight of the weapon —not just the weight of the black metal, but the power it carried.

A boiling hatred pulsed through me as my emotions warped, suffocating all thoughts but one: *Where the fuck is Ayanna?*

She'd killed my mother. She'd destroyed this land. And now she thought she'd break through my magic? *Fuck that.* I wouldn't allow it. I'd cut off her vines, and then I'd cut off her head.

Without a word, I turned and strode through the gap.

"Are you sure you're okay?" Mel prodded as she joined me.

I tightened my grip as the axe's fury twisted and bored into me like ribbons of fire. "I'm fucking great. Tell me what you need."

Doubt flickered in her eyes, but she turned to survey the infestation of vines. "Clear them back thirty feet. That should allow me enough space to set a ward strong enough to keep them off this section of the wall."

I tested the axe in my hands. It was heavy, but not too heavy to swing. As I lifted it up, I hesitated for a fraction of a second. The more vines I cut, the more innocent people Ayanna would sacrifice to grow them back.

Fuck it.

She'd kill them all anyway. She'd been playing this game for centuries. I'd just have to find a way to kill her first.

Their blood is on her hands, not mine.

With a guttural snarl, I swung the axe high and brought it down, cutting through a vine a foot thick with the hiss of searing metal. The cut ends of the vine leapt apart like twisting snakes and splattered me with purple sap. It seared my skin like a branding iron, yet where the drops landed on the ground, slender blades of grass sprang up—restored to life by the blood of the vines.

I shook the stinging sap off my arm and turned to Cadean. "Pull the vines back across the barrier. Let their blood nourish your lands."

My stomach twisted. Their life restoring magic came from stolen power and the blood of sacrificed fae. It was an abomination, but it would have been worse to let it go to waste.

A storm raged in his eyes, but he nodded, then grabbed the severed vine and heaved it through the hole. Blood spilled in its wake, leaving a trail of tiny green flecks of life. It wasn't much compared to the destruction the vines had caused, but it was hope.

I tightened my grip on the axe and pushed into the thick of the vines, hewing at Ayanna's creations. If I couldn't kill her, I would lay waste to the source of her strength. I imagined every vine was Ayanna's throat and lost myself in the destruction and the punishing sting of the sap, even though I knew it would be futile in the end.

The only way to permanently kill the vines was to cut them off at the roots. I'd had my chance, but I couldn't do that without destroying the city of Dreamspire itself and all the people in it. Even fueled by the bloodlust of the axe, that was something I would not do. I wasn't Ayanna or Cadean. I wouldn't condemn innocents to die. Just her.

I lost myself in the bloody work until Cadean's voice shook through my body like an earthquake: "I said get back!"

I stumbled over the vine I'd just cut and looked up, stunned. Cut and bleeding vines lay everywhere, my skin burned like wildfire, and my entire body ached. How long had I been at it? Minutes? Hours?

"We've got company!" Fang shouted, unsheathing his sword and pointing to the sky. "Time to get the fuck out."

Deathwings.

I whipped my head around. Mel stood in the middle of an arcane circle formed from white power. She had a smoking goblet raised in one hand and blood dripping from the other. Her eyes were closed, and her lips moved in an inaudible chant. The vines at the edge of the circle were beginning to wither and squirm away like dozens of headless snakes.

"We're not leaving until Mel is done!" I shouted back.

Cadean stepped to the edge of the barrier, his expression contorted with pain. "You're more important than a spell! Get back across the border!"

But without the spell, the vines would quickly regrow. More to the point, I wanted to kill something that would scream when it died. I twisted my hands around the haft of the axe, its darkness seeping deeper into my soul. "Help if you want!"

I sprinted to the edge of Mel's circle as one of the monsters dove out of the sky. Seizing my power, I summoned a shield of moonlight, blocking its poisoned stinger as I spun and cut through its cluster of pink eyes with the axe's wicked blade.

The deathwing screeched as life left it in a curl of smoke, and I laughed with utter joy.

Cadean's magic crackled through the air like lightning, and the hair on my arms and neck rose. A gust of wind swirled around us, kicking up leaves and fragments of bark. The sky turned gray with whirling debris, and the deathwings became giant, mothlike shadows beating helplessly against the wind.

I cherished the protective shield of his power wrapped around me, but I hated it as well. I craved blood.

Shadows burst out from the gloom—fae soldiers with pikes. I summoned a wave of moonlight in front of me and dove into them, cutting through the spears and butchering those who wielded them. Men who killed for *her*. Men who had driven shifters from their homes and laid waste to villages. Men who had chosen to be monsters.

Instead of growing weary, my strength surged with each kill. Black flames began to belch from the blade, and all I wanted was more blood.

"Get out of there!" Cadean roared with an intensity I'd never felt before. His voice burst across me like ice water, waves of energy that demanded submission, obedience. The black madness strangling my thoughts shattered, and I gasped in revulsion as I looked at the slaughter around me.

Kass's arm wrapped around me, and he pulled me back toward the barrier. "It's done!"

I swallowed the spit flooding my mouth as nausea twisted my gut.

"Run, godsdamnit!" Kass boomed in my ear.

Suddenly, all three of us were running toward the wall. As soon as we were through, I threw out my hand as warriors and monsters charged the gap. Freezing sunlight surged through me as I poured my magic into the barrier. The gap closed in a thunderclap, crystal once again, silencing the sounds of battle and the cries of wounded men.

I stepped away from the barrier, safe for the moment, but as I tried to catch my breath, Cadean stormed toward me. "Next time, you get the fuck back when I say so," he thundered.

I ignored him, unable to tear my eyes away from the scene of devastation on the other side of the wall. The mangled bodies of broodlings, deathwings, and fae were strewn among the severed vines. The ground was covered with red and purple blood and the white lymph of the monsters.

I let the axe fall from my aching fingers, and it vanished in a wisp of smoke. My gaze settled on the contorted expression of one of the warriors I'd slain. My stomach lurched, and I vomited right there.

In the madness of the battle, all I'd seen were Slaine and Ayanna and monsters, but these were just men and women serving an evil queen.

I dropped to my hands and knees and heaved again and again until there was nothing left. Cadean knelt beside me and placed his hand lightly on my shoulder. "Let the poison out."

As if his permission mattered, I retched again. My face was hot with grief and shame, but I refused to cry. Anger beat through me. I was supposed to protect the Dreamlands, the fae included. Not this.

Cadean's magic tingled lightly over my skin, not pushing, but simply as a calming reassurance that he was with me. My heartbeat began to slow.

"Fuck, Wolfie." Fang whistled. "Remind me not to piss you off. That was some bloody work."

"Why were there so many soldiers there?" I rasped. "How did they get to us so quickly?"

"Ayanna has always guarded the border," he said. "I know their kind. They were butchers and mercenaries, accustomed to raiding villages and taking pelts for sport. They were probably out hunting for any shifters caught on the wrong side of the wall."

I braced against my knees as I waited for my guts to stop spinning. "Yeah, well, you can use the axe next time. I think I prefer my blade."

"There's not going to be a next time," Cadean said roughly.

I wiped my mouth and straightened. "We have a narrow window until Ayanna realizes what we're doing and stations an entire division in each place the vines are attacking. We have to cut them while we can."

"No," he said with a ferocity that made me take a step back. "We are not doing this again. We will find another way."

10

Cadean

For a long time, we rode in silence broken only by the pounding hooves of the tireless striders. The scent of frustration hung in the air and was reflected in the stooped shoulders and unfocused gazes of my companions. Of my mate.

My chest ached with anger and self-recrimination. I should have never let Samantha wield the axe. Her face was pale and drawn, strained by a mix of exhaustion and fury—a poison I knew all too well. The axe took everything. It thrived on destruction and stole your strength, compassion, and willpower in return. It would keep pushing until you had nothing left to give.

Few people could have carried it for as long as she had.

Yet how could I have asked that of my *mate*?

The axe was the manifestation of everything I'd come to despise about myself since meeting her. The rage, the hatred, the delight in death. It had been *its* magic that I'd used to sow chaos in Magic Side and to force Samantha's packmates to attack themselves. The thought of her wielding it, of having that part of my soul flowing through her, of her seeing the monster I truly was...the weight of my shame pressed down on me, an unbearable burden.

The axe was everything she hated, but without it, I didn't have the power to defend my realm from the Moon, the queen, and the Three Fates.

"Ayanna will triple down on protecting the vines after this," Kass said from behind me, drawing me from my dark musings. "She'll pull forces away from other assets, leaving them exposed. With Samantha's power to control the wall, we can slip a pack through and strike—"

"No," Samantha said, the exhaustion in her voice making it sound almost feral. "No more attacking fae villages, and no more raiding. You tried that for years, and it never made a difference."

Kass shrugged. "When we cut through the vines, they grow back. If we cut off fae heads, however, I doubt they'll do the same."

She spun Elowyn around to face him, forcing him to pull up short. "Do you think Ayanna gives a fuck how many of her people we kill? She doesn't care. She's more than happy to sacrifice them to feed the vines or let them bear the brunt of our wrath. *She* is the one we need to kill."

The ferocious glint in her eyes finished her thought for her: *I'm going to be the one to do it, even if it kills me.*

"She's right," I said. "The only thing Ayanna values is power, so that's where we must strike."

We returned to the silent road until Melanthe spoke. "When Samantha and Sarion escaped the queen's lands, Ayanna summoned a storm to stop them—that was your magic, Cade. I think draining the magic from your lands doesn't just giver her power, but access to your powers."

I nodded. "I also have the power of regrowth. That may be how she's spreading the vines so quickly."

"Right. But now the queen is siphoning magic from your wall. That might give her access to the Moon's magic as well."

My blood went cold. "If that's true, she could become powerful enough to control the wall, just like Samantha can."

"That would be fucking catastrophic," Kass said for all of us.

"Maybe there's a way to make the wall defend itself," Samantha said.

"Is that possible?" I asked warily.

"I don't know, but the Moon would. The wall is her spell. Maybe I could contact—"

"*No*," I snapped as a thousand years of resentment burst out. Samantha's eyes widened, and Mel winced as the echo of my voice died away through the trees. My shoulders were shaking, but I seized my anger and forced my heart to slow. "She would never help."

"She helped me before."

I shut my eyes, forcing myself to remain calm in the sea of bitter memories. "She assisted you when you were trying to restore my prison. If she knew you were trying to help me, she'd find a way to take her power back or even kill you."

"She wouldn't want the queen siphoning her magic from the wall," Samantha insisted, pulling alongside me. "Not after everything we did to restore the barrier."

I turned and met her eyes with a stone-cold glare. "If the Moon knew what Ayanna was capable of, she'd make a deal with her to destroy me."

"I doubt—"

"You don't know her like I do!" I snarled. "She conspired with the Three Fates to trap me here. You can bet she's just as ruthless as Ayanna, if not more."

Her betrayal lanced through me, a millennium too short a time to dull its bitter edge. We'd been lovers, but she'd turned on me and imprisoned me here. Perhaps she'd never felt anything at all. Perhaps it had always been a game to her. Had I known what real love felt like, perhaps I would have seen through the illusion of her smile.

I knew it now. What I felt for Samantha was nothing like the carnal lust I'd shared with the Moon. It was fierce. Unrelenting. It filled my every waking moment and haunted my dreams. It was not something I could walk away from, but lived within me, a wildfire that I couldn't tame or control.

Samantha was looking back at me with an expression I couldn't quite read. How could I ever explain what I felt for her?

How could I ever explain what had happened with the Moon?

I looked away. "I'm sorry, little wolf. Gods don't change, and she can never be trusted. There must be another solution."

I looked from her to each of my advisors in turn. "I have faith that you can find it."

11

———

Cadean

A solemn desperation accompanied us on the ride back to Shadowstone and followed us into Mel's workshop, where we brought Wulfric up to speed.

"Then there are only two solutions," the general said after we'd laid the problem out before him. "We kill the queen or destroy her vines. I know which I'd prefer—ripping out her throat with my claws."

"Wulfie, you're a hell of a fighter," Kass said, as he slumped into a chair and kicked his feet up on the table. "But you and the entire army couldn't take on the queen. Cade's the only one that can, and something tells me Ayanna's not going to accept an invitation to settle this by single combat."

Wulfric grunted dismissively at Kass while Mel crossed the room and pulled an age-worn book from the shelf. She paged through it, her attention elsewhere.

Samantha drew a hand over her face. "Then vines it is."

Exhaustion weighed on her features, but she was still the most beautiful creature I'd ever laid eyes on.

"I should have done it before," she said quietly, staring down at the floor between her feet.

"Done what?" Kass asked.

"Destroyed the vines." She met my gaze, a mix of sorrow and frustration in her eyes. "You were right, Cadean. I should've cut them off at the roots when I had the chance."

My chest ached for her. My beautiful little wolf had a heart of gold, and I'd tried to corrupt it. I'd made her doubt herself.

Drawing near, I tipped her chin up to me. "I should never have asked that of you. I was wrong."

She pulled free of my touch, shaking her head. "But we wouldn't be in this situation right now if I had. Ayanna would have been cut off from her source of power. Perhaps I would never have had to make the barrier impermeable."

"If you'd severed the roots, you would have destroyed everything built upon them. They would have withered into dust, and Dreamspire would have collapsed in on itself, killing everyone in the palace, the city, and beneath it, including you. Do not question your choice. It was the right one. I was simply blinded by hate and eager to strike."

I suspected this had been the reason Ayanna had entwined the city with vines in the first place—her court could never cut off her source of power without dooming the city and themselves.

"But Ayanna—"

"She probably would have escaped like she always has while I'd still be trapped in this prison, but without you."

"It wouldn't just have been Dreamspire," Mel said as she flipped through her book and then added something powdery to the copper pot bubbling on a small burner.

Samantha looked up questioningly. "What do you mean?"

Mel sprinkled some ingredients into the potion she was

crafting, and a hiss of steam billowed up. "Not only have the vines infested the realm, but they've embedded themselves in the fabric of the land. If you'd killed them, they would have undermined much more than Ayanna's palace."

I scrubbed a hand across my jaw. "Fuck, you're probably right. Half the realm would have been affected."

My sorceress shot me a pointed look. "Thank you. I hope you remember that in the future when I counsel you."

I bit off the retort on the tip of my tongue and crossed my arms. "So, what's your advice now, sorceress?"

"We need a way to stop the vines without bringing down the entire realm."

Kass folded his hands behind his back. "Sounds simple. You've got a solution, then?"

"Maybe. Give me a minute." Mel turned her back and began shuffling through tinctures on her shelf, her irritation thick in the air. "I'd have a better idea already, but *someone* has been meddling with my supplies."

Samantha's brows lifted, her eyes glittering as they darted around the room. "Rune?"

The blood sorceress went rigid as she was reaching for another bottle. Her head whipped around toward Samantha. "You'd better tell that goblin to stay out of my apothecary or he'll be sorry."

My little wolf's lips pulled into a soft smile, and she nodded. "I'll relay the message if I see him."

I'd also have a few words to say to the little thief.

Mel went back to her project and began grinding something foul with a pestle. Wulfric and Kass pulled out a map of the border lands and began to study it, while I paced the room, trying to think.

Samantha sat alone, staring at her hands, summoning small

bursts of moonlight, and then dismissing them as if somehow, she could summon the solution from thin air. I could see the weight she was carrying, and it pressed on my heart like a stone. It was because of me that she was suffering. The Fates may have bound our souls, but I was the one who'd brought her here in the first place.

The sickening part was that if I had a choice to do it over again, a chance to ensure that we'd never meet, I wouldn't. She was mine now, and I could never let her go.

That was proof enough that I was a greedy fucking bastard who didn't deserve her.

Mel slammed a ladder against the wall and climbed up to the high window. She retrieved a potted plant from the ledge and came back down. Only then did it register what she had.

"You're growing some of Ayanna's vines?" I growled. "In here? Inside my domain?"

Kass looked at Wulfric. "The witch has finally lost her mind."

Mel ignored him as she set the small pot on the table. "Samantha brought back some of the fruit—well, technically, the fruit was smashed, but the seeds were viable. I sprouted them."

"For what fates-damned reason?" I asked.

"For finding a fates-damned solution. Just watch." She clipped off a small section of the vine and placed it on a plate. Using a glass dropper, she sucked up whatever potion she'd brewed and placed two drops on the tendril.

Immediately, the skin of the vine changed in hue from purple to gray as the tendril petrified.

"Incredible," Samantha whispered, approaching.

Excitement flickered on Mel's face. "We need a way to destroy the vines without undermining Dreamspire and the surrounding lands. If we turn them to stone, then problem solved! The city stays standing, and the queen won't be able to siphon magic from the wall anymore."

"Holy shit," Kass said. "That's actually brilliant."

"All my work is brilliant. I can't help it if you're too dense to understand," Mel said as she picked up the petrified vine and tossed it to him.

He caught the stone instinctively but immediately dropped it. The tendril shattered across the floor. "Shit, Mel! Are you trying to kill me?"

She smirked. "Relax. Once the process is complete, it's not contagious."

"How certain are you of that?" Kass asked, inspecting his hands.

She shrugged.

"Can you make more of that potion?" Samantha asked the sorceress. "And would it be enough to kill all of the vines?"

"Yes and no. Comparatively, it wouldn't take a lot to petrify the whole lot of them. Once the potion touches something, the petrification will quickly begin to spread. However, to make enough, I will need a *lot* more of the key ingredient," she said, holding up a nearly empty vial. "And it's a bit difficult to get."

"Which is?" I asked.

"Blood of a cockatrice."

Kass whistled low.

The vicious beasts lived in the western peaks that bordered the Moon's barrier. One sting from their multiple barbed tails would turn you to stone.

I placed my palms on the table and leaned forward, considering the potential of it. "Assuming you have this blood and can make the potion, what does this plan look like? Do we pour it on the vines along the barrier and let the blood do its work?"

Mel hesitated and set the vial down on the table, her expression exhausted and forlorn. "No. There's no way I could make enough to kill them all that way. We need to kill them from the roots."

"The Well of Life," Samantha said softly. "I'll have to break back into Dreamspire."

"Not you," I said roughly. "You got out once. You're not stepping foot in the queen's domain again."

"Only those with fae blood can enter the queen's palace or the Well of Life," Samantha said, crossing her arms. "And last I checked, I'm the only one here who has it."

"We'll find someone else."

"But I've been there—"

"My word on this is final," I snarled. After what had happened in Mistwind, I wouldn't allow it.

"Let's focus on the problem at hand," Mel said, stepping between us. "We need to get cockatrice blood—as much as we can. That will be perilous enough to start."

Perilous was an understatement.

I fetched one of the maps that Mel had stacked against the oaken bookshelf and unrolled it on the table, glad for a chance to avoid the argument with my brave little wolf. "The only cockatrices in my realm winter in caves in the high peaks of Mistveil," I said, pointing to the far western mountain range depicted on the moth-eaten parchment. "I'll head out at first light."

"Alone?" Kass scoffed.

I looked up at the faces of my counselors, and then at my mate. "There's no coming back from a cockatrice's strike, and I can't afford to lose any of you. They are vicious, territorial creatures, and their numbers have multiplied since the Moon constructed the barrier. I'll go myself."

"Then you're immune?" Samantha asked.

My jaw ticked in annoyance.

"You're not, are you?" she said, her voice suddenly leaden.

"A strike will slow me," I said, "but I don't intend to get stung."

That was as close to the truth as I wanted to admit. I'd been stung before. It had been blinding agony, and a chunk of my skin had hardened. If I were attacked in a nest...

"I don't like this," Samantha said, the tight lines at the corner of her mouth telling me she suspected the truth.

"I appreciate you being a hero, Cadean, but your plan is fucked," Kass said, gesturing to the map. "This chart is outdated. The barrier has shrunk since it was made."

My fist clenched. He was right. The barrier had started retracting when Ayanna had begun draining power from my land. Dozens of shifter villages were now on the other side of the wall.

Wulfric tapped on the parchment. "The barrier is here, on the wrong side of the caves and the pass. Kass and I will have to go the long way around. It should take us an extra two days.

I shook my head. "Time that we don't have and a risk I don't want to take."

"Then take me," Samantha pressed. "I'll push the barrier back, just like *you* used to do with the moonshard."

I flexed my fist in agitation. If I still had the moonshard, this would have been no problem—but Samantha had used it to heal the pylons.

"We'll find another way," I said, preoccupied with plotting the route Kass and Wulfric would have to take to get to the pass. "You're not going."

Moonlit flames leapt around her hand, and she stalked forward. "I'm sick of you treating me like I'm made of glass. I am an asset, and I can help. Stop disregarding me."

"I'm not—"

"You *are*. No one else can extend the barrier, but I can. I'll push it back far enough for you to enter the caves and track down one of those creatures. I'll stay back, perfectly safe, while you do the hunting."

A muscle in my jaw popped. "Nowhere in the Mistveil Mountains is safe."

Or the Dreamlands. Not for her.

Frustration flashed in her eyes as she dismissed the light around her. "You don't believe I can handle things my own, but I can."

I reached out to touch her. "Trust me, little wolf. I believe in you—"

Samantha slapped my hand away. "Then trust *me* and stop trying to cut me out of this war, because I'm a part of this, whether you like it or not. I'm choosing this path because I believe in it."

Every fiber of my being rebelled against the thought of putting her in danger. But she was right—she wasn't my prisoner any longer. I couldn't keep her locked in Shadowstone anymore.

Kass's voice broke the tension that stretched between us. "It's not a bad plan, Cade, and the only option if you want to enter the caves yourself. Otherwise, it'll take Wulfric and me a day or two to circle around the pass and make the ascent, even if you fly us to the border yourself. It'll be slow going, particularly in winter."

Fuck. Winter. The mountains were dangerous enough without snow.

"I'm up to this," Samantha said resolutely, though her eyes were pleading.

How could I tell her no? The Fates had put her on this path, and I knew keeping her from it would kill her just as much as the sting of a cockatrice, only far more slowly. She'd wither like the vines, cut from their roots.

I scrubbed my hand through my hair. "If I let you come with me, you must promise to stay behind the barrier and *obey* me. I'll find our target and bring it down. Do you understand?"

"I understand."

I pinched my brow. "Fine. Then we'll fly in the morning with an escort of fire drakes. The cockatrices won't come out into the cold, but there are other dangers. You are not to leave the drakes behind."

The little dragons would be able to fly her to safety, if needed, and their heat would keep her warm. They were the best bodyguards I could think of, given the limitations of getting there quickly.

Samantha nodded, a weight falling from her shoulders. "Got it."

There was a sudden radiance about her, a lightness I understood well. Nothing was worse than having your hands tied. Being trapped and helpless within my prison had eaten away at my soul. It meant everything to be able to fight back.

"Don't forget about Elydora," Mel said. "You'll need to pay your respects to her...especially if you're bringing Samantha. You should make an offering for safe passage."

A heavy silence fell over the room as I cursed the Fates for fucking me over at every single turn.

"Elydora?" Samantha looked between Mel and me.

Kass snorted. "She's a mountain deity. Also vicious and territorial."

And jealous.

Auren had once been her plaything, but she'd taken more than an interest in me over the last few centuries. I hadn't crossed paths with her for decades, but I had no doubt this reunion would be unpleasant.

"Gather up whatever you think would appease her," I said, trying to keep the irritation from my voice.

"There's only one thing that will appease her, Cade," Mel said dryly.

I looked over at Samantha, who was scrutinizing the map. "That's not an option anymore."

"Well, then you'd better be prepared for a fight."

12

Samantha

I headed through the halls of Shadowstone as dawn broke over the fortress walls. I'd dressed in a heavy fur parka and boots and strapped my sword over my back.

I hadn't slept well again, and my head was pulsing with a low, aching throb. My muscles ached, too. It was probably just lingering exhaustion from the day before. Cadean could probably restore me with his magic, but I didn't dare mention it before we left. I was certain he'd use any excuse to cut me out of the expedition. If it didn't clear up, I'd ask once we arrived.

"It will be brutally cold up in the Mistveil, my lady," Lorsha said as she and the rest of my escort followed me through the silent halls.

The tall, curly-haired captain was my favorite. Out of all Cadean's guards, she'd actually warmed up and carried on conversations with me since she'd first been posted.

She was still far too formal.

"Just call me Sam."

"Here," she said, passing me her heavy red scarf. "You're going to get windburn if you go like that."

I took the beautiful red piece. "Thank you. You don't need it?"

"I'm not assigned to the barrier today."

When we reached the great hall, a young doorman leapt to his feet. His cheeks flushed when he recognized me, and his fingers fumbled as he unlocked the heavy wooden door. "There's a bitter cold northerly wind today, my lady."

A rush of frigid wind kissed my cheeks as I stepped out, my eyes tearing up, and I was instantly glad for Lorsha's gift, which I wrapped around me. This was like the arctic blasts that blew through Magic Side in the winter.

The ground was covered in a light dusting of snow. Wulfric and Kass were speaking to Cadean, who appeared to be furious. His shoulders were tense, and he shook his head.

"Ready a garrison of soldiers—" A gust of wind lifted my hair in a frenzied mess, and Cadean stopped mid-sentence and looked back at me. "Little wolf," he rumbled in acknowledgement.

Three pairs of eyes bored into me, but only the Dark Wolf God's felt like they were penetrating my soul.

A thin veneer of snow crunched under my boots as I descended the steps. "What's going on?"

"Ayanna has responded to our attack on the vines. She's massing forces along the border," Cadean said.

"For now, I assume they're just protecting the vines," Wulfric offered. "But if she's able to breach the wall, those forces will become a spearhead."

My stomach tightened at the thought. "She won't be able to breach the barrier."

The wall was mine.

"You're certain?" Kass asked, but I didn't respond.

"Position your forces to respond, if necessary. Pull everyone from the south that you can spare," Cadean said to Wulfric, then turned to Kass. "There are plenty of fae in our realm. I want you to assemble a team of fae defectors who have the training and knowledge to get into Dreamspire. Ayanna probably has plenty of spies among the fae in our realm, so make sure it's done in secret and that you ask the right questions."

A team to go instead of me. I balled my fists to stop myself from saying something that would no doubt only further antagonize Cadean. He was stubborn and proud, and I knew that once he made up his mind about something, it was damned near impossible to change it. I had to pick my battles wisely, and at that moment, getting the blood of the cockatrice was more important than winning this argument. We'd discuss Dreamspire once I'd proven my value.

Cadean turned and glanced down at me. His mood was dark, and the shadows cast across his face only added to his deathly aura. "You're prepared to ride?"

"I'll ready Elowyn and Vega."

A sly smirk crossed his lips. "No need, little wolf. You'll be riding me this morning."

I lifted a brow. "Will I, now?"

"And *that* is our cue to go." Kass rolled his eyes and placed a hand on my shoulder. "Remember the footwork we practiced. If you do find yourself face-to-face with one of those winged devils, stay ahead of it and try not to get stung."

With a wink, he turned and headed back toward the great doors of the fortress.

Wulfric simply eyed me. "Your magic will protect you better than any footwork that ponce has taught you. Stay safe. Return quickly."

It was probably the most tender thing the general had ever said to me.

I nodded, and he left us alone.

The Dark Wolf God stalked up to me and cupped my cheek.

"I know you're furious with me—I can feel it. I'm sorry, but this is how it must be for now. I risked too much last night."

His words were soft and his touch tender, and my chest throbbed. We'd worked so well together when I was in Dreamspire, but since I'd been back at Shadowstone, it was like there was a fissure in our relationship.

"Has something changed between us?" I asked softly.

A blaze of emotions smoldered beneath his composed exterior. "Why would you ask that?"

"You've just been acting...different."

Distant. Suffocatingly protective. Disappearing each night.

He leaned down and dragged his nose up my jaw, breathing me in before whispering, "When Ayanna is dead and the threat against you is gone, I promise I will make it up to you, my beauty."

I closed my eyes, relishing the way my skin pebbled under his touch. "It'll take a lot of making up."

He pressed a kiss against my neck and then grinned down at me. "Then I'll start tonight."

"I'll hold you to that, Wolf God," I said. "Speaking of which... what's this about riding you?"

"The fastest way to Mistveil is to fly," Cadean said as he retrieved a strange collection of harness and tack and threw it over his shoulder. Then, without warning, his magic exploded through the courtyard. In a swirl of shadows, his human form shifted into a majestic bird of prey, a black phoenix with feathers as sleek as obsidian.

He looked back at me with a pair of amber eyes.

"Incredible," I whispered.

He'd taken this form to fly me to the pylons, but my memories of the journey were little more than broken fragments. Seeing him like this in person, without terror and desperation clouding my mind—it was breathtaking. And daunting. I'd held on for dear life and buried my face in his feathers. The world had seemed so small below us. It would be a very, *very* long fall.

Maybe I should have let Fang and Wulfric go after all.

As if reading my mind, the phoenix—Cadean—stretched his wings, revealing the harness and tack he'd slung into place. A saddle.

I've had the stablemaster working on it since our last flight, Cadean said in my mind. *Buckle the strap around my chest.*

I stepped forward and ran my hand along the silky feathers of his wing. His body quivered, and he looked back at me. *Touch me there again, little wolf, and we won't be leaving my citadel.*

I pulled my hand back, and then I saw the heat in his eyes and understood.

My cheeks burned. "Right, sorry."

He chuckled.

I reached underneath and secured the billet straps, trying not to laugh.

Tighter, Cadean instructed. *I don't want you to slip off.*

I did so, and then awkwardly, I swung up into the saddle. I'd never seen anything like it. The saddle was made of several parts: a harness that I sat in, a set of suede straps that fitted over my upper arms, and two smooth pommels to hold on to. Once I was seated and cinched into the harness, I leaned forward and slid my arms through the straps. Though it was a strange position to be in—sprawled out on my belly—it was remarkably comfortable. The stablemaster was clearly an unappreciated genius.

I pulled against the straps, checking them one last time. "All right, I'm all set."

Cadean glanced back with those amber eyes. *Hold on tight. Flying is not like rock climbing. If even for a second you feel unstable, let me know.*

He reached out and grasped a large chest that had been left beside the wall with one of his huge, taloned claws.

"What's that?"

Offerings for the goddess of the mountains. If the Fates are kind, we won't see a sign of her.

With that, Cadean exploded into the sky, his massive wings beating the air. His muscles rolled and strained beneath me as we rose above the walls of Shadowstone.

13

———

Samantha

Cadean circled the fortress as we gained altitude. The dark stone of the castle sucked up the sun's rays, and drips of melted ice flowed in sparkling rivulets down its sides. The white claw-like spires that rose from the heart practically glowed in the dawn.

"Fates," I whispered, "it's beautiful."

It is.

Several of the staff who were up and milling about spotted us overhead. One waved, while the others looked at us in wonder.

Cadean cried out as we passed one of the spires. Three shapes burst forth from a small roost and began flying toward us: little black dragons with red wings and wide, fanlike tails. They belched bursts of flame into the sky as they fell into formation.

Fire drakes—my new bodyguards.

With the fire drakes drafting behind us, we soared over the great lake beside the castle, which had a little forested island at its heart. Beyond the lake, I could see for miles in the hazy morning light. The landscape was a patchwork of different terrains with dozens of hamlets, villages, and towns tucked in—and far above and beyond us, the golden barrier that had come to mean so much.

"If I were you, I'd stay up in the sky and never come down," I said absently, watching the sunlight glistening over the lake.

No matter how beautiful it is, I wouldn't be able to stay away from you for long.

As soon as we crossed the mountains surrounding the lake, we turned our backs to the sunrise and began flying west. Far off to the left, I could see Mistwind Harbor, and I could almost smell the cooking fires on the wind.

We flew on over the marshes and then into the wide, forested vale at the heart of the realm. Despite the bright sunlight, the three pylons shone like lighthouses in the midst of the darkness. Each of the orbs emitted a steady beam of light that rose into the air, powering the now impermeable dome high above.

We passed directly over the one that had been erected in the middle of a small lake.

Down there is where we first met, Cadean said, his voice mournful.

The memory pierced through me. I'd attacked him with one of the moonstones the Moon Goddess had given us to recharge the pylons. I'd had no idea what I was doing when I threw it, but somehow, I'd trapped him in a sphere of light.

Then he'd used his magic to force my best friend to kill me.

My eyes watered. I passed it off to the biting wind and not to the well of sadness that suddenly felt like it was suffocating me. "We've come a long way since that day."

It felt like years but had only been four short months since the attack and three since he'd abducted me. So much had changed.

The phoenix looked back briefly, but in that flash, I saw the same emotion in his eyes. *I've done horrible things to you. I've imprisoned you, interrogated you, and used you. But nothing haunts me more than what I did down there. I don't think I could ever be sorry enough for it.*

I looked away from the pylon and the little lake. "I've forgiven you, Cade. I forgave you long ago."

I don't deserve your forgiveness, nor do I want it.

His voice was so bitter, so filled with self-hatred, it felt like the words had stabbed me through the heart.

"I don't care. I've forgiven you all the same." I rested my face against the soft feathers of his back. "If you hadn't killed me, I would never have had the power to stop what's happening here. I would've never learned about my past. I wouldn't have you or my magic. It was a small price to pay."

What came of it doesn't change what I did.

"We were enemies then. We were at war. We're different people now." I wiped my damp cheek on my shoulder. "Let's not be enemies anymore."

I swear I will never hurt you or anything you love again, little wolf. You are worth more than the sky and lands to me.

"Why?" When he didn't respond, I asked. "Is it because I'm the key to your prison? Is that why you're so protective?"

The phoenix lurched beneath me as if suddenly hit by a downdraft. *No!* he snarled in my mind. *You aren't the key, because releasing me would kill you, and you're worth more than my freedom. Or my magic. Or my honor. You are worth more than all of that to me.*

"Then why?" I asked, shocked at the fury of his denial.

We rode in silence for a while, but at last, he spoke. *Because you are precious. Because you're everything that I cannot be. This place needs you, and so do I.*

Deep in my soul, I knew what he'd said was true. That he truly cared for me.

Yet there was also something he was hiding. The way he spoke in my mind wasn't exactly with words, but with meanings and images and thoughts. And in that collage of meanings, there was a shadow—something he wasn't saying.

For some reason, I was afraid to ask. Maybe because I sensed that whatever it was, it made him afraid. What could do that to a god?

We didn't speak again for a long while, and I contented myself to watch the changing landscape below. The wind chilled me to the bone, but the warmth of the sun on my back and Cadean beneath me staved off the worst of it.

After what seemed like hours, a rugged range of snowcapped peaks rose up from the golden-brown grassland rolling before us.

"Are those the Mistveil Mountains?" I asked.

Let's take a closer look.

Cadean pivoted his wings and soared downward, leaving the fire drakes behind.

My stomach dropped as we plummeted. I screamed with delight as the golden plains raced toward us, letting the exhilaration clear my thoughts. Cadean pulled up just before we crashed, and we glided silently above the dry grass.

I laughed, relishing this brief moment of joy—the heaviness that had been hanging over me was completely vanquished.

How does that compare to a...rollercoaster? That's what you call them, yes?

"Better. A rollercoaster's got nothing on you."

I could almost feel him preen. *I should hope so. I am a god, after all.*

Cadean began beating his wings faster and faster. The height at which we'd been traveling had concealed our earlier speed, but now that we were only twenty feet up, the land was moving by so quickly that I was beginning to feel queasy. We raced over a flock of sheep, scattering them across the plain in a white, bleating wave. The shepherd bravely stood his ground as they stampeded by, his hand raised to block out the sun. I glanced back to shout an apology, but he hadn't moved.

He was stone.

I saw them now, scattered here and there across the hillsides. The shattered gray remains of sheep, men, and wolves. All stone.

"The cockatrices did this?" I asked as we swooped up the face of the foothills.

Before the Moon created the barrier, the cockatrices were kept in check, and they didn't venture so far from the peaks. But now their numbers have spiraled out of control, and they're a persistent threat to the shepherds and shifters who dwell in these lands.

"Are there no natural predators?"

Not anymore. The great mountain gryphons disappeared long ago, hunted by fae for pride and glory. Now the cockatrices roam free. There is always a balance, Cadean said solemnly. *That's the way of the wild.*

I tried to ignore Auren's warning that replayed in my mind: *Millennia of beliefs have shaped who he is and what he is striving for. My brother would annihilate civilization and return the land to an untamed state.*

Auren could go to hell.

As we left the foothills, the fire drakes caught up with us, emitting a burst of flame as acknowledgement.

The wind buffeted us as we sharply rose on an updraft. The Mistveils were rugged and majestic. We soared over the steep and varied slopes. Some were rough, jagged rock, while others were piles of loose, crumbled stone. Thick snow blanketed the upper peaks, but lower down, there were drifts and exposed patches of grass and scree.

Cadean deposited the chest on a saddle of rock midway up two of the tallest spires, then landed beside it. I slid my arms out of the straps and climbed down, then looked around as Cadean shifted back to human form and discarded the harness.

"This place is magical," I said, wandering among the hardy shrubs and admiring the brilliant orange lichen that clung to the rocks.

"In more ways than one," Cadean answered.

Wisps of clouds flew overhead, but otherwise, the sky was bright blue in stark contrast to the black volcanic rock. A hundred yards uphill, the Moon's barrier rose. It was still solid and impermeable, much to my relief. Thousands of ice crystals had formed along it and glistened in the sun.

Further up the slope was the mouth of an ominous, dark cave.

"That's where you're headed, isn't it?" I asked.

"All monsters are drawn to the darkness," Cadean said, as the shadows rose around him. "But first, we must deal with a danger of another kind."

14
_____

The Misveil Mountains, on the border of Cadean's realm
Cadean

I heaved the chest of offerings onto my shoulder, and we hiked uphill toward Elydora's shrine.

It was simple—a cluster of weathered standing stones surrounding a flat slab that overlooked the steep scree slope. They'd been erected and carved by the shepherds who dared to enter the peaks, though few came this way anymore. Pilgrims and travelers had left small cairns around the shrine. Most were toppled. Elydora knocked them down out of spite.

She was a fickle goddess.

Praying that she wouldn't show her face, I said a short mountain blessing in the way of the shifters of the valley and laid my offerings on the slab: a deer I'd brought down in the citadel's woods; smoked fish from seas she would never visit, cheese and wine from the Summerlands, foreign silks woven from vibrant reds and yellows, and a tincture of perfume that Mel had bought in the harbor. All the things Elydora couldn't get.

I hoped it would be a fair exchange for not getting me.

She'd developed a keen interest in me when we'd met almost a century ago. Over the years, that interest had turned into an obsession, and ultimately, possessiveness. At that point, I'd abandoned the borderlands to the cockatrices and her.

I looked around uneasily. I didn't like having Samantha anywhere near this place.

"Do you think she'll accept the offerings?" Samantha asked as she arranged the silks with a little more care than I had shown.

"The sooner we can leave this shrine, the better."

"Is she dangerous?"

"She's possessive like an avalanche and bitter like the mountain wind when she doesn't get her way," I muttered as we began to descend.

If Elydora so much as touched my woman, I'd annihilate her.

Samantha's shoulders were tense, and I placed a hand along her back as we crossed the rocky slope. "Be wary of her, but do not fear her. Your power is equivalent to if not greater than hers. She's a minor deity, though she holds sway over these mountains."

"How do you know her? Is there a pantheon of gods and lesser deities and spirits or something?"

"These are my lands. I know all the beings who dwell here."

"Mel implied that you used to give her a different type of offering."

My neck flushed, and I raised an eyebrow at my mate. "Are you jealous?"

"If that means what I think it means, abso-fucking-lutely."

Good. I loved her bluntness, and I craved her covetousness. I couldn't hide the grin pushing at my cheeks. "Don't worry, little wolf. There's nothing between us. Our paths crossed many years ago, and she took a liking."

"A liking?"

My beautiful mate was *quite* jealous.

"A liking is nothing," I said, and pulled her to me. One hand on her hip, the other tangling in her hair, I leaned down and kissed her, slowly and deeply. A soft moan rose in her throat, and it was enough to undo me. I broke the kiss and looked down at her. "You're my queen, Samantha, and that is everything. There's no one else."

"Okay, then," she said breathlessly.

Everything about her set me on fire. I wanted to pin her up against a boulder and ravage her right there, but given Elydora's predilection for violence, nothing could have put my mate in more danger.

I pulled away. "Let's go."

We headed back down the slope toward the barrier until Samantha stopped short.

I looked down. Below us was the hardened corpse of a goat, a gaping hole in the middle of its chest.

She glanced up at me with a look of horror. "The cockatrices did that?"

I flexed my hand, wondering how much I should explain. All of it, if it would keep her safe. "Once stung, the petrification process begins from the outside, paralyzing you as your skin slowly hardens. They peck through the rock and feast on your innards."

The color drained from her face. "They eat you like a hard-boiled egg?"

I winced at the accuracy of her description. "Stay here, and don't go anywhere near the cave. They roost for the winter, but if anything or *anyone* besides me ventures out of the cave, take cover and stay out of sight."

I would never have brought her if she couldn't summon her

moonlight shield. I knew she could defend herself, but on some base level, I needed to protect her.

Samantha's gaze remained fixed on the shattered stone body. "Cadean?"

"Yes?"

"Be careful."

I lifted my brow. "I appreciate your concern, but lest you've forgotten, I'm a god."

"All the same, be careful."

I brushed her cheek and then lightly kissed the top of her head. "I will."

"Good." A warm glow emanated from her palms as her magic sparked to life. "Then are you ready to do this?"

"Extend the barrier just beyond the mouth of the cave. No further." I gave her one last glance, then summoned my axe, letting its darkness consume me. Shadows rose from the weapon, along with the overwhelming desire to destroy, and my thoughts narrowed to a singular focus.

To protect my mate, I had to destroy Ayanna and her vines.

That began with this hunt.

Samantha unleashed her magic on the barrier. A detonation of light spread from the impact site, and the barrier began advancing up the slope, extending my realm beyond its limit. No matter how many times I'd witnessed her do it, it was no less incredible.

Once, I'd been able to work this magic with the moonshard. Now, the barrier was hers alone.

I strode forward, following the crystalline wall as it retreated. The Moon's magic rushed over me, burning my skin like frostbite, but the pain only fueled my determination.

A stream of warm, putrid air flowed from the mouth of the cave, carrying the scent of decay and shit.

Inside, it was a nightmare landscape. The walls were covered with feces and deep gouges from the beasts, and all around, as far as I could see, were the remains of stone corpses. I knew the cockatrices overwintered in shelters, and I'd once witnessed a pair inhabiting an abandoned bear cave, but I'd never seen anything like this.

I shadow-stepped through the darkness. As I descended further into the mountain, the air grew hotter and ranker and became punctuated by a cacophony of snarls, screeches, and squawks.

My boot crunched something underfoot, and I glanced down at the hollowed-out petrified remains of a male fae. I rolled the unlucky fellow over with my boot, and a stone face, mouth agape in terror, gazed back at me. The poor fool had still been alive when the cockatrice had pecked away his skin and feasted on his entrails.

Like a hardboiled egg. I would never be free of that particular image.

A light source emanated ahead, and I shadow-stepped to a patch of darkness near it.

"Fates be damned," I muttered above the racket.

A sprawling cavern opened below and above me, lit by a turquoise pool at the base that bathed the space in a pale blue light. I reached out over the ledge on which I stood and touched the damp, warm air that rose from the hot spring.

The walls of the space were painted with streaks of gray excrement and, like a honeycomb, pocked with at least a hundred holes large enough for a griffstryder to fit through.

It was a fucking hive of cockatrices. No wonder the slopes of the mountains had become a sculpture garden.

"Impossible," I whispered as I gazed into the cavern below. "They're completely out of control."

"It's amazing what happens when you neglect your duties," a soft, feminine voice said from behind me.

Silently cursing, I turned toward Elydora. There was no mistaking her signature as it wrapped around me—the bitterness of blackthorn bark and the sweet fragrance of forget-me-knots.

Ironic, as all I wanted to do was forget the mountain deity.

"Elydora," I said warily.

She smiled at me coyly. She wore a long purple shift and a large fur cape that swallowed her petite frame. "I'd thought you'd forgotten about me, Wolf God. I'm so pleased you came looking."

Dealing with her was a highwire act, one I had little patience for.

"You're not easily forgotten, but I'm not here for a visit. I've come for a cockatrice."

A flicker of disappointment flashed in her icy blue eyes, and beneath that, a razor of warning. "*You* should know better than to enter my domain without bringing me something in return."

"I placed an offering at your shrine and said the words."

She laughed heartily. "*That* pitiful display? You dishonor me, Cadean." Elydora stepped close and traced a finger along my arm. "My hunger cannot be sated with food and silks. You know what I crave."

I grabbed her wrist and pushed it away. "Then you'll be sorely disappointed. I promise to send something more fitting later but leave me while I hunt. Time is short."

I turned back to the lip of the cavern to find a path down, but her voice stopped me in my tracks. "Who is that woman outside? Is she part of the offering? If so, that changes everything."

In less than a heartbeat, I'd clasped my hand around Elydora's neck, the urge to snap it beckoning me. "Touch her, and I will end you."

The deity's face contorted in shock, then jealousy.

I instantly knew I'd betrayed my hand, but I was committed now. "Leave, Elydora. Do not speak to or meddle with that woman outside. If you cross me, I swear that I'll make your last moments in this world agony, and then I'll banish you to an eternity in the worst of the hells."

"Let me go!" she spat, sinking her nails into my arm.

I didn't let my gaze waver. "Promise."

"I won't speak to her or touch her."

I released her and turned back to the cavern. I should have felt remorse and disgust for handling her like that, but I didn't.

"You're a monster, Cadean!"

"In more ways than you know."

"I will leave you and your whore, but not before I cause you the same pain as you have caused me."

A torrent of magic slammed into me, a frigid gale that knocked me off the ledge. "I hope they eat your heart out!"

My shadows billowed around me as I fell. Cursing, I twisted in the air and managed to grab a handhold on the wall and swing into one of the openings in the cavern. Before I could launch myself back up onto the ledge, the whole cavern shook. An avalanche of stone fell from above, knocking me back and sealing me into the small space.

Dread and an all-consuming rage swallowed me. I would not be imprisoned.

Something shifted behind me in the darkness.

I spun around. A hulking form moved at the back of the cavern, barely visible even with my dark vision. Tightening my grip, I summoned a ball of flame into my left hand.

For a second, the fire reflected in the glossy black eyes of the monster. It raised its wings as it reared up, serpentine neck coiled back and razor-sharp beak open wide.

Then it struck with all three tails.

I twisted out of the way, hewing through one and dodging the second. But the third pierced my arm. Pain exploded through my shoulder, and my bicep stiffened as my magic fought against the creeping petrification.

"I don't go down so easily," I snarled, then charged headlong at my prey.

15

Samantha

"Come on, Cadean," I said, my body quaking as I pushed more magic into the barrier.

He'd only been gone ten minutes, but holding the wall back was taking far more of my energy than I'd thought.

The mountains seemed far more ominous without him at my side. Here and there, the remains of stone corpses stood, gruesome reminders that winter or not, this was the cockatrices' domain. But they weren't the only danger.

I searched the slope for the snow leopard I'd seen shortly after Cadean had left. It was a magnificent creature, but I didn't want it sneaking up on me. The last thing I needed was to be made a meal of by a giant cat.

At least the fire drakes were flying patrol, circling high above me, watching the rock and snow.

I wiped the sweat off my cheek with my shoulder. "Just a little longer."

Exhaustion flowed over me like waves, but I was strong enough still. I was an idiot to assume that I could manipulate the barrier as easily as I had in the past. It was solid now, and I'd started the day fatigued.

A low rumble erupted underfoot, and I stumbled on the loose stones.

The barrier raced toward me as my concentration faltered.

"Shit!" I pushed more magic forward, and it slowly retreated.

What the hell had that been? An earthquake? Hopefully, it was Cadean slaying a cockatrice. I didn't have a whole lot of strength remaining.

A sweet floral fragrance drifted on the cold mountain wind. I glanced in the direction of the scent and jumped.

A woman wearing golden-brown fur was perched on a boulder, staring at me with an expression that was either curiosity or hatred. She was beautiful. Her striking blue eyes were the color of the sky, while her raven hair matched the mountain rock.

"Elydora?" I asked.

She slid off the boulder and strolled over to one of the statues, gently tracing her fingers over its stone skin. "The pretty thing knows my name, but I don't know hers. Unfortunately, the Wolf God made me promise not to speak to her."

Fear streaked up my spine, and I shuffled to the side. "Don't come any closer."

Everything about this woman screamed *crazy bitch*.

One of the drakes landed beside me, clearly of the same opinion. It raised the spines on its back, hissing.

"Pity, so few interesting people come here. I've no one to talk to," she said to the statue, then began to slowly prowl toward me.

That look she'd given me earlier was definitely not curiosity. Nope. This woman really didn't like me. I could smell her animosity like a burning dumpster fire.

Trouble I didn't need.

Cadean had told me not to fear her, but hell, I knew a woman scorned when I saw one. He'd also either underestimated her strength or overestimated mine. She might have been an even match for me if I wasn't holding the weight of a gigantic magical wall, but in my current state, I had little reserves to protect myself.

I had to stall her. I cleared my throat. "The Dark Wolf God told me all about you. He spoke of your unrivaled beauty. Of your eyes that mirrored the sky. Your hair that reminded him of the shadowed peaks."

Fates, I was terrible at this.

"He said that you two met many years ago," I continued, "and that you had a special relationship."

"Special," she mused as she eyed me with suspicion, but at least she'd stopped stalking toward me.

"How do *you* know him?" she asked directly, no longer keeping up the guise of speaking to the statues. "What is your relationship? *Special*?"

Her words dripped with venom.

Honesty was always the best choice when it came to dealing with supernatural creatures. They usually could detect lies, but it didn't mean I had to tell the whole truth. Just the one she needed to hear.

"The Dark God nearly killed me," I said. "And then he imprisoned me in Shadowstone."

"Then you're his captive?"

"In a way." He'd begun as my most reviled foe but had somehow managed to capture my heart.

She smirked and clasped her hands behind her back. "Then you will be happy to learn that I've trapped him. You're free to go. I will take care of the beast for you."

A deep, primal growl escaped from my throat, as adrenaline and anger flooded my system. Magic reserves or not, I would kick this bitch's ass if she'd harmed Cadean. "I'm not going anywhere until he walks out of that cave."

She flung her hands up, and a gust of wind hurled snow and razor-sharp shards of rock at me. Stinging cuts welled up across my bare skin and the force of the gust knocked me over the boulder, tumbling me a good ten feet along the rough slope. The fire drakes beat against the wind, breathing fire but the gust pushed them back further and further away from me.

I rolled to my side. Pain blossomed when I breathed but nothing felt broken.

"These are *my* mountains, mortal. Leave or I will be the last thing you see," Elydora said bitterly.

I quickly glanced up at the barrier. It had fallen back to the opening of cave. Cadean would be trapped. Panic lanced my chest, and I pushed more magic toward it as I stood on wobbly legs. It slowly retreated, taking more effort than before. "I'm not leaving."

Elydora's lips quivered with anger. "You dare defy me, you idiot girl? Do you know who I am?"

My patience withered, and I strode toward her. "Do you know who *I am*? Samantha Bennet, bitch."

I devoured the shocked expression on her face, then unleashed a bolt of moonlight from my palm. It hit her squarely in the chest, sending her tumbling ass over teakettle across the snow and scree.

While she lay stunned in a pile of her furs, I braced my feet and drew everything I had left in me. Currents of my magic flowed into the wall, one of my them holding the barrier in place behind the cave entrance, and the other pulling a section of it downslope toward Elydora and me. I'd gotten the drop on her, but I needed to get the wall between us before she recovered.

My arms screamed, and it felt like an inferno was eating up my insides, but I kept channeling my power. I heard the cries of the drakes, and they flew back against the fading wind.

But before they made it, Elydora crawled onto her hands and

knees, a stream of blood flowing from her temple. Anger flushed her cheeks, and her magic sent shards of stone flying into the air.

I dove behind a boulder, ducking the storm of debris.

"You'll see what happens to defiant little wolves!" she shouted as her magic boomed through the earth, followed by the rumble of an avalanche.

I was officially out of time. I needed more power.

Reaching deep to the source of my magic, I pulled all I could from that place of light and warmth. My right forearm fractured as Moon's magic coursed through me. I screamed as I tried to keep my focus on the barrier, pulling it to me as quickly as possible.

Although it was crystal, it moved around me and over the rocky slope like butter, forming an impenetrable wall between the goddess and me.

A half breath later, the avalanche hit the barrier, spreading in a cascade of snow and sparks, but didn't break through.

But now I had bigger problems. I'd pulled the wall below the cave entrance. That meant Cadean was trapped and had to be suffering something unimaginable.

Elydora sat upon an isolated spire of stone amid the snow and kept flinging her magic at the barrier, but it was to no avail. She screamed in fury.

I struggled to push the barrier beyond the cave. "Come on!"

But I'd spent too much of my magic to move it anymore from this distance. I had to get closer. I got to my feet and began climbing, using each step to push the barrier a little further. Elydora realized what I was doing, but she was too late. By the time she reached the entrance to the cave, I'd already sealed it off from her.

Ignoring her insults and curses, I stepped into the dark

entrance. A massive pile of rock filled the passage. He was trapped.

Despair filled the emptiness inside me, but I wasn't going to give up now.

"Cadean!" I shouted. "I will never forgive you if you leave me on this godsforsaken mountain!"

16

______

Cadean

My chest tightened. Samantha's voice echoed distantly from the chambers beyond the collapse. Her pain and exhaustion resonated through our bond and dread consumed my mind. She was hurt, and her strength fading.

Fear for her drove me on like wildfire. I stumbled through the jumble of rocks, my body still fighting the toxins after getting stung a half dozen times. Summoning my power, I hurled myself against the collapse and rammed the blade of my axe down into the pile of stones. The earth shook, and shards sprayed through the cavern beyond. I swept the rubble away with a blast of wind.

Elydora had defied me, and she would pay.

Dust swirled in the blue light of the turquoise pond that lay beyond, and the cries of cockatrices echoed off the cavern wall.

Seizing the corpse of the one I'd slaughtered, I hauled myself out of collapse and climbed up the cavern walls. The cockatrices circled in the air and began to dive down at me, but I called a savage windstorm to keep them at bay, buffeting their bodies against the stone walls.

Nothing would keep me from her.

I sent my shadows forward, streaming through the darkness, seeking the presence of my mate. Like a compass, they pointed back through the winding chamber toward the entrance of the cave.

What the hell was she doing there? I'd told her to stay *away*.

With the heavy body of the cockatrice slung over my shoulder, I scrambled forward as her pain became more intense. If any of the creatures got to her before I did...

A glimmer of white light appeared, and I shadow-stepped to the mouth of the cave.

Samantha was down on one knee in the entrance of the cave, silhouetted against the white snow beyond. Her head hung in exhaustion, but her hand was raised, inches away from the golden barrier that was encroaching along the side of the cave and searing my skin.

"Samantha!" I shouted, running forward.

Panic choked me when she didn't respond. I dropped to her side. Her arms quaked, and she didn't look up or acknowledge I was there. *Fuck.*

She was pouring herself into the barrier, but utterly spent and her magic was waning. The barrier was inching closer to us by the second.

I heaved the cockatrice out through the mouth of the cave, then scooped up my mate in both arms and charged through the opening.

I ground to a halt in shock as soon as I emerged into the bitter wind.

Samantha had reshaped the entire wall, creating a bubble around the cave—and on the other side of the barrier, there was Elydora.

"What have you done?" I roared at the spiteful deity, but I

had no time to take heed of her response. The barrier appeared behind me as the bubble rapidly collapsed.

Tremors shook Samantha's body.

"Release the damn wall!" I shouted as I transformed back into a phoenix.

Samantha's back arched, and the barrier roared toward us like a tidal wave of crystalline light. I scooped her up with one claw and the cockatrice with the other, then hurled myself into the air.

Searing moonlight crackled over me, igniting my nerves and nearly blinding me, but I beat my wings as hard as I could and soared ahead of the wall.

A blast of arctic wind shook through me, and the mountain rumbled.

Elydora. She had the nerve to attack me, now?

I banked hard to the right and soared down the slope as a rumbling avalanche of snow and rock followed us.

I would deal with the mountain deity another day. All that mattered was getting my little wolf to safety as quickly as I could.

Once we were in the foothills and out of Elydora's domain, I plunged toward the first shelter I saw: a shepherd's cottage, used in summer when the sheep grazed the high foothills.

I dropped the cockatrice and then gently alighted with Samantha. I transformed and picked her up, then kicked open the door of the cottage. Dust stirred and swirled through the dim space. We were alone.

Samantha was ice cold, trembling uncontrollably, and barely conscious.

"What did you do to yourself?" I asked as I knelt on the ground.

Grinding my jaw, I poured my magic into her. Tendrils of fire and life roared along the mate bond we shared. Her back arched as she groaned with the ecstasy of it. I didn't stop. I focused my power, heating her frozen limbs, closing the red wounds that cut her hands and cheeks, restoring her strength. Everything I had, I gave to her.

When I was done, her head rolled back lazily so she could look at me. "Did you get it?" she choked through chattering teeth.

"What?" I growled in utter confusion.

"The cockatrice."

That was what she was worried about at this moment?

"Of course I did," I scoffed.

Her lips pursed. "Cocky bastard."

We didn't speak much on the way back, and I'd sunk into a black mood by the time we finally returned to Shadowstone in the late evening. Samantha was still exhausted and shivering from the flight. We hadn't had time to retrieve the harness before it had been consumed by the avalanche, so she'd had to cling to my bare back and hold tight against the cold wind. Kissing her frozen lips, I left her in my chambers to recover with a hot bath while I headed to Mel's workshop, a dark anger building around me.

I dropped the half-frozen corpse of the cockatrice on her workbench without a word.

"You got it," Mel said, eyeing me carefully. "Judging by the look on your face and your generally shitty disposition, I'm guessing it didn't go smoothly."

"Samantha nearly died," I growled, then turned my back on her and began to stalk the room. "If I hadn't gotten to her in time, either Elydora would have killed her, or her own power would have burned her alive."

"Then it's lucky you got to her when you did."

"Lucky? Samantha is the *unluckiest* woman in this forsaken realm. I nearly got her killed. *Again*."

A storm of sensations clashed inside me, rolling in on waves of anger.

She sighed. "First of all, will you stop pacing my workshop like a rabid animal?"

"If I stop moving, I'll either break something or murder someone." I gave her a withering stare. "I don't want it to be you."

"I understand why you're upset."

"You know nothing," I snapped. She had no idea what it was that I was feeling. I couldn't even pinpoint the emotions I felt other than the desire to rage.

"You're furious because you believe that you can't protect your mate," she said. "Or am I wrong?"

The bitter truth of her words halted me like a blade to the chest.

"You feel helpless," she continued. "Powerless, in a way. It goes against every fiber of your being."

"I've been helpless for a thousand years! I cannot protect my own kingdom, let alone a single wolf. I'm an expert in powerlessness by now."

"You're pushing her away. We can all see it. You need to tell her the truth before the rift between you grows too deep."

My shoulders rose and fell as the weight of her words sank in. "I can't tell her. The Fates know I've wanted to, I've tried, but..."

"And why not?" Mel asked matter-of-factly.

"She won't accept me."

The sorceress's eyes rounded, and she laughed. "The Dark Wolf God is afraid of being *rejected*?"

"Watch yourself."

"I'm watching *you*, and I'm telling you what I see; a god who is afraid to face the truth and afraid to show a little faith in his mate."

Her words ripped through me like a saber. My forearms clenched as I held back my claws. Her honesty was why she was my most trusted advisor, but she could be ruthless.

She could be wrong.

Samantha would never accept me as her mate after everything I'd done. I gazed down at my palms. They'd had so much blood on them, including hers. "She claims she's forgiven me, but there comes a point when the sins you've committed are too great for forgiveness. She'll never forget."

"Then you need to prove to her that you've changed, and that begins with trusting her. It begins with the truth."

I looked up at my sorceress and shook my head. "I don't even trust myself with that."

17

Samantha

My body was still steaming from the bath when Cadean returned. I pulled my damp hair back and quickly pulled on a nightgown. When I entered the bedroom, the scent of lingering smoke and cedar drifted lazily over me, but no one was there—just strange shadows cast by the flickering glow of the sconces.

"Cadean?"

No answer, but the deep thrum of his signature pulled me toward the balcony. A chilly draft blew through the open door, along with a few flakes of snow. I padded past the warmth of the fire, its flames licking up the chimney. Outside, Cadean stood like a statue. Gentle flurries dropped silently around him, looking like stars where they clung to the black cloak that covered his broad shoulders.

I stopped at the doorway, the cold dampness biting my toes. "Cadean?"

He didn't move or speak, but I felt his darkness. It slipped around me like an oil slick, acrid and suffocating. He was furious, and I didn't know why.

"What's the matter?" I gently prodded.

After a moment, he said, "You disobeyed me today."

His tone was harsh and void of warmth. Colder than ice.

I frowned as my mind did gymnastics but came up empty. "You'll have to elaborate because I have no clue what you're getting at."

He turned and faced me with a glacial expression that stopped my heart. Shadows billowed from him like flames, pouring from his fingers and licking up his arms.

Fuck.

I slowly stepped back. I'd never seen Cadean like this before, and it was a stark reminder of why he was so feared. I lifted my chin, refusing to be intimidated.

His eyes tracked the movement, and his lips curled into a hard line. "I cannot trust you to keep out of trouble. I told you stay put, and yet I found you *in* the cave, nearly dead because you drew too much power. You can't take risks like that."

I blinked twice, and a shocked laugh tore from my throat. "I stayed put *until* I needed to save your ass."

His brows rose as his pupils dilated. "Save *my* ass? I'm a god. I'm immortal."

Red-hot anger seeped into my veins. "Yes, you remind me of that every day. But what would have happened if I'd dropped the barrier while you were stuck inside of that damned cave?"

His jaw worked, but he said nothing.

"You would have been trapped by rock on one side and crushed by a burning wall of magic on the other. That's what."

I retreated into the warmth of the bedroom as he slowly prowled after me.

"I would have survived," he said, his tone sharp as glass.

"Sure. Encased in eternal agony."

"The agony would have been far worse for me if you had died," he growled, so vicious and low that the hair on my arms stood. "I told you to stay away and stay out of that cave. You never obey."

I couldn't believe that *he* was angry with *me* over this. Any fear I'd had was long gone and replaced with a fiery rage for that hard-headed ox.

I stalked forward and jabbed my finger into his solid chest. "I stayed back until your sweet ex-girlfriend showed up and unleashed an avalanche on me. Whatever you did to piss her off, that's on you, not me—I just did what I had to do to keep us both alive."

His hungry eyes darted to the rapid rise and fall of my chest, leaving a trail of heat in their wake.

"She kindly gave me the option to leave your sweet ass," I continued. "But regretfully, I didn't."

Something savage flashed through his eyes. "You should have manipulated the barrier and stayed out of the cave. You could have been killed by a cockatrice."

I glared up at him, furious at how easily my body betrayed me. "I didn't have enough power to hold her off and keep the barrier from cutting you in half. I was too weak. Is that what you want me to say? Because I was. *Weak.*"

"You are anything but weak," he said as he clasped my arm with a firm but gentle grip and pulled me toward him. His smoky leather scent wrapped around me, and my traitorous body leaned into him. "I promise you that."

"Then don't treat me like it." I twisted out of his hold, needing oxygen.

Cadean turned away from me and braced himself against the stone hearth, looking deep into the flames. He sighed and pinched the bridge of his nose. "I'm sorry. I'm furious with myself. I should never have brought you there," he said remorsefully. "I shouldn't have put you in that danger."

And there it was. The underlying cause of this argument—his overbearing and unrelenting protectiveness over me.

"I knew what I was getting myself into," I said defensively. "We're at war. We have to take risks."

"I will not stand by while you throw yourself into danger at every available opportunity!" he said, prowling back toward me. "You've risked enough already. You're done."

My shoulders quaked. "You don't dictate that, you domineering asshole! I am my own woman, and I will choose what risks I take, not you! Why must you be so suffocatingly protective all the time?"

"Because you're my fates-damned mate, that's why!" he boomed.

The feral intensity of his words thundered through the floorboards and sent the walls of my world crashing down like an earthquake.

His mate?

Cadean's shoulders heaved. "That's why I can't stand to see you in danger, or even imagine you in pain. Because you're precious to me above all things. Because you are my mate, Samantha, and there's nothing either of us can do about it."

My pulse throbbed in my ears, and the room swirled around me like I was stuck on some strange carousel that was about to throw me off.

"Your mate," I said, my voice suddenly weak. "That's impossible."

But it wasn't impossible. It was true. Despite everything I wanted to believe, I felt it in my gut and in my bones. Our connection. His power to heal me. The magnetic draw he had on me. They way our magic entwined when we were together.

I looked up at the lethally beautiful man before me.

The Dark Wolf God was my mate.

A wash of conflicting emotions fell over his face as he searched my eyes for something but was left wanting.

Confirmation? Acceptance?

I could barely accept the idea, let alone him.

"How do you know?" I asked, resisting the urge to collapse onto a chair.

"Sigrun confirmed it. But I've suspected for a long time."

My claws tingled in my fingertips. "Then why the hell didn't you tell me?"

"Because how could you accept the monster who killed you?"

I couldn't answer that.

When I didn't speak, he shook his head. "I didn't ask for this any more than you did. I even considered rejecting the bond…"

His words gutted me even as fury blinded me. "Did you ever consider what *I* might have wanted?"

"That's why I said nothing!" He strode toward me and grasped my arm, pulling me close. His body vibrated with restrained tension as he looked down at me with a volcanic expression. "It is *all* I think about each and every waking moment when I'm not consumed by soul-crushing guilt and terror for your safety."

I glared up at him, my heart hammering against my chest. "Maybe you should have asked me instead of presuming to know what I want."

He slid his hand to the back of my head, fingers tightening in my hair as he tipped my head back further. His smoldering eyes darted to my mouth as he glided the tip of his tongue across his own lip. "Tell me, little wolf. What *do* you want?"

Pain and something else arced down my spine. My treacherous body angled toward him, and I was suddenly very aware of his own desire.

"I want you to stop regarding me as your responsibility, godsdamnit, and to start treating me like someone worthy of being your mate."

"*My mate.*" His gravelly tone nettled my sensitive skin. "You truly think you could handle being my mate?"

"Try me," I shot back.

He arched a brow at my challenge. "You chafe at your bonds now, little wolf. Pray tell, how will you survive my singular fixation if you accept the mate bond?"

The wind whistled through the open balcony doors, sending a gust of swirling snowflakes into the room. The cold bit through my thin linen nightgown, and goosebumps pricked the backs of my thighs.

I tilted my head and glared up at him defiantly. "I don't let alphas boss me around. Not even my mate."

His lips unfurled in a slow and deliberate curve of approval as his hand slid up my nightgown and cupped my butt cheek. "Then you're willing to accept that your body and soul will be bound to mine? That you cannot decide one day down the road that you've tired of me and wish to leave? That you'll never be free of me again?"

His words probably should have frightened me, but it was quite the opposite. They stirred something deep and primal inside me. To be wholly possessed by this god and to possess him in return. To be rid of all the pretense, all the games, and all the doubts. To let the beast within me take over.

To claim him.

To claim a *god*.

An aching heat pulsed deep inside, but it couldn't match the radiant glow that had enveloped me—the knowledge that he was my path, my fate, and my destiny.

I pressed closer to him. "You'll be stuck with me, Wolf God. I won't submit. I won't stay locked away. And I will defy you if you keep me from what I want, mate bond or not. You sure you can handle that?"

He lowered his head to my exposed neck. "It will be a struggle, no doubt"—my eyes fluttered closed as he planted a delicate trail of kisses from my collarbone to my jawline—"but I shall persevere."

"I expect my mate to stand with me. To believe in me. To never hold me back."

His expression grew serious. "I believe in you more than anyone I've ever met, little wolf."

"Then come here and claim me," I said in a breathless challenge. "If you dare."

With a bestial growl, he ripped my nightgown open, then grabbed me by the hips and pulled me to him. Our bodies surged together, united by a force far more intimate than love and more powerful than desire.

Cadean's mouth crashed into mine, his lips devouring and punishing me with his kisses. I tasted the lingering traces of summer wine on his tongue and drank him in while my fingers fought with the buttons on his trousers.

As soon as I'd released him, he hoisted my hips up, and I guided him into me. I was wet and readier than I'd ever been. When he thrusted into me, it wasn't gentle or sweet, but primal and overwhelming, and my body responded with an animalistic need to be touched, filled, and consumed by him. My nightgown was already torn to shreds on the ground, and I clawed at his shirt, needing there to be nothing separating his flesh from mine.

Our magic rose around us—beams of light and wisps of swirling shadows intertwining and merging in a haunting dance —and the world fell away. It was just Cadean and me, joined in body and soul.

I ground against him, but somehow, it still wasn't enough.

Sweat dampened our bodies, and the taste of salt lingered on my tongue. A raw, untamed power grew as I dug my heels into Cadean, driving him deeper inside me. It spread from my center, ecstasy filling every space in my body and fiber of my being.

Then panic gripped my chest as this feral power overwhelmed me, yearning to be released, but with nowhere to go.

"It's too much," I gasped.

"I've got you, little wolf. Come with me."

It wasn't a command but an unspoken invitation to accept the bond that would seal our fates together. My mind, body, and heart were ready, but I wasn't prepared.

But it was too late, far too late. I'd made my choice long ago.

Agonizing pleasure ripped through me, my spine arching as radiant light streamed outward, converging with the velvety tendrils of Cadean's magic in an explosion of crackling sparks. Cadean held me tightly as spasms of his own delicious pleasure racked his body. My heart squeezed, and I feared it might give out, as wave after wave rolled through me, each binding me closer to Cadean.

The waves of ecstasy slowed, and the symphony of our magic ebbed, leaving us tangled in each other's arms and completely spent.

I was connected to the world around me in a way I'd never been before. My skin tingled with new sensations, like I was suddenly attuned to the forests outside, to Shadowstone itself, and to Cadean. I could sense his emotions more deeply now in inexplicable ways. The firelit room seemed to drift in and out around us like waves each time we breathed together.

I was a part of him now. A part of the Dreamlands itself.

I gazed up at him, and his lips pulled into a languid smile of genuine pleasure and approval. "You are mine, Samantha Bennet, now and forever."

18

———

Cadean

That night, my mate rode me like a wild animal, relentless and unquenchable, until the bedframe cracked, and we lay there, exhausted.

I was at peace in a way I hadn't been for centuries. Perhaps ever. I felt a sensation of rightness, of harmony that had never been there before. I knew I would be made to pay for the fleeting moment, but I would cherish it as long as I could.

With a deep rumble of satisfaction, I rolled over to look at my mate and lazily dragged my thumb along the dark mark that was emblazoned into the soft skin under her left breast. "You're shadowkissed now."

Samantha jerked her head up and peered down her naked body. A faint shadow in the shape of a wolf was imprinted on her skin. Her eyes flicked to mine. "What is it?"

Grinning, I leaned forward and gently kissed the mark. "I've marked you, little wolf."

"What?" She pushed herself up and lifted her arm to get a better view of it. "You marked me like a dog marks a tree?"

I tipped my head back and laughed, and then pulled her

onto my lap so she was straddling me. "You're so irreverent. It's not quite like that, but sure, same idea."

She pushed me down onto the bed and began surveying my body. "So where is my mark, then? It's not fair if I don't get to mark you."

"You'll find it sooner or later."

She narrowed her eyes at me playfully, and then pulled the fur blanket back to continue her search.

Resting my hands under my head, I watched in amusement until she found her mark. It was a band of golden light woven seamlessly into the tattoos along my chest.

"It's beautiful," she whispered, lightly tracing her fingertips over it.

"And so are you." I gripped her bare hips and rolled her under me, bracing my weight on my forearm. "It proves that I am yours and you are mine, and none can question that."

A delicate worry line graced her otherwise smooth brow. "What is it, little wolf?"

She shook her golden hair. "It's nothing. Forget it."

"What is it?" I asked suddenly alert.

"Just a dream. Nothing more," she said, sliding off me, the mood suddenly fractured.

I rolled over and propped myself up on my arm. "Dreams are never nothing in this place. Tell me, or the incessant curiosity will keep me from ravishing you again."

She turned to her side, facing away. "It was a week ago. I dreamed I was fleeing the vines and calling for you, and then a black jackal appeared and tried to claim me. He said that I wasn't yours, but his."

Like Elydora's avalanche, crystal-cold dread rolled through me and left me churning with anger.

The Opener of Ways.

What the fuck was that bastard doing in her dreams? I

forced a liar's smile on my face. "You are mine, little wolf. Don't let any dream convince you otherwise."

I would destroy him for this.

She eyed me carefully, looking for a tell. "The dream was real, wasn't it?"

I hesitated a moment too long.

"Don't lie. I'm your mate," she said, searching my expression.

"The visitor was real, but you don't belong to him. You are *mine*."

"He was death," she whispered, but it was an arrow through my chest.

Just like that, the peace I had was shattered, and I doubted I'd be able to find it again for a long time.

"He is not," I grated out, trying to keep my anger at bay. "Just a god who doesn't know his place. You'll never be his."

Samantha brushed her fingers along the side of my face as if *I* were the one in need of comfort. "I can't hide from death, Cadean. I'm going to die one day—I'm hoping it's after I've had a long run at life, but I will die. Nothing can change that."

My jaw clamped shut as hard as a vise. I would do whatever I had to do to keep that day at bay.

She nestled into my arms, and we lay back down together. I breathed in the scent of her sweat, cherished the warmth of her form and the feel of her heartbeat against my skin.

She sighed softly. "Maybe that's why the Fates gave me to you. To teach you how precious mortal life is."

My heart breaking, I brushed her golden hair gently from her neck. "You're already more precious to me than all the stars in heaven or all the souls on earth. And as for the jackal, don't worry about him. I'll make sure he never bothers your dreams again."

∾

Three hours later, I dropped the body of a freshly killed stag in the middle of the torchlit clearing I'd prepared. Its splattered blood was nearly black against the thin layer of white snow.

I hated to leave the warm embrace of my sleeping mate, but I had a score to settle, and it had to be done. The Opener of Ways had better stay the *fuck* out of Samantha's dreams.

Pitching my head back, I released a howl into the night sky, infusing my voice with the weave of my magic. The howl reverberated down through the roots of the trees and deep into the earth, then died away—a summons not meant for shifters or mortal ears, but for the gods themselves. It was an act of sheer desperation, but I'd do anything to protect Samantha, even if it meant bargaining with old enemies.

At first, there was nothing, and then an unearthly silence filled the woods. The six torches that ringed the clearing flickered as if blown by a strong wind, even though the air was still. The flames shifted from red to blue, and the air filled with the scent of parched earth and incense. The shadows slipped and shifted unnaturally, as if something were prowling just beyond the edge of the light.

My fists tightened. The Opener had arrived.

A pair of golden eyes appeared in the darkness, and I raised up my blood-covered hand. "Come and claim what is yours by right, Opener."

He hesitated for a breath, then stalked into the ring of light. He wore his jackal form, with fur as smooth and black as obsidian. He wasn't as large as my wolf, but his muscles were lean and powerful. He stopped beside the still-warm body of the stag and looked up with a glare of unrestrained malice that was almost as strong as the waves of power that rippled off him.

For a moment, I thought he was going to leave, but he opened his jaws and inhaled the ephemeral tendrils of soul light that coiled off the stag's body.

I bowed my head with what respect I could manage. "Thank you for accepting my offering."

He bared his teeth, and his words formed in my mind. *I guide all souls into the netherworld, even those offered by you. Its soul belonged to me the moment it was born.*

My muscles tensed at his arrogance. He was not death, only the ferryman. I steeled my expression, hoping my contempt didn't show.

Why have you summoned me, mighty Wolf God? he asked, making no attempt to shield the vitriol beneath his words.

Flames of fury flickered under my skin. "Stay out of Samantha's dreams. These are my lands, and the dreamworld belongs to me."

The jackal grinned. *Just as she belongs to me.*

My black axe materialized in my hand, appearing in a dance of shadows. Smoke billowed from the edge of the blade, and it was all I could do not to lunge forward and strike. "Samantha is mine."

She should be dead, but the Fates stole her from me. I will take her back, and I will take her soon.

Never.

A searing heat flushed my neck, and darkness crept into the corners of my vision. Yet I had to control the rage. I needed him.

"I offer you a trade."

The jackal's eyes bored into me. *You have nothing I want except the girl.*

My mate.

Every instinct I had urged me to strike, to tear into him, if only for a moment while he remained in my domain. But my anger wouldn't help Samantha, and she was all that mattered.

Hand practically shaking with fury, I dismissed my axe, and my mind began to clear.

"You're worried about Samantha, but you let the Queen of the Undying Court defy you."

The queen will be mine in the end, the jackal said. His stance was casual, but I could feel the irritation in his voice. Good.

"She and her court have defied death for centuries, and as long as she's able to steal the magic from my land, she'll never be yours. She'll dole out immortality to whomever she chooses and continue making a mockery of you."

The Opener shifted into human form in a blur of darkness. His black fur became a robe of midnight, but his eyes remained those of a jackal, yellow and full of hate. "You make a mockery of me, harboring that *girl*."

I circled him, knowing that I had his interest now. "I've seen into the heart of Ayanna's palace, and I know how to take immortality from her grasp. I offer you the queen and her court in exchange for Samantha's life."

"You can do nothing while locked in your prison, Wolf God," he spat.

I stepped close, reminding him whose domain we were in. "I can do enough. I know how to break her. Samantha is the key. But I won't risk her unless I'm certain she will survive," I said. "Release your claim on her soul, and you'll have a hundred more that have defied your reach for centuries."

The Opener's lips pulled back into a sneer. "I'm a patient god, Cadean. I will claim their souls in the end, just as I will claim *hers*. There's no escaping fate."

A guttural growl reverberated through me. "Think of what I'm offering! Ayanna stands in defiance of you, and yet you quibble over a single soul?"

He stepped forward so that we were inches apart. "I will do my duty because I respect the rules of our world, even if you and the Fates do not."

I gritted my teeth, my jaw cracking under the strain. "Surely one soul is worth hundreds? Samantha means nothing to you."

"She didn't until the Moon and the Fates pried her from my grasp. Now, she means everything. My honor will not be defied. I will claim what is mine by right."

"You are not the god of death, despite what you might believe," I snapped. "She's not yours."

Fury flashed in his eyes, as my words dug into old wounds. "Samantha is a mortal. She died. It is my duty to ferry her soul into the darkness, and I will do my duty—a concept you seem not to understand."

I scoffed. I understood duty. It was not to rules, but to my land and people...and to my mate.

With a derisive look, the Opener turned and strode toward the shadows.

Fuck. I couldn't believe I was doing this.

Cursing under my breath, I shadow-stepped to the edge of the ring of light and spread my hand wide. "Surely there must be something I can offer you."

"You've already given me the only thing I ever wanted from you, Cadean: *suffering*. Whatever this woman is to you, it's tearing you apart. The desperation is written on your face and echoes in your voice. That's music to my ears, Wolf God." He revealed his teeth in a triumphant and predatory grin. "When I finally take her from you, I'll watch you mourn and rage and weep, powerless to stop me. That day, my soul will be full."

My claws tore free from my left hand as the axe formed in my right in a wreath of shadows. "I'll never let you have her, you fucking bastard."

He backed up, remembering the power I wielded in my own realm. With a final glance, he leapt toward the edge of the circle, taking the form of a jackal once more.

She will be mine in the end, Wolf God. I promise you that.

His form vanished into the shadows, and the flames turned back from blue to red. The Opener was gone, but his malicious grin lingered in my mind, mocking me for having failed my mate once again.

I pitched my head back and roared.

The branches quaked overhead, yet my throat couldn't release the rage boiling up inside of me. I hurled my axe through the night. It sank deep into the trunk of an oak, and I pushed my magic into it, channeling my hate and fury though the dark streams of shadow that bound me to the blade. The tree shuddered and twisted, and then its trunk split in half. Shards of wood rained down around me, but the destruction brought me no relief.

I would find a way to defy him, no matter the cost.

19

———

I woke with a pounding headache, tired and exhausted, yet somehow still wrapped in the afterglow of last night. I slowly opened my eyes and stretched my arm out, finding only empty sheets and a cold pillow. As always, Cadean wasn't there.

Except he was—his presence filled the room, rumbling through the wood and stone, wrapping around me like a parka against the cold, and his scent mingled with the aromas of sweat and blood and smoke.

I rolled over, and a deep satisfaction warmed my breast. Cadean sat in a chair against the shadowed wall, watching me with a ferocious intensity I'd never seen before.

My mate.

The thought of it sent a shiver over my skin. My mate was a god, and not just in bed. A fucking deity from the depths of time. A savage beast and noble warrior and entirely mine.

The Fates must absolutely be off their rockers.

Stretching, I studied my solemn watcher with lidded eyes. "Where have you been all night?"

"Hunting."

His scent told me that was both the truth and a lie, but I was in no mood to press him.

"Must you always leave my side?" I reached out lazily toward him, murmuring, "Come back to bed."

A soft laugh slipped from his throat as he crossed his legs. "I'm covered in blood and soot. I'm hardly in any shape to join you."

"I'll be the judge of that. Come into the light for a closer inspection, Wolf God." I turned back the covers and stretched out languorously. When my inviting motions didn't have the intended effect, I slipped my bare legs over the edge of the bed and sat up. "Fine. I guess I'll have to come to you."

I stood, but a sudden wave of vertigo raced through me, and I slumped back onto the bed, grasping the post for support. "Gods, did we have a lot to drink last night?"

Cadean rose. "What is it?"

I shook my head and sat back. "Nothing. Just a moment of weakness. It'll pass."

His expression darkened as he approached. "You expended too much power yesterday. You're going to kill yourself trying to manipulate the wall like that. I don't want you doing it again."

My neck heated, and pride forced me to stand, even though my legs ached with exhaustion. "You were in danger."

"I'm immortal."

"That doesn't mean you don't need protection," I said, stepping into the sunlight and running my fingers over the solid outline of his chest.

He tensed as if my touch were ice.

I flicked up my brow. "What's wrong?"

Cadean grasped my arm and turned it over.

"Hey, that—" My words were cut off as I saw what he had—glowing purple-blue lines spreading across my forearm.

My stomach plunged. "It's—"

"The same curse I had." His magic sparked, and all the lamps in the room came to life. He turned me around, then traced his fingers gently down my spine. "It's here as well."

My thoughts moved in a fog.

"How is this possible?" I asked, turning my arms over in a daze. The spiderwebs of light stretched from just above my elbows to the backs of my knuckles. "Is this because the vines are attacking the wall? Because of my bond with it?"

"I don't know—but you can be certain this is Ayanna's work." He turned me back around and brushed his thumb gently along my jaw. "But fates be damned if I'm going to let her witchery take you. You stopped my curse when you healed me. Perhaps I can do the same."

He pressed his hand firmly over the pale veins of light covering my forearm, and my skin ignited with his power, a river of electricity flowing endlessly back and forth between our souls. I gasped and sank into him as his lifeforce shuddered through me, turning my muscles to gelatin. My heart raced, and it felt like I was falling and flying and dancing through sunlight. I moaned and arched my back, overwhelmed by his power.

He didn't stop until his own arms began to shake.

"Enough," I gasped weakly as I slumped into his embrace. "Cadean, it's enough."

It took us a moment to catch our breath, but when it felt like I could stand on my own, I slipped out of his grasp and stepped back, holding up my arm.

My stomach sank. The veins had retreated, but not far. "It didn't work…" I whispered. "Why didn't it work?"

He strode across the room, grabbed my clothes, and tossed them to me. "I don't know, but we can't risk wasting any time. We're going to see Mel."

Unbridled tension rose off Cadean like heat waves as we strode down the hall. He'd descended into a hush of a black mood, and the shadows swirled around us as he moved.

When we reached Mel's door, he pounded on it with his fist. The blows echoed down the corridor, and it was a wonder the wood didn't split.

For a while, there was nothing, but after another round of pounding, the door was wrenched open. Mel glared back at us with a look that could have withered fruit on the vine. "What the hell do you bastards want? I just got to sleep after staying up all night refining the poison sacks from your damn cockatrice."

I flinched in spite of myself. Mel was not at her best before late morning.

Cadean gently pushed me into the room. "Samantha has been afflicted with the same curse I had."

"That's impossible," Mel said, and snapped her fingers. Lights flared to life in the small antechamber that connected her sleeping quarters to the workshop.

I held out my arms, and her breath caught. She grasped my left arm and stretched it out, examining both sides. "How long has it been like this?"

"We just noticed it," Cadean said gruffly. "I tried healing her, but it had little effect."

Mel's lips pursed as she studied the lines. "How do you feel?"

"Better now after Cadean healed me. My head was throbbing before. But I still feel achy and weak—honestly, I've felt that way for days."

"The curse nearly took everything out of me," Cadean said. "Constant pain. Headaches. Toward the end, it was almost impossible to think straight. Had Samantha not cured me before she'd fled, I would've been reduced to a raging beast, driven mad by pain." He met Mel's eyes. "I won't have the same thing happen to her. We need to find a solution, quickly."

She nodded with a grim expression and opened the door that led into her workshop, motioning us through. Early morning light streamed through the ornate windows that ringed the octagonal chamber. "I'm concerned it appeared so quickly. As a mortal, she might not share your resistance to the magic. We'll need to act fast." Brushing her black hair back over her shoulder, she went to her library and pulled a messy stack of papers off a high shelf.

"I was hoping I'd never need these again," she grumbled as she sat and spread the pages out over the uncluttered end of her workbench. The parchment was covered with careful illustrations and arcane symbols, surrounded by a sea of tight, precise script. I couldn't read her cursive, but I recognized the writing for what it was: her notes about Cadean's curse.

There were several sketches of his torso and arm, documenting how the curse had slowly spread across his body. Each picture was marked with the date and a few notes—most likely what I had done to heal it, or when I'd burned him with the Moon's magic and made it far worse.

Mel rubbed her forehead. "Cadean's curse made him susceptible to the blight of vines infesting our realm. Every time the vines spread, the blue lines expanded across his body, like a mirror of the land—draining his life like they drained its magic."

"So...they're attacking me through my bond with the wall?" I asked, though I'd reached that conclusion already.

"I suspect so," Mel said. "But what I don't understand is that Cadean only became susceptible to the curse after you attacked him with the Moon's magic."

"But no one's attacked me other than those assassins, and this isn't poison or fae magic, is it?"

She examined my arm again, clearly at a loss. "I don't think so…"

"You nearly killed yourself drawing the Moon's magic last night," Cadean said, his voice dark and vibrating with worry. "Perhaps that's what did it."

My breath stilled. "You think I did this to myself?"

Their silence spoke volumes. I looked down at my hands in disbelief. "Perhaps I made it worse, but I think this has been going on longer. I've been exhausted for the last week—from even before the assassins attacked."

Mel gave me a pitying look. "I suspect that whatever you did at the pylons tied you and your magic to the wall, along with your fate."

"So how do we get rid of it?" Cadean asked sharply. "My magic failed."

"Perhaps it can only be cured by the Moon's magic," Mel suggested.

"You had me make a balm from moon blossoms before," I asked. "Would that help?"

Mel shook her head. "We can try, but I don't have much hope. It wasn't so much a healing balm as a method to help draw your magic out when you didn't understand your own powers."

Cadean shook his head, his anger palpable. "The vines are the root of the problem. If we destroy them, then we defeat Ayanna and the curse at the same time."

I glanced at the black cauldron bubbling on Mel's hearth. "Then our plan remains the same. I infiltrate the queen's palace and poison the roots with your potion. They turn to stone, we win, and I'm cured."

Cadean narrowed his eyes at me in warning. "You're not going anywhere in that condition, let alone the queen's palace. You could barely stand this morning."

"I'm better now," I said, straightening my spine. "Your magic gave me some of my strength back."

"I was better, too, after the first time you healed me," Cadean said, his voice grinding like gravel. "But by the next morning, the curse had come back, worse than before."

"Cadean's right," Mel interrupted. "If we're going to pull this off, you need to be at the top of your game, not a shadow of yourself."

"We'll send someone else," Cadean said.

"No one else can get it in," I protested. "Only fae can enter Dreamspire, and I'm the only one who knows the secret passage into the Well of Life."

"There's Sarion," Cadean suggested.

"Sarion is amazing, and he helped me escaped, but—"

"He's not you."

The room fell silent.

I was certain I was the only one who had a chance of pulling it off, and even with my knowledge and the Moon's magic, it was going to be dangerous beyond belief. And right now, I knew I wasn't up to the task. Not in my current state.

Mel stirred the potion bubbling in her cauldron, the delicate features of her face drawn and tight. "This won't be finished brewing for at least another two days," she said. "If we have any hope of affecting all the vines, it will need to be extremely potent, and I've barely begun the first round of infusion."

Cadean sighed. "Then we either need a cure or a different solution to deal with the vines."

Mel tapped her long silver ladle on the edge of the cauldron and dropped it in a bucket. "If Samantha were stronger, she could revert the wall. That might stop the curse from spreading."

"Or make the curse worse," Cadean said as he began to pace. "She nearly killed herself last night shifting a small section of the wall. I'm not letting her anywhere near the pylons."

Mel returned to her notes, flipping through them as if a solution would leap off a page like an imp, but I knew it wouldn't. The solution wasn't here in Shadowstone, or even in the Dreamlands.

The answer was clear, but I knew Cadean wouldn't like it. I braced myself for the outburst I knew would come and looked the Dark Wolf God in the eyes. "I need to visit the Moon Goddess."

20

Samantha

Cadean stopped in his tracks like he'd been hit by a ballista bolt. "We are not bringing the *fucking* Moon into this."

His fury rolled over me, but I held my ground. I knew I was right.

"The Moon's magic might have the power to heal me, or perhaps she has a way to protect the wall. She might even be able to teach me how to make the wall defend itself. Either way, she's our best shot."

"I told you she can't be trusted. If she knew you were helping me, or worse—that you were my *mate*—she would lock you away until the end of time."

"Then I won't tell her."

"I'm not going to listen to this insanity!" he growled.

"Then what *will* you listen to?" I snapped, my patience at its limit. "You've turned down every suggestion we've made."

"Because they're too dangerous!" I could feel the dread vibrating beneath the surface of his anger, like a low and rolling earthquake, permeating every corner of the castle. No matter how much he tried to hide it, he was terrified of what was happening to me.

I crossed my arms. "Your magic doesn't work. It's too dangerous for me to revert the barrier. It's too dangerous for me to infiltrate Shadowstone. But I *can* visit the Moon, and I'm certain she *can* cure me, just like I cured you. It's messy, sure, and I'll have to be cautious, but we're out of options."

Cadean's expression tightened with frustration, and shadows spiraled around his clenched fists. "She can't be the solution."

He looked to Mel for support, but she remained silent. She knew the truth of the situation as well as I did: we were desperate.

I stepped forward and took his hand in mine. "Do you trust me?"

"Of course," he snapped. "But—"

"Then trust me *now*," I pleaded. "The Moon is the answer, Cadean—to the curse, to the barrier, to ending this war. I feel it in my bones, like the Fates themselves are pulling me to her. This is the way—you just have to decide which is more important, me, or your vendetta against her."

"You know the answer to that. You are more important, above everything."

"Then it's settled."

Cadean gave me a look that screamed that it was not, and pulling free, began prowling the perimeter of the room. "The Moon cannot enter the Dreamlands—not since she created the barrier. Her temples have all been abandoned here."

That was why my friends and I had to recharge the pylons on her behalf the day that Cadean had killed me. The Moon had told us that she was the anchor, keeping the door of Cadean's prison shut.

"That's why I have to return to the Waking World. My pack's

loremaster summoned the Moon before, and she can do it again."

Cadean's expression was incredulous. "Your pack will help after everything that happened? After everything I did?"

"They're not helping you, Cadean. They'll be helping me."

"Then you will lie to them? Because the moment you mention me or the wall or the Dreamlands, they'll lock you away in an asylum."

"Then you refuse to let me go? You'll keep me here, your prisoner, and watch me wither?"

His face tightened with fury and guilt. "Of course not. But you're too important to me, and there's too much at stake. I don't want you out of my sight."

"I know you want to protect me, but you can't—not by keeping me here under lock and key. The best way to protect me *and* your lands is to let me go. Let me get help because we can't do this on our own."

"She's right, Cadean." Mel shivered in the silence that formed between us.

"I can't believe you're taking her side in this!" he snarled, turning on her.

"I can't believe you're *not!*" Mel snapped back.

It was like she'd struck him across the face. He stared back at us, stunned. I could practically see the guilt twisting in him.

The only sound was the potion sputtering on the hearth.

I stepped forward and placed my hand on the coiled muscles of his arm. "I need you to trust me, Cadean."

My touch calmed some of the fury rippling beneath his skin. "I do. I will always believe in you. You've done more here than I've ever imagined possible."

"This will work. I'll return cured or with a solution for the wall, I promise."

He brushed the hair along the side of my face, and my skin tingled at the tenderness of his touch.

Slowly, he set his jaw with resolution. "If sending you back to Magic Side and the fates-damned Moon Goddess is what it takes to break this curse, so be it. But I'll be damned if you're fucking going alone."

~

I was going home. To Magic Side.

I honestly couldn't believe Cadean had conceded. The thought of it all was elating, and frankly, overwhelming.

As soon as the decision was made, we began making frantic preparations. We didn't know how much time either I or the wall had, but we knew we had to move quickly. It felt like time was a rip current carrying me home. Cadean summoned Fang and Wulfric to join our council, and we began hashing out details and contingencies.

Cadean pointed at his two generals. "I want you with Samantha at all times. We don't know if Ayanna has a way to track her, but if so, she'll send assassins."

I glanced at the dark-haired werewolf. "The alpha will recognize Wulfric's scent—he tried to drag me away during our final battle with you."

It was a long time ago, but I knew that Jaxson, the alpha of Magic Side, wouldn't forget.

Suddenly stiff as a suit of armor, Wulfric bowed his head. "I never apologized for that. I'm sorry, Samantha."

"I ordered him to capture you," Cadean said. "The fault is mine."

I shrugged. "Fang's never apologized for half the shit he's done. I'm over it. It's just that I don't want Jaxson going off the rails and attacking before I have a chance to explain the situation. I should take Sarion instead. He can attest to what the queen has done, and he has no ties to you."

Cadean nodded. "Speak to him. See if he'll help."

We finished making the last arrangements for my journey, and then I headed to Sarion's quarters.

The shifters guarding his door let me enter. Sarion wasn't a prisoner—he could move about the castle freely. But he wasn't *not* a prisoner, either. Despite everything the fae warrior had done for me, Cadean was slow to trust and kept him under close observation with sentries wherever he went.

Just like he had done with me, once.

However, rather than chafing at the chains, Sarion seemed resigned to his current predicament. He was lounging casually by the window, legs up, and staring at the horizon. He turned and smiled broadly as I entered. "Samantha, to what do I owe this pleasure?"

I leaned against the wall, arms crossed. I'd visited him often enough to chat, but there was no point beating about the bush today. "I'm looking for a favor."

He lowered the book in his hand and frowned. "I'm not sure how much use a wingless fae is to anyone in Shadowstone, but I'm happy to do what I can."

"I feel bad asking anything more of you, after everything you did for me"—my voice wavered—"and my mother."

He shut the book with a snap. "I'm currently spending all my time in a fortress full of extremely suspicious shifters who trust me about as far as they can throw me—which, considering the Dark Wolf God, is probably a considerable distance. Either way, at this point, I'd volunteer to dive into a volcano if you needed it."

"Not a volcano—but a situation that might be similarly explosive. I'm returning to Magic Side and the Waking World."

He raised his eyebrows. "The Dark Wolf God is letting you go home?"

My gut tightened. *Home.* Did I even think of Magic Side that way anymore? What was left of my old life? My apartment? My old bedroom with the roller derby trophies on my shelf? A fridge with rotting yogurt? I hadn't paid rent in months.

The extent of it all slowly sank in. I'd lost my wallet, my phone, and everything from that old life. The only possessions I had were ones I'd earned here, and that was a handful of clothes and a sword that had once belonged to a fae I'd killed.

My old life was in Magic Side. My pack was there. But my mate and my destiny were in the Dreamlands.

"He knows I'll come back."

Sarion studied me appraisingly. "My, how things have changed."

"Things are pretty fucked."

I explained the situation, and Sarion whistled low. "Fucked, indeed. But that's Ayanna for you—takes the life out of everything."

"I'm afraid the people I'm planning to ask are going to be a little reticent, given their prior experience with Cadean. I need someone who can testify that I haven't been brainwashed, and that Ayanna is, well..."

"A power-hungry psychopath sucking the life from the Dark Wolf God's land and even her own people?" Sarion offered.

A crooked smile broke across my face. "You're going to be perfect."

He rose and stretched his arms. "So, when do we leave?"

21
———

Cadean

I leaned against the balcony and dug my fingers into the stone as I gazed out over the wintery landscape beyond.

I was letting her go.

The bitter taste in throat was as much as I could stand. I would have rather given up my axe, my magic, or my ability to shift than give up her.

It had been agony while she was in the queen's realm. This time would be far worse. Now that we knew what we were. Now that we'd both accepted it.

The Fates had given me a mate for the span of a single life-time, and I was going to cherish every second we had left. I knew those would be far too few. And now, I was letting her go.

It was infuriating. It clawed against every instinct I had and made a mockery of everything I'd done to bring her back and convince her to stay. I wanted to rage and rip the stone railing right off its foundation, but I knew the truth: letting her go was the best chance to save her.

Because I couldn't do it. Just like I couldn't save my own kingdom.

I was less than a king. Far less than a god. Just a prisoner with illusions of grandeur.

Fuck Ayanna and the Moon and the wall and the Fates. Fuck all the gods—

The warmth of Samantha's signature brushed over my skin, and her scent stirred the blood in my veins. Footsteps echoed down the hall and through the open door to my chambers. They paused for a moment, and then there came a tentative knock.

"You never have to knock," I murmured, keeping my eyes fixed on the horizon. "This is your room now as much as it is mine."

"You seemed lost in thought. I wasn't sure if I should disturb you."

I shook my head. "I was simply lost."

The footsteps resumed, shifting from the dull beat of boots on the heavy oak floor to the gentle clap of soles on stone as she stepped onto the balcony behind me. Even though I could barely stand to look at her, I forced myself to turn around.

She was bundled in breeches and the leather jacket I'd had made for her in town, and had a small pack slung over her shoulder. I repressed the instinct to frown. "You're ready to go."

She nodded. "Just need to stop by Mel's for a disguise."

I appraised her with a lingering glance, and my brow furrowed. "You're not taking the sword?"

"It would raise too many questions," she said, then extended her claws. "I'm better with these, anyway. And my magic."

She was one of the best fighters I'd met, but she was also drained and exhausted. Would it be enough if Ayanna's assassins learned where she was?

"You still don't like this," she muttered.

"Of course not. I hate to see you go. I hate not being there to protect you."

"I'll have Sarion and Fang."

"It's not enough."

"Cadean—"

I lifted my hand dismissively and turned back to the horizon. "I know. You have to go. If there's any chance that the Moon can help you, I'll pay whatever price she demands. I don't have to like it, though. I don't trust her, and I never will."

"What happened between you?"

"The less you know, the better. You can't risk giving away our relationship or even our association. She might not be a shifter, but she's a goddess and can tell when people are hiding something. If she suspected...I don't know what she would do."

Samantha's fingers gently touched my back, sending currents of electricity along my spine. "Part of my task is to persuade her that Ayanna is a bigger threat than you are. If I'm going to do that, if I'm going to understand her and her magic, then I need to know what happened. Why did she lock you away? We've never really talked about it—not expressly."

"To protect the world from a monster," I said bitterly.

"Our pack legends say that you wanted to annihilate the world, so the Moon drugged you and imprisoned you here. But that's not the truth. I know that much."

The winter wind cascaded over the balcony and filled the silence between us. Samantha didn't press, but I knew she deserved an answer.

With a growl of frustration, I thrust myself away from the balcony and strode back inside. "We need wine."

I shut the door behind her, then pulled a dusty bottle off the shelf. Fae wine from the Summerlands. I poured two glasses and raised mine to her. "Never trust legends or anything my brother has to say."

"Then what *is* the truth?"

I braced against the fireplace and closed my eyes, savoring

the rich taste of sunlight and ripe fruit as I dredged the memories up from where I'd buried them.

"You and the queen visited an oracle outside of Dreamspire. Well, I visited her myself a thousand years ago. It was one of the worst mistakes I've ever made."

"Ayanna suspected the oracle has been in your lands a long time."

I laughed softly, shaking my head at what *long* must mean to a mortal. "The oracle was living in those woods when these lands were still islands of dreams scattered in the mists, long before my brother and I united them to forge our realms."

"Why did you seek her out?" Samantha asked.

"Because I was a fool. Only fools wish to know what fate has in store for them." I dragged my fingers through my hair, lost as to how to explain it all to someone who'd only witnessed a few decades of life. "The world was changing quickly, and I was concerned. I'd watched mankind since they first learned to tell stories, as they invented tools and grew in power. But the discovery of bronze and iron made them bold. They lost their fear of the wolf, and with it, their respect. As their numbers swelled, they uprooted the wilderness and began hunting the beasts they'd once feared for sport."

I glanced over at her. "I did nothing because shifters could wield iron as well. I thought they'd take a stand, but they didn't. Your kind became the hunted. Fates only know how many of you were murdered or burned at the stake."

Samantha set her wine down and leaned back against a wooden pillar, arms crossed. "Our loremaster claimed our pack fled southern France because the Church paid for shifter skins by the pelt, child or adult."

The wine suddenly tasted sour. Humans never changed. I set my glass down as well. "I asked the oracle what would become of the wilderness, and what would become of men and shifters.

She gave me a vision of what was to come—the next thousand years of history."

My throat tightened as the memories flooded back, and I found it hard to speak.

"The vision lasted only a moment, but it felt like a century. I saw men spread across the earth, driven by greed and hatred. Everywhere they went, they brought plague and death. They leveled mighty forests and paved them over with stone. I saw endless war becoming more and more brutal until it felt like there were more dead men than had ever existed."

I wove my magic with the shadows, forming images of tanks and planes and men screaming.

"The last thing I saw were weapons more powerful than any magic the gods had ever imagined, explosions that devoured cities like they were paper. I thought that maybe the whole world had been consumed."

The shadows formed into a city, swept away by fire.

"Hiroshima and Nagasaki," Samantha whispered.

My chest tightened. I could sense her sadness and horror, but it was nothing like the mad terror that had taken me when the oracle had first shown me the visions. She and her people had become so accustomed to this kind of destruction that they felt no true terror. They lived with it. They'd seen it over and over until they accepted it without question. She whispered the name of the cities, but she should have wept.

The shadows of the room lengthened as the terrible truth sank in, and my stomach knotted. The waking world was lost. They'd learned to live with nightmares that not even the Dream-lands could conjure. How could I explain myself to someone from that world?

Samantha stepped close and laid her hand on my arm. "It must have been hard to bear that knowledge alone."

"I was arrogant. I thought I could stop it. I told the Moon

everything I'd seen. I told her that I was going to wake the beasts of the earth and stop mankind in their tracks. I would take the secret of steel from them and teach those who survived to fear the wilderness again."

My anger and magic rumbled through the room, and Samantha braced herself against the wall. Silence stretched between us as my words sank in. I could almost hear her thoughts.

I would've culled humanity to stop them from doing it to themselves. It was irony, but how could I explain the *balance* to her?

But she didn't speak. She didn't accuse me of being a monster. She simply reached out and took my hand.

The shame of it all twisted in me.

"The Moon said we needed to trust mankind. That they weren't capable of such evil. That they were still children, and they would learn." My muscles knotted as the shadows billowed around me. "She was wrong. Humankind needed to be tamed and taught, not allowed to spread unchallenged."

Samantha swallowed. "And that's why she trapped you in the Dreamlands?"

"I told her that I'd stop it, whatever the cost. And since I didn't listen to her counsel, she conspired with the Fates to imprison me forever."

"Maybe after all this time, she'd be willing to set you free. Your vision was true, and humankind is in more danger than ever."

I laughed bitterly. "She won't release me. When she learned my barrier was weakening, she sent you and your friends from Magic Side to strengthen it. As long as I remain locked away here, she can lie to herself that I was the greater evil. That there was nothing we could have done to stop it. That she wasn't wrong."

Samantha rested her head against my shoulder, but I lifted her chin to meet my gaze. "If you ever suggest releasing me or even hint at the vision to her, she'll kill you. You must never speak of this to another, do you understand?"

She nodded, then pressed her hands against my chest and pushed up on her toes to kiss me. Her soft lips brushed against mine and tasted of summer and spring. When she gently pulled away, it was like a mountain had crumbled from my shoulders, like the heavy roots pinning me down had suddenly released.

There was an emptiness in my chest where my fury had lived. It wasn't gone, but for the first time in a thousand years, it was a little lighter.

Samantha brushed her fingers along my cheek and smiled faintly. "I didn't ask for the Moon, but for myself. I wanted to know my mate. To understand him so I could love him better, while I can."

22

Samantha

Three hours later, my fate stood before me.

We climbed up the stone stairs to the portal in the center of Mistwind Harbor, the market bustling around us. Most of the townsfolk had their heads down, pretending to go about their business, yet when I looked away, I could feel the heat of their eyes on my back. The Dark Wolf God making a second visit to their town in less than a week was going to keep the local rumor mill running for a long time.

I scanned the crowd out of the corner of my eye. Were Ayanna's spies watching?

Hopefully. That was the plan.

Once we reached the top of the dais, Cadean waved the sentries back. After everything that had happened, they were more than happy to give him ample space. Cadean pressed his hand against the gateway, and a pulse of magic thundered through the ancient stones. The runes around the ring flared to life, and the portal filled the gateway, flowing like a quicksilver mirror.

I tensed at my reflection, though I'd known what to expect—

with a vibrant purple dress, long dark hair, dusky skin, and perfect lips, it wasn't my own face that stared back at me, but Mel's.

I touched my cheek without thinking. The resemblance was uncanny. Being half fae, I could see through most illusions, but Mel's blood magic was another matter.

"I know I'm beautiful, but don't be so obvious about it," Mel whispered from beside me.

I glanced at my friend, who wore my own face, along with a black leather jacket. She brushed her short blonde hair back and smiled, though it wasn't quite like mine. "I did pretty well, huh?"

"It's perfect," I said under my breath. Hopefully, if I couldn't see through it, it'd be enough to fool the fae.

"Well, it'll fade as soon you step through the portal. I've got to keep this up until you get back, so please hurry."

Switching appearances had been Mel's idea. Even though Cadean had rooted out the nest of assassins in Mistwind Harbor, we had to assume that Ayanna had more informants. They'd report that the five of us had ridden into town, and that Mel, Kass, and Sarion had gone through the portal while the Dark Wolf God and I returned to the citadel. Hopefully, Ayanna would be thrown off my scent, and her assassins wouldn't come for me while I was in Magic Side. The problem was that taking on my identity left Mel a sitting duck.

"I still don't like this," I muttered. "If anything happens to you—"

Mel scoffed, then lowered her voice. "I'll be able to pass as you as long I don't have to speak to anyone. I'll never be able to do a Chicago accent."

I blinked. I had a Chicago accent? How did she even recognize that?

"I know the risks, so quit worrying. This was *my* idea, and I'll be safe with Cade in Shadowstone." Crossing her arms, she cocked her hip out playfully. "Anyway, I'm his right-hand woman. If Ayanna had assassins who could take me out, they'd have done so decades ago. Frankly, I hope they try."

There was no doubt that Mel was a badass bitch, but I was afraid that with so much at stake, Ayanna would take risks that she hadn't in the past.

Unfortunately, it was too late to change Mel's mind. We were committed.

I looked up as the crowd on the far side of the market parted, making room for Fang and Sarion, who'd been making last-minute arrangements. They nodded slightly to me as they approached, and I swallowed. This was it. Showtime.

As if reading my mind, Cadean's mouth drew into a thin line. "Are you sure about this?" His voice was low and gravelly, but beneath it, I could almost imagine a half-whispered plea for me to say no, to give it up and stay.

"I'm ready." I tilted my head closer, then whispered, "I don't want to leave your side for a minute, but this is about more than my curse. The Moon may know a way to protect the wall forever. I have to do this for your people's sake as much as mine."

His jaw hardened, and he nodded reluctantly. "It's you I'm worried about most."

My chest ached. I knew Cadean would be able to shadow-cast to me, like he'd done while I was in Dreamspire, but it wasn't the same as having him near. I wanted to throw my arms around him, but posing as Mel, I couldn't do anything of the sort without blowing our cover. We'd said our goodbyes back in our bedroom, coupling together one last time in breathless harmony. But what I'd taken then and what I needed now were very different. All I wanted was to feel his arms around me one more time. I wanted to pull his lips to mine, to drink deeply of his scent and power and presence, and to never let him go.

But I couldn't. As long as Ayanna's vines still infested the wall, neither I nor Cadean's people could be safe. I had to find a way to stop her.

Cadean turned to Kass, his expression dark. "If anything happens to her—"

"I'll be dead already, so your threats won't matter," he said. He looked up at the giant glistening dome above us. "Something tells me she's not going to need much help from me."

Cadean stepped closer, pitching his voice so low, it was closer to a rumble in the earth. "Keep. Her. Fucking. *Safe.*"

With one last warning look at Kass, Cadean closed his eyes and slammed his hand against the gateway. The silver surface shuddered and turned black, then slowly resolved into a view I knew well.

Magic Side.

I recognized Exposition Park in the heart of town. Summer and fall had gone. The trees were bare, and a gray winter sky hung over the jagged city skyline. It was home, yet alien and unfamiliar. I suddenly felt all three months that I'd been trapped in the Dreamlands. It had seemed both forever and no time at all.

And now, after all this time, the way out was flickering before me.

My heart began pounding against my chest, and I suddenly felt a sense of dread. Of wrongness.

I glanced back at the Dark Wolf God, almost believing that it was all a trick. That he would never truly release me.

He smiled softly. "Time to go."

I straightened and forced a smile. "See you in the shadows, Cadean."

Then I stepped through.

23

———

Magic Side, Chicago

Samantha

I spun through the infinite gray of the ether, then stumbled into the dim winter sunlight of Magic Side.

The scents and sounds of the city hit my senses in a torrent. I'd spent three months living near wilderness and primitive towns, and the comforting aromas of forest and woodfires had suddenly been replaced by exhaust, asphalt, and garbage. While I'd thought the bustling market square in Mistwind Harbor was noisy, Magic Side was deafening, buffeting my ears with the sounds of engines and horns, sirens, and the roar of planes overhead.

Had all this really just been background noise before? Even Exposition Park, which had seemed like a gorgeous greenspace once, now appeared painfully small and crowded. How did our pack survive with only this little patch of grass to run in?

Fang stepped through the portal behind me, with Sarion close on his heels. The shimmering disc was hovering in the air just above the grass, a window into a dreamworld I'd never truly believed existed.

The Dark Wolf God looked back at me with an expression I couldn't quite place, and then, with a single nod, the portal vanished. I took an involuntary step toward the place it had been, yanked forward by the unseen bond between us. It was like having the breath knocked out of me, and despite my allies and the bustling park around me, I suddenly felt very much alone.

He'd still be there in the shadows, wouldn't he?

I took a deep breath of city air, then quickly scanned the park. A couple glanced in our direction as they jogged past but ignored us otherwise. An old man sitting on a bench was watching us more intently, though from his hawkish features and gaze, I suspected he did that to everyone.

The reality was that no one cared. Magic Side had the densest concentrations of supernatural people in North America—shifters, sorcerers, vampires, you name it. Strange things were always happening, so if nothing was exploding or on fire, Magic Siders generally kept to their business and didn't ask questions.

The city itself was an island suburb of Chicago, located a mile and a half offshore of Southside—though of course, no one in the human city had any idea our world existed. You had to have magic in your blood to see our island.

Sarion looked as shellshocked as I felt, but Kass seemed unphased by the crowded park and towering skyscrapers in the distance.

"So, this is the big city, huh?" Kass said with an unnerving glint in his eyes. "What a banquet of delights."

I gave him a pointed look. "Non-consensual feeding is against the law, so keep your fangs to yourself."

He smirked. "Pity."

While we'd drunk wine together, I'd never seen the vampire feed. I cleared my throat uncomfortably. "Uh, should you need it, most of the bars around here sell synthetic blood. If you get a little peckish, gold is accepted everywhere."

That was an economic necessity in the magical world.

Fang's lip curled up in something between horror and disgust. "Synthetic blood? It's a wonder anyone can stand living in this place."

I shrugged as we headed for the nearest trolley stop. "Admittedly, it's...not great."

Sarion raised his eyebrows. "You've tried it?"

"I was a bartender, remember? Maybe curiosity got the better of me. Let's go."

Fang gave me an appraising look as we headed for the trolley. "Samantha, you have depths I never imagined."

"Keep your imagination to yourself."

It took forty minutes to reach Dockside. Cadean could have likely sent us directly into the heart of pack territory, but I wanted a chance to think and read the wind first. I leaned against the window, watching the old familiar streets of Dockside roll by. Memories clung to them like lichen tangled in the branches of trees, but none of them could escape the shadow of death and destruction Cadean had caused when he'd tried to seize the city. Even if the city had been rebuilt, it was still burning in my mind.

"You look troubled," Sarion said.

I shrugged, keeping my eyes out the window. "Rough memories. I lost a lot of packmates here."

"Ah," he said. "This is where the Dark God attacked when he tried to break into the waking world."

I glanced at Fang in the other seat, who was now pointedly ignoring the conversation. "He didn't come through himself. He created a rift and sent a black mist. Every werewolf it touched came under his power. They turned on the city, attacking everyone."

I couldn't shake the memory of those savage red eyes charging out of the mist—of having to shoot people who'd once belonged to my pack.

"I made a last stand with sorcerers on the southside, but if my friends Jaxson and Savannah hadn't been able to stop him, I think the entire city might have fallen." I turned away and leaned against the window again with a soft but bitter laugh. "And now, I've got to ask them for help. It feels like a betrayal of everything we fought for."

Sarion put a hand on my shoulder. "I understand, but you're asking for yourself, not for him. This is about curing your curse and protecting the wall from Ayanna—and protecting thousands of shifters as well, don't forget. I don't know these people, but if they're anything like you, they'll understand."

"I'm not sure they will."

"Lying is always an option," Fang muttered.

"I'm not going to lie to my alpha and my best friend," I snapped. "They deserve better than that. Plus, werewolves can smell lies, and Jaxson knows me better than anyone."

Fang shrugged. "Your funeral."

His resigned indifference gnawed at me, the cancer of doubt.

How much should I conceal? If Savy and Jax refused to help, I had no one else I could turn to. Wasn't defeating Ayanna more important than the truth?

The old trolley shuddered and slowed to a stop, and I forced a smile despite the knot in my gut. "This is us, boys."

We shoved through the packed carriage and out into the sun across the street from Eclipse, the upscale club that served as the seat of our pack. It had been my second home for the last decade.

As it was early in the afternoon, the bouncers weren't out yet, which was a relief. I wasn't in the mood to explain myself or my companions to anyone.

"Wait here," I told the others. "I need to set a few things straight with the alpha before I start mixing vampires and fae into the cocktail."

Kass squinted painfully against the sun and stepped into the shadow of an adjacent building. "Cadean won't like it. He told me not to let you out of my sight."

"Eclipse is the safest place for me outside of Shadowstone. This is my pack and my turf. If anyone gives you trouble, say that you're waiting on a meeting with the alpha, Jaxson Laurent, but that he's attending to other business."

Before he or Sarion could protest, I slipped through traffic and made my way toward the black door. I wrapped my fingers around the handle and hesitated, still uncertain what I wanted to say.

Shit.

I strode inside.

It was like falling back in time. The place was empty, but everything was exactly how I remembered: the small stage in the back, the cocktail tables, the marble bar top and the massive mirror behind it. Even the high-end bottles in the racks were in the same place. I probably could've slipped behind the bar and served up a cocktail with my eyes shut.

I turned around, drinking it all in. The scent of the bar, the taste of the air, even the feel of the tile beneath my feet.

This had been home. Not Deerhaven or my apartment downtown, but *here*. And fates, was it good to be back.

"We're not open," a girl's voice called from behind me.

I turned, and my eyes widened in recognition at the skinny sixteen-year-old with dirty blonde hair. It was the girl from the fighting ring in Deerhaven.

She set down her tray of limes and lemons as her eyebrows shot up. "Holy shit. It's you! Everybody's been looking for you. I thought you were dead."

"Nope, just AWOL. What the hell are you doing here?"

She shrugged. "Well, after you took my place in the fighting ring, I took the five hundred bucks you gave me and found Jaxson in Magic Side, like you suggested. You said he took better care of his pack. You were right, so I stuck around."

I shook my head in disbelief. "I didn't think you'd actually do it. You were pretty pissed at me."

She shrugged. "I was, but when you disappeared, everybody in Deerhaven just looked in the other direction. The alpha—I mean Wyland—said that you got what you deserved. I kinda figured you were right about him and the pack, so I headed here to give your friends a heads-up that you were missing and to see if there was anything they could do. After that, I didn't have anywhere to go, so Jaxson gave me a job."

My throat tightened. That was exactly how I'd gotten my gig here—except it had been Jaxson's father who'd helped me out after I'd fled Brent and the Deerhaven pack.

My chest hurt as memories of my mother flooded through. She'd stayed behind when I'd left, and now—

Footsteps sounded from the back, and I looked up as a woman with brilliant red hair and tight jean shorts swung around the corner with a case of beer. My heart skipped a beat.

Savannah. My best friend in the world. The friend Cadean had forced to kill me. The one who'd convinced the Moon to bring me back.

She stopped short, mouth hanging open. The case slipped from her fingers, shattering on the floor. "Jesus H. Christ! Is that you, Sam?"

Savy leapt over the mangled and leaking box of beer and rushed into my open arms. "Holy fucking fates, you're okay!"

My throat tightened, and I squeezed her in turn. Just like that, my old life had come rushing back in a tsunami of feelings. Whirling in memory and doubt, I was barely keeping my head above water.

I held her awkwardly, but finally, she pushed back and wiped her eyes. "Where the fuck have you been? We were worried sick and had people looking everywhere for you."

Before I could answer, the hair on my neck rose as the alpha's presence filled the room behind me. I turned. Jaxson's muscled frame filled the doorway. His coffee eyes were hard and unyielding, and his alpha presence vibrated through the room. "You have a lot of explaining to do," he growled low. "Savy's been worried sick."

I straightened my shoulders. "And what about you?"

The alpha glared at me from the doorway. "You fucking left without a word and then ditched my truck in the middle of backwoods Michigan, so pretty pissed, I'd have to say."

We held each other's gaze until at last, his scowl broke, cascading into the broad grin I knew so well. He crossed the room in two strides, and I laughed in delight as he wrapped me in his arms and spun me around.

Jaxson set me down and fixed me with a stern look. "But seriously, that's the last time I ever lend you my truck, Bennet."

"Fair enough," I said, grinning from ear to ear.

Jaxson clapped me on the shoulder. "Gods, it's good to see you back here—if not for your sake, then for mine. I've been half blind without you running things. I knew you'd be okay, though. You're as tough as nails."

"He was worried, he just wouldn't admit it," Savy said.

"What the hell happened to you?" he asked. "You look like you're still all in one piece."

My grin faded. "I think you're both going to need a drink. Seriously."

Savy snatched two glasses with ice from behind the counter, then filled them two fingers full of Breckenridge Burbon. She passed them to us but didn't take one herself. "Whatever it is, we'll do everything we can to help."

I threw my jacket on the back of the barstool and rolled up my sleeve to show them the blue lines tracing along my arms. "I have a curse, and I think the Moon Goddess is the only one who'll know what to do."

"Shit," Savy whispered.

Jaxson stepped forward, examining my arm. "Why her? What have you gotten yourself mixed up in?"

My chest tightened. This was the fork in the road. The truth or the lie.

Fuck it.

I'd been to hell and back with the two of them. They'd been there when I died and when I was brought back to life. They were my people. If I couldn't confide in them, then, well, fuck all three fates and the road they'd set me on.

This was *my pack*.

I drained my glass and set it down hard on the bar. "You couldn't find me in Deerhaven because I was abducted by the Dark Wolf God. I escaped from him, then his brother, and then from the evil fae queen who was trying to drain his magic. I control the Dark Wolf God's prison now, and it's under attack. The curse will kill me first, but if we can't find a solution, the barrier will fall."

24

Samantha

Shocked silence reverberated through the room, and then Jaxson's eyes flashed a vivid gold.

"Shut all the doors," he growled to the girl from Deerhaven, whose name I still hadn't gotten. "And make sure no one else from the staff comes in here."

The power in his voice made her jump, and she rushed to do his bidding.

Savy slumped down on one of the bar stools, her face ashen with shock. "Jesus. I thought the Dark Wolf God was out of our life for good."

"Is he trying to break free?" Jaxson growled, his wolf suddenly very close to the surface.

I shook my head. "No. It's the work of that fae queen. She's trying to steal power from the walls of his prison."

"You said you can control it," Jaxson mused as he studied me intently. "How?"

I called a little moonlight to my hand, creating a spinning orb of light. "I have magic now."

Savy's eyes widened. "You never had it before..."

"Apparently, I have a little fae blood in me, but this isn't fae magic—it's the Moon's. I suspect I bonded with it when she brought me back from the dead."

"And you're in danger because of this magic?" Jaxson asked.

I dismissed the ball of light. "I turned the Dark Wolf God's prison into a solid barrier to protect his people and his lands from the queen, but now she's draining power from the wall, and with it, my life."

Jaxson's grip tightened on his glass, and his expression grew dark. "What do you mean, to protect *his* lands?"

I licked my lips nervously, but at this point, I was committed. "There are tens of thousands of shifters in his realm, and they were in danger. The fae were raiding their towns and sucking the life from his realm."

The muscles of Jaxson's neck tightened as his eyes narrowed. "Are you telling us that you're *helping* that fucking monster?"

"I'm not helping him escape, if that's what you mean," I snapped, surprised at my sudden anger. "I did what I had to do to protect his people. Shifters like us."

Jaxson slammed his fist down on the bar. "His people? How can you do anything for the bastard and *his* people after everything he did to *our* pack?"

I dug my claws into my palm as I steeled myself against his fury. "Because like it or not, he's not the worst thing in the Dreamlands. Not by far."

Jaxson stared at me, stunned, then shook his head. "Fates. He's got you brainwashed."

My neck heated. "He doesn't. I am my own wolf, here of my own accord."

The alpha stood, knocking his chair back. "You're one of the smartest and toughest women I've ever met Sam, but he's a god. He can *fuck* with your mind. He's manipulating you to do his bidding. Whatever this is, it's part of a long game to set him free."

I shook my head. "No. I just need to find the Moon, to see if she can heal me and teach me how to protect the barrier—"

"But you were with him before you came here?"

There was no lying to the Magic Side alpha. I nodded.

"Fuck!" he snarled. "He sent you here, didn't he?"

"It's not like that!"

Savy's eyes widened with panicked desperation. "He's using you, Sam, just like he used me. I thought I was fighting against him, but he tricked me into loosening the bonds of his prison. He forced me to attack you, for fates' sake! You are being *used*."

"I'm not. I know what's real and what is a lie," I said firmly. "And if he had the power to force me to release the wall, he would have used it months ago. I can resist his magic."

"Can you?" Jaxson growled as his alpha presence flared, pushing me into submission.

Fueled by my rising anger, I shoved back against the alpha's compulsion with my own power, just as Cadean had taught me.

Moonlight streamed around me, circling my arms and shoulders. "Don't you dare try to dominate me, Jaxson Laurent. I've stood up to queens and gods, and by the fates, I am more than strong enough to stand up to you, too."

Jaxson stepped back, eyes wide with shock.

The hair on my neck was up, and my wolf was very close to the surface. "You want to make sure the Dark Wolf God never returns? Then help me," I growled. "This is about protecting the walls that keep him locked away. It's about protecting other shifters."

I looked from one to the other. "Please, I need you to trust me. I'm here of my own accord. It's not a trick. I'm not his puppet. I just need help."

Savannah and Jaxson glanced at each other, their faces pale and drawn with worry.

"Please, after all we've been through, I need you to believe me," I begged.

The silence stretched out between us, and the growing chasm felt like it was going to shatter my heart.

Then a quiet voice piped up from the corner of the room. "I'll help."

I glanced over in surprise. It was the girl from Deerhaven, leaning against the wall, half hidden in shadow. I'd forgotten she was even there, and apparently, so had the others.

"This doesn't concern you!" Jaxson said in rebuke, wheeling around. "You shouldn't even be in here."

The girl raised her chin and pushed away from the wall. "I don't understand half of what you're talking about, and I didn't experience what happened here, but Sam stood up for me when no one else would have. So if you won't stand with her, I will."

We all stared back, stunned.

There was one person who believed me. A person I'd spoken to *once* in my life, and here she was, ready to face a goddess with me.

Savy's voice broke with a sudden sob, and she put the back of her hand over her mouth. "What are we saying? Of course we'll stand with you, Sam. We love you. Whatever you need, we're here."

She reached out across the bar and gasped my hand. I could smell her sorrow and shame and fear, but her touch was as warm and familiar as it had ever been.

Jaxson's shoulders dropped, and he ran his fingers through his hair. "Fuck. I'm sorry, Sam. I just got caught up in the past. Savy's right. We'll do anything we can to help you." The alpha put his hand over his mate's and mine. "You're part of our pack and our family. Whatever this turns out to be, we'll help you find a way through."

Of course, there were some finer points to explain—like Sarion and Fang. Jaxson had them hauled in and interrogated, then made me walk him through everything again.

"You've gotten yourself in some fucked-up situations, but this takes the cake," he said after I'd explained things for a third time.

I rubbed my temples. "I know, I know. I wouldn't have come to you if I wasn't desperate—but it's desperate."

He looked between Sarion, whom he clearly mistrusted, and Fang, whom he clearly despised. "I've got a bad feeling about this."

I glanced around the room. We'd all crammed into Jaxson's office to speak privately, along with the pack's loremaster, an old woman with a cantankerous attitude. She'd inherited memories and stories from her predecessor and probably had more wisdom than the rest of us combined, but so far, she'd been content to listen and ask questions.

That had always been her way. Let the alpha lead, guide him when needed.

The girl from Deerhaven—Jen, apparently—wasn't present. Despite her offer to help, Jaxson had to set a few things straight about eavesdropping and challenging the alpha. I voiced my objection, but I was secretly relieved. We could be walking into danger, and I didn't want her blood on my hands. She'd just gotten out of a bad situation and had her whole life ahead of her.

At least one of the Deerhaven girls would make it.

I surveyed the group. "Does anyone have any better ideas?"

Jaxson shifted uncomfortably in his large leather chair. "We could go to the Order of Magica."

I gaped. He had to be desperate. Jaxson hated the Order, and I was dumbfounded that he'd even suggested it.

The Order kept peace between the magical peoples of the waking world and upheld our laws. The pack, which spent a great deal of effort breaking those laws, didn't have a good relationship with them. Hell, when the Dark Wolf God had tried to take the city, the Order had barely lifted a finger until the last desperate moments. If we approached them about the queen of the fae, the pretentious old mages would try to take control and put us on lockdown, telling us they'd "handle the situation themselves"—which likely meant doing nothing, or at least waiting for an opportunity to leverage the situation for their own gain.

"No," I said emphatically. "The Order has no stake in this— the only thing they'll care about is keeping trouble out of the waking world. The Moon is our best bet. If the queen isn't stopped, she'll drain all the power from the Moon's barrier. Not only would that set the Dark Wolf God free, but the queen would become as powerful as a goddess herself. The war between them would set the Dreamlands on fire."

It was all the truth, minus a few specific details.

"If that's not enough motivation for her to help us, then I doubt anything will suffice." I held up my arm, displaying the blue lines of the curse. "And on a selfish note, I'm hoping she'll be able to cure this, because I'm feeling—how did Bilbo say it? Like too little butter that has been scraped over too much bread?"

"Who the fuck is Bilbo?" Fang asked, to Jaxson's annoyance.

"I'm sure the Moon will help," Savy said. "She did before."

"Then it's settled. We go to the Moon," Jaxson said, rapping his knuckles on the desk. "But from everything you've told us, time is short." He turned to the loremaster. "Is there any way to call down the Moon without having to visit one of her temples?"

We'd been banned from ever returning to the last one we'd visited, and it had taken a lot of effort to find in the first place.

"Perhaps," the loremaster said, drumming her fingers on the table. "Now that I've performed the ritual once, I understand it better. If we bring the pack together, we may be able to call her down right here in Magic Side." The old woman's eyes flicked to Savannah. "If your family would help, it would increase our chance of success. We need our voices to reach into the heavens themselves."

Savannah's family were sorcerers and weapons dealers of extremely dubious reputation. They'd been a thorn in the pack's side for centuries, but when Cadean had attacked, they'd stood with us to defend the city.

"They'll help," Savy said. "Even if I have to twist or break a few arms."

"Good." The loremaster tapped her walking stick resolutely on the floor and rose. "Then we should try tonight. I'd rather the moon be full, but it's already waning, and the ritual will be harder each night we wait."

Jaxson nodded. "Then tonight it is."

She looked up at the alpha. "I'd organize a pack run first. Make sure everyone is in high spirits. We'll need everything we can get."

He pushed back from his desk. "If we're going to do this tonight, then we don't have much time to organize."

"What about us?" Fang asked.

"Sarion, go with the loremaster and help her prepare a ritual site at Exposition Park," the alpha said, then glanced at Fang with unrestrained malice. "As for you, I don't have any coffins for you to sleep in, but I could arrange to put you in one."

Fang snorted. "Hilarious. But I'm not letting Samantha out of my sight—at least not until you summon the Moon. I'm her sworn bodyguard, whatever else I might be."

Jaxson gave me a disapproving look, then glared at Kass. "Then I hope you can keep up when we run because the pack isn't going to wait for you."

The vampire folded his hands behind his head. "How sporting."

As the room started to clear, Jaxson grabbed my arm. "I don't want you getting pulled any deeper into this mess, Sam. After we speak to the Moon, you're staying here in Magic Side. You will not return to the Dreamlands."

The hair on my neck bristled. Once, I would have obeyed any order the alpha had given me, but that was a long time ago. "I know you want to protect me, but I have to go back, Jax."

"I'm your alpha," he growled low, but not out of anger or malice. His voice was vibrating with a deep and earnest protectiveness.

I met his eyes. "Then don't make me defy you. I have a duty to the shifters there. I've got to return to help end this war."

"This isn't your war. They aren't your people. Your people are here, in Magic Side."

I gently pulled away from his grasp. "No matter how much I care for you and Savy and the pack, my fate lies in the Dreamlands. The people need someone to protect them, fae and shifter alike."

And my mate.

"And that person has to be you?" he asked, his voice pained.

"The Fates brought me back for this reason, Jax. I feel it in every bone in my body. Gods and queens have tried to stop me. Don't be the next in line."

Savy clapped me on the back. "We understand. That's why we're coming with you."

Jaxson's head snapped toward her, his eyes suddenly a deep gold. "No. Not you. I'll go with Sam. You're not to go anywhere near the Dark Wolf God's realm."

The alpha's presence was pressing through the room, but Savannah crossed her arms with an expression I knew all too well: *watch where you're about to step.*

"I have magic, Jax, and you don't," she chided. "I'm not letting Sam march back into the Dreamlands on her own."

He clenched his fists and gave her a pleading look. "You know why—"

"I do. And if you want, we can take this argument outside, *dear husband.*"

The room thrummed with tension while they glared at each other with half-feral expressions.

You tell him, girl, I thought, trying to restrain a smile.

Jaxson was just as protective of his mate as Cadean was of me, and Savy was just as defiant. I almost felt bad for the alpha. She had a fiery streak as intense as her red hair, and I'd rather face the queen of the fae again than take an upbraiding from Savy.

"Why don't we table that point until we speak to the Moon?" I said, trying to diffuse the situation for a moment. "We don't know what she'll suggest."

"Fair enough," Savy said, hooking her arm around mine. "We'll sort it out then. For now, let's get a drink."

I followed Savy out to the bar as the irritated alpha began making arrangements.

The happy-hour crowd had begun pouring in, and a guitarist on stage played a little Chicago blues for the folks at the high tops. The sound of glasses and bottles tinkling behind the bar mixed with the music and the scents of people of every type—

mostly werewolves, but vampires, devils, and even some sorcerers brave enough to come up from the Indies, the local name for the south end of the island.

It was overwhelming. It felt like home and absolutely alien at the same time.

Fang took a spot at the far end of the bar, and Savy poured him a blood martini. He sniffed it dubiously, then took a sip. Glancing at me, he didn't make any attempt to hide his expression. "I can't believe vampires drink this, let alone you."

I shrugged. "Warned you."

He pushed it back across the bar. "I think I'll settle for a little red wine, preferably something that doesn't taste like a three-day-old goat."

Savy rolled her eyes and got him a drink, then poured me a whiskey. "What's it like being back?"

"I'd say a lot's changed, but I think it's just me."

"Plenty has changed," she said, giving me a playful expression that I couldn't quite read. "The place isn't the same without you here."

With arrangements for the ritual made, Jaxson joined us, and Savy slid him a whiskey as well.

"Thank you for doing this," I said.

He raised his glass to me. "I should never have doubted you, not for a second. You're family."

"Here's to family, then—always getting you in and out of messes, one after another." I clicked my glass against his, then turned to Savy, my hand still raised.

She snatched a rocks glass and filled it with a press of soda water, then saluted. "To family. It's damn good to have you here again, though really, we should be on opposite sides of the bar."

"Toasting with soda? Isn't that bad luck?" I laughed.

She glanced at Jaxson for a moment, and then patted her stomach. "Good luck, in this case."

For a second, I stared dumbly, and then my eyes rounded. "Holy shit! You're pregnant? That was fast."

Now that I knew, I recognized it in her scent. It certainly explained why Jax was so adamant about her not going.

Savy couldn't stop a smile from breaking across her face. "After everything that happened here, we headed for Colorado for a while, but we didn't get out of the bedroom as much as we expected. Now we have twins on the way."

I looked between them, almost unable to believe it. "Damn, you guys are going to have some cute pups—but I have to say, I hope they get Savy's personality. And looks. And smarts."

The alpha grinned at the familiar ribbing, but Savy's face fell. "That was all before we knew you were missing. We would have come back from Colorado sooner if we'd had any idea that you were in trouble. Maybe then—"

I put my hand on hers. "Stop it. There was *literally* nothing that you or anyone else could have done other than get yourself killed. I got myself out, anyway."

"And straight into more hot water, it seems," Jaxson muttered, then took a sip.

I shrugged and matched his grin. "When has it been any different?"

"I hope these two are as tough as you," Savy said. "You're going to make a great aunt."

I laughed and kept the smile on my face as my heart crumbled into dust.

If I was being honest with myself, this was probably the last time I'd ever step foot in Magic Side. The last time I'd run with my friends or the pack. I could feel my fate driving me forward toward my purpose and into the waiting jaws of death himself.

I instinctively glanced toward the comfort of the shadows, but Cadean wasn't there. Instead, I swept my gaze across the room, taking it all in again and letting myself get lost in the drone of voices and laughter as people from across the city indulged in their early evening cocktails.

"What's the matter?" Savy asked.

"Nothing," I lied. "It's just like I'm seeing everything and everyone here again for the first time."

25

Cadean

I watched the pack run through Magic Side that night. Seeing into the waking world was always difficult, murky and indistinct—except when *she* was there. Samantha was a spotlight in the darkness illuminating everything around her.

Of course, she was also the only thing I cared to see.

I moved shadow to shadow, observing as the dozens of werewolves shifted and charged through Magic Side, howling and raising hell. People leapt off the sidewalks and out of the way but showed little fear. Apparently, in a city enraptured with magic, a pack of snarling wolves was nothing too out of the ordinary.

I had to give credit to their alpha for keeping them in line.

Samantha's wolf was beautiful, sleek with flecked brown fur and piercing yellow eyes. Even when she was running in the midst of her pack, I could always pick her out. She was unmistakable and enrapturing.

She was racing against another male. Their heads were down as they ran neck and neck, feet pounding against the concrete. My palms itched. Had I been there, I would have slammed the bastard into the nearest tree. They wove through live traffic like it was nothing, furious horns blaring around them. He pulled up short as a car came around a curve, but she vaulted over it, leaving him in the dust.

Good girl.

The pack tore down the green midway that ran east to west through the heart of Magic Side, then burst out into a vast park on the eastern shore of the island. It was filled with magical creatures of all kinds—shifters, fae, and devils, all of whom gave the wolves a wide berth.

Samantha had almost caught the alpha and other leaders when they reached the shore—and then, to my astonishment, they leapt into the lake, shifting as they plunged naked into the icy water.

My little wolf burst to the surface, gasping and scrambling up and out as quickly as she could claw her way. "Holy shit, I'd forgotten how cold it gets in winter."

"It's not even Christmas yet," her friend Savannah replied, laughing, as she wrapped a towel around Samantha's shoulders and handed her dry clothes.

I wasn't the only one watching, and my blood began to boil. Had I been there in person, I would have heaved every male in the park straight into the lake. Of course, Samantha didn't mind the looks. She was wolfborn, and these were her people. They'd been running like this since birth. They shifted the old way and had some of the wilderness still left in them.

These were my children, trapped in a prison of concrete and stone. It sickened me to my core.

I prowled the edges of the pack, keeping back in the shadows of the trees. None but Samantha could see me, but I still didn't want to draw too close. This was her time with them. She laughed and spoke idly with the werewolves around her as they toweled off and dressed. Someone passed her a drink, and she laughed again.

My neck heated with jealousy. I hadn't ever seen her this carefree and happy—not since she'd entered the Dreamlands. My envy turned mournful, and the shadows laced about me as I withdrew a little from the waking world.

I had taken this from her. All of it.

Werewolves needed their pack. It was part of their soul, part of who they were. Yet greedily, I'd kept her to myself. Had I known what that happy beauty looked like, perhaps I would have freed her long ago.

Samatha patted someone on the back, and then her eyes flicked up and looked directly at me—as if she'd felt me watching among all the other gazes around her.

My chest pulled, and every nerve in my body came alive. To be seen by her was to plunge into cool waters on a scorching summer's day.

She slipped out of the throng of werewolves and began making her way to me.

Stay with them, I wanted to shout. *Be with your pack one moment longer. Savor the joy.*

But I didn't say anything because I was a covetous bastard, and I'd steal her for myself every chance I got.

She made her way closer, veering slightly toward the terraced seawall that protected the park. Checking over her shoulder that no one had followed, she took a seat on one of the upper stones and patted the spot beside her.

I left the trees and sat, both of us facing the Chicago skyline. "Your pack misses you."

"I missed them," she said softly, then looked over. "I could feel you watching as we ran."

"You're fast—almost as fast as the alpha."

"I should be faster, but I'm out of practice. Too much

running around on two legs, swinging swords. My paws got a little roughed up on the asphalt."

I didn't respond, but my face must have betrayed me.

"What is it?" she asked.

I hesitated, then looked out at the lights of the city on the horizon. "It breaks my heart, having to watch you and your people run like that."

"What do you mean?"

My lip curled. "Barreling through the city, breathing poisons and dodging cars, desperately trying to make it from one small patch of green to another. I can't imagine wolves willingly living in this place."

She put on a playfully offended look. "There are plenty of packs living in the wilderness up north and in the south, but we all chose to be here." She nodded at the lake. "Look at that skyline. Isn't it beautiful? I love seeing it like this. I wish you could see it the way I do."

Skyscrapers lined the shore, pillars of light reflecting off the water, drowning out everything around them in their brilliance. I looked up at the light-bleached sky. "I prefer being able to see the stars."

"The city is amazing," she said, and laughed quietly. "If I had time, I'd show you. I *loved* living here. Great food. Rocking bars. The shopping. The magic. *Roller derby*—you don't have that in the Dreamlands."

I grunted, unimpressed. None of it meant anything to me, but if she loved the city, then there must be something there worth loving about it.

Samantha sniffed in mock disdain. "Well, I don't suppose I should expect a feral brute to appreciate the finer points of civilized life."

"Would you stay here, then?" I asked, trying to keep my voice as casual as I could.

She looked down at her feet, dangling over the stones. "I have a job to do."

"I know you do, but if you could stay..." I gestured at her packmates, circling around a roaring bonfire. "I haven't seen you so happy."

Samantha placed a hand atop mine, and a shiver of magic traced its way between us, from her world into the land of dreams. "You make me happy, Cade. My place is with you in the Dreamlands. That's my home now."

I couldn't repress my smile. It was the answer I wanted, but by the fates, I didn't deserve it.

A grin cut her face. "But I'll be desperate to visit. There are some things you just can't get in your realm, like silky underwear and really good ramen."

"I'll never prevent you from coming here."

Samantha didn't respond, and I realized that it hadn't been what I'd needed to say.

I looked out over the black water and the city, everywhere but at her, before finally meeting her eyes. "I should never have taken you or stopped you in the first place. Everything I did to you was wrong, and everything I did to your pack was worse. I shouldn't have tried to force my way into the waking world or attack Magic Side."

Samantha didn't pull her hand from mine, but her fingers had become iron. The memories were still raw. She'd witnessed me at my worst.

I flexed my free hand, searching for some way to explain. "I was blind while I was imprisoned. I couldn't see into the waking world. Knowing what would happen and being powerless to stop it drove me into a kind of madness. When the barrier began to weaken, and I could see again..."

I thrust myself up off the stones and stepped to the edge of the concrete, frustration pounding through me. How could I explain what a god sees?

I gestured to the lights of Chicago on the far shore. "A thousand years ago, before this island existed, there used to be people living where those skyscrapers are now. They were all murdered and driven off their land. The forests and wetlands are gone, too, replaced by asphalt and concrete and hazy, polluted skies. The world was unspoiled, and now, barely a fraction is unchanged." Shadows drifted down the shore, building around me in a weave of darkness. "I was consumed with rage. It was an abomination of all that I loved."

"I can imagine," Samantha said. She hadn't risen to join me, and I knew as much as I tried to explain, it would never be enough.

But I didn't need to explain myself or justify my actions. I had to own them.

I returned to her and lifted her chin. "None of that matters. What I did, what I was *going* to do, that was wrong. If I could undo it, I would, but I can't."

Her expression was dark and unyielding. "You need to tell them that one day."

I shook my head. "Nothing I say would change anything. Words won't rebuild or bring back the dead. Your people will never forgive me, and I don't blame them. I wouldn't forgive myself, either."

"Then find a way to make it right."

"I don't know that there is a way." I took her hand. "But I will leave them be. You are the only thing I desire in the waking world, and once you return, there will be nothing for me here."

"You can just walk away?"

I gave her a mournful smile. "The truth is, the world I loved doesn't exist anymore. It's moved on—not just from me, but from all the gods. Our place is in myths and dreams. The realm I need to protect is my own. It's up to your kind to protect this one, and they shouldn't have to protect it from me."

She squeezed my hand.

I shook my head, in sad wonder. "I didn't think there was any hope for your world, but seeing the pack thriving here, amid all the concrete...maybe there is."

"People are better than you give them credit for."

I brushed the hair back from her face. "You give me hope of that. You're better than anyone I've ever met."

She opened her mouth, but a voice cut through the night. "Sam? Is that you? What are you doing sitting over here? I've been looking all over."

Samantha waved at Savannah, the one who'd sealed my prison again. She had shadow magic herself, which might mean she could see me.

I withdrew into the darkness until I was nothing more than a silhouette against the dull black sky. "You need to be careful, little wolf."

"I will be," she whispered, not wanting to give my presence away.

"I know the Moon helped you before, but she is perilous. You saw her light side, but she also has a dark one, and her moods shift on a breeze. We were close once, and in the blink of an eye, she imprisoned me for a thousand years. She's more dangerous than Ayanna ever has been, so keep your wits about you."

She nodded as her friend arrived. "I will."

I looked at her one last time. "I believe you can do this."

With that, I slipped back into the world of dreams.

26

Samantha

"Is everything okay?" Savy asked me. "I've never seen you pass up a party."

Actually, I'd slipped out of plenty of parties to meet a guy, but this was a little different. I shrugged. "Just taking a moment to get my head right. It's a lot being back—a bit overwhelming."

"I bet."

"And yeah, I'm a bit nervous, to be honest. There's a lot riding on me convincing the Moon to help."

"I brought these," Savy said, digging a pair of pearlescent white stones out of her pocket—two of the moonstones the Moon Goddess had given us to recharge her pylons. Each had been a little nuclear battery of her power. When she'd first given them to us, they'd been radiating with so much power that we'd only been able to carry one each safely. Now spent, they no longer glowed or thrummed with her magic, but they were beautiful to behold, nonetheless.

"You still have them?"

"I recovered these two from the first pylons we recharged, but the others got left in the Dreamlands—the one you threw, and the last one we used," Savy said, holding them up so they were backlit by the city lights. "I was going to give them back as an offering to the Moon."

Right. The last time we'd called the Moon, we'd learned too late that we were supposed to provide offerings. I'd given her an old cheap bead bracelet that I should've tossed years before.

The Moon had not been impressed.

Hell, I was probably going to have to give her my new jacket this time. I loved it, but it was the only cherished possession I had other than the sword, and I'd left that with Cadean in the Dreamlands.

Savy held the two moonstones out for me. "I think you should have these instead—I've been carrying them around with me for good luck. So far, I've got twins on the way, and no one has tried to kill me in months, so that's about the best luck I've had my whole life."

She slipped the moonstones into my hands, each the size of a golf ball but far heavier than they looked. The first time I'd carried one, it had been on the verge of exploding with the Moon's energy. It had pulsed through me and made me feel alive in a way I'd never felt before. I would have killed to have power like that.

Now, that magic was mine and with me all the time. I smiled down at the stones. Despite the curse and the assassins and nightmare my life had become, maybe I'd been blessed a little, too.

"Thanks. I think I'll need all the luck I can get." I rolled them against each other in my palm. "They make pretty good worry balls."

And boy, did I have a lot of worries.

"This is going to work," Savy said. "The Moon will listen and help. She helped us once before, and she brought you back from death."

Yes, but that was when I was trying to lock up her homicidal ex-boyfriend. Now I was screwing him.

I let out a low, unsteady breath.

Maybe the Moon would just kill me.

"Jaxson and I believe in you," Savy said, putting her hand on top of mine. "And even if the Moon can't help, we'll find a way to get rid of your curse and help you stop the queen."

A commanding howl reverberated through the air, and we snapped our heads around. *Jaxson.*

"They're ready for us," Savy said.

We headed back toward the crowd of werewolves. Most had shifted back to wolf form and formed a circle. I knew almost all of them by sight and scent—friends and allies I'd fought alongside in my other life, before Cadean had swept me up into the world of dreams. A few humans milled warily around the perimeter of the pack—sorcerers, members of Savy's family. I recognized her cousin and aunt, but not the others. Once our archenemies, they'd become the pack's allies while fighting the Dark Wolf God.

My mate.

Fates, how things had gotten fucked up.

The loremaster, still wearing her human form, had taken a position in the center of the circle of wolves beside the bonfire. With one hand knotted around a heavy oaken staff, she beckoned us to hurry.

I looked toward the trees, where Fang was standing guard, watching me like a hawk. The wolves didn't like having him close, but I could tell from his irritated stance that it was driving him crazy to be positioned so far off.

Jaxson was waiting with Sarion just outside the ring. He patted my shoulder. "Good luck tonight."

"I can't thank you enough for trusting me on this, Jax," I whispered as the four of us entered the ring.

"You were always there for us. I should never have doubted you for a second," he said, grinning.

My stomach knotted. I knew what I was doing was right, but why did it feel like a betrayal of everyone there?

I tightened my fist. This wasn't about what had happened before. This was about stopping Ayanna and a war that was bigger than Magic Side alone.

The pack had put their faith in me, and I would earn it.

"Ready, alpha?" the old woman asked, eyeing the sorcerers warily. "Because keeping all these folks standing around and in position without a fight breaking out is nearly impossible."

Jaxson nodded. "Let's do this."

The loremaster raised her hands and turned to the assembly, stilling them and hushing their voices. "Tonight, we call the Moon Goddess down from the heavens. She helped our pack defeat the Dark Wolf God when he threatened our city, and now, we need her help for one of our own."

A sea of golden eyes measured me, and I dug my fingers into my palms.

Pacing the circle, the loremaster met the eyes of all assembled as if assessing their conviction. "This time, we cannot seek the Moon at one of her temples, but instead, we must call her here. Our devotion must be her temple. We will show her that while the world has forgotten the goddess of the Moon, we have not!"

A burst of noise resounded from the wolves, but the loremaster raised her hand and staff to quiet them. "The pack requires your voices tonight! When I begin to chant, I want you to call out to the Moon with your hearts. Our friends, the sorcerers, will amplify your voices to the heavens! Together, we will call the Moon down to us!"

Savy must have seen the doubt flickering across my expression because she squeezed my hand, and I forced a smile.

Slowly, the assembly fell quiet. The loremaster let the silence fill the air, then whipped her staff high above her head and began chanting in a low drone. The flames began to dance and flicker. I couldn't make out the ancient words, but I felt their meaning: devotion, praise, and need.

Regina, Jaxson's second-in-command, tilted her head back and began to howl. It wasn't a piercing cry, but rather a rolling, mournful sound—the call one makes to summon a lost wolf home. The hair on my neck rose, and I shivered as one by one, my old packmates joined in. Their echoing voices became a chorus, almost a song.

Magic flared at the edges of the circle as the sorcerers' magic burst to life, amplifying the loremaster's chant and the howl of the wolves until I felt like I was drowning in sound. It shuddered through me, dancing and wild, and it took every ounce of control I had to stop myself from shifting and joining them.

These were my people, calling for me—a lost wolf.

As the ritual reached a fevered height, I lost sense of the sound. It became like ice and sunlight, like stars in the sky turning into rain, filling the circle with limitless, beautiful light.

I shielded my eyes as the flare rose into the sky, a waterfall of light that slowly melted away into the glowing form of a woman standing where the fire had been.

Her presence was silent, as every one of us caught our breath, wolf and human alike. I felt her power pulsing through the crowd. Scents of wonder and fear and trepidation filled the air. For all but the five of us in the center, this was the first time they'd ever witnessed a god.

I let my hand drop away as the afterimage faded, and my chest tightened in awe, despite myself. Like a Roman statue with perfect lips, flawless cheeks, and impossibly long blonde hair, the woman who stood before us was as breathtakingly beautiful as she was powerful.

I remembered what it was to feel small and insignificant before her.

The Moon stepped forward, shattering the illusion of her almost statuesque presence. She was flesh and blood, and very much alive. Her luminescent white dress was far too modern for ancient sculpture, with a revealing slit along one leg. It hugged the curves of her body and moved like the rolling waves of the sea with each step she took as she circled us and eyed the gathered pack.

The loremaster stooped and lowered herself to her knees. "Moon Mother, you are the guide and strength of our people. We come before you, pleading for help in a time of darkness."

The Moon looked from one of us to the next, and her lips drew into a hard line. "You four—again? And not even in one of my temples?"

What confidence I'd had began to quickly slip away. Apparently, we weren't a fond memory. I wrapped my suddenly damp fingers around the jacket I was preparing to offer. Hopefully, our gifts would be enough.

The loremaster shuffled forward and placed a small ivory statue of a wolf at the Moon's feet. "We've brought—"

The Moon waved her away dismissively. "I've received gifts from you once and have no use for your offerings now. I already know who you are, and the only thing you've ever brought me is trouble. What disaster has befallen you this time?"

My companions all slowly turned their eyes to me, and the Moon followed. Her lips pursed in displeasure. "Ah...I thought as much. Once you bring someone back from the brink of death, they just keep coming back for more."

I'd stood before Cadean and Auren and the queen of the fae, but it was far harder to stand before the Moon. While their power had been overwhelming, she was the embodiment of perfect womanhood, beautiful, strong, and confident. Every word resonated with purpose and power, and every movement sang with grace. And even though I'd learned to wield her magic, it suddenly felt like I couldn't live up to it.

The Moon Goddess folded her arms. "Out with it, little wolf. What do you need?"

The hair on my neck bristled. I was no little wolf, naïve and begging for help. Not anymore. I could wield her magic. I had shaped her wall. I'd fought gods and queens, and I was here on a mission to save the Dreamlands.

Suddenly, I felt my doubts fade. She would help us. I would find a way.

Lifting my chin, I stepped forward. "With your help, our pack restored the Dark Wolf God's prison and drove him back from Magic Side, but now, the walls of his prison are in danger."

Her eyes became arrow slits. "How so?"

"A fae queen rules over the lands adjacent to the barrier. She's found a way to drain power from the wall. While she grows stronger, the barrier is weakening. I don't know how long it would take for her to drain it, but eventually, the Dark Wolf God will go free."

The goddess's gaze hardened, drilling into me, searching for the truth—and when she found it, the light about her darkened. "You're certain of this?"

"Yes," I said, matching her measuring stare.

"Then there is no time to lose." The Moon turned and traced her hand through the air like a knife, creating a slit of light. She reached out and parted the darkness like curtains or the flaps of a giant tent, revealing a bright room beyond. She stepped into the glowing triangle of light, then glanced back. "Come along, then, little wolves. Let's sort this mess out."

~

I stepped through into a dazzlingly bright space, followed closely by Savy, Jax, and Sarion. As my eyes adjusted, I turned slowly, trying to take in the beauty that surrounded me. We'd emerged into a large octagonal room with a floor ringed by low walls of smooth, milky marble. Pillars rose at each of the eight corners, along with a ninth mounted on a plinth in the center of the room. I craned my neck up, following the pedestal skyward. There was no roof above us, only brilliant black sky and stars.

With a wave of her hand, the Moon closed the doorway behind us. The sky rippled as the stars moved in a long, gentle wave.

I blinked, suddenly seeing the illusion for what it was. The pillars supported a vast obsidian canopy illuminated by sparkling points of light. It was like the night itself had been woven into fabric and stretched between the columns to create a giant pavilion. After the light-bleached skies of Magic Side, it felt like we were suddenly perched on a spire in the middle of deep space itself.

"Wow," I breathed out like a prayer.

The Moon glanced up. "Yes. It's always breathtaking, even for me. It reminds me of where I belong."

For a second, she kept her gaze skyward, then turned and reclined languidly on a crescent-shaped throne. "But this is not where you belong, Samantha, so let us sort out this predicament so that you and your trouble can be on your way. Who is this fae queen, and how is she stealing my magic?"

"Her name is Ayanna, Queen of the Undying Court," I replied. "She's infested the Dreamlands with vines that bleed magic from the land. At first, they were draining the power from the Dark Wolf God's realm, but after I turned your barrier solid, they attached and began feeding from it."

Her lips turned up in an incredulous smile that didn't reach her eyes. "After you *what*?" she half-laughed.

My neck heated. "I've inherited some of your power, and I can control the barrier now."

The Moon scoffed. "That's ridiculous. Mortals—"

Breathing in sharply, I summoned my magic shield in a burst of dancing light. I quickly spread it to encompass my friends, then shaped it into a single ball in my hand before dismissing it again.

The Moon Goddess gaped—perhaps for the first time in her life. "How is this possible?" she whispered, as if to herself, and then to me, "What have you done?"

Heartbeat rising, I began the dance of words I'd rehearsed over and over since leaving the Dreamlands. I lied with the truth, telling her exactly what she needed to know, but obscuring every sign that I might be partial to Cadean's cause.

It was a more precise duel than I'd ever fought with Kass.

I told her how the Dark Wolf God had captured me, interrogated me, and locked me in a cave—but not that he had let me out or sought my help. I told her that Auren had helped me escape and that I'd stopped the Dark Wolf God at the border, but not that I had healed him first.

"You really stabbed the Dark Wolf God in the chest with a fragment from my pylons?" the Moon asked in disbelief.

I shrugged. "I missed his heart, but it gave me enough time to cross the barrier. That was the first time I was able to crystalize the wall."

She drew her fingers through the air, and a shimmering barrier appeared between us. "Show me."

Meeting the challenge in her words, I closed my eyes and reached out to touch the barrier. There were no whispers like in the Dreamlands, but I felt the familiar pattern of the Moon's magic. Grasping the threads of her spell, I pulled the weave of magic tighter and felt it crystallize beneath my touch.

"Extraordinary," the Moon muttered beneath her breath.

Her imperious attitude had faded, leaving an expression on her face that wavered between curiosity and delight. "I didn't think the weave was strong enough to do this."

"This power and my defiance of the Dark Wolf God were why the queen sought me out. I assumed she wanted my help to defeat him."

"But she didn't?" the Moon asked, voice suddenly edged with suspicion.

"She wanted to take your magic from me, just like she was stealing it from the land. She claims that she's doing it to help her people, but she consumes the power herself." I met the Moon's eyes. "She wants to become as powerful as a god, and she has the means to do so."

The Moon folded her fingers, looking from one of us to the next. "You must understand, this is difficult to believe."

I nodded to my fae companion. "This is Sarion, one of her court. He brought me to the Dreamlands on her orders, and he helped me escape in the end. He can corroborate everything I've said."

The Moon grilled us both about the Well of Life and the queen's powers. About the murder of my mother. I explained that we had escaped across the border—but of course, we didn't mention that Cadean was there to grant us passage.

"And so," she said, her voice rising as her earlier irritation returned, "you solidified the *entire* wall to stop the queen from hunting you down?"

"And to protect the people living in the Dark Wolf God's land."

Her eyes widened. "To protect *his* people?"

"They're shifters, just like me," I said quickly. "They don't deserve to be trapped in a war. Someone has to look out for the packs since you can't be there."

Her expression went ice-cold. "Indeed."

I was walking a very fine line, but hopefully, my anger would cover the deeper truth: they were my people now. I was his, and he was mine.

"How was it that you evaded the Dark Wolf God again and returned to Magic Side?"

"Sarion and I slipped through a portal in Mistwind Harbor. I'd learned of it from a werefox while I was the Dark Wolf God's prisoner."

Everything we told her was true, but in the end, it was no more than a lie—but one that could mean the difference between the safety of Cadean's realm and its destruction.

The Moon sat back, considering us in silence.

I pushed up my sleeve and showed her my arm, which was covered with purple-blue veins of light that had spread further than the day before. "I don't understand my connection to your magic, but once the vines began attacking the wall, they began draining me as well—my strength, my stamina, my magic, nothing is the same as before. It's the best proof I can offer."

She motioned me forward. "Show me."

The Moon gently took hold of my wrist and drew her fingers over the infection. Her magic dragged along my skin, cool and warm all at once, sending a shiver through me.

"It is as you claim," she murmured at last. "I can feel your bond with the wall, and through it, I can feel the vines feeding. I don't know how you forged the connection, but if we do not break it or stop the vines, they will consume you."

27

Samantha

I stepped back as the Moon released my wrist, looking uneasily at Jaxson, Savy, and Sarion. Their faces were dark and downcast.

"There must be something we can do," I said. "Is there a way to make the barrier defend itself from the vines?"

"Perhaps," the Moon said, waving her hand dismissively, "But unfortunately, I'm the anchor that keeps the door of the Dark Wolf God's prison shut. He cannot leave, but I cannot enter —otherwise, this situation would be much easier to deal with, and I would not have needed you to recharge my pylons in the first place."

"Then can you teach me how to manipulate the barrier? Is there a way to make it repel the vines, like it repels the Dark Wolf God?"

Her eyes flashed, and her expression was as cold as the dark side of the moon. She leaned forward on her throne. "Let me make this clear: you will never touch my pylons again—fates only know what damage you would do."

The force of her words stole my breath like a slap across the face.

"But I can do it. I've done it before," I protested.

She thrust herself to her feet. "I sacrificed nearly half my power to create the pylons and trap *him* there. It was either insanity or arrogance that you ever tried to wield that kind of power."

My wolf stirred at the rebuke. Cadean had warned me that she was temperamental, but I hadn't expected such sudden vehemence.

Forcing my claws to stay in, I straightened my spine. "It wasn't arrogance. It was desperation—and I succeeded."

"And look at the predicament *you* put us in," she said, her voice dripping with accusation. "My barrier is in danger, as is my magic—potentially, the entire waking world."

"There must be something I can do."

"Yes," she said, seizing my wrist roughly. "And it starts with you giving back the power you stole from my pylons."

I jerked, but before I could pull away, her magic exploded around us, whipping her dress and long blonde hair like a storm. A surge of warm sunlight and cold ice raced over my arm, and I gasped as her power poured though me.

I was lost in sensation, suddenly feeling both her connection with me and ours with the wall, the three of us entangled across space and time. For a second, I heard the whispers again, but then, like wires snapping under tension, the bond began to splinter and unravel.

I grasped for clarity amid the burst of pain.

"Release the power you stole and your connection to the wall," the Moon commanded through her clenched teeth. "It will free you from your curse, fool girl! Do it for yourself, if for nothing else!"

My mouth slicked with the wrongness of it, like the taste of rancid oil. If cutting off my connection to the barrier and the Dreamlands was what it took to be healed, then I didn't want it. I would rather wither and die than relinquish what I'd been given.

Given. That was the truth of it. I hadn't stolen her power. The barrier had chosen me. It had been given to me for a purpose. *To protect.*

I seized the glowing source of energy with my soul, refusing to release it, pouring all my strength and will and determination into the connection we shared. The Moon's magic poured over me in a raging torrent, and then it collapsed and faded away like a mighty wave breaking and dissipating upon the shore.

The Moon dropped my wrist as if it were a hot kettle and stumbled back, her face enraged. "You dare defy me, girl? I am a *goddess.*"

"The magic was given to me to protect the Dreamlands. I will not let it go until that realm is safe. Someone has to stand for the people there if you cannot!"

"Protect the Dreamlands?" She laughed, rage smoldering in her eyes. "They're in more danger than ever *because of you.* The barrier is weakening, and soon, if I do nothing, the Dark Wolf God will be free—*because of you!* You've done immeasurable damage with magic that doesn't belong to you because *you do not understand it.*"

My blood simmered in my veins. "*You* don't understand what's at stake! The queen is far more dangerous that the Dark Wolf God!"

The corners of her mouth turned down in a mix of pity and bitterness. "You prove what a fool you are, poor wolf."

I pulled myself up to my full height. "I will not give up my power."

"Then you will be its prisoner." She whipped her hand into

the air, deftly weaving the signs of a spell. A burst of moonlight exploded from her palm and wrapped around me, forming a glowing sphere. The shock of it pinned me in place. It was just like the spell I'd used to trap Cadean the first time we met.

I stared back at her in disbelief. "What are you doing?"

"What needs to be done to set things straight," she said bitterly.

"Release her!" Jaxson roared, leaping forward. I glanced over as Savannah's magic flared, and Sarion's hand reached for his absent blade.

Terror filled me. Were they mad? They couldn't face down a goddess.

The Moon turned to them. "I will overlook this for the sake of your pack, but we will have no more business together." She flung up her hand, and with a crack of lightning, they flew back, consumed by the darkness of the pavilion.

"No!" I screamed, throwing myself against the walls of my prison. "What have you done to them?"

"I returned them to their place," the Moon said, stalking forward.

My stomach tumbled as despair choked my throat. Not only had I not convinced the Moon to help, but she'd decided that I was a thief. I'd failed catastrophically, and now I was her prisoner, just as Cadean had warned.

I slammed my hands against the sides of the sphere. Ice burned my fingers as her power cracked over me, trying to drive me back. I gritted my teeth, feeling for the weave of the spell.

This wasn't just her magic, after all, but my own, and I knew the spell well.

"Don't be a fool," she said, but I ignored her.

I found the thread and began to pull. Power and light poured through me like wildfire, and I gasped, falling back against the side of the shimmering orb.

"You may control my magic, but you barely know what you're doing," the Moon said, looking on with a sad expression. "To unravel a spell like this, you must reclaim its power, and there is more magic in this casting than you could hope to draw and hold in a dozen lifetimes. If you try, you'll die—and for now, I need you alive, at least until I learn the extent of what you have done."

The Moon turned her back on me and glided over to a silver basin standing by the pillar in the middle of the room. She danced her hands over the liquid within, and her power surged. Steam began to rise from the surface, and three orbs appeared in the mist.

I shoved myself up onto my side. "What are you doing?"

"I might not be able to enter the Dreamlands or recharge the pylons, but I'm still connected to their magic. I'm hoping I can undo the changes you made." She glanced back. "At least this should free you from your curse—not that I expect thanks from a thief."

Her hands moved faster and faster as she rewove the spell. I didn't care about the curse consuming me anymore, just Cadean and his people.

My stomach knotted as the room filled with the radiance of her magic. If she returned the barrier to a wall of light, the queen's armies would flow across, and her vines would begin feeding off Cadean's lands, sapping his strength just as it had stolen mine—and I wouldn't be there to protect them.

They'd have no warning before it fell. No chance to prepare.

"Please," I begged. "I need you to listen—"

"I don't need to listen to fools or mortals," the Moon responded, not turning from her work. "They have a rather short-sighted view of the world, I've found."

"You're a goddess. Isn't that what you do? Listen to us?" I

dropped to my knees, clasping my hands before. "Please, listen to me *now*. The Dark Wolf God's people are in danger."

"Do you think I care about them? They sealed their fate when they knelt before that monster."

Sick to my bones, I shoved myself to my feet. "Are you heartless? Without the wall, the queen will slaughter them!"

The Moon spun on me. "No, I'm not heartless. But I care about the people of *this* world. They are the ones I'm sworn to protect. I will not put the safety of a few traitorous shifters in the Dreamlands above the lives of my *children*."

The fury and passion she put into *children* lanced through me like an arrow. Suddenly, everything shifted, and I saw the truth.

She wasn't cruel or capricious. She was terrified.

The Moon was a mother bear, fierce and wild, doing what she had to do to protect her cubs. She knew what the Dark Wolf God was capable of and what he'd once wanted to do, and it was enough to keep her scared for a thousand years. Enough to make her give up half her power to keep him at bay.

My throat tightened with grief. The Dark Wolf God and the Moon were the same—both ferociously protecting a people they loved. Both afraid that they weren't strong enough to do so, and of what would happen if their power failed.

That's why she was so furious that I controlled some of her magic.

My mind spun as I searched for a way forward—I couldn't persuade her by putting his people first. I had to make this about protecting the waking world—about protecting her children and her power.

"Ayanna is the key!" I shouted through the walls of the orb. "She's the one stealing your power—perhaps she's been draining it this whole time. The barrier was weak before my friends and I recharged it. She might still be able to steal your power, whether you revert the wall or not."

"If so, it still lasted a thousand years. I'll find a solution."

"She'll keep stealing his magic. She's ruthless. With the strength of a god, she'll be more of a threat to the waking world than he ever was."

"If the fae queen becomes a problem, I'll deal with her just as I dealt with him," the Moon said, breaking off her weave. "Until then, I couldn't care less if she drains the last wisps of his soul."

She spoke with the malice of a spurned lover. She wanted to see him dead.

I dug my nails into my palms as my heart tore itself apart, desperately trying to keep the emotions from my face.

Her eyes widened. "You care for him, don't you?"

She circled me like a shark, and my heartbeat quickened. "No! He nearly killed me! He imprisoned me! He's a *monster*."

You didn't have to be a werewolf to smell the lie.

Pain and anger and delight danced across her face. "Of course," she said, almost laughing with a bitter voice. "How did I not see it immediately? A little wolf under the Wolf God's spell. He always had a penchant for blondes," she muttered.

"I'm not under his spell," I protested.

"You are," she snapped. "I can see the truth written across your face. You care for him. This isn't just about my wall or his people. You're trying to protect *him*."

We both knew the game was up, but I had to keep fighting. "I care for his *people*. And for the fae. That's who I'm trying to protect."

But she wasn't listening. A millennium of resentment had broken through the surface, and it wouldn't be tamed. She stalked around me, her shoulders shaking with fury. "You're more a fool than I could ever have imagined. He's a monster who will destroy the world if let out. The fact that you feel anything—"

"He's changed," I pleaded. "He only wants to protect his people—just like you!"

"Gods do not change," the Moon said. "We are born from belief. We are shaped by belief." She stepped close to the shimmering orb of my prison. "Tell me, little wolf, what do your people believe about the Dark Wolf God?"

I clamped my mouth shut.

"Tell me!" she commanded as she unveiled her full presence. I fell to my knees, crushed beneath the overwhelming press of divine power. It was like drowning in the Arctic Ocean or being burned alive by an inferno of light.

Compelled by her power, I choked out the truth. "They believe that he's a living nightmare. That he's darkness and destruction lurking in the shadows. That if he's ever freed, he will destroy our world."

"Then that is what he is," she said. "Gods are what you believe us to be."

Heart aching for the fate of my mate, I forced my head up and met the Moon's unwavering gaze. "I don't believe that."

"What?" she said, her voice rising to a fevered pitch.

"I believed it once, but not anymore. I believe he's a fierce protector of his people—that he cares for them and his lands more than anything. I believe—I *know* that he regrets what he did to Magic Side. I believe that he *has* changed and that he's worthy of a second chance. More importantly, I believe his people are worthy as well."

The Moon looked at me, her anger and resentment melting into an expression of pity. "I wish that were true, but you're one little wolf." She shook her head. "Your beliefs don't matter."

Her words were a knife.

The Moon flicked her hand, and I stumbled against the side of the sphere as it levitated into the air. "What are you doing?"

"I must find a way to undo everything you've done," she said sadly. "But for now, I need you out my sight and my thoughts. I have a barrier to repair."

With that dismissal, she flung her hand forward, and I hurtled backward through the walls of the pavilion and deep into the night sky.

28

Dreamlands, The Northern Border of Cadean's Realm

Cadean

My world was coming undone. Samantha had disappeared, the wall had collapsed, and Ayanna's forces were marching across the border, burning villages that had been safe behind the wall.

Chaos reigned, and I could do nothing but try to stem the tide.

I'd rushed to the border as soon as the wall fell, joining my army and cutting through the queen's men and monsters without mercy. They posed little threat to me, just a mass of bodies to slow my blade. But the vines were another story. Like something from my nightmares, they'd come alive like snakes slithering across the landscape. They lashed out wildly, seeking to entangle themselves around my arms and limbs. Each grasping strike sent a dull, freezing ache shuddering through me as they began to bleed my strength and my power.

Fuck Ayanna and her magic, she couldn't have mine.

With a roar of fury, I tore my arm free of the grasping

tendrils and hacked through them with my black axe. Their blood burned where it landed on my skin, but anything was better than the chill of their touch.

Yet even the hungering vines were nothing compared to the fear I had for Samantha. What had happened? I'd watched her disappear into the Moon's realm, and then a matter of minutes later, the wall had reverted into a barrier of light.

Samantha would never have willingly released the wall—it was too important to the safety of my people. It had to have been the *fucking* Moon.

I'd tried shadow-casting, but the Moon's magic had cut me off from my mate, just like the barrier cut me off from the lands I'd once ruled. If she'd harmed Samantha—

My body shook with uncontrolled rage, and I hurled myself across the battlefield with a hurricane wrapped around me like a shield. I cut through soldiers, broodlings, and scuttling monsters from the queen's dungeons, showering the earth with their blood.

They would pay. The queen would pay. The *fucking Moon* would pay.

Shadow-stepping from tree to tree, I slipped through the forest until I found my quarry: a fae warlock standing at the edge of the barrier in glistening silver armor. Hands raised and eyes glowing with an unholy light, he chanted the spells that controlled the monsters ravaging my wolves. He was surrounded by a bodyguard of nightmarish scorpion-like creatures, a shield of flesh and poisoned stingers to keep my wolves at bay.

I'd show them a true nightmare.

I sent an earthquake ripping through the forest, driving both the fae and my own warriors to their knees. Jagged stone exploded from the earth behind the warlock, blocking his retreat.

I raised my axe and charged, but the vines were already

there, pulling him back behind the safety of the shimmering wall. Were they acting on their own, or was Ayanna there, hiding in the shadows and controlling them? It didn't matter.

Barrier or not, the warlock wasn't safe from me.

Drawing on the power of the earth, I summoned the last reserves of my strength, and a thundering maelstrom of power built around me. With lightning cracking and leaping between the clouds, I slammed my axe into the ground. A massive fissure ripped the earth apart, creating a wide chasm that tore its way beneath the wall and raced toward the warlock. Trees, earth, and men poured down into it as the mists began to rise from within.

The warlock scrambled to his feet and grasped for the sentient vines, but he was consumed by the avalanche of dust and bodies. The deathwings under his control halted, then raced back across the border. The entire front devolved into chaos as the queen's monsters went berserk and turned on their masters, no longer enslaved.

Run, bastards.

The fae were deadly because of their precision and control, but my wolves would feast in the chaos. I allowed myself a thin smile. This skirmish would be ours.

The cry of a hawk above tore my attention from the destruction before me, and I raised my arm for it to alight. Its talons dug into my skin as it landed, and it screeched. *Three two-legs on four-legs, heading for the king's roost.*

Shadowstone.

My heart leapt. "Is Samantha with them?"

Three males, the hawk responded.

Fates be damned, what the hell had happened?

Dread coiling in my chest, I launched the hawk back into the air. "Thank you, friend."

Then, abandoning the front to Wulfric and my captains, I took my phoenix form and followed the messenger into the sky.

Pillars of smoke rose from further along the border, all testaments to my failure to protect my lands. I couldn't be everywhere at once, yet somehow, it seemed the queen of the fae could. She'd grown strong feasting on my power and the Moon's, while I felt weaker than I ever had before. She had to be stopped, but she and her armies could wait.

My mate came first.

The doors of the great hall of Shadowstone slammed open before me as I arrived. The galleries were filled with refugees fleeing the border—a fraction of the waves I'd seen still approaching as I flew. My citadel would not be able to hold them all.

At the far end of the hall, three figures stood waiting before my throne of bone and antlers, watching as I approached: Kass, Sarion, and the Magic Side alpha, Jaxson Laurent.

I shadow-stepped to my seat of power, and the three men whipped around to face me.

"Where is Samantha?" I growled. The sound rose from the feral part of my soul and boomed through the hall.

"Fucking trapped by the Moon, as far as we know," Kass said. "I brought these two as soon as they returned." He shoved Jaxson forward. Or at least, he tried.

The alpha didn't move an inch.

"This is your fault, you fucking bastard," the werewolf snarled, fearlessly meeting my gaze. The accusation shook through the crowded room, leaving silence in its wake.

My lip curled, and I released my power like an earthquake,

shaking the pillars of the hall to their roots. I pinned the alpha to the ground with my presence.

"Brave wolf," I growled. "But now is not the time to challenge me. Not in my hall, not in the lands I created, not in the middle of a war to protect my people."

"It's a fact," he said, barely able to speak. "This is your fault."

"It is," I said, crouching down beside the prostrate alpha. "But I care for her above all else, so trust me, there is nothing I will not do to get her back."

"Why should I ever trust anything you say?"

"You're a good alpha but let me make this clear. You would be dead right now if she didn't care for you."

"Dead like so many of my people."

I stepped back and dropped onto my throne. "I don't blame you for hating me, alpha, and I can't bring back the dead, but I have the power to get her back if you help me."

"*If* she's alive."

"She *is* alive. I can feel her with my soul. So if you give a damn about her, then put aside your hate and tell me what you know."

After a moment of hesitation, he turned his gaze away in submission.

I released my power over him. "Why did the Moon take her?"

"She defied the Moon Goddess." He slowly stood, dusting himself off. "The Moon accused Samantha of stealing her magic and putting the Dreamlands in danger."

"Then the Moon's a *fool*," I snarled. "Samantha would've risked anything to defend the Moon's fucking barrier. She could've found no better bearer of her power."

"Yeah, well, that's not the way the Moon saw it," Jaxson said. "She tried to take her magic back, as well as Samantha's hold on the barrier, but Samantha resisted."

"Good girl," I said with grim satisfaction, my chest swelling with pride. My mate was tenacious and a fighter to her core. She might be part fae, but she was all wolf.

"Good?" he shouted. "That's all you have to say? She defied a *goddess*, and now she's a prisoner. If you care for her as much as you claim—"

"The mother of your children has shadow magic," I interrupted, and the alpha's voice instantly stilled, his eyes wide with shock.

I leaned forward on my throne. "If I demanded she give it up, if I claimed it as *mine*, would you have her do it?"

"If it meant her life? Yes. Unequivocally."

"Now ask yourself—would *she* do it without a fight? Would she ever willingly give up that part of herself?"

The alpha glared at me, his teeth clenched, the answer clear from his silence. Never. I'd faced the woman before, and she hadn't hesitated to stand up to me.

"Samantha has earned her power. She has ferociously protected the people of the Dreamlands with it. I would never wish to see her give that up, for my sake or anyone's." I leaned back on my throne. "I would rather give up my ability to shift than see her bend the knee."

I wouldn't take her purpose from her. I wouldn't let the Moon take it either—or anyone.

"Then you'd better have a fucking good idea of how to get her back," Jaxson growled. "Because I will *not* lose one of my pack. Not for this, and certainly not for you."

My fingers tightened on the bone arms of my throne, crushing them in my grip. "Do you know where the Moon took you?"

He shook his head. "It was a giant pavilion."

"That's her traveling court, and it could be anywhere. Did you see outside?"

"No."

Sarion confirmed their ignorance.

Fuck. No clues as to where she might be, and I couldn't shadow-cast to her. How was I going to find my mate?

"Can your pack call the Moon again? Can you get back there?" I asked.

Jaxson's expression turned grim. "I doubt the Moon Goddess will answer our prayers ever again."

"Then your lives will have changed little," I said darkly. "Gods have no answers for the problems of mankind."

The Moon, like most gods, honored her vows of non-intervention in the realm of man. My threat to change the course of history was enough for her to turn on me. I doubted she'd ever done anything for the shifters except help them stop *me*.

"Then what are we to do?" Jaxson asked.

Samantha was in the realm of the gods now, and the truth was, there was little he or his pack could do to help.

I knew who might, however…and unfortunately, I also knew the cost.

Frustration tearing at me, I thrust myself up and off my throne. "Go back to your people, alpha. There's nothing more you can do here. I promise I will get Samantha back, and once this is over, I promise I will let her return to you."

"What does a promise mean from you?" he asked, his voice as gray as winter. "You've brought nothing but death and ruin to my people—and now, Samantha may have to pay that price as well."

"She will not," I said, my voice grinding in anger. I strode down the steps of the dais until I was standing squarely before him. "You question my honor, so I will give you a *god's* oath. I will never threaten you, your people, or Magic Side again, as long as I exist. Samantha loves you, and I will honor that love until time tears itself apart."

I turned and walked away from the alpha, dismissing him and the others. "*That* is what my promise means. Take my oath back to your people. Tell them they can sleep well because of what *she* has done."

"And what happens to Sam?"

I glanced back, my gaze burning like molten steel. "There's nothing that I won't do to get her back."

29

______

The Moon's Realm

Samantha

"Fuck!" I slammed my hand against the side of my shimmering sphere, pain coiling up my arm.

The godsdamned irony of it all was sickening. I'd trapped Cadean this way once, and I could cast the same damn spell, but now that the Moon had done it to me, I had no idea how to break out from the inside. It was one thing to shut a door, another to pick the lock.

Not that I'd know what to do or where to go if I got out.

The Moon had sent me hurtling over an eerie and uninhabited landscape of starlit dunes. My floating prison had finally come to a halt in the middle of nowhere, hovering twenty feet off the ground. Even if I managed to break out, I was bound to land headfirst in the sand.

Where the hell was I? The waking world? The Dreamlands? Mount Olympus? Only the gods knew. *Literally.*

I'd tried reaching for Cadean in the shadows, but the Moon's spell was like a leaden wall between us. I'd tried unravelling the spell, but just as the Moon had warned, the power surge had nearly knocked me out and left my palms raw and blistered from pressing them against the side of the orb.

I was screwed.

As minutes turned into hours, I grew more and more desperate, in part because I had to fucking pee which made it impossible to think straight. Problematically, I was in a ball, so there was only one place for it to go: right to the middle, where I had to sit.

The miserable cave Cadean had kept me in suddenly seemed far more civilized, with its ample leg space, corner to piss in, and pool of fresh, clear water to drink. It was practically the Ritz.

Unfortunately, peeing was the least of my worries. I shoved the sleeve of my shirt and jacket up, checking my forearm for the third time. The lines of purple-blue light had continued to fade, and despite my exhausting attempts to break out of the glowing sphere, some of my strength had returned. The curse was fading —and that was a bad thing.

It meant that the Moon had successfully turned the barrier back into a wall of light. Ayanna might not be able to drain it or me anymore, but Cadean's lands would be exposed, and she'd be able to siphon his power and attack wherever she wanted.

I'd risked everything to find a solution, and instead, I'd made things worse.

My gut was in knots. I'd been so certain that the Moon was the answer. Hell, I'd practically felt the Fates yanking me along like a pup on a leash. Yet she'd given me nothing.

I'd once admired her. Believed in her. Prayed to her. I'd taken a huge gamble on that faith, and my hand had busted.

She wasn't the woman I'd expected her to be.

"Let me out of here!" I shouted to the deaf sky, releasing a blast of moonlight into the side of my prison. It just crackled over the surface and reverberated through the orb, but when the ringing in my ears had stopped and my vision had cleared, I couldn't find any sign of weakness. Hell, it was possible I'd just made the walls stronger by infusing them with more moonlight.

My chest rose and fell with ragged breaths, so I braced against my knees and put my head down as I tried to calm my churning mind. *Get a grip, Sam.*

I couldn't let the rage and betrayal take over. I was better than that. I'd spent my whole life getting myself in and out of jams, and this was just one more. There had to be a way out of this prison. I just had to find it.

Think.

As far as I could tell, the orb was almost like a smaller version of the wall. I'd been able to transform the barrier with my power, so why had I succeeded then, when I was failing here?

Because I wasn't trying to break out.

That was the heart of it. If I'd tried to completely dispel Cadean's prison like I was trying to do to the orb around me, I probably would have released enough energy to vaporize myself and half the kingdom in a second. Instead, I'd shifted the nature of the spell. Could I do that here? Make the orb permeable like the wall?

Hell, anything was worth a fucking try.

I reached out and gingerly pressed my blistered palms against the sides of the orb, wincing. I could sense the tight weave of the Moon's magic flowing beneath my fingertips. Strands of magic crisscrossed and encircled me like spiderwebs, but I recognized some patterns in the chaos.

It was just like the wall, right?

Closing my eyes, I pushed a stream of my magic into the spell. I began to manipulate the weave, envisioning the solid orb that was imprisoning me turning back into moonlight. *Transform, damn it!*

At first, I encountered only resistance, but then the sides of the orb began to loosen and shift. Elation flowed through me, and I pushed more power into it the spell. *Transform!*

The smooth sphere bent beneath my hands, swelling outwards.

Then, it snapped back.

A blast of moonlight erupted from the spell, hurling me backward. My head cracked against the wall in an explosion of pain, and everything went black.

I came to some time later, my head throbbing and my vision blurred. I was lying crumpled in a twisted heap at the bottom of the orb, staring up at the night sky through the translucent glow of the orb. Hopefully, I hadn't given myself a concussion.

"Okay, I get it. Don't fuck with your spell," I grumbled to the Moon, wherever the hell she was.

How long had I been out? Judging from my aching shoulders and stiff legs, a fairly long time. There was also a stabbing pain in the small of my back where I was lying on something hard.

I yanked the corner of my jacket out from under me. It clunked against the side of the glowing sphere, and then the two moonstones Savy had given me slipped out. I stared as they rolled around and came to a stop.

My heart stopped for a damned moment, too.

"Holy shit!" I jumped to my feet and reached for them as they scooted around the bottom of the orb. During all the *betrayal* and *getting fucking imprisoned by another god*, I'd forgotten I'd had them.

Hope flared in my chest, and my heart accelerated. I couldn't hold enough of the Moon's magic to unravel her spell—but could the moonstones? They'd been little fragments of her soul and had held an unbelievable reservoir of power. Could they do so now?

I scooped them up and turned the small orbs around in my palm.

The Moon probably hadn't ever thought about them again after she'd made them—they were just dead, discarded batteries. She didn't need a reservoir for her own power, and no one else could wield her magic.

A slow grin spread on my face.

But I could.

I drew in a shaky breath, then began to push a little of my magic into one of the stones.

It absorbed it instantly.

"Thank you, Savy," I whispered. That girl had been guided by the Fates—that was, if the Fates were actually on my side.

I shoved one of the stones back in my pocket, and gripping the other in my palm, I closed my eyes and pressed my hand against the wall. "Let's see what you got."

I reached out with my power and began to pull the weave of her spell apart. Moon's magic rushed out like sand from an urn, filling me with a radiance that felt like flying, like falling through the stars. The euphoria didn't last. Soon, the power flowing into me began to burn, fire and ice racing over my skin, just like it had the times I'd tried before. I gritted my teeth against the pain. This time I didn't have to hold it all. The moonstone could.

Focusing my mind, I guided the power through my body, letting it flow down my arm into the moonstone like a stream of water. The small orb grew hot in my tender palm, but it didn't burn. I channeled more and more, as the moonstone consumed it all.

I've got you now.

I tore into the weave of the spell, ripping it apart strand by strand. Soon, I began to see the structure of it and understand how it worked. It wasn't just a single spell, but several bound around each other: one to repel, one to contain, and one to hold the magic together. Up till now, I'd been using my magic instinctively, just like hopping behind the wheel of a car. But this was like watching the demon girls down at Jaxson's autobody tear an engine apart. I began to understand how the whole thing worked. Instead of lashing out blindly, all I had to do was pull the right thread and—

The spell dissipated in a burst of heat and light, revealing the full black of the night sky.

A second later, my back slammed into the ground. My spine cracked, and the wind burst from my lungs.

"Fuuuuck!" I gasped as I tried to draw in air. Pain lanced through my arm over and over, and I nearly blacked out when I rolled to my side.

Left arm, broken.

It was a small price to pay for freedom. I was a werewolf. A fracture would heal in a matter of hours.

I choked out an agonized laugh as I looked up at the night sky, crystal clear now without the intervening glow of the orb. I was free.

Pushing myself off the ground with my right hand, I stood. Every joint in my body screamed, and I felt more exhausted than I'd ever felt before, but it couldn't smother the elation of the moment.

The moonstone had been knocked from my grip when I fell, but it was easy to find. It glowed with a soft white light. I staggered over and picked it up. It was warm to the touch, and I could feel the power coursing through it—probably more power than I'd ever be able to summon at once—but it wasn't even a fraction of the way full.

That wasn't surprising. They'd been created to hold enough magic to power Cadean's prison, after all.

I pulled a little of the magic from the stone, and my hand

began to glow. The exhaustion began to fade, drowned in the warmth of the Moon's magic. Of *our* magic.

"Cadean!" I shouted to the darkness.

There was no response.

I shouted again and again and tried to pull him to me through the shadows as I'd once done, but that leaden wall was still there, keeping us apart.

This was *her* realm. And just as the Moon couldn't enter his, it seemed he couldn't shadow-cast here.

Well, fuck.

My bladder reminded me I had very pressing matters to attend to, so I took a pee right then and there, in the middle of the open desert—an act that the wolf in me found extremely satisfying.

Then I started walking.

There was absolutely nothing around, just starlit sand as far as I could see. But in that darkness, I saw a dull glow on the horizon. That had to be the Moon's pavilion, and if there was any way out of this gods-forsaken place, it would be through there.

30

Two hours later, I crested the top of a dune and got my first look at the Moon's pavilion, now just a white speck on the far horizon.

Apparently, the orb had been moving very quickly, and the Moon had wanted me very, *very* far away.

"You've got to be kidding me!" I shouted at the miles ahead.

We should run, the wolf in me urged for the umpteenth time.

It would have been faster, for certain. Unfortunately, unlike some shifters who transformed completely through magic, wolf-born shifted the ancient way, the original way, with snapping bones and stretching flesh. It meant we couldn't take our clothes with us, and at that moment, I had two precious moonstones in my pocket and no great way to carry them without pants or my jacket.

The wind stirred, kicking up a trail of dust along the dunes and carrying with it the familiar scent of ripe wheat and the distant sounds of battle.

"You seem a little lost," a velvety voice said behind me.

I spun around, unleashing my claws and calling a shield of moonlight in front of me.

Auren.

Dressed in white with a flowing gold cloak, he stood atop the ridge lit by a light that wasn't there. A sickeningly self-satisfied grin was plastered across his face. "My, my. Feeling a little jumpy, aren't we?"

I released my shield and sent its residual energy blasting forward in a crackling ball of light. Sand exploded into the air as moonlight slammed into the golden god, flinging him backward over the top of the dune.

"You fucking bastard!" I charged up the crest, drawing power from the moonstones until my insides burned. The pain couldn't extinguish the sheer joy that came from knocking the treacherous ass off his feet. After all his betrayals and games, laying into him was pure delight.

Moonlight rippled around me and licked across the ground like tongues of flame. "What are you doing here? Are you working with the Moon?"

That would explain why he'd never lifted a finger to help Cadean. How long had they been scheming behind his back? Hell—what if he and the Moon were lovers and it was all some sort of sick plot?

Endless possibilities raced through my head, but the truth was, if he was working with the Moon, there'd be no way to run. I'd have to trap him like I'd trapped Cadean once. Like the Moon had trapped me.

Auren gave me an icy but largely unperturbed look as he picked himself up. The wind stirred around him, whisking away the clinging grains of sand from his clothes. "For your information, Cadean sent me to rescue you—though at this point, I may reconsider."

"*Rescue* me? You've never done anything but lie, coerce, and play games with me," I said as I skidded down the slope, moonlight still at the ready.

He held his hands out apologetically. "I'll admit I haven't been the best of friends."

"You left me to find my own way out of the queen's palace! You had no intention of getting me out of there unless I had your little seedlings." My fingers flexed as my wolf stirred within me. "My mother died during that escape."

"For that, I'm sorry," he said with an authenticity I still couldn't trust. His hands dropped slowly. "I can't bring her back, but I can help you get out now."

"I got myself out," I snapped, my blood still boiling, despite the frigid desert air. "Just like last time."

"Have you?" he asked, looking at the vast sea of sand around us. "Doesn't look like it to me."

I glared back at him. "How did you know I was here?"

"Cadean, though he didn't say how he knew you'd been captured—or why."

A part of me desperately wanted to believe him, but there was no denying that he was treacherous and two-faced and prone to manipulating the truth. "Why should I trust anything you say?"

"Because he gave me this." A golden ribbon of light danced between his hands, lengthening and brightening. Then it faded away, revealing a sword and scabbard. *Wolf's Vengeance.* The golden god tossed it to me. "Cadean said you have work to do."

Releasing my moonlight, I caught the sword and scabbard and staggered on the uneven slope of the dunes.

While I was infuriated that Cadean had *ever* entrusted my blade to his bastard of a brother, I knew there was no other way Auren would have it.

"Cadean also said that in the *highly probable* scenario that you still didn't trust me, to drag you back kicking and screaming, and he'd make it up to you later."

I shifted into a fighting stance, scabbard in one hand, calling the moonlight back to the other.

Auren raised his arms in mock surrender. "I'm just putting all options on the table so that you can weigh them equally. I know how much you appreciate openness."

"What's in it for you?" I asked. Auren never did anything from the goodness of his tiny little heart.

His lips split in a covetous grin. "Don't worry, Cadean promised to make it worth my while—and trust me, I won't be handing you over until he fulfills his half of the deal."

The moonlight spinning in my hand brightened. "So then I'm your hostage, *again*?"

Some relationships never changed.

Auren glanced at my palm and then back to me. "My. You've grown confident since we last met."

"I have good reason to be."

His eyebrows went up. "You remember I'm a god, right?"

"Yup," I said, not giving an inch. "Not a problem."

I had no doubt if he decided to abduct me, he could best me. But the kicking and screaming part wouldn't go well for him. If I could trap Cadean, I could make life miserable for his brother for a while.

Auren nodded thoughtfully, then shrugged. "How about we go with the option where you decide to trust me based on the available evidence, and I cordially escort you back to my clearly *besotted* brother?"

I despised the idea of going with him, but I was certain Cadean hated it more. He would've never asked Auren unless it was clearly the only option.

And what other option did I have? Hike another ten miles to the Moon's pavilion and try to find a portal through there?

I sighed and dismissed the ball of light, then fastened the sword belt around my waist. "So how do we get out?"

"There's a portal in a ruined temple several miles from here," he said, then turned and started off. "Do try to keep up."

~

"Helping you escape once again," Auren said as he casually strolled over the dunes with his hands clasped behind his back. "It brings back such pleasant memories."

"No, it doesn't," I panted, trudging forward. The ease with which he practically glided over the sand was infuriating, and likely intentional. I was just over half his height, which meant I had to practically run to match his pace, and my feet kept sliding and sinking into the soft drifts.

"You could always shift," Auren said, clearly amused by my struggles. "You seem to be breaking a sweat despite the delightful night air."

"I'm fine." I clawed myself over the top of another dune. It would have been far easier to shift, but there was no way I was going to give him the satisfaction of stripping naked. Moreover, I didn't want to hand my things over for him to hold, and I *certainly* didn't want him to learn about the moonstones.

"If Cadean didn't tell you, then how did you know where to find me?" I asked between heaving breaths.

"The Moon Goddess has an active social life, particularly when she's attending her traveling court. A few well-placed questions got me the general location. A blast of moonlight from the middle of the desert pinpointed where you were, and your tracks led me straight to you. Speaking of which..." Auren raised his hand, and a little dust devil swept over the sand, erasing our footprints. He smirked, revealing a dimple that was a near match to Cadean's. "I really don't want her finding us. If she learned I had a hand in this, I'd never get invited to another of her parties, and trust me, they are to die for."

"Fuck her and her traveling court," I grunted, bracing myself to catch my breath. "No one has ever disappointed me more. And that includes you."

"What in the hell possessed you to go to the Moon Goddess, anyway? You certainly got yourself into a predicament."

My neck heated. "The wall was in danger, and we were out of options. I thought that the Moon would be desperate to protect it, and since I could control her magic, she'd be willing to teach me what to do."

"I can see why you took the chance. It was a big bet, but a good gamble."

"Well, I lost," I said. "I'd thought that she would trust me. I put my life on the line—hell, I *died* trying to recharge her pylons. She trusted me with her power then, but not now."

Auren glanced back at the far horizon. "She trusted you with power you didn't have the ability to use. The fact that you can wield it now changes everything."

I followed his gaze back to the glow of the distant pavilion. "Why?"

"Gods are created by belief, and thus, we are beholden to those beliefs—think of it as a set of rules that govern our actions and how we use magic. The Moon knows how I will behave and how Cadean will behave, which is why she locked him away— because she *knows* who he is and what he is capable of."

He looked over, a hint of accusation in his eyes. "Mortals —*like you*—have no such constraints. You can wield power without principle. Just look at what you've done to your world with the power you have."

"We're not all the same," I said, shoulders still heaving from the climb up the face of the dune. "I would have sworn an oath to the Moon if that was what it took to protect Cadean's realm."

"You might have good intentions, Samantha, but you have free will in a way that gods don't. That makes you extremely unreliable. It's why the queen is dangerous. She has stolen divine power. She's a goddess without all the safeguards."

"I'm not the queen. I'm trying to stop her," I said defensively.

"To the Moon, you aren't that much different. You wield power you've taken from her without having the bonds of her moral code. Your intentions don't matter."

"Since when do intentions *not matter?*" I asked, at my absolute limit with divine beings.

"Gods are jealous beings, and I find that we're not always considered rational by mortal standards," Auren said, giving me a wicked look. "I assure you, if someone had control over my magic, I would eliminate them, no matter what they believed. It's not fair, but fair doesn't matter when you're a god."

"Then what about Ayanna? Why don't you kill her? She'll steal your power, just as she's stealing Cadean's."

"Ayanna is a problem."

"Then why haven't you done anything?" I asked, my blood rising to as I tried to keep up. "Why didn't you do anything when the Moon imprisoned your brother?"

"Because I was fucking *delighted* by it!" Auren snapped, turning on me with a sadistic glint in his eyes. "The day she locked him away, I opened a dozen casks of mead and killed a pair of boars to feast in his absence. I drank and ate and fucked with abandon because the biggest headache in my life was gone."

My stomach twisted. "But you fought wars together. You visit him at Shadowstone and get each other drunk!"

"We fought side by side against the other gods, but we fought more among ourselves," Auren said, his expression darkening. "Trust me, Cadean is much easier to deal with when he is locked safely behind a wall. He's become rather enjoyable now that his hands are tied."

My hands trembled with outrage. "And so you left him there to rot for a thousand years? You just let Ayanna feast on his power?"

"Ayanna kept his power in check and my lands free of trouble."

I was so furious I wanted to vomit. My fingers itched to summon my magic and show Auren just what it was like to be trapped in a prison of the Moon's power, but I needed his treacherous ass to get me out.

I settled for shooting daggers at him with my eyes. "You're a twisted, self-serving prick."

Auren grinned, clearly satisfied with himself. "I am, but my brother was an absolute asshole. There's a reason no other gods came to his aid."

I clenched my jaw and started walking in the general direction he'd been leading me.

Auren followed. "You don't know him."

"I know him well enough."

"Don't fool yourself. The Cadean that wanted to annihilate Magic Side was my brother. The man who has emerged since meeting you—he's different. I'm not sure I trust it, but you've changed him."

I dug my fingers into my palm to keep my claws from coming out. "If anything has changed him, it's the Moon's betrayal, being abandoned by his own brother, and the world moving on while he was forced to watch his nightmares come to life."

"No, Samantha. It was you."

Auren's footsteps stopped, leaving an ominous silence behind me.

I paused and turned around. His intense gaze burned through me, peeling me like an onion and searching for answers. Sweat formed along my palms, and my throat tightened.

Fuck.

Had he realized that we were mates? That could completely change the equation of whatever deal he and Cadean had made.

I licked my parched lips as I searched for a response, but before I could speak, Auren's head whipped around, and he held up his hand. "Quiet. We've got trouble."

I followed his gaze, and the hair stood on the back of my neck. The silhouettes of giant winged creatures blackened out the stars in the direction from which we'd come.

"Those aren't desert creatures. Those must be the Moon's scouts," he whispered. "She knows you're gone, and she's searching."

31

Samantha

My heart beat faster as I watched the mothlike forms cutting back and forth across the sky, sweeping the desert below them. "Do you think they've seen us?"

"Not sure," Auren hedged, "but we need to get to cover as quickly as possible. Come on! There's a rock formation up ahead. Our exit is there."

He hurried across the rolling sands, while I half-staggered, half-ran beside him. The going had been rough before, but now the dread of being intercepted made the shifting sands maddening.

Auren's magic swirled around us, stirring the sand and burying our tracks. "Quickly now!"

"I'm going as fast as I can!" I gasped. I had werewolf stamina, but keeping up with a god was another thing, particularly one so adept at avoiding problems.

I scrambled over the dunes, periodically shooting glances over my shoulder. The moon was just rising, casting the sand in its low-lying pale light. For my whole life, it had always seemed a protective presence, a reminder of a goddess watching over our people. Now the rising moon was a menacing sight, a reminder of betrayal and the danger that I was in. Its soft light left us exposed.

"The temple isn't far now!" Auren urged as he pulled me to the top of the next rise. Ahead lay a craggy outcrop of stone spires and tumbled boulders, which protruded from the desert in defiance of the endless dunes.

I looked back.

Moonlight tinted the edges of the creatures' wings. They were no longer weaving back and forth in their search pattern.

"They're coming straight at us!" I said breathlessly.

We plunged down the slope, and it was everything I could do to keep on my feet. My boots were filled with sand and my shirt soaked with sweat, despite the icy desert air and my unzipped jacket.

Auren pulled me forward as the desert became firm beneath our feet, then gave way to gravel and bedrock.

The boulders and jagged outcrops rising around us cast long shadows in the low light. Once we were deep into the formation, Auren pulled me behind a large, slab-like spire, and we watched the horizon.

After a minute, pale green wings glided over the top of the dune and began weaving over the boulder field. A second of the things appeared two hundred feet further down. They must have been twenty feet across, with three sets of pale wings and half a dozen long tail-like streamers dancing behind them.

"Moondancers," Auren muttered. "They're telepathic, so the Moon will know as soon as they spot us."

"Haven't they already?"

"I'm hoping we were far enough away that they couldn't make us out."

There was no way I was going to let the Moon take me again.

I began to draw my magic, but Auren grabbed my arm. "No magic. They'll know we're here."

"They can't report us if they're dead."

"The Moon likely knows they've spotted something near here, and if we kill them, it will confirm it. She'll know you've made your way to the Dreamlands through the portal ahead." He released his grip on my arm. "We need them to keep searching the desert as long as possible."

If only Cadean had been there to hide me in the shadows.

As it was, we crouched in the shadow of the spire. I glanced over at Auren in his bright white outfit and golden cloak. "You're really not dressed for clandestine operations."

He rested his head back against the rock. "Yes. Likely an error of judgement."

I peeked around the spire, tracking the weaving trajectory of the moths. "They're still searching, but they're getting closer."

Auren's brow wrinkled. "Perhaps I can convince the locals to help."

He closed his eyes, and a pulse of magic swept out across the rocky ground, stirring up little spirals of sand. The dust settled, and nothing stirred, but Auren kept sitting with his eyes closed.

I peeked around the rock again.

My hands grew clammy despite the cold desert air. The giant moth-like things were almost on us. I popped back around, and my heart leapt. Two tiny foxes with giant ears were sniffing Auren's fingers. They were so cute, I thought I might die.

With all of Auren's civilized pretensions, it was easy to forget he was a shifter god like his brother with command over nature.

He closed his hand and sat back against the spire. "If you would be so kind, the big buggies up there are looking for a pair of creatures out in the desert," he whispered. "Perhaps you could lure them away?"

The foxes hesitated for a second, eyes on me, and then trotted off into the rocks, going back the way we had come.

"With any luck, the Moon's spies will think the foxes were all that they saw," Auren said, his voice barely audible.

"They're awfully small body doubles," I muttered under my breath.

"We were far away, and the moondancers—well, they're essentially giant moths, so not a lot of advanced reasoning going on." His head rolled to the side to look at me. "But if you have a better plan, by all means, execute it now."

I slumped back against the stone and tried listening for the sound of those giant wings, but all I could hear was my thundering heartbeat. I looked up and readied myself, waiting for their shadow to pass over.

We'd have to kill them quickly. Tipping off the Moon was better than having her spies hovering over us.

But nothing came.

After a few minutes, I slowly leaned over to look around the side of the spire.

The moths were circling away.

I let out a slow and steady breath. "I think it worked."

Auren checked over his shoulder, then rose. "We shouldn't waste any more time sitting around in the desert. Cadean's already had one run-in with Ayanna's forces, and from what I gather, it didn't go well."

Auren's words weighed on me as we made our way to the center of the formation. We kept to the shadows, even though the moondancers were far in the distance.

"What happened to Cadean?" I asked as I picked my way carefully over the rocks.

"He seemed weaker than I've ever seen him. He warned me that Ayanna can control the vines now and make them attack, just like he can control the forest and trees. He says that they're voracious and begin draining your power the moment they touch you." He paused. "Cadean thinks the queen is using his own magic against him."

My foot skated on the rocks, and my chest suddenly felt like it was caving in. My mate was in danger, and it was my fault. I had to find a way to stop her.

Would Auren really take no side?

He leapt to the top of a rocky outcrop and knelt, offering me his hand.

I extended my claws and quickly climbed up the face, heaving myself up beside him. "And you're still not afraid of her?" I asked bitterly. "You're still content to let her feed off your brother and be a check on his power?"

The only sound was gravel crunching beneath our feet.

"No," Auren said at last with a sigh, "I'm not. I'm hoping you two have a plan because I have no intention of going anywhere near those vines."

Anger raced through me, heat that had me sweltering in the cold air. *Fucking coward.*

If I hadn't needed him, the fates only knew what I would've done.

Auren didn't offer me a hand up the next outcrop. It was a good thing, too, or I might have bitten it.

I was beyond furious with him, but also at myself. That guilt rested on my shoulders, becoming heavier and heavier as I thought of what was happening to my mate—the life and power the queen was taking from him.

I needed to help him.

We continued in silence, higher and higher, until we emerged on a shadowed plateau in the face of the formation. Toppled columns lay all around, the ruins of an ancient temple.

There was a tiered platform at the center, and on it, an ornate archway carved from the local rock.

Auren climbed the steps and placed his hand on the gateway. His magic pulsed, the sound of steel clashing against steel and the scent of fresh wheat.

A silvery portal materialized.

He gestured with a slight bow. "Your ticket out of here and back to the nightmare that is the Dreamlands."

I hesitated and swallowed, meeting his eyes. "I had a chance to stop all of this, you know? I could have destroyed the vines and saved Cadean and his people—but I didn't take it."

Auren's outstretched hand didn't waver, but his eyebrows rose. "Did you, now?"

"I had Cadean's axe in the Well of the Vines. I could have cut through all the roots and killed the vines forever."

Auren stared back at me in utter shock. "Cadean let you touch his *axe*? His *black axe*?"

"I used it to kill General Slaine and destroy the queen's throne."

His expression turned wild, and he ran his hand through his hair in exasperation like Cadean so often did. "My brother's actually gone mad. Do you have any idea of the willpower it takes to wield that weapon?"

His voice was verging on hysterics.

"Obviously. I *used it*."

"Then what in the hells stopped your from destroying the godsdamned vines?"

My back stiffened. "Because if I had, I would have destroyed the entire city. It's built on the vines. Tens of thousands of fae would have died."

Auren studied me a long time.

"What?" I snapped, the weight of his judgement finally becoming unbearable.

"The axe is destruction and hatred made manifest. It takes unnatural willpower to wield a weapon like that and not use it."

"Maybe I should have. Maybe someone else—"

"No," Auren said with a sudden vehemence that shook me to my bones. "No one else was in that room. Did *you* make the right call?"

Images of Dreamspire and the city flooded my head. The busy tavern. Shoppers and merchants bustling over the cobblestones embedded in the vines. Beneath it all was the polluted undercity with its droves of repressed and forgotten people. Deeper still were the little erdelfen, whose very homes were nested in the vines. None of them were evil, just trapped in a system the queen had created.

"I made the moral one," I said.

He nodded, looking at me as if he were seeing me again for the first time.

"The greater good is a seductive thing," Auren said. "I remember a time not long ago when the people of your world chose to annihilate two cities to end a war the quick way. Funny thing about that. When people talk about killing for the greater good, it always involves killing someone else's people, not their own."

Suddenly, Auren looked far older than I'd ever seen him, and I could almost see the bodies and ash reflected in his eyes. Cadean, the Moon, and Auren. They'd all had to watch it from afar.

"Never doubt yourself, Samantha. You're a mortal, but you've been given the chance to wield divine power—both the Moon's and Cadean's, through the axe. You must believe in that power and believe in yourself. That is the nature of divine magic. Belief." He motioned me toward the portal. "Now come on."

I mounted the stairs, but he laid his hand on my shoulder, stopping me before I stepped through. "I guarantee the Fates chose the right person to be in that room in that moment. Power should be held by those with the conscience to use it."

With that, he slipped through the portal, and I followed, stepping back into the Dreamlands and the war that awaited.

I had the moonstones now even if I didn't have the Moon. I would find a way to turn this war around.

32

Dreamlands, the southern border with Auren's realm

Cadean

I galloped toward the border and Auren's realm as fast as Vega would carry me.

Ayanna's blight hadn't reached these lands yet. The hills on either side of the Moon's barrier were thick with tall pines silhouetted against a bright dusting of snow. A flock of birds burst into the sky as my strider charged through the trees. They flew off toward Auren's realm, passing through the shimmering barrier with ease. And yet I—_a fucking god_—could not.

The cursed thing rose before me. No longer the crystalline wall Samantha had formed, it had returned to a wall of dancing moonlight, as it had been for so many centuries.

It was beyond maddening. I could feel my mate there on the other side, so close and yet impossibly far away. I could almost taste the jasmine and honeysuckle of her signature and imagine the warmth of her lips pressed against mine.

I'd been a fool to let her go, yet how could I have stopped her? I doubted any prison or person could hold that woman for long. Not me, nor Auren or Ayanna. Not even the treacherous Moon.

I spurred Vega faster. The pull of the bond between us grew stronger the closer I got until it dragged me relentlessly forward like an anchor plunging into the depths of the sea.

I yanked Vega to a halt as the barrier loomed ahead. The freezing heat of the luminous wall seared my skin, driving my thoughts into a furious rage.

How could anything keep me from *my mate*?

But it did.

A pair of riders descended the hills before me. My chest tightened as Samantha pulled her hood down and shook out her blonde hair, giving me a broad smile. My blood turned into fire as unrestrained joy cut through the specters of helplessness and rage.

I dismounted and approached the wall, and they did the same, with Auren keeping his hand firmly on Samantha's shoulder. *Fucking bastard.* If I could've reached him, I would have broken his fingers and rammed them into his eyes just for touching her like that.

And yet my brother had returned her to me. That was all that mattered. *She* was all that mattered.

I tried to calm my anger, but it was almost impossible in the presence of the Moon's toxic magic. It had become red-hot coals pressed against my flesh and frostbite burning through my body, but I didn't slow my pace. I wouldn't show Auren my weakness before the barrier.

Auren halted five paces away and pulled Samantha close to his side. "I think I found something that belongs to you, brother."

"She doesn't belong to me," I snarled. "She's a free woman. Now let her through."

"Not until you give me what is mine." His hand tightened on her shoulder, and my blood churned.

Anger flashed across Samantha's face, and streams of moonlight trickled over her hand. I could almost read her intentions. *Trap him. Walk across. Solidify the wall.*

"No," I growled at her. "Auren and I have a deal."

Auren glanced down at her, and the corner of his mouth curled up. "And you think *I'm* the treacherous one?"

"You're the asshole holding on to my shoulder, so I'd advise you to let the fuck go before I put you in a cage of moonlight that'll make a kennel look like the Ritz."

"What is the R—"

"I will honor the deal," I said, and held out my hand. Black tendrils of mist swirled around my arm, taking the form of my obsidian axe. Its rage and hatred poured through me, and I envisioned slamming it into my brother's head. I'd done so before.

We hadn't been kind to each other over the years. I only understood the true cost of that now.

Samantha's eyes widened. "You can't give up—"

"I can," I growled, my voice shaking through the earth. I walked closer until I was a foot from the wall, gritting my teeth as its magic rained over me like droplets of fire. Every part of my being urged me to recoil and back away, but my bond to Samantha was stronger still—so I stood there among the flames of light, waiting for my brother to claim his prize.

Auren grinned and wrapped his hand around the haft. "I heard you let her use this. You're fucking insane, brother."

"She killed a man and then set it aside before she killed a city. She has more conscience and willpower than most of the gods in the Dreamlands."

Auren released a cold laugh. "That doesn't take much, now does it?"

He pulled the axe, but I didn't let go. "Samantha first."

"Break your bond with the axe, then you get the girl."

"Enough bullshit Auren," Samantha said as she struck his hand from her shoulder. Moonlight swirled around her as she leapt across the border. "I'm not your plaything."

Auren's magic surged, but I clasped my hand over his arm. "The axe is yours. Act fucking worthy of it, you bastard."

With that, I broke the bond.

Screams ripped through my mind, and my jaw clenched in agony. Thousands of voices. My vision was flooded with blood and death and corpses. Everyone I had killed. Everything I had destroyed.

My hand slipped away, and I staggered back—away from the searing moonlight wall and away from fucking nightmares I'd made. The world collapsed in on me as the strength rushed from my limbs.

And then she was there, glowing hope in the midst of the endless nightmare, holding me. Earthquakes of regret shuddered through me, but I didn't move—it couldn't bury me as long as I was in her arms.

I forced myself to look up at my brother.

He held it aloft, admiring the cruel curve of the blade with a covetous look in his eyes. "My, what a beautifully evil bitch you are. And now, you're mine."

Swirls of sunlight wrapped around his arm, entwining with its darkness. His signature surged, and a thunderclap ripped over us. I held Samantha tightly, shielding her from the blast. When I looked up again, the axe was gone—dismissed into the ether for the first time in fifteen centuries by a man who wasn't me.

"It's tainted. Don't let it corrupt you," I said.

"Father should have given it to me in the first place," Auren replied as he turned back to his mount and grabbed the reins. "You and the axe were always too close in temperament."

Samantha's hand tightened on my arm. "How can you give it away? It's the only thing that'll cut through the vines—"

"Because I need *you*," I rumbled. "You're the strongest part of me. Not that axe. You are what the Dreamlands needs."

Auren had paused, his hand on the saddle. Did he suspect the truth about us? Well, fuck him and his suspicion. I didn't have time for it.

I touched the graceful curve of her cheek and inhaled the dusty scent of the desert in her hair. "I should have never let you go."

She brushed her lips across mine, giving me the softest of kisses, before stepping away with a wide grin. "I'm back now, and stronger than ever."

I exhaled in relief. "And not a moment too soon. Ayanna's forces are spilling over the border. She's created a large swath of vines that are heading straight for the pylons."

"Good luck, Cadean," Auren said as he swung up into the saddle. "And thank you for the marvelous gift. I hope you won't be needing it."

My neck heated with rage, but Samantha's hand clamped down on my arm.

"We need you!" she shouted, stepping back into the radiance of the wall of moonlight. "Fight alongside your brother like you used to."

Auren gave her a knowing smile, then looked to me. "That wasn't part of our deal."

"Cadean isn't the one asking, I am."

My brother guided his strider back toward the barrier. "He's not asking because he's asked before. I don't do anything for free."

Samantha crossed her arms. "Then let's make a trade."

I stiffened.

"I already have everything I want from Cadean," Auren said.

A malicious smile crossed his lips that made me want to claw them off. "Unless you're offering yourself."

I leapt forward and extended my hand to summon my axe, but there was only a deep weakness and unrelenting agony where it had once been.

Samantha seized my open hand, and immediately, the anger flooded away. She looked Auren defiantly in the eye. "You get your lands, your power, and your dignity. Because if we fail, Ayanna will take them all."

"*Are* you going to fail?" he asked, raising his eyebrows in a way that had always made me want to break his teeth.

"Not if we have your help," she said.

She was right. As much as I hated it, we needed my bloody brother.

"You were a true god of the battlefield once!" I called, stepping as close as the barrier would allow. "But look at you now. You've gotten fat and lazy lying in that palace of yours. Where's your wolf? Don't you miss the smell of battle or the taste of blood on your teeth?"

It had been long years since he'd been that man, but I knew that warrior was still in there somewhere. I just had to find the right words.

Auren's expression darkened. "The smell of battle and the taste of blood? You've held the axe too long, brother."

"And you hold it now," I growled.

"I *do*." He summoned the axe in a swirl of light and shadow. Turning it in his hand, he examined it carefully. "It is a wicked thing."

"Power should be held by those with the conscience to use it," Samantha said softly. "For fates' sake, use it to help us stop this war."

He looked away with a silent laugh. "You'd turn my own words against me?"

"Do something worthy of that weapon," I challenged. "Show Ayanna what happens when she tries to catch the sun."

I saw the dam cracking.

"Just think," I said, "if you're the one to defeat the queen, you'll be able to lord it over me for the next thousand years. What sweeter reward could there be?"

A thin smile I knew too well formed on his lips.

His lands, his duty, his power—they were merely appetizers. But the chance to humiliate me was a *feast*.

33

Samantha

Our deal with Auren sealed, Cadean pulled me close. He held me there among the whispering pines as the cold wind whipped around us. I savored the heat of his body. He was powerful and strong and iron against me, and he was all mine.

My mate.

I didn't care that Auren was watching and waiting. After everything that had happened, I just wanted to feel and be felt. To be with my mate and shut out the rest of the world and its problems.

But I knew I couldn't. Ayanna was drawing ever closer.

"We need to go," Cadean said as held me out at arm's length and inspected me. "Are you certain you're okay?"

"I'm fine." I said, suddenly uncomfortable. "The Moon didn't hurt me, and the curse retreated when she dropped the wall. Now that the vines aren't feeding off its magic, I feel better."

The truth was, it hadn't just been the barrier's magic they were feeding off, but mine as well.

A shadow cut across his face. "But some of the curse remains?"

I nodded. It was just a few thin, glowing veins, but it was there. "Ayanna must be able to draw power from the barrier even when it's a wall of light."

Maybe that's why it had weakened in the first place—why Savy and I had to repair it all those months ago.

Cadean released me and grabbed Vega's reins. "If you're still infected, we need to hurry, even more so than before. If Ayanna's vines reach the pylons and infest them—"

"Then the curse will return in full."

Or kill me.

Cadean swung into the saddle and pulled me up in front of him. I nestled in against the hard strength of his body. "How far have they reached?"

"Just past the mountains. It seems she's pouring all her resources into creating a conduit of hundreds of vines and guarding them with her army. They're like a pipeline for siphoning power from my land and a highway for her monsters. Her aim is clear: drain the pylons or draw me out and drain me in battle."

My body tensed at the thought, and my blood went cold. The queen had tried to steal my power when we'd battled in the Well of Life. Could she do the same to him, even without the vines?

"Is Ayanna leading the army?" Auren asked, circling us on his strider.

"Uncertain," Cadean answered. "Though I have no doubt that she'll appear as soon as we attack."

"That is exactly what we want. Hopefully, her highway of vines has made her confident enough to venture deep into your lands. We can swing behind her and get between her and the barrier, cutting her off. We'll crush her between us."

"It's good to have you back, brother." Cadean chuckled. "I just hope you're still in fighting form."

He spurred Vega, and we lurched forward into a run.

"Don't get used to it!" Auren shouted as he followed. "There's only one evil queen to kill. Then it's back to business as usual."

"One is enough." Cadean muttered, though his voice was likely lost in the din of the striders' hooves and claws churning the forest floor.

We rode straight for Mistwind Harbor in single file, weaving through the pines and leaping over fallen trees until we reached the southern road. I was thankful that Auren was hanging back, as it gave me a moment to be with Cadean alone.

He sent a hawk to Mel and Sarion to meet us, and I reached down on occasion to touch the sword at my side for reassurance. I wasn't going to be kept out of the coming battle, though I knew he would try.

"If you and Auren pin the queen, she'll make for the wall," I told Cadean. "I can transform the barrier to stop her."

"No." He tightened his arm around my waist. "The last time you manipulated the wall, you nearly killed yourself. I don't want you near the queen."

My blood heated. "I'm not going to stand down and leave you unprotected. I know how the Moon's magic works now, and I can transform the barrier without killing myself."

His body tensed behind me. "I thought the Moon refused to help."

"She didn't intend to. She trapped me with her magic, and I had to unravel the weave strand by strand. I've learned the pattern now."

His arm became iron around me. "Unbinding a spell like that could have killed you."

"It would have been too much power to draw, but I have these." I pulled the two small stones from my pocket, holding them tightly against the jarring ride. "They're moonstones Savannah used to recharge the pylons. I can channel the Moon's power into them and pull it back out without getting burned alive."

He let out a slow breath. "How much power?"

"A fucking lot," I said as I tucked them safely away. "It took three moonstones to recharge the barrier. With two, I should be able to manipulate a huge section."

"I don't like it."

I placed my arm over the one he'd wrapped around my waist. "They're the solution we've been looking for, and we need one now more than ever."

He was silent for a moment, and then he said, "Fates know we do."

The remorse in his voice reminded me of just how much he'd sacrificed to get me back. Guilt clawed at me, and I glanced at the golden god riding behind us. "I'm sorry you had to give up your axe for me."

"You're worth it, a thousand times over." His words warmed my neck and sent shivers down my back. "And to be fair, I doubt Auren would have ever agreed to help without the axe or more importantly, you guilting him into it. I think he must have a soft spot for you."

There was more than a flicker of jealousy in his tone.

"You must have been *very* desperate to send him."

"I was. But I also knew Auren had a price, and that if I paid it, he would hand you over, no questions asked—no matter how important you might seem to me."

I leaned back against his chest, appreciating its strength and warmth. "How did you even know to send him?"

Cadean shifted uncomfortably in the saddle behind me, suddenly tense. "As soon as the Moon took you hostage, Kassian brought Jaxson and Sarion to my hall. They told me you'd been trapped."

My throat tightened. "Jaxson?"

"Don't worry. I may have humbled him, but I didn't hurt him."

Humbled did little to assuage my fears.

"Is he still here in the Dreamlands?" Visions of the dank cells beneath Shadowstone leapt to mind. Of the way Cadean had used his power to force the truth from my lips, and how Kassian and Wulfric had shoved me around.

"No," Cadean said, his voice suddenly a hammer. "I didn't hurt him. I sent him back to your pack with an oath that I'd never threaten you, your people, or Magic Side again."

My mate had given Jaxson an oath?

Cadean took my hand, rolling his fingers gently over mine. "I should have sworn the same oath to you long ago." His grip tightened. "I will never threaten your pack or the waking world again. I swear it on the strength of our mate bond and by my respect for you. I will look after your people and never harm that which you love for as long as I breathe."

A rush of power flooded through my fingers and along my arm, entwining around my heart. I felt his magic flowing into me, radiant like sunlight dancing through leaves and as strong as folded steel. It mingled with my power, twisting and knotting, forging a vow that could not be broken. A bond of love and devotion.

My people would be safe, not just for my lifetime or theirs, but for all the centuries ahead—regardless of what happened to me in the battle to come.

My breathing quickened, and I bit my lip to keep it steady.

My pack no longer had to fear.

A heavy weight fell from my shoulders like snow slipping from pine boughs in the spring. I'd borne it for so long, I'd forgotten what it felt to be without it.

"Thank you," I breathed, my heart swelling in gratitude. "I don't know what to say."

"Say nothing, little wolf," he purred. "Just be with me. That's all I ask."

I closed my eyes and nestled in against him, losing myself in the sensations of relief, the heavy beat of his heart, and the rhythm of the ride.

I woke when we reached Mistwind Harbor. Apparently, the midnight march across the desert had completely taken it out of me.

"My ass hurts," I murmured, feeling dazed. "I can't believe I fell asleep on the back of a griffstrider."

"If it makes you feel any better, my arm is dead from holding you in place." The Dark Wolf God chuckled, still a surprising sound coming from him.

The people of the town crowded the streets. There had been commotion enough the day before when Cadean and I had ridden through the port, but now Auren was with us. *Two* gods. The town would have gossip for months.

We met Mel along with Sarion and the group of fae Kass had recruited.

I gratefully, and somewhat painfully, dismounted and wrapped my arms around Mel, and then Sarion. "You don't know how good it is to see you both." I gave a stiff nod to the vampire. "Kass."

He grinned. "You missed me the most."

"Maybe."

"Well I'm glad you decided to return from your little vacation. Things are getting a bit dicey here." Kass pointed to my sword. "You remember which end to use, right?"

I drew my fingers lovingly over the scabbard. "The sharp end goes in you."

I was relieved to be reunited with my friends, but it was Elowyn whom I was most grateful to see. I loved riding next to Cadean. Hell, I'd fallen asleep on his chest—but by the fates, my butt was ready for its own damn saddle. She ruffled her gliding wings in acknowledgement, then nuzzled my hand affectionately with her large, skull crushing beak.

Since Cadean had given up his axe, the armorer had sent along a wicked-looking glaive—a long, heavy spear with a blade and spike at one end. It looked custom-made for lopping off heads. It must have weighed sixty or seventy pounds, but Cadean could spin it with a single hand.

I purchased a sturdy belt pouch from a terrified leatherworker to hold the moonstones, then mounted up on Elowyn.

"Did you finish the potions?" Cadean asked Mel.

She produced a heavy leather bandolier with six steel bottles slipped through the loops. "I would have liked more time, but this'll do. I'm not sure how powerful the potions are, but I have one for each of the six men going in. They're all sealed with a spell, so they should be safe to carry."

I wasn't going to push it at this point, but I was definitely going to be one of those six *men*. But first, we had to deal with Ayanna's column of vines and the army marching south.

We led the striders through the portal at the center of town, emerging in the heart of Frostfall—the portal I'd once hoped to use to escape.

A deep sorrow settled into my bones as I looked across the familiar sod roofs of the abandoned homes. The winter had set in weeks before, but no smoke rose from the hearths. The light dusting of snow was marred only by the footprints of birds and small animals.

The place felt deeply hollow without Selene and her people.

I breathed deeply and furrowed my brow. The earthy undertones of a fire lingered in the air. I looked to the north and spotted a single plume rising into the sky.

Cadean followed my gaze. "Sigrun. For some reason, she seems to have a great deal of faith in us."

"At least someone does."

We met Wulfric and his werewolf scouts on the ridge that overlooked the surrounding grassland. Snow covered the bushy tufts, turning them into a featureless expanse of white closer to the dead forest and barrier in the distance.

My gut tightened with dread as my eyes drifted across the scene below.

An enormous conduit of vines cut straight through the center of the plain. There must have been dozens, weaving back and forth and entwining together, a purple-green highway through the snow. Like the headwaters of a stream, it emerged from the cover of the dead forest and wound its way southwest toward the mountains at the heart of Cadean's realm—the last barrier standing between the vines and the pylons.

"Holy fuck," I whispered as I pulled Elowyn to a halt.

A bright column of fae soldiers marched four abreast along the side of that corrupted highway. Banners waved from the tops of shining pikes, and I could see riders mounted on deathwings scouting the hills ahead.

"*Holy fuck* is right," Wulfic said, stepping up beside us. "We can't face this kind of army. Maybe in the mountains, but not here in the open. Not with shifters alone. It would be a bloodbath."

"I don't know, Cadean." Auren circled his griffstrider around us. "I might feel in the mood for a bloodbath today. It's been a long time."

Cadean didn't move, surveying the scene with grim resolution. "Is the queen here?"

Wulfric pointed. "Yes. She's at the heart of the column. As far as we can tell, she's using her magic to grow the vines."

"She's using *my* magic," the Dark Wolf God growled, the earth suddenly vibrating with his rage. "Regrowth is *my* gift. Not hers."

"Well, it looks like she's got it now," Kass said, then quickly looked away to avoid Cadean's gaze.

It made sense. It was how she'd infested the wall. The more power she stole, the more powerful Ayanna got.

My skin prickled, and I tightened my frozen gloves on the reins. How much of the Moon's magic had she taken? Could she control the wall?

Cadean turned to Mel, who'd ridden Dawnfire. "We're fucked if these vines reach the pylons. Can we use the potions to petrify them?"

She hesitated. "Is it still your intention to kill them from the roots?"

"Yes."

She shook her head. "Then it's not worth the risk—we need the element of surprise. If Ayanna suspects we can petrify the vines, she'll flee and barricade the Well of Life with enough defenses that even you and Auren couldn't break through together."

"I don't intend to lose," Cadean rumbled.

"And neither does she."

He turned Vega back to the ridge, gazing out over the plains below.

My mate was impossibly beautiful, sitting like an ancient warrior upon his steed. His glacier-blue eyes shone like diamonds, framed by dark hair that whipped in the winter breeze. The shadows clung to him, leaning away from where they should be and seeking him out. I knew them now not as things to be feared, but as protectors that had hidden me from danger and provided comfort when I was alone.

"Wulfric is right," he said not breaking his gaze. "It will be a bloodbath, and I can't risk any of you. Auren and I will go, and if the queen escapes, then we'll strike Dreamspire and poison the vines."

I urged Elowyn forward. "There's no way I'm letting you go down there without me."

"There's no way I'm willing to risk *that*," he snapped, turning back.

"This is my fight too, Cadean." I unsheathed my sword. "And I will have vengeance."

"Vengeance isn't worth your life."

"I know a spell that can trap a god, and I can trap her, too. Which one of you can do that?" I asked, circling the two gods on their steeds. "Which one of you can manipulate the barrier if the queen tries to escape?" Cadean glared at me, and I glared back. "If this is our shot at the queen, then you'll need all the help you can get. Otherwise, why did you let me seek out the Moon? Why did you even bring me along? Why not just lock me up in a cell and visit me when you want?"

He turned Vega away from me and rode back to the ridge-line, fury visibly pulsing off him like heatwaves in the desert.

"Do you believe in me?" I shouted after him. "Because if not, what am I doing here?"

The Dark Wolf God spun around. "You are not to join the battle unless there's a shot to take out Ayanna, are we clear?"

I nodded. "Crystal."

"You will wait with Wulfric and his outriders. Do not engage until I call for you. And for fuck's sake, remember you are *mortal*."

I opened my mouth to protest, but he pulled out his glaive

and turned to Auren. "What the hell are we waiting for? Let's show them what it is like to fight the gods."

He spurred Vega and charged down the hill toward the column of vines and soldiers below, shadows trailing behind him like a cape in the wind.

My breathing quickened as I watched my mate disappear. I might know the spell to trap a god, but Ayanna knew how to steal their strength and drain them dry.

I turned to Mel and held out my hand. "Give me the potions. I think I'm going to need them."

34

———————

Cadean

I raised my glaive above my head with a roar, then charged across the grassland with my brother riding at my side. Streams of sunlight and shadow wove through his fingers, and the black axe materialized in his hand. The ground thundered beneath the hooves of our striders, and soon, all who lay before us would learn to fear.

It was like a thousand years had never passed.

This was *true* war. Not men and shifters dying for me because I had to hide behind a wall. Just my brother and me facing down the world.

Auren pointed the axe ahead. "Since all you have is that whittling knife, I'll take the vines and the queen. You handle the riffraff and keep them off me."

The bastard laughed and broke away before I could respond, taking the left flank.

All that I had? I'd show him all that I had. Summoning my power, I called the storm. Clouds began to swirl above the queen's column, and thunder cracked. Lightning flashed as bolts rained down, exploding into men and beasts. The neatly formed ranks of fae pikemen began to scatter as we approached.

Concealed archers rose from the grass to rain poisoned arrows and magic down on us. Broodlings skittered out from the vines on their long, spindly legs with giant carrion eaters close behind, their maggot-like mouths filled with thousands of teeth. There were even lumbering krai'tan with their pincer jaws. All the horrors of her kingdom. All here for me to kill.

I ripped into them like a hurricane. The winds rose around me like a shield, scattering arrows. I swung the glaive, cutting down men and monsters both as we pushed forward.

The white snow turned brown and red with the churned earth and streaks of blood.

The wall of fae broke before us and fled, revealing a clear path to Ayanna and her vines. She floated above the chaos on silver wings, power rippling around her.

"Take her down!" I shouted to my brother as I cut the head off another of her raiders.

Dirt burst up around us as vines and roots ripped free of the earth. Auren cut through them with the axe, but they wrapped around Vega and pulled us down.

My bones shook as I hit the ground, but I was on my feet in the next breath, hacking away at the grasping tendrils. Vega rose and began clawing at the vines as well, but I smacked his rump and shouted "Away! Hunt the archers!"

He turned and sprinted back toward the fae warriors, ripping through armor and crushing skulls with his savage beak.

The vines kept coming, slithering toward me, and wrapping around my arms. The glaive was sharp but unwieldy. More and more vines grabbed hold, and my body grew numb as they drained my strength and magic alike.

"What a feast you have prepared for me, Dark God!" the queen shouted from above. "Two fat wolves to be fed to my children!"

I roared as I ripped at the vines, but they were like the ocean pouring over me.

I felt Samantha before I saw her. The heat and light of her signature entangled with the power of our bond.

A brilliant explosion flashed before my eyes, and the vines loosened. Samantha charged past, her sword streaming with flames of moonlight as she cut through the vines entangling me.

Fury and gratitude churned within me as I pulled free of the last tendrils. She was a warrior born, but how could I watch my mate risk herself for me?

Where *the fuck* was Wulfric?

A quick glance told me she'd left her bodyguard far behind in the mass of fae. Godsdamn that woman to hell!

A vine whipped around her throat and yanked her from the saddle, and I lunged forward. Deathwings dropped from the sky toward her as she lay gasping for breath, the murderous barbs aimed straight at her heart.

I heaved my glaive like a spear through the chest of one of the beasts, and then I shifted and seized the form of a wolf.

Samantha summoned her shield of moonlight around her as she dove for her blade. Elowyn tore the wings from another deathwing while I crushed the last with my jaws, shaking off their paralytic stings in my rage.

Get out of here! I roared at my mate.

"Auren needs us!" She grabbed Elowyn's reins and mounted up.

The queen had circled high above my brother. The vines struck like vipers at her command and wrapped around his limbs. He hewed through them with the axe, but they simply multiplied like the necks of a hydra.

I called down lightning. It flashed around the queen, and she dodged and wove, then raced back over the battlefield on her luminous wings.

Samantha cut through the last of the vines around Auren, then turned toward the queen.

"Fuck those things!" Auren shouted as he mounted back up. "And fuck the queen. I'll teach her to try to steal my power."

Samantha raced Elowyn forward on the other side of the conduit of vines. "I'll pin her! You take her out!"

She raised her hand, and a blast of moonlight streaked across the sky. It exploded into Ayanna's side, and a billowing sphere of light formed around her—a burning prison I knew all too well. The queen pounded her fists against the glowing walls and screamed in defiance.

I roared in adoration for my mate.

This time, Ayanna wouldn't get away. I bared my jaws, killing men and beasts alike as I fought my way to her.

The queen stared at us as we converged. Her monsters formed a teeming barricade of deadly fangs and razor-sharp claws, but we wouldn't be kept from our prey. Auren crashed into them on his strider, hewing through flesh and vines with his black axe. Shadows and crackling sunlight trailed behind it, and everywhere was carnage.

Ayanna simply laughed at the massacre below her, then threw her hands skyward.

The ground shook as dozens of vines ripped free and coiled into the air. I braced for the strike, but instead, they wrapped around the sphere of moonlight that had imprisoned their master, folding over it like a flower closing at night.

"What's she doing?" Samantha shouted as she reached my side.

I ripped a fae soldier from the air, then looked back at the queen. She was fully enclosed by vines. This was our chance.

The potion, now! I roared in the mind of my mate.

Comprehension dawned, and she grasped for the bandolier of potions. She pulled one free, but it was too late.

The vines dropped away.

The ball of light imprisoning the queen was gone. The vines had consumed every shard of magic, freeing their master. The queen threw up her hands, releasing a thundering wind, then soared upward on her lacelike wings, racing toward the barrier.

"We can't let her get away!" Samantha hurled another fireball of moonlight, but this time, it went wide.

I sprinted forward, bounding over clawing monsters and twisting vines. Auren appeared on my left, a golden wolf, a bright mirror of my own dark form. We broke away from the queen's army and raced over the grasslands, moonlight, shadow, and sunlight streaming together.

I called the winds to stop the queen, but Ayanna kept flying faster and faster, fueled by stolen power. She curved to the northwest, over the dead woods, leading us away from her vines.

Dread filled me. She was almost to the wall.

Samantha thrust her hand into the air, and moonlight began to billow around her fingers. It grew brighter and brighter until she released it in a jet of light. It slammed into the wall in a crackling blast, then spread across the surface like frost, transforming the wall of light into pure crystal once more.

The signature of her magic pulsed through me, and I growled in praise.

The queen pulled up sharply before the wall and spun to face us—yet instead of terror, it was a look of triumph. "Do you not realize that I've taken your power, you foolish girl? All that you can do, I can do as well."

The queen pressed her hand into the wall, and it melted away beneath her touch. She slipped through the barrier seconds before I slammed into the place where she had been.

A torrent of the Moon's power exploded through me like flames and ice, repelling me from the wall. I crashed into the ground and collided with the trunk of a fallen tree. Gritting my teeth against the agony of the Moon's magic, I shifted back to the form of a man and thrust myself to my feet.

"Godsdamnit!" Samantha screamed as she leapt from Elowyn and slapped her palm against the barrier. Magic rushed across its surface, and the wall began to dissolve as light spiraled down her arm and into the moonstone in her hand.

"Hunt her down and kill her!" I shouted at Auren as he charged through the widening gap. Sunlight exploded around him. Wings burst forth as he took the form of a giant golden drake and flew after his prey.

Frustration and hope fought in my chest.

The queen was isolated, away from her army and vines. She wouldn't stand a chance if he could catch her. But while Auren was an unparalleled hunter, she was in her lands, and if she knew them as I knew my own, she would lose him in the end.

But she would never have lost me. I'd forged those lands from dreams themselves.

And now, they were hers.

I called a ball of pulsing magic to my hand and slammed it into the earth. The ground shook beneath me, and dirt and stone sprayed into the sky. "Fuuuuuck!"

Samantha grabbed Elowyn's reins and jammed her foot in the stirrup.

"Where are you going?" I growled before she could hoist herself into the saddle.

"To chase down the queen."

"The hell you are. You're staying here. I won't have you out there on your own, and you'll never catch up." Auren was a bright speck in the sky, disappearing over the dead trees.

The fury in her expression told me she knew I was right.

"Damn it all!" she swore, her chest still heaving. "Are you going to lecture me about joining the battle, too?"

The gods knew I should. I wanted to tie her up and leave her in my room. But the truth was, she was the only reason we'd stood a chance of catching the queen.

Samantha stalked a few paces away and looked at the wake of destruction we'd left in our path.

We'd been so *close*.

I closed my eyes, drowning out the sight of the barrier that had made a mockery of me for a thousand years. "You almost had the queen twice. You were right to join."

Samantha sighed and rubbed her forehead. "I'm sorry about crystallizing the wall. I thought I could stop her. It only stopped us."

The scent of her guilt was utter torture.

"The fucking Moon put it there, not you," I snapped, looking away. "There was no way to know Ayanna had learned how to get through."

"I wish I could steal her magic," Samantha said. "I'd drain her dry."

The shock of our failure was ice in my veins. I felt the weakness from the power Ayanna had stolen from me, a cold, creeping sensation that had invaded every muscle. "What a fucking mess."

Samantha stalked toward me, her expression resolute. "We need to kill the vines. They're the only reason she can challenge you. Without them, she's nothing."

I looked back the way we'd come.

The network of vines stretched across the plains as far as I could see, draining my lands and creating a protected highway for the monsters that raided my realm. They were a living fortress, and once they had a hold, I knew we would never be able to dislodge them.

If they reached the pylons, Ayanna would drain them dry.

It would kill Samantha, I was sure of it.

"I need to go to Dreamspire and poison the roots," she said.

I shook my head. "Not you. Kass organized a team of fae warriors for this."

"We only have one shot. You know I'm the only one who can do it."

I didn't care. I'd nearly lost her tonight. The terror of seeing her going down beneath the vines and deathwings was more than I'd ever felt.

"This is not a negotiation," I said, and turned away.

She seized my arm and pulled me around. "For fuck's sake, Cadean, look what they're doing to your land!"

"I know what they're doing!" I roared, my heart close to breaking. My shoulders shook with wrath, and shadows swarmed around me.

My mate backed away.

I pressed my palms against my temples and gritted my teeth. My head was pounding, and my skin burned from being so close to the wall.

I was so fucking powerless.

Lightning cracked above me as my rage boiled. Ayanna. The Fates. The Moon. The sword hanging over the head of my mate. Fuck them all. Fuck everything.

I reached down into the roots of the earth and summoned my strength. It became white-hot inside of me as it merged with the anger coursing in my blood and veins. I called it from the trees and hills and stones until I could hold no more.

Then I drove my fist into the earth.

A quake shook the forest, dropping Samantha and Elowyn to the ground. Thundering aftershocks kept them pinned as the land heaved and a fissure split the earth, swallowing grass and trees and stones. Devouring them like the queen had devoured my power.

The jagged crevasse spread across the landscape and cut through the great conduit of vines where they crossed the border. They stretched and pulled, then split apart, their ends dropping into the abyss below.

Mists began welling up from the bottomless seam.

Chest heaving, I pulled my mate to her feet.

She looked up at me in shock. "What have you done?"

"I created this realm," I growled. "I'll break it apart if that's what it takes to protect it from the queen."

35

Samantha

Horror knotted in my chest as the chasm kept widening before us. Rocks and trees and bodies of fae soldiers slipped over the edges as it widened, a waterfall of death. Eventually, the subsidence slowed until only the vines were dangling over the edge and down into the darkness.

My mate may have torn the land apart, but it was him that was breaking. I could see the cracks like thin fractures in a massive sheet of ice.

Cadean snarled and shifted back into his wolf form, then began pacing along the edge of the barrier like a caged beast. His dark fur rippled with every stride, and his feet shook the ground. He was power incarnate, capable of ripping the very earth in two—and yet he couldn't hunt down the queen like his brother or even defend his realm.

My throat tightened as if strangled by a noose, but I forced the words out. "You can't do this."

Shadows exploded around him, and he took the form of a man again. "I can, if that's what it takes."

"She'll find a way to bridge this chasm or make conduits

elsewhere. The vines are everywhere along the border," I said, not backing down. "You know we have to kill the roots, and we have to do it now. Auren has Ayanna on the run, but she'll return to Dreamspire. We have to go *immediately*, while she's gone."

Cadean ran his fingers through his hair and closed his eyes. "I know. Just let the others go. I can't lose you again. It would break me apart."

But he *would* eventually lose me. And it *would* break him.

Death was coming—a black jackal lurking in my dreams, a waiting presence just beyond my sight. Tonight or tomorrow or ten years from now, I was going to die. And when I did, I'd leave my mate trapped and even more broken than before. My death would shatter him like he'd shattered the land. It would leave him with no way to control the walls of his prison, no way to ever find the freedom he deserved. The mighty god would crumble and wither away until he and his kingdom and his people were consumed.

Because I had been afraid. Because I hadn't done the thing he would never ask but needed more than breath itself.

Because I hadn't done what I knew I needed to do.

I kissed my mate lightly on the lips and stepped back. "If you don't want to risk me going to Dreamspire, then take me there yourself."

A shadow crossed his face as I slowly retreated into the warm light of the barrier.

"What are you talking about?"

He was impossibly beautiful and utterly frightening. Streaks of blood covered his perfectly muscled skin, and he wrapped shadows and anger around him like a cloak. I'd just watched him butcher countless men and monsters in front of me, then rip the earth itself in two. He was ruthless and terrifying...and absolutely not the monster I'd once believed him to be.

He was the *protector* of this place. And now he'd sworn to protect my people as well—to never threaten the waking world again and help my pack, whenever they needed, as long as he lived.

He took a step forward into the burning light. "Samantha, what are you doing?"

I gave him a wistful smile. "I was brought back to protect the Dreamlands, Cadean. And freeing you is the best way I know how."

His face contorted, and he lurched forward into the wall of light, pushing through the barrier inch by inch. "You can't do this! You'll kill yourself! I've *seen* it."

"I'll die if I have to watch you eaten away by the queen's magic for one day longer," I said as I backed to the far side of the wall. "Your people will die, and your lands will die. We'll all die if she isn't stopped—and I can't stop her without you. Without my mate."

"I forbid it!" he roared.

I slipped the moonstones from my pouch and took one in each hand, then met his eyes. "I see you, Cadean. I know who you are, and you deserve to be free."

Moonlight streamed like fire around him as he struggled forward, billowing in waves like he was a meteor plunging through the sky.

"I don't need to be free!" he called out. "I need you!"

But this was what I wanted—for him and for the Dreamlands, for my pack and my soul.

I thrust the moonstones into the air and seized the power of the wall. Its magic surged through me, and the world turned white as time slowed.

An endless expanse of light spread in all directions, and at its center were the three pylons, now separated by yards instead of miles. They resonated with the power I'd once called the

Moon's. I knew my body was still in the Dreamlands, inches away from Cadean's grasp. But I was also here, within the magic of the wall itself.

The familiar cacophony of voices pummeled me like the roar of an unceasing storm. Were they the voices of the wall or of the Dreamlands itself?

"Who are you?" I asked. "What are you?"

Who are you? What are you? the voices responded, echoing where they shouldn't in a space without walls. It felt almost like they had spoken first, and my own voice was the echo.

Their purpose raged though me, a mirror of my own.

The Oracle had once told me, *your purpose is within you, waiting for you to grasp it. It's not an act or a mask you wear, but the thing that drives you forward—the thing that will not let you stop when every part of you wants to die.*

"I protect the Dreamlands," I whispered.

We protect the Dreamlands, the voices echoed.

But they didn't. Not anymore. Their power was a prison.

Free us, the voices begged, as they had since I'd first heard them. *Become what you were meant to be.*

I tightened my grasp around the moonstones and closed my eyes. "Then come to me."

I saw the Moon's spell in my mind—a thousand iron threads of magic woven tightly together. I knew the spell like I knew the sound of Cadean's voice or the feel of his touch against my skin. A weave for strength, a weave to repel, and a weave to bind a god.

I reached out with my power and pulled the golden thread to unravel them all.

Magic cascaded through me as the spell collapsed like a building falling into rubble and dust. My body exploded with agony, and sensation ceased to have meaning. There was nothing but pain and light and the roar of the voices in my mind.

It was more power than any mortal was meant to bear.

My teeth and muscles clenched, but I focused all of my will and strength on the moonstones. The pain vanished, and suddenly, I was no longer being torn apart, but an open conduit. My body quaked as the Moon's magic rushed through my body and into the stones. Power poured into me from all directions, and I felt myself rise from the ground.

The moonstones grew hotter and hotter, but I didn't stop. It was past the point where stopping was possible. I was the heart of Charybdis, a whirlpool drawing the entire ocean down into me. I would channel the magic, or I would die trying.

And then, suddenly, the moonstones were full.

It happened in an instant, without sign or warning, leaving me as the only place the power could go. It became a firestorm, burning me from the inside out. I screamed, but there was no sound—just infinite light pouring through me and out of me and consuming me as it poured into my soul. I absorbed all that remained, every last bit of power within the wall.

Then the light vanished, and I was falling beneath the dark winter sky.

36

———————

Cadean

Samantha floated in the center of a storm of magic, wreathed in a halo of light. The entire barrier was collapsing, and it was collapsing onto her.

"Stop!" I bellowed as my darkest nightmares took shape.

Waves of crackling energy spilled across the surface of the wall, descending on my mate. She couldn't absorb the magic. No mortal could.

Visions of her death flooded my mind, memories of the way the pylons had left her burned and broken in my arms. I couldn't kill her again. I couldn't let her die to set me free.

I forced myself forward, each step like fighting against a turbulent sea.

A blast of magic ripped through the air and drove me to my knees, burning me like frost and fire.

And then—all of it was gone. The pain. The ceaseless thrum of the barrier. The shimmering wall.

In its place was only the twilit sky and the body of my falling mate.

I rammed my feet into the earth and flung myself toward her.

She dropped into my outstretched arms, and I crashed to my knees, cradling her.

Moonlight streamed off her skin, and her eyes were wide and glowing with light. I pulled her to my chest, anguish choking my voice. "What have you done?"

Closing my eyes, I called the power from the land and poured it through our bond, willing her to heal, to live, to release the storm of power surging through her body.

Her back arched, and she gasped. "Holy fucking shit!"

She wrapped her arms around me, pulling her head to my chest. I moved my hands over her body, stunned beyond words. She was whole. Unburned. Unscathed.

Disbelief shuddered through me.

She'd nearly burned to death at the pylons when she'd transformed the wall. The vision of her charred skin and milky eyes had haunted my dreams every night since.

But now?

It was impossible.

She pushed out of my arms and stumbled back to brace against her knees. "I thought I was going to die there for a minute."

The laughter in her voice flipped a switch, and my relief turned into an inferno of rage. "What were you thinking?"

My anger crashed over her, but the laughter didn't leave her eyes. "I knew I could do it!"

I clenched my fists as my arms shook and shadows of my wrath rose. "You could have died!"

She grasped my arms, practically beaming. "Then I would have died knowing my mate was *free*. That he would protect his people and mine. That there was one fucking god in this place who gave a damn."

"Your life—"

She shook me. "You're free. Do you hear me? You're free."

My chest tightened as the word rammed home like the blade of a spear. *Free.*

It was almost as if the word was in a foreign tongue, sounds without comprehension or meaning.

Free.

I turned slowly as if seeing the forest around me for the first time. The shimmering dome of my prison was gone. Nothing stood between me and the limitless sky or the lands I had forged so long ago.

I tried to speak, but I could barely draw a breath.

Samantha took my hand and pulled me forward, leading me across the place where the barrier had once been.

The Moon's wall had been wide, but the dividing line was as sharp as a knife. One side, death: desiccated trees and brown grass, now hidden beneath the snow. On the other, life: strong limbs, vibrant pines, bushes, and mistletoe, all still green against the winter expanse.

I brushed my fingers over the bow of a pine, letting the needles bend and spring back beneath my touch.

"It's been a thousand years since I set foot here last," I said in wonder.

There was no pain. There was no crushing presence pushing me back. Only the wilderness surrounding me.

"How does it feel?" she asked quietly, the amusement in her voice extinguished.

I closed my eyes and reached out with my spirit, searching for the rhythms of the lands I'd long since forgotten: the bitter chill of the snowcapped mountains in the north and the fierce winds shaking the ceders on the eastern shore. I felt the frigid water running beneath the frozen rivers of the hill country and heard the heartbeat of living things tucked away for winter, deep in their dens.

It had all been mine once, and now, it was mine again.

Power that I hadn't touched in years pulsed through me. The winds danced at my command, and snow spiraled into the sky. When I inhaled, the trees raised their branches, and when I exhaled, they bowed before me.

Yet nothing was more powerful than the gratitude I felt for my little wolf. Her faith in me and her strength had freed me.

I stepped close and cupped her cheek in my palm. "I feel whole for the first time in a thousand years." I bowed my forehead to hers. "Thank you, beyond all things."

Pushing up on her toes, she gripped my arms and kissed me. It was a soft and gentle caress, tender and filled with longing.

She was my mate and my love, and now my savior.

All anger was forgotten as my heart filled with joy and pride. My mate was strong and fierce and powerful enough to free a god. And I was lucky beyond all others to have her.

I brushed the windswept hair from her face and lips and smiled. "You've given me more than I could have ever asked for, my little wolf. How can I repay you?"

The wind rose just slightly, and the edges of her mouth hardened, becoming almost sad but resolute. "You can take me to Dreamspire and help me destroy the vines. Let me free you and your lands forever."

Her words sank into my gut like a blade of ice, and the world turned cold. My chest tightened as the fears I'd harbored for months came roaring back. She'd risked her life to free me. Could I really let her do it again?

I stepped back, reining in my emotions. "Things have changed. I'm free. Auren and I can hunt the queen down together. There's no reason—"

"Look at what she did today," Samantha said. "She'll never fight you unless she's certain she can win. Until then, she'll keep stealing power, getting stronger and stronger."

I set my jaw. I couldn't risk her now, not after what she'd done.

She grasped my hand. "This is our one chance. Ayanna is on the run and away from the palace. We need to go, *now*. You and your kingdom won't be safe until the vines are dead."

I turned to look at the swath of vines winding its way toward the mountains. I'd had to break my land apart to stop them, but there would be more. This was just the beginning.

"You know that I'm right, Cadean."

Of course she was right. What Ayanna had done tonight was proof enough. I could almost feel the vines wrapped around me, sucking the life from my body.

"I'll send the others," I said.

"No. You'll send me. We have one shot, and you know I'm the best one to do this. That I'm *meant* to do this."

My muscles knotted, and I clenched my teeth against the horrible truth. *She was returned for one task,* Sigrun had said, *and when that task is complete, the thread of her life will unwind.*

"Samantha—"

Her eyes flashed with a determination I couldn't deny. "You asked me how you could repay me. This is it. Stop fighting me. Stop trying to hold me back. This is my path, and I will *not* forsake my purpose or my fate."

Her purpose is her spark. Without it, she will wither into nothing.

In my heart, I knew Sigrun was right, but I wanted to fight and rage. I wanted to tear the world open again. My mate was racing as fast she could to her doom, and there was nothing I could do—not without defying her. Not without disregarding all that she had done and risked for me.

Not without taking her choice and power from her like it had been taken from me.

I knew the truth. I was greedy. I wanted her more than anything—more than my lands or my freedom or my honor. I stepped close and took her hands, then pressed my forehead to hers. "I'll have nothing if I lose you."

Her fingers tightened around mine, becoming steel. "I'm mortal, Cadean, and one day, I'm going to die. Until you accept that, you'll never see me for who and what I am. You'll never be able to accept what it means to be my mate."

Her mate.

What kind of mate would I be if I shut my ears to her voice? If I denied her vengeance? If I stood in her way at every turn? It would mean that I cared more about myself than her.

Greedy wolf.

I closed my eyes, feeling the closeness of her body and the strength of her spirit. The pull of the unbreakable bond we shared.

Death comes to all mortals, Sigrun had told me. *But if I had a mate, I would stand by them against the world. Whatever the cost. Whatever their fate.*

I took a deep breath, inhaling the jasmine and honeysuckle scent of her body. I'd accepted our mate bond for now and forever. If the cost of standing by her was my heart, then fuck it, it would break. And if it was my soul, then let it be torn apart.

"You've done more for me than I could ever ask," I whispered. "I will honor your wish."

She grasped my neck, pulling my forehead tighter against hers, until we were like two iron pillars. I felt her strength, and it was mine. If she could bear the burden of her purpose, then so would I.

Samantha kissed me softly, then stepped back, slipping from my arms. "Don't look so sad. I have no intention of dying today." A wisp of moonlight traced around her hand, and she smiled. "I plan to win."

Her eyes were bright and her shoulders straight. She was beautiful and brilliant and unstoppable. The Moon's magic may have given her power, but I knew that in the end, it was her heart and purpose that gave her strength.

I'd never believed in anyone as much as I believed in her. She'd defied the gods and set me free. Whatever her fate, wherever her path would lead, all I knew was that I would be right there by her side, ready to *fight*.

37

———

Samantha

A cold wind had risen as night set in. Cadean stood against it, his expression hard and unyielding. I knew his heart was breaking.

Mine was, too. Chances were that this would be a one-way trip. But this was my chance to save him, to return his power, to protect him if the Moon ever tried to imprison him again.

The moment I'd chosen to release him from his prison, I'd stepped onto a path that I couldn't leave. My destiny was pulling me forward, and I doubted I could escape the shadow of the jackal from my dreams.

"We should go," I said.

Cadean turned and began walking back toward the battle-field of severed vines. "Get Elowyn, and I'll call for Vega. We'll need to collect Sarion and his team."

"No. Just us," I said softly.

I wouldn't take the rest down with me. Sarion was a good warrior, but he'd nearly died getting me out. I didn't want to have to carry that burden again.

My voice stopped him dead in his tracks. He turned, his jaw

set and his expression like iron. "I'll take you to Dreamspire, but I'm not sending you in there alone."

"Sarion and the others would just slow me down and make it harder to sneak in. I'll be worrying about protecting them when I need to focus on my mission. That much, I think you'll understand."

Cadean never took his eyes off me for long. He was always more worried about my safety than about the dangers that faced him.

He started walking back to me across the snow-covered grass. "You need protection in there. Someone to guide you through."

I called the moonlight to my hand, a crackling force that warned me against the winter chill and restored the strength to my tired limbs. "I'm holding two moonstones charged with enough power to trap a god. As long as you lure the queen away, no one in Dreamspire will be able to stand against me."

"And if the queen returns? Or if she's there already?"

"Then you draw her and her army out. If you can keep her away from me, I can kill the vines." I laid a hand on his arm. "I need you to trust me as you have before. We can do this, the two of us, together."

He measured me for a long time with a gaze that suddenly felt ancient and cold.

At last, he swore and tore the shadows from a tall pine. Pulling the darkness to him, he wrapped it over my shoulders, forming a cloak of shadow. "It will last only until the dawn, but it'll hide you in dark corners, just as I can."

"Thank you," I said, and kissed him again.

"This is your path, little wolf," he said, stepping back. "And I'll follow where you lead. You've defied gods and queens. If anyone can do this, it's you. I believe that with all my heart."

Before I could respond, shadows rose up from the ground

and cloaked him in a storm of darkness. They billowed out and became the great outstretched wings of his phoenix form.

He bowed low before me. *Let's end this.*

I touched the bandolier of potions still slung around my chest. This was it. We were going into the breach.

Heart pounding in anticipation, I crawled up onto his back and threw my legs over his neck. The saddle would have been easier, but I'd flown this way before. Now there would be nothing between us, and I would be able to savor the warmth of his body and the sweet taste of his magic. Perhaps for the last time.

Three beats of his wings sent us up into the twilit sky.

We soared over the forest, then after a quarter of an hour, we turned north toward one of the banks of mist that flowed along the seams of his realm. In moments, it consumed us, and the world became gray.

It wasn't as cold in the mists, and the air was still. Glimpses of the forest faded away below me until I could make out nothing but the occasional spire of rock or the tip of a tall tree.

"How long will it take to reach Dreamspire?" I asked.

Escaping though the mist had taken the better part of a day, and we'd even had to sleep. I was afraid the queen would beat us back.

Don't worry, little wolf. All places connect in the mists through paths that mortals cannot walk, even the queen. We don't have long.

Every so often, I would see something move below us. Shapes like tentacles or white lights that floated through the endless gray. An unearthly howl rose up, and I tightened my grasp on Cadean's neck.

I'd seen the horrors of the mists below.

I am the Wolf God. Nothing here will dare approach us.

I closed my eyes and tried to purge the ominous shapes and eerie noises from my mind. I had to focus on the task ahead. I retraced all the corridors of the palace in my mind, mapping pathways to the queen's gardens and to the Well of Life.

I couldn't find my way in again through the undercity—not without Sarion or help from the little elves that lived in the tunnels beneath. Those had probably been closed off after my escape.

"How close to Dreamspire can you get?" I asked.

Like the sacred glade, only those with fae blood could enter the palace.

I don't know. Never tried.

I breathed out. So much could go wrong, but it was our best shot. On my own, I could slip through the shadows and make my way to the heart of the palace.

News of the barrier's fall would have spread quickly, and I was certain that the fae would be scrambling. But they'd be expecting an attack from a god. Not a lone operative slipping through the night.

It would work. I had faith.

Prepare yourself, Cadean said, and slowed. *We've already left the seam, and I'm driving the mists ahead of us. They won't see our approach.*

My heart clenched. "Already?"

Suddenly, a part of me wasn't ready. I'd expected it to take hours. I'd expected more time to plan.

All seams connect, Cadean said. *You just walk between them instead of through them.*

There was only one path left for me to walk, and I didn't know how it would end.

At least we'd probably overtaken the queen—if she'd escaped Auren.

My hands tightened, and I pressed myself closer to the warmth of Cadean's back as dark shapes loomed up out of the mists—the towers of Dreamspire, no longer brilliant purple and glistening in the sun, but shrouded in gray. Blurry lights shone in some of the windows and from a few of the high balconies, and there was an indistinct glow from the city below.

Cadean pulled up sharply, and I grabbed hold. "What is it?"

I can't land. The spells that protect the palace extend far beyond its walls.

"How close can you get?"

He swooped low over the dim glow of the city and palace grounds, then circled the towers again. I had to cling tightly as he wove around them, probing the extent of the wards.

I can set you down outside the walls. Otherwise, the roofs of the high towers will be closest.

Well, fuck.

I'd either have to navigate through the tunnels beneath the city and pray that they hadn't been barricaded or jump for it. Time was short, and the queen was probably on her way.

"What the hell, let's go for an aerial assault. It's faster, less chance of getting spotted, and we'll know if I fuck it up real soon."

Amazingly, it wouldn't be the dumbest stunt I'd pulled in my life—though perhaps, it would be the last.

Cadean climbed upward, then slowed as we neared a roof. Beating his wings vigorously against the air, he hovered unstably about twenty feet above.

I peered over the edge at the slanting tile below. "Whose idea was this?"

Don't worry, little wolf, Cadean rumbled in my mind. *You're carrying the power of a goddess. You will succeed. I've never believed anything more.*

"Well, we'd both better be right."

Then I jumped.

38

———

Samantha

Cadean's magic wrapped around me, a wind from below, guiding me down and breaking my fall.

I reached for the spire but slammed into the roof of the tower, the impact driving the breath from my lungs. Gasping, I dug my claws into the clay tiles as I skittered downward.

A foot from the edge, I came to a stop. I lay there for a moment, my muscles screaming and chest aching. I waited for shouts or an alarm, but there was nothing but the whistling of frigid winter wind.

Opening my eyes, I glanced over the edge of the roof. The mist was thick enough that I couldn't see the bottom of the tower, and my mate was just a shadow in the gray sky, fading away.

I will be watching, he said as he disappeared.

I took a deep breath. Time to go. Luckily, I'd done this bit before.

I shimmied around to the lee side of the roof. The last thing I wanted was for my cloak of shadows to turn into a sail and send me careening downward to my doom. Once in position, I extended my claws and flipped over the edge of the roof. Handhold by handhold, I began scaling down the surface of the spire.

As long as I didn't think too much about it, it was no different than climbing down Red River Gorge, or even sneaking out of Cadean's tower at Shadowstone—except if I fell and survived, I'd be executed on sight.

I looked down again, and despite the mist, my stomach swam with vertigo. Why had I ever thought climbing was a good form of recreation?

I forced my breathing to slow and concentrated on the feel of the stone beneath my palms, searching for strong holds to sink my claws into. I slowly crept down the surface of the spire, praying that Cadean's cloak of shadows and the cloying mists would protect me from watchful eyes.

I moved faster and faster as my confidence grew, until I was able to drop to the top of the roof of one of the main halls.

A dim shadow swept over me, and I pressed myself down against the tile.

Nice landing, Cadean said.

The bastard nearly gave me a heart attack.

I waited for a minute, then dropped onto a darkened balcony below that was similar to the one I'd once had here. Then, I'd been able to see the city, but now, there was only the haze of dim light.

I looked around, then tried the door.

Locked.

Well, fuck. I slapped my hand against it, then released a burst of magic. My arm jerked back, but the door crashed open, hanging precariously on one hinge.

So much for stealth.

I drew my sword and entered. My werewolf vision allowed

me to see in the near dark, and I breathed a sigh of relief when I realized it was a disorganized study and not someone's bedroom.

I paused at the door to listen, then slipped through and out into the hall. I looked around. It was a floor I'd never been on, so I chose a direction and started moving, thankful I was on my own.

Werewolves have sharper vision than most supernaturals, a keen sense of smell, and pin-drop hearing. It was like we were custom-built for this. No matter how good Sarion's crew was, they would have been a mass of loud bodies.

I was almost to the stairwell when footsteps echoed down the corridor. I ducked into an inset doorway and waited with Cadean's cloak wrapped around me. Not long ago, he had hidden me with his power in these very same halls, and while the cloak served its purpose, it was a cold and lifeless replacement.

The sentries moved on, and I slipped into the stairwell, sword out. There would be no hiding here.

I wound downward, moving quickly now. I'd used this stairwell to visit General Slaine. That put me on the map. The walks I'd taken with Sarion and the queen, the time I'd spent scouting the palace at night—it all fell into place.

My momentum built until I was practically running, certain of my target...but then my luck began to run out.

The palace was on alert, and the lower levels were bustling with fae sentries rushing about. They had to know Cadean had escaped. Were they expecting an attack? If so, it could play to my favor. The soldiers would be distracted, and maybe they'd pull guards to the palace walls.

Fates, please be kind.

It took me another five minutes to reach the hall where General Slaine's office had been, and beside it, the secret entrance to the Well of Life.

Hopefully, the door hadn't been sealed forever.

I peeked around the corner, and my heart fell. There was an honor guard in plate mail posted outside of the general's old office—either to protect the queen's new commander's quarters or the secret door. Perhaps both.

I sighed. It was either this or I'd have to retrace my steps and go through the queen's garden with its massive, enchanted doorway and heavily armed guards.

Time was running short, so the direct approach it was.

In the light of the hall, my cloak of shadows would make me even more suspicious than I already was, so I dropped my hood and pulled the cloak behind me, then repositioned my hair to hide the tips of my ears. It was a shitty attempt at a disguise, but I had nothing better on hand.

I strode down the hall with confidence, my hand casually resting on the hilt of my sword.

There were six guards standing at attention. At first, they didn't move, but then one turned to me. "No one is allowed on this floor."

"I'm on official business," I said, trying to buy half a moment more to close the distance.

His eyes dropped to the sword hanging at my side, and his hand flew to his weapon. "That's Wolfeater, Slaine's—"

I snapped up my palm and sent a bolt of moonlight into his chest. "It's called 'Wolf's Vengeance' now, assholes."

He crashed to the floor, his armor smoking, as the others unsheathed their weapons.

"Kill the traitor bitch!" the captain shouted as he slashed out with his longsword.

I leapt back, but pain erupted through my left arm as the blade tore through my muscle. Snarling, I backpedaled out of the way, and drew Wolf's Vengeance as his next blow grazed past me.

As soon as the sword was in my hand, I dropped into scorpion stance out of instinct. The guards were all better trained and in plate, so my sword was only useful for parrying blows. But I didn't need it to kill—I could do that on my own.

He lunged, and I parried, then spun to the side, and slammed my hand against his armor. Moonlight roared through me, and the steel went white-hot, searing the skin of my palm. The captain screamed and crashed to the ground, crawling in pain. The others were on me instantly, one swinging a pair of twin war hammers like a tornado. I danced away and summoned my shield of moonlight around me as their blows rained down.

The vines growing along the sides of the walls pulsed with purple light. Some kind of warning system?

I had to end this quickly.

Sucking in a breath, I pulled a surge of magic from the moonstones in my pouch, then dismissed my shield and unleashed a searing blast of moonlight. The wall of white fire swept down the hall, incinerating flesh and heating armor to lethal levels. The guards crashed to the floor one by one, some screaming, others already dead.

I staggered to the wall and heaved, then wiped my mouth. I was a fighter, but I wasn't cut out for this shit. I was meant to defend. To protect.

These fae were soldiers just like Sarion, yet they were also part of a machine that had ravaged the Dark Wolf God's lands. I was going to put an end to that machine forever.

Shouts rang out from the end of the corridor, and several forms vanished down the stairwell. Time was up.

Cadean! I shouted through our bond.

I felt the sudden heat of his gaze on me and his presence in the shadows as they began to move. *What happened? Are you okay?*

My sleeve was soaked with blood from the captain's strike, but the wound would heal quickly—I was a werewolf, after all. It didn't compare to the evil I'd caused.

I looked at the corpses and chaos around me, and my stomach knotted. "Things went bad. There are alarms sounding, and the alert has been raised. I need a distraction—a big one."

The darkness before me rumbled like a thunderstorm. *I'll remind them of what it means to anger a god. I will show them what it means to touch my mate.*

"Don't—" I started, but his presence vanished, a hurricane collapsing into stillness.

And now, there was no more time to lose.

Stepping over the soldiers, I felt along the wall for the hidden door Slaine had used. When my finger couldn't detect it, I released some of the moonlight I was holding. It flowed over the wall like water, and a glowing seam emerged where it pooled. Closing my eyes, I put my hand on the wall and forced my magic through the widening crack. I poured more and more into it until the door exploded open in ball of luminous fire.

I staggered back, looking at the unlit space within: the secret passage to the Well of Life.

A dark certainty descended over me like the weight of the sea. The paths of fate had led me here, but they didn't lead back out. The Oracle had once told me that if I found my true purpose, it would destroy everything I was. So be it. I was ready.

I sheathed Wolf's Vengeance, then stepped over the threshold and pulled the secret door shut behind me.

The Well of Life descended before me, a vast pit lined by pillars that concealed a descending staircase, which wrapped around and around, corkscrewing to the bottom. Roots and vines covered the wall, snaking downward and entwining around the columns.

This was the heart of Ayanna's power—her means to steal power from Cadean, but also to fool her people, to drag them along under her spell with the promise of eternal life.

It was time to break that spell.

I flung myself over the edge and dropped to the ground below, releasing a burst of moonlight to soften the bone-jarring landing. A quick check told me nothing was broken, so wincing, I shoved to my feet and called a wisp of moonlight to my hand. The light swept over the room as I turned, illuminating the closed portal that led to the garden and the queen's throne. Although I'd shattered it with Cadean's axe, it had been repaired with seams of gold.

In front of it, a stone grate covered the queen's sacrificial pit. I'd hidden there when Ayanna had slit Asta's throat and fed her blood to the roots. As much as I'd hated Asta, she hadn't deserved to be murdered.

My hand clenched with rage, and I prayed that Kirin and the others in my cohort hadn't met a similar end. It was time to stop this bloody fucking farce.

Hand shaking, I pulled one of Mel's potions from my bandolier and said the spell to release the seal. I pulled the cork free and raised the bottle high. So many had been sacrificed to feed the vines.

Never again.

"Time for one last drink, you bloodsucking bastards," I said as I poured the blood potion through the grate, watering the roots below. A gentle rustling, like something large moving through the underbrush of the forest, filled the air as the vines pushed up through the bone-flecked earth and began to lap up the falling drops.

I held my breath and cast more moonlight down through the

grate. The twisting roots began to turn gray, and the sound of fracturing stone reverberated through the space.

A malicious grin split my lips. They would never feed again.

I cast the bottle aside and yanked another free. I doused the roots creeping up the wall and laughed as their purple-brown flesh began to turn smooth and gray. "This is for Cadean."

I flung my arm out, spraying the contents of the third potion across the walls. "And this is for me!"

Everywhere the potion splattered, blooms of gray began to form, spreading faster and faster as the living nightmares turned to stone.

I grabbed the last potion...and then the room shook.

My head snapped up as a half-petrified vine ripped free of the wall. It had broken off where the tip had turned to stone, but it still moved with the grace of an eel. I gaped as it curled back above me like an octopus's tentacle, searching for prey.

Then it struck.

The petrified tip raced for me. I summoned my shield of moonlight, but the blow drove me to the ground.

"Shit!" Stone fragments scattered against the walls.

I rolled out of the way as it struck again, fracturing the stone floor.

Heart thundering, I scrambled to my feet as it swept through the room. Pain screamed up my side, and I was thrown against the wall. I blinked through the agony and watched as another tendril ripped free.

The petrifying vines along the wall thrashed and twisted, trying to fight their stone-cold fate. Dozens of tendrils snaked through the air, clearly sentient and pissed as they sought me out.

Bracing my cracked ribs, I rolled as the stone tip of a root lanced past my head and shattered against the wall.

"What the fuck?" This wasn't like the simple transformation Mel had done with the sprout. Suddenly, it was Samantha Bennet, a very small werewolf, against the angry pit of death.

A thick, half-hardened root swept just over my head, scraping against the wall. I darted out of the way and dove through the gaps between the columns of the chamber. Another dying root crashed into one of the pillars, sending a cloud of shrapnel ripping through the air.

Shards of stone tore my skin, and a heavy chunk rammed me back against the wall.

My hand came away from my face soaked with blood, and my ribs felt like I'd been hit by a bowling ball. Clearly, hiding behind the pillars was almost as dangerous as being in the center. With no way to escape up the stairs, I scrambled back down and leapt for the passage that led to the pit below the stone grate.

Something caught my foot, and I tumbled down the steps, crashing face-first on the floor. I coughed out a mouthful of dirt, gagging at the thought of what it was.

The grate above cracked, sending dust and debris raining down as the roots beat against it in a shuddering rhythm, pummeling the only protection I had.

"Not good," I whispered, eyeing the hairline cracks that slowly began spreading. Against the vines, the grate wouldn't last long.

I looked around wildly, but the truth was clear: I was trapped like a rat.

Cadean

I began raining hell down on Dreamspire the moment they

attacked my mate. I called lightning and thunder and earth-quakes to shake the palace to its roots. I was the wrath of nature, and after a thousand years, I'd awoken once more.

A hail of ballista bolts whistled through the air around me as I soared between the towers of Dreamspire. I twisted out of their path, but my body lurched, and pain exploded in my wing.

Roaring in anger, I spiraled down toward the artillery crews safely ensconced behind the powerful palace wards. They wouldn't be safe from my power. I raked the battlements with steaks of lightning, and defenders leapt to their deaths.

I dropped low over the city, driving the screaming crowds before me. I would be the monster in the darkness and the terror at the palace gates. I would be chaos and pandemonium. I would draw all the city's defense to me while my mate slipped through the shadows, a subtle knife. The only danger that mattered.

Warriors on deathwings poured into the sky to give chase as steel-clad soldiers marched into the forest below.

I plunged downward to meet them in battle. They'd honed their skills hunting wolves and raiding villages.

I would show them what it was to face a god.

I crashed into them like an ocean wave, a whirlwind of death, shredding flesh and carapace with claw and magic alike. I hurled my head back and unleashed a roar that shook the woods around me. I poured my magic into the forest, waking the trees and commanding them to serve as my bodyguard.

The leafless ashes and oaks shuddered to life. They struck down the queen's monsters with heavy limbs and strangled her archers with their roots.

Then the forest lit with a glow of shadow and moonlight.
There was the evil bitch.

Ayanna rose before me, lifted on a throne of vines. "I didn't think you fool enough to attack me in my domain, Wolf God."

I stalked forward through the destruction. "These are my lands. I created them, and I will claim them again."

"You will have *nothing*."

Vines exploded toward me from every direction, streaking through the trees faster than a hail of arrows.

I tore and ripped at them, shifting from wolf to bear to bird, as I slipped through their grasp. But with every strike that landed, I slowed, a little weaker.

It didn't matter. As long as Ayanna was here, she wasn't in Dreamspire. She wouldn't stop my mate.

A low rumble grew in my chest as I called a hail of meteors down among the trees. The blood of severed vines sprayed across me, but they kept coming, relentless as the ocean waves. One lashed around my neck, and another around my arm. They swarmed me like constrictors, pinning me back and draining my magic.

"I will take every shred of power you possess," Ayanna said, her words slick with venom. "Then I will take your brother's and the Moon's. I won't stop until Death itself bows before me."

The tendril encircling my neck constricted, choking off my air. I tried to rip it away with my free hand, but my claws skated across the surface. It had become a noose of stone.

I grinned at her. Pure delight filled me as the vines around my waist went ridged, one by one, compressing my lungs and growing harder with every second that passed.

Samantha had won, and now, I would finish the queen.

An expression of utter shock racked her face as I pressed my limbs against the vines that held me captive. They slowly fractured and cracked, then exploded away from me, their fragments spraying across the forest floor.

Flooding myself with power, I braced to face the queen.

But Ayanna was gone.

Panic seized me. *Samantha.*

I surged toward the palace, cutting through men and beasts, until I slammed into the wards that only permitted fae to enter. I hurled my magic against it, a thunderstorm of power and lightning fueled by terror.

Somewhere beyond that barrier, Ayanna was hunting my mate, and I'd been too slow to stop her.

39

Samantha

The stone grate above me shattered as a crumbling fifty-foot length of vine collapsed down on top of it. Shards of stone scattered off my shield of moonlight, but the weight of falling slabs rammed me into the ground.

Thanking the gods for werewolf strength, I heaved them off and staggered back against the wall. My hidey-hole wasn't safe any longer.

Dodging another falling chunk of stone, I climbed up the face of the broken grate and back into the main chamber. A vine slammed into the wall behind me, but it was slower now. It shattered where it bent, and a twelve-foot length broke away.

Fragments of falling vines crashed into the floor around me, breaking off wherever they tried to twist and turn. The petrification was spreading faster and faster, and they'd all be lifeless soon—but not soon enough. There were still too many thrashing around the room to risk scaling the wall, so I'd have to brave the spiral staircase once again.

I turned toward the steps but stopped in my tracks as

Ayanna emerged from the portal with a storm of light and shadow whipping around her.

My breath slowly slipped from my lungs.

She'd grown more powerful than I'd ever imagined, and I felt the signatures of Cadean's magic and my own entwined with hers.

She strode toward me, her eyes almost alight with fury. "What have you done to my vines?" she screeched.

"You had a way to help your people, but you betrayed them. Your vines have had their last meal, and so have you."

I released a bolt of moonlight, but she spun out of the way with impossible grace, the shadows of Cadean's magic streaming behind her.

"My people have nothing left to give me—but you do." A web of pink lightning burst from her hand, enveloping me in agony as it burned my skin everywhere it touched.

Horror clenched my heart as I watched the wisps of my magic spiral back to her.

Ayanna's eyes flashed with greed. "I will drain you dry and use your magic to make the Dark God grovel before me. He will beg for mercy in a prison of his lover's magic."

Fuck that.

Fury fueled the moonlight racing through me, and I summoned my shield. The pink lightning crackled across it, draining its energy, but a moment was all I needed.

I seized the last potion and uncorked it, then dismissed my power, and flung it at her.

The beads of toxic blood sprayed through the air in a wide fan.

And then they burst into smoke as the queen summoned a moonlight shield of her own.

My mouth dropped open in shock, and the queen gave me a cruel smile. "How do you like the taste of your own magic?"

Moonlight flashed in her hand, and the blast drove me back into the wall. A pale sphere of light crackled around me, closing in tighter and tighter.

She was using my favorite spell against me, only she'd twisted and corrupted it.

"I can take anything I want," the queen said, stalking toward me. "Thanks to you and your power, I now have the means to trap a god."

Cadean.

The golden sphere tightened around me with a thunderclap, knocking me to my knees. The walls seared my skin like ice and fire, and I gritted my teeth.

"Does it burn?" The queen laughed maniacally. "What a *shame*. I wonder how loud the Dark God will howl when I bind him."

"Not with my magic, you won't." I pressed my hand against the sphere and ripped apart the weave, knowing it better than any other spell. The magic roared through me, crackling over my skin like hot wires. "I told you long ago, this power is mine." I snapped my wrist forward, and the light exploded into the wall.

The queen had vanished in a cloud of shadows.

I spun around, searching for her as her voice echoed off the walls. "Then I'll use your lover's and kill you just the same."

A shockwave rolled through the ground, flipping stones and knocking me backward. My head ricocheted against the wall, and Wolf's Vengeance flew from my hand and skittered across the floor.

Stars swam through my vision...and then everything was dark.

The warmth of Cadean's magic surrounded me, and I could almost taste chocolate and smoke—but beneath it was the sickly taint of Ayanna's power corrupting it, just as she'd corrupted mine.

I formed a glowing orb in my palm and held it aloft, driving the darkness back.

Wolf's Vengeance lay before me, a perfect trap. I dove for it as a bolt of light cracked against the stone.

Sword in hand, I rolled to my feet and slapped my hand against the blade, filling it with moonlight. Vertigo churned my stomach as I swung around and glimpsed the queen sliding back into the shadows.

I lunged with my moonlit blade as she threw up her hands and unleashed a dark storm of shadows and stone.

The wind pushed me back as rubble pelted me, but I summoned my shield and stood my ground. Our power billowed and clashed, and streams of shadow and light swirled in the space between us.

Lightning bolts burst against my shield one after another, the thunderclaps echoing so loudly that I could no longer hear myself screaming. Each strike chipped away at my power, and I knew my shield wouldn't last much longer.

This was what I had come for. My moment of vengeance, and I wouldn't be denied.

Shifting into the iron tower stance, I braced back against the storm. I seized the magic within the moonstones and poured it into the blade and shield, more and more, until we were both glowing like the sun. I could barely see, but I knew where the queen was. I could feel her, a vile presence in the darkness hiding behind a whirlwind of power that didn't belong to her.

The room shuddered, and stone roots ripped off the wall, tumbling end over end in massive fragments that battered the sphere of moonlight protecting me. My feet skidded back as the stones beneath them trembled.

Ayanna was using Cadean's magic at its worst. At its most destructive.

But I would be stronger. I had to be.

With a sharp breath, I drained the power from the moonstones. The magic burned through me like rivers of lava, but I kept drawing until it felt like my soul itself was on fire. Closing my eyes, I released my fury.

It ripped through the weave of the queen's spell, tearing it apart thread by thread. The tornado protecting her burst into ribbons of shadow, and I plunged forward, blade first.

The sword slipped between her ribs, and with a cry of rage, I pushed all the power I had left through it. "This is for my mother!" I cried. "For Asta and Kirin! For all the people in your kingdom that you've betrayed!"

Magic surged through me like the sun itself, and Ayanna's scream cut off as the blade was incinerated within her.

"This is for the Dreamlands," I whispered, letting the melted hilt slip from my blistered hands.

Ayanna's form disintegrated into light and shadow and streams of magic, and in a blinding flash, the font of her stolen magic was released.

It hit me like an avalanche, all-consuming and suffocating.

I reached for what little moonlight remained and poured it into my shield, but the blast tore the weave away, layer by layer.

And then, with a thunderclap, the storm was gone. Centuries of power, released in the span of a breath.

Shadows danced across my vision, and a single tone rang in my ears. I staggered forward, half blind, and dropped to my knees.

The Well of Life had become a cavern of molten stone. The remaining vines and columns had melted together, and the queen's shattered throne was reduced to a pile of smooth and featureless slag.

Reaching down, I grasped a fragment of the shattered moonstone—and my heart stilled. My hand was black and burned and pulsing with light from within. My arms, my legs, my whole body shone with light, building and building and only growing brighter.

Panic flooded me. This was too much power.

Moonlight burned though me like wildfire, like a volcano, like a tempest of lightning.

I struggled to stop it, to release it, to do anything, but I had no control over it. Tears wet my burning cheeks.

I'd drawn it all. More than any mortal could ever hold. And now, I knew the price I'd pay.

This was the death I'd seen crossing the mists, the vision in the water—an inferno of light consuming me, and Cadean on his knees at my side, mourning me, begging me to return.

But I knew I would not.

40

Cadean

The world shook beneath my feet, and I looked up as the spells barring me from the palace collapsed in a waterfall of crackling magic.

I had only a second to brace myself before I was overwhelmed by the concussive explosion of power. The fae army was swept off its feet, and the trees around me were torn up by the roots.

Yet the force of the impact was nothing compared to the shock of the truth: the barriers had fallen. Ayanna was dead.

I looked up at the unprotected battlements and lifeless vines. We had won. Samantha had done it.

One moment my soul was alive with euphoria. Then next, there was only pain. A jolt of unrelenting agony lanced through my heart and brought me to my knees. *Samantha.*

My mate was dying.

Her pain tore through my soul, driving my mind to the edge of madness.

The mate bond yanked me forward like a leash of fire, and I charged, heedless of all that stood before me. I called meteors to annihilate the sides of the palace, then seized the form of a falcon to fly through the smoldering gaps. I shifted to a wolf and raced through corridors, tearing into anyone foolish enough to stand in my way.

Terrified fae courtiers and soldiers fled as I killed and cleared the path before me. I switched forms again and again, slipping through the shadows, and taking any form that would bring me to her faster.

All that mattered was her.

I turned down a hall filled with corpses of armored men and pulled up short beside the hidden door. I shifted and slammed my palm against the wall. Magic coursed down my arm, and the stone wall quaked and shattered, sending rubble spraying across the hall. I flung myself through the gap and out into the well, plunging a hundred feet down toward the crumpled form of my mate below. The walls flashed by as I fell, twisted spindles of molten rock where vines and columns had once been.

The floor cracked and buckled as I landed beside Samantha's prone form. Waves of magic pulsed off her like a lighthouse, almost blinding.

I rolled her over, and my throat caught. Her eyes shone up at me, pure white and filled with radiating light. I could feel the Moon's power boiling within her like the sea in the midst of a storm. It was more power than I'd ever imagined she could hold.

"You've drawn too much! Return it to the stones!" I ordered.

"I'm sorry." Her fingers opened, and the fragments of a shattered moonstone clinked across the floor.

My stomach plunged. She'd drawn it all—every shred of power that had made up the Moon's barrier.

"I killed the queen, but I think...myself." She choked on the crimson stream running from the corner of mouth.

I pulled her up against my chest and poured my power into

her, willing her body to heal, defying the storm of magic within her. "I refuse to let you die. You are my mate!"

It was too much, too much for me to heal, too much to control.

She smiled up at me, the pain gone, almost content. "I'm glad it was you."

Then the light in her eyes dimmed, and she fell limp against my chest.

"No," I choked out.

A blast of moonlight burst out from her, shaking the room and searing my skin, but I didn't let go. I clutched her harder to me, my anchor in the middle of a churning ocean. "*No.*"

She was burned and tattered and had endured more than any mortal possibly could, but still, I refused to believe she was gone.

She died once before, and the Moon brought her back.

Gritting my teeth, I summoned the power of my lands, pulling strength from the trees and rivers and lands I'd woven together to make the realm. I drew it in until my blood had become an inferno of power, then pushed it into her bones and flesh, commanding her to heal, to wake, to come back to life in my arms.

"You aren't done here!" I snarled, squeezing her as tightly as I dared. "Your purpose is not complete!"

My magic coursed through her like an earthquake, but her heart didn't stir.

"The Dreamlands still need you!" I shouted, and then, with a choked-off sob, I pulled her against my lips and kissed her forehead. "I need you."

The right words. *I need you. I love you.*

Once, Mel had commanded me to find them, but I'd said them too late and too weakly. I should have shouted them from every mountain in every corner of my land when I'd had the chance.

I prayed to the Fates in a thousand tongues, begging and pleading, but I knew the truth: my mate was dead, and I couldn't bring her back. The grief and guilt of it tore at me like wolves, savagely ripping the flesh from my bones and my heart from my chest.

My mate was dead, and it was my fault. I'd failed to protect her. I'd failed to be the shield she needed me to be.

I threw my head back and howled. Unbridled anguish entwined with my power, and it exploded out of me in a thunderclap that raced up the walls of the chamber. The stones of the ceiling rained down around me, and molten pillars cracked and shattered, creating rifts that climbed skyward like the roots once had.

The echoes slowly died away, leaving me in a lifeless chamber, surrounded by motes of dancing dust. I was suddenly alone in a way I'd never imagined, a shipwrecked soul floating in a meaningless sea.

And then, I was no longer alone.

The dark shape of a man stepped from the shadows. He wore a cloak as black as midnight, but his fingers shone with gold.

My breath stilled as the Opener of Ways parted his lips in a malicious grin. "You failed, Wolf God. Samantha is mine now—just as I promised you she would be."

41

Samantha

The world slipped into darkness, drowning the afterimage of Cadean's glacier-blue eyes. The strong embrace of his arms faded into nothing, and the familiar warmth of his magic drifted away like a heavy blanket sliding to the floor. I clawed for the sweet chocolate and heat of his signature, but it was gone, and I was alone in the dark.

"No!" I cried as his absence crushed in like the ocean depths.

I could still feel my body, but it was only the memory of having form. I knew that my real body was lying on the cold stone, not far from where Ayanna had died. Not far from where Slaine and Astra and the countless others who had died before her had fallen.

Now I'd joined them.

"I'm not ready..." I whispered to the darkness.

A part of me had known I wasn't coming back from Dreamspire.

I'd accepted my fate and considered my life a fair trade for Cadean and his people. But now, faced with the darkness, I wasn't prepared to enter eternity without him, to never see the corner of his mouth turn up in a smile or feel his strong hands holding me and anchoring me to the world.

A part of my mind registered the subtle tingle of another presence in the void, but it didn't matter. Nothing mattered but him.

"You did well," a young girl whispered from somewhere in the sea of shadow. "We knew you would."

I looked around, but the void was featureless. "Who's there?"

"The queen is dead," a second voice said, this one an old woman. "The Dreamlands is safe from her tyranny, and the balance of life and death is restored. You have done everything we asked of you."

The words meant nothing. I felt no sense of triumph or victory or joy, even though it was everything I'd been fighting for. There could be no triumph without him. All that mattered to me in that moment was the heartbreak I'd seen in Cadean's eyes. I couldn't face eternity knowing I'd left him broken, knowing that the pain building in my soul would devour him as well.

"Please send me back!" I begged.

"We cannot," a third woman said. "You cannot cheat death again. I'm sorry for it, and for everything you suffered, but one chance was all we could give."

Her voice was hard, but beneath the iron there was an undercurrent of tenderness that reminded me of my own mother breaking bad news—calm and stern, but ready to wrap me in her arms.

The Child, the Mother, and the Crone. The Three Fates.

There in the embrace of the darkness, I could recall everything that had happened before—the conversation that had been lurking in my memory in scattered, dreamlike fragments since I returned to life.

When they'd given me the choice to return, they'd warned

me there would be a price to pay. The old crone had handed me a golden thread.

The cost, she'd said.

They wouldn't tell me what it was, but I knew it now: the thread of fate that had bound Cadean and me together, our mate bond. I could feel it still, binding us through the ocean of eternity.

Once, I would've thought that the cost was being bound to the monster who had killed me and destroyed my city. But the true price hadn't been to be Cadean's mate, but to spend eternity apart from the man I'd come to love so fiercely—to never even be reunited in death. Two souls, completely and utterly alone.

It was a price I'd accepted.

But Cadean hadn't been given a choice. It had been thrust upon him by the inevitable weaving of fate.

The horror of it all clenched my throat, and I grasped our bond as if by pulling it, I could climb back from death like I'd scaled those cliff faces long ago.

"I have to get back to him! I can't leave him this way."

"You cannot return," the old woman said.

Although I couldn't see her, my senses prickled. I could almost feel her pacing around me in the gloom like a circling hyena. "Samantha Bennet is gone. She tried to wield the power of the gods, and it utterly destroyed her. There is no healing that."

The words turned bitter in my mouth, and my thoughts clouded with fury.

Everyone had warned me, but the magic had been *mine*. It had *chosen me*. It had wanted me to use it, to change the world with it. Hadn't that been what I was supposed to do?

I reached for the source of my power, but I couldn't grasp it. I tried again and again as my rising despair choked me—it was just beyond my touch, near, but no longer a part of me.

I had become nothing, no one, just a broken spirit floating in the dark.

"What will you do with me now?" I said, forcing back a sob. "Now that I've completed your task and paid your price?"

"The Opener of Ways has come to guide your soul into the Deadlands," the motherly woman said from my left. "He'll take you to the ghost pack. You'll run with your ancestors once more."

Visions crafted from soft moonlight slipped from the darkness—wolves running, circling me in the hundreds. Thousands. My packmates. Jaxson's sister. My mother.

My heart leapt at the sight of her.

She slowed as she spotted me, leaving the group. At first a ghostly apparition like the others, she became more and more opaque as she approached. Her eyes sparkled with light and joy. *Samantha? My love? Is that really you?*

I reached for her, but she vanished in wisps of shadow, and my stomach tumbled.

"Where did she go?" I asked the Fates, but they didn't respond.

More wolves raced past me, and I recognized more and more that I knew. Savy and Jax and the girl from the ring in Deerhaven.

"Why are my friends here?" I cried.

Had they died? Had I been trapped for years in this place between life and death? I saw more and more, even wolves I knew would be Savy's twins one day.

"Time is not linear in the realm of the dead," the woman's voice said. "This is a glimpse of what is and what your fate could be."

"*Could* be?" I asked.

"There's another path," the Child said. "But to walk it, there is another price to pay. You must forsake the Deadlands forever."

Forsake the Deadlands? But that would mean...

My chest tightened. I'd never be reunited with my friends or my mother. I'd dreamed of seeing her again one day. She thought she'd been a bad mother, but she hadn't. She'd been brave and had the strength to raise me on my own. She'd borne the pack's wrath because of me, and she'd sacrificed herself in the end. How could I leave everything that I needed to tell her unsaid?

My heart felt like it was trapped in a vise. "What is the path?" I asked warily.

"An eternity of toil," the Crone responded, a deep sadness hanging on every word. "An eternity of relentless loss and battle. I would not wish it on anyone—but it is not our path to offer or rescind."

"Then whose is it?"

"Theirs."

A light flickered in the darkness, then another, and another —like candle flames springing to life in the middle of night. More and more appeared, and then I heard their voices whispering in my mind. The voices of the wall.

Samantha...

42

Cadean

I gently laid Samantha's broken and burned body on the cold stone floor and rose to face the Opener of Ways. "Stay away from her."

Pity and amusement flashed in his eyes. "You cannot heal the dead, Wolf God. What will you do with her corpse? Because that is all she is and all she was ever destined to be. Let me pass and let her go with the dignity she deserves."

Guilt and despair swelled in my chest until my ribs felt like they would break. My fists knotted, and streams of shadow and magic wrapped around my arms. She was *not* a corpse. She was my love. *My mate.*

"I'll never let her go," I growled, stepping between him and her body. The grief was madness now, a delirium driving all sense and logic from my mind.

"You think you can stop this? That you can defeat death itself? Her fate is already sealed!"

His merciless laugh tore me from the fog that had clouded my mind. I snapped my hand to my side, and the wind rose, spiraling around the Well of Life until it became a storm.

"Death is your brother—you're only the ferryman, doing his bidding."

The Opener braced against the windstorm and drew his khopesh, a wickedly curved blade of bronze that he used to sever the souls of the dead. "I know my place and will do my duty, even if you do not."

He leapt for me, swinging his blade for my throat.

Twisting my wrist in the air, I reversed the storm suddenly, and the Opener lurched to the left, his blow swinging wide. I pivoted and drove my fist into the side of his face.

He reeled sideways, and the gusting wind knocked him to the ground. Claws ripping from my fingertips, I lurched forward to press the attack, but the Opener slipped out of the way and sprang to his feet, khopesh leveled at my chest.

I thrust my hand to my side to summon my black axe, but it didn't come. Of course—I'd given it away. For her. For the only thing that mattered.

The Opener's lips turned up in a cruel smile at my mistake. "What's your endgame, Wolf God?"

My throat tightened as an earthquake drummed in my head. There wasn't one. He'd take her soul eventually. Even if I fought him to a standstill, I'd tire. I'd slip up, and he'd have her.

It didn't matter.

Every second I defied him, I honored her. Every minute was another moment where I didn't have to face the world without her.

"I'm a man with nothing left to lose," I snarled. "I'll fight you for a thousand years to keep you from taking her away."

"You won't last a thousand years. You won't last an hour. You're half the man you used to be." He pointed his khopesh at my empty hand. "You gave up the strongest weapon you possessed."

"You're wrong. It was always the weakest part of me." I leapt forward on the wind, raking at him with my claws, but the Opener spun away.

"What are you without your darkness and hate?" he shouted as he lashed out with his blade.

"What I should have been all along!" I feinted left in a burst of shadow, then seized the form of a cave bear, doubling in size. I slammed his sword arm out of the way with my massive paw, then rammed my full weight into his side. He flew back into the wall, and his blade skittered over the floor, lodging in the open grate. I swung my claws for his head, but he ducked, and my paws shattered the molten stone vines where his skull had been.

I wheeled around as he snatched his sword off the ground and darted toward Samantha's body. With a roar, I bent and hurled a broken column at him. As he dodged the spray of rubble, I shifted to the form of a man and seized the twisted wreckage of Samantha's sword, Wolf's Vengeance. There wasn't much left, just the hilt and a hunk of melted steel where the blade had been, but that would have to suffice.

Making sure there was no way for him to slip between me and the body of my mate, I lunged. The Opener spun to parry my strike, and the clang of metal on metal echoed through the room. The edge of his sword skated down mine, but I twisted my hilt, trapping his khopesh with the savage spikes rising from her blade's cross-guard.

"I gave up my axe for her," I said as we circled her body. "I'd give anything to bring her back. Name your price to relinquish your claim on her life. I could give you power like you've never imagined. Storms. Earthquakes. Shadows."

"This is desperate, even for you, Wolf God." The Opener sneered. "All the magic you possess isn't worth a sliver of my honor. I'll do my duty and take her from this world, and then I'll watch as you break—that is the only thing I'll ever want from you."

He kicked my foot out from under me, and with the speed of a viper, he spun and raked his wicked blade across my arm, cutting deep into my bicep. Samantha's sword clattered to the ground as my arm dropped to my side, lifeless below the shoulder.

He'd cut the fucking lifeforce from my body.

The Opener laughed. "Don't worry, Wolf God. Your body will heal with time—if not your heart."

He lunged.

I shadow-stepped behind him and seized the form of a giant wolf. I slammed into his back before he could turn, tearing at him with tooth and claw. His body crashed into the ground, and I felt his ribs fracture beneath my weight. My right foreleg was still stiff and useless, but I could feel a trickle of pain—a sign it was returning to life. Still, I didn't need my claws to maul him; my fangs would suffice.

I clamped my jaws around his head, and he screamed in agony as I shook him left and right. As I towered ten feet at the shoulder, it was nothing for me to hurl him against the wall.

Although I couldn't kill him permanently, I was going to savor ripping his bowels out while he watched.

Jaws wide, I leapt in for the kill.

At the last second, the Opener threw up his hand, and the air filled with the scent of sand and incense. Lightning erupted from his fingers, driving into my chest and lifting me into the air. Agony spiked through my chest, then exploded through my spine as my back cracked against the floor.

"You cannot defeat me, Wolf God," he said as he rose like a spirit from the grave. "Give up and keep what little there is left of your dignity."

I shifted and stood, glaring back at him. "Never. Not while there are still stars in the sky."

43

———

Samantha

More and more of the lights flared to life around me, their voices whispering in my mind. I turned about in wonder. "Who are they?" I asked the Fates.

A shadow moved in front of the lights, and I recognized the dimly lit form of the Crone, hunched and beaten down by the weight of eternity itself. "They're beliefs—abandoned power, left to imprison the Dark God forever."

Join us, the lights whispered as they multiplied.

It was bright enough now that I could see all three Fates silhouetted against the lights. I turned to the Mother, who didn't speak in riddles. "I don't understand."

"Gods and goddesses draw their power from beliefs," she said. "To imprison the Dark Wolf God in the Dreamlands, the Moon had to sacrifice part of her power and imprison it in the pylons. When you released the Dark Wolf God, you released the beliefs that powered the wall as well."

You released us, and we will release you. Join us.

I felt them all around me—sensations of warm sunlight and

cool night air. Thousands of beliefs, power waiting to be claimed. *Needing* to be claimed.

Become one with us, they beckoned. *Help us.*

I felt their desperation, an urgent need to act. Rather than making a difference in the world with their power, they'd been trapped, tasked with holding back a god for all eternity—a god who didn't deserve to be chained.

"And if I go to them?" I asked, dreading the answer.

"Then everything you were ceases to be—you'll no longer be a shifter or fae, but a bearer of belief. A goddess, in a way," the Mother said.

Goddess. The word rang through me like the peal of bell.

"You must choose quickly," the Child said. "The Opener of Ways has come to take your soul. As soon as he does, you'll join him in the Deadlands and lose your choice forever."

"Why me?" I whispered as my mind grew numb with shock and the urgency of the moment. "How am I worthy of this?"

We see the beliefs you carry, the lights whispered. *We knew you'd be strong enough to carry us as well.*

"Beliefs?"

Beliefs, the voices echoed. *They have been a part of you always, but you have never fully embraced them—not like you embraced us.*

It was like their words pulled a veil from my mind. Thousands of tiny lights appeared around me like fireflies dancing in the wind, a thousand flickering moments, each with a belief pulsing at its heart—a belief in me, in what I could be.

I reached out and drew my fingers through them, a new vision rising as each touched my skin. I saw the crowd in the barn roaring as I entered the fighting ring as a girl, cheering as I put down a wolf twice my size. I saw my mother watching from the shadows, though I'd thought she'd never come—believing that I had the strength, knowing that I would make her proud. I saw Savy and Jax a dozen times over as we fought bikers in bars or bloodthirsty demons and even the Dark Wolf God himself. They'd trusted me, put their lives in my hands, knowing I would stand with them against the world when no one else would.

I saw Selene crying after I'd saved her brother, and Sarion and Kass and Mel shielding me from the queen's monsters. I saw my mother giving me one last look as she leapt for Ayanna's throat. All of them had believed in me, been willing to risk their lives, certain that if they could just buy me a little more time, I could triumph, make a difference in the world.

My throat clenched, and my body shook. A thousand beliefs, and I felt so profoundly unworthy.

You carry the beliefs of gods, the voices whispered as the firefly-like lights entwined around my fingers.

I felt Auren's awe as I battled his brother, Sigrun's eye judging that I was worthy, and even the Oracle, knowing I was strong enough to face the future she'd foreseen.

And everywhere, everywhere around me, there was Cadean. Fighting against me. Testing me. Following me in the shadows. Pulling me across the barrier. Willing me back to life when I lay limp in his arms.

Thundering through it all was the power of *his* belief—unwavering, unfaltering, and drowning out all the others. He'd feared for me, but he'd never once doubted what I was capable of, what I could become.

I felt him then, still fighting for me, still believing that somehow, I could return to him, despite knowing there was no chance.

I felt his pain and suffering through our bond, raw and untamed and furious. I knew then that it would be his unrelenting belief in me that would break him in the end.

My chest clenched. "I have to get back to him."

"Do not choose eternity for a man," the Mother cautioned as

she stepped close. "The path before you is hard, so do not choose it lightly."

"Your life will become a litany of loss," the Crone added, her voice bitter and tired. "You'll watch as mortals make foolish choices again and again, helpless to change their fate. You'll watch as everyone you know and love grows old and sick and dies, but you'll be barred from the Deadlands, never to run with them."

I'd never see my mother again or thank her. I'd have to watch Savy and Jax die, their children die, their grandchildren die. Mel and Kass, too. One day, they'd be ripped from me, while I lived on and on and on.

"Once you accept the burden, you'll never be able to put it down. Your duty will no longer be to yourself or your own hopes and desires, but to the Dreamlands. It will be relentless, unending, and in time, you'll think of the Dark Wolf God's imprisonment as a release."

The young girl grasped my hand. "That is why you must choose this life for yourself."

The choice stood before me like a yawning chasm, ready to swallow me up. But I had no time to think, no time to consider. The Opener was closing in, and my mate was still in the Dreamlands, fighting for his life.

My mate.

No one had ever believed in me as fiercely as he had—but I believed in *him*. I would stand against the world, not for a single lifetime, but until there was nothing left of the earth but dust among the stars.

I looked up at the waiting beliefs, a sea of candles drifting in the night. I could feel their desire to make a difference, just as fierce as mine.

I knew the truth now. My purpose hadn't been to free Cadean from his prison, or to destroy the vines, or to even kill

Ayanna. My purpose still burned within me, a wildfire that couldn't be put out, that would *never* be put out. *The thing that will not let you stop when every part of you wants to die.*

"I accept the cost," I said as I held out my hand. "Help me protect the Dreamlands. Help me protect the man I love."

44

____

Cadean

Pain exploded down my spine as the Opener of Ways slammed me into the ground and pinned my deadened right arm to the stone floor. He pressed his blade within a millimeter of my throat, and my left arm quaked as I held it back.

"Why do you still fight? She's dead, and you cannot change her fate! Yield!"

Never.

It didn't matter that it was hopeless.

I fought now because I hadn't fought hard enough while she'd been alive. Because I hadn't been fast enough or wise enough to stop this. Because I hadn't been strong enough to break through the queen's magic and protect her.

I fought because this fight was all I had left of her.

I wanted to hold her one last time before he took her soul. I wanted to pull her to me again and never let go.

"She's mine!" I growled, shoving him off me.

"Then you will have nothing!" His khopesh flashed in the light as he raised it high, and then he brought it down swiftly like a headsman.

For a second, there was only the blade.

Then the world went white as a shockwave of magic ripped over me. I was suddenly tumbling in a sea of power, gasping for breath, unsure where my body began and ended.

The Opener of Ways bellowed as he was lifted into the air. He crashed into the wall, pinned by streams of moonlight—by more power than I'd ever imagined possible. Waves of force rippled through the air, prickling my skin like the sting of an icicle or a numbed hand held too close to the fire. I tasted honeysuckle and the sweet perfume of jasmine—a signature I knew as well as my own.

Her signature.

It was impossible. It couldn't be, and yet I *knew*.

Flipping over in the rubble, I shoved myself to my knees, and my breath stopped.

Samantha.

She was a supernova of light floating in the air above my head.

I could barely look at her, but neither could I take my eyes away. Sheathed in a flowing silver dress, she was whole, her skin smooth and healed. Her blonde hair danced in the wind, as long now as when we'd first met. She was breathtaking and beautiful and unbelievably powerful.

She descended to the earth like an angel, her eyes blazing with the white-hot fury of hell. With a snap of her wrist, the Opener flipped off the wall and crashed down onto the stones, sliding across the floor to her feet.

As I gaped in awe, she jammed her foot down on his chest and bared her teeth. "Keep your *fucking* hands off my *mate*."

～

Samantha

The Opener of Ways glared up at me, his face contorted with rage. He pushed against the bonds of my magic, his power hammering into me like a wrecking ball. "Who do you think you are?"

"I am the guardian of the Dreamlands," I gritted through clenched teeth.

"You should be dead! You are mine by right!"

His arrogance soured my mouth, and without fully understanding what I was doing, a thread of my magic wrapped around my foot, taking the form of a stiletto heel. I pushed the point against his chest. "The only god I belong to is my *mate*, and he belongs to *me*."

Cadean.

He knelt in the dust and rubble of the Well of Life, a shocked expression chiseled into his face. His flesh was covered with blood and lacerations, and his right arm hung limp. I could feel the pain shuddering through his body as if were my own. It *was* my own.

My throat tightened as the reality of it all sank in.

You have the power to bring him to his knees and bind him with bonds that cannot be broken.

The oracle's prophecy had come true, but not how I'd imagined. I'd bound him with bonds of love that had pulled me back from death itself, bonds that I cherished more than any power ever given to me.

Once, I'd hated him more than anything in the world, but now, he was the only one I wanted to see when I opened my eyes in the morning.

And I'd nearly lost him forever.

Whatever pain I had yet to endure, he was worth it, a thousand times over.

"How?" The word fell from Cadean's lips like a prayer.

"The Moon gave up part of her power to imprison you. She abandoned it and *you* and the *Dreamlands*. That power chose me to bear it and be the protector of this place—a new Moon, as it were."

How could I even begin to explain what had been asked of me or what I'd given up?

How could I explain that even if the Fates had offered me a life of relentless torture, I would've taken it just to come back to him?

"You're nothing but an abomination!" the Opener snarled as he shifted beneath the bonds of magic that pinned him to the floor. "The gods have gone mad. I will make your life hell, and you will wish that you hadn't forsaken your fate."

Cadean leapt forward with a growl and seized the Opener's sword. He swung it high, but I raised my hand to stop him.

I glanced down at the furious god pinned beneath me. "Let me make this crystal clear. I know the weave to bind a god. You're not getting up until we reach an understanding."

The Opener spat in contempt.

"First, you will leave this realm forever and never trouble our dreams again." I leaned forward a little so that the point of my stiletto heel dug further into his chest. "My second demand is for the fae. They die young because of the withering curse. You will release your claim on them, and I will release you from your bonds."

"Their souls are mine, even if yours will not be," he said sharply. "I will not give them up."

I'd defeated Ayanna and destroyed her source of power, but I'd also taken away the only way the fae had to prolong their lives against the curse. Rather than living for centuries on end, they wouldn't even survive as long as a human. Even if Ayanna hadn't shared the fruits of her garden fairly, I'd taken away the only hope they'd had.

I had to do something. The fae here were my people now, my responsibility.

I lifted my eyebrow at him. "I could bind you for a thousand years, just like Cadean was."

It was a hollow threat. I didn't have the skill yet to replicate the wall, and more importantly, I would never imprison beliefs the way the Moon had. But the Opener didn't need to know that.

His yellow eyes flared with anger—but also a flicker of doubt. "You cannot keep me here. I serve a purpose. I have a duty!"

He strained against my magic again. I stumbled back against the sudden rush of power, but Cadean grabbed me, supporting my magic with his own.

"And I have a duty to *them*. How long are you willing to rot?" I asked.

"Whether I rot or not, there is nothing I can do. The Undying Court were cursed by the lord of Death himself, and they must free themselves." The Opener let his head fall back, a wolfish grin cutting across his face. "It is not for the gods to decide, but them—and it seems you are some kind of excuse for a goddess now."

Cadean released my hand and stepped forward so that he loomed over the prone form of the Opener. "You play by the rules, so bend them. Stay your hand for fifty years. That's nothing to the gods or the fae. Give them a chance to find the cure to their curse. Put fate back into their hands, if only for a time."

"I will not negotiate with you!"

Cadean knelt beside the Opener and tapped him on the nose with his own blade. "The other gods didn't lift a finger when I was imprisoned. What makes you think they'll come for you, *old friend*? In fact, your imprisonment would be rather convenient for some of them that we both could name, or am I wrong?"

The Opener gritted his teeth and thrust with his magic, but I was ready for him this time and drew the bonds tighter. Every muscle in my body screamed with exhaustion, and over-whelming relief poured through me when at last, he dropped his head back in submission.

"Fifty years if I never have to see either of you again," he muttered, shutting his eyes.

Cadean gave me a questioning look: was that acceptable to me?

The shock of it made me almost drop my weave. I had the fate of a god in my hands. I was the one calling the shots, the one controlling the situation.

Would fifty years be enough? Would a century?

In all the time that the fae had been in the Dreamlands, they hadn't found a cure. But Ayanna had been focused on her own power and not the fate of her people. Maybe they'd find a way. I would help them find a way.

"Fifty years," I said as I released the weave restraining the Opener. The moment my magic retreated, the air flooded with the scent of incense, and my mouth went as dry as the desert.

Cadean's feet spread into a battle stance, and he summoned his magic. I mirrored him, preparing to chain the Opener once again if he made a move to attack.

Paying us no heed, the Opener simply rose and dusted himself off. "I'll not forget *any* of this."

"That's rich, coming from a god who just tried to behead my mate and steal my soul," I said. "Never set foot in the Dreamlands again."

He regarded me with an expression as cold as iron, and then a reluctant smile curled the corners of his mouth. "I think the

Fates have done me a favor in the end. I doubt I could've borne eternity with you dwelling in the land of the dead."

Cadean threw the Opener's sword as his feet. He retrieved it, and then, with a rush of cold desert air, he was gone, and I was at last alone with the man who mattered more to me than the whole world.

45

———

Cadean

Samantha stood before me, radiant with light and power, but I could barely believe she was real. That she'd returned.

She took my hand with a smile, warm and beautiful and utterly enrapturing. "Are you okay?"

I gaped in utter shock.

"Me? You ask about *me*?" I grasped her hand and pulled her close. "Everything I feared came true, and yet here you are. I still can't believe it."

My beautiful mate traced her fingers along the line of my jaw. "Here I am."

She pushed up onto her toes and kissed me gently, her soft lips like warm silk slipping against mine. It was long and sweet, and I lost myself in her touch, in the unmistakable and irrefutable knowledge that she was here. That she was mine.

The Well of Life shook, and loose stones clattered to the ground, but I was too overwhelmed with wonder to give it any heed.

"How is this even real?" I asked as I searched her eyes for the impossible.

She entwined her fingers with mine. "Because you believed in me, Cadean. Because I couldn't face eternity without you."

"But you're not..." I shook my head. "You're a *goddess* now."

That made the corner of her lips turn up in a rueful smile. "You realize, of course, that means you're stuck. You'll never be free of me."

"I'm free *because* of you." I wrapped my arm around her back and pulled her tightly against me. "My people are free. Forever will not be long enough for me to make it up to you."

"Then you'd better start."

I lifted her chin and kissed her again, as if somehow, it was all a cruel trick of the Fates, an illusion, and that she would vanish from my arms at any moment.

But she didn't.

The room shook again, and more stones rained from above. A stone pillar snapped free, and I spun Samantha out of the way as it shattered across the broken and jagged floor.

She glanced at the unstable ceiling above. "On the other hand, forever is going to be a very long time if we get buried alive. There's a portal to the garden, but I don't know how to open it. Can you?"

"Yes. I'll teach you how, but for now, let's get the fuck out of here."

Protected by its magic, the ornate archway was the only thing in the chamber that hadn't melted away. Placing my hand against the stone, I poured my power into it, igniting runes around the edges. The portal materialized.

I glanced back at the Well of Life and its twisted columns. It was a place of death and murder and sorrow—a macabre temple to Ayanna and her ambition. Standing aside, I drew the power of the earthquake until my muscles hurt and every bone in my body was shuddering with its thrum, then released it into the stone.

The quake rippled up the wall like the stones were water. The melted forms of vines and columns shattered, raining slabs of stone down around us. I pulled Samantha through the portal as the Well collapsed, burying Ayanna's sacrificial pit, her broken throne, and what traces remained of her body.

We emerged into the queen's garden with aftershocks rumbling beneath our feet. The massive fruiting vines that had once filled the place with life had all turned to stone. Like a thousand flying buttresses, they cascaded down the terraces winding out into the city below.

Samantha gripped one of the dangling fruits and snapped it off the vine at its narrow stem. She turned the stone over in her hand. "I took away their cure. I hope fifty years is enough time for them to find another."

"That was never a cure," I said, kicking over one of the vines. "It was fruit grown from power and blood taken from unwilling victims. It was little more than a trick of the queen to keep her court in chains and blind her people with hope. You will help them find a way. I believe that there's nothing you cannot do."

She looked up at me, doubt in her eyes for the first time since her return. "The Fates and the Opener said not to interfere. That I'm bound by rules now."

I laughed. "Gods, Samantha. When have you ever listened to the rules?"

Her eyes twinkled as she let the petrified fruit slip from her fingers. "A fair point from someone who would know."

I took her by the hand. "Come, let's see the city you saved."

I closed my eyes and shifted to my phoenix form, with plumage as black as night. She swung her leg over my neck and seized ahold of the feathers covering it. With her a goddess now, she no longer needed a saddle. I launched myself into the air, and we soared up out of the garden.

With the sun just breaking over the horizon, I circled

the base of the palace, sweeping low over the city. The streets had cracked and buckled where they lay atop the vines, and the corners of some houses had collapsed, yet it was a far cry from what would have happened if the vines had died.

We will help them rebuild, I promised.

The fae below us fled in terror as my shadow swept over them, and I took a grim satisfaction that I knew Samantha wouldn't share. Despite her affection for them, they'd been preying on my lands and people for centuries.

Let them run.

"It'll take a long time to earn their trust," Samantha said.

You're their protector now. You'll help them, and you'll keep the Dark Wolf God at bay.

She tensed. "You haven't forgiven them?"

They have no need to fear me, but the balance needs light and dark. Let me remain the villain of their legends and the nightmare that stalks the shadows. You can be their hope and guide in the years to come.

Whether they realized it or not, she had saved them from their queen. One day, I was certain, she would help save them from their fate.

I turned to the southeast, toward Shadowstone, marveling as I looked to the horizon. The wall was gone, and I could fly as far as I wanted. I'd never again hit the edge of the barrier or beat my wings against it in frustration, unable to climb higher.

For the first time in a thousand years, I would be able to roam these lands. We'd do it together, discovering the world anew.

Samantha leaned forward, pressing her face against my feathers. I savored the warmth of her body and the soft touch of her arms wrapped around my neck. She was my freedom and my joy, and she was mine.

We soared low over Frostfall and the Red Mountains, but we didn't stop until we'd reached Shadowstone.

I swooped upward in front of the wide balcony leading to my room, then shifted back into the form of a man. Samantha cried out in surprise as we dropped the last few meters down onto the stone, and I twisted to catch her in my arms.

"We need to work on our dismount if we're going to do that again." She laughed, eyes sparkling. "You nearly gave me a heart attack, shifting like that in midair."

"Who said anything about dismounting?" I asked, setting her down on the stone railing and slipping between her legs.

"Fates, Cade!" she said, glancing down over her shoulder. "It's three hundred feet to the bottom. If I fall—"

"You'll be fine because you're a goddess now. Because I will catch you. Because there's no danger that you cannot face, mortal or divine."

I pulled her head to mine and kissed her fiercely, with the force of all the pent-up emotions knotted in my chest. Hope. Desire. Terror. I'd held so much in for so long—but no longer. Samantha was mine, now and forever.

Her lips parted, and her tongue traced over mine, sending waves of delight racing along my skin. I leaned into her, and she gave a squeak, breaking off the kiss to glance back at the abyss behind her. "Fucking hell, that's a long way down."

I brushed the hair out of her face and turned her chin back to me. "You don't have anything to fear anymore, my queen. You're limitless now. Never forget that."

～

Samantha

My heart was beating a hundred miles per hour.

Limitless.

I didn't even know how to fathom that. I might be a goddess, but damn, I still had mortal instincts, and sitting three hundred feet in the air was enough to make my head spin.

I'd climbed down this same wall once to escape Cadean, but that was far different than sitting high on the balcony with a god between my legs.

There was an impossible thrill to it, and I had to admit, the part of me that loved danger was excited beyond reason. I dug my fingers into his back and pulled him closer, wrapping my legs around his waist.

"Show me what it is to be limitless," I purred.

He swept me off the balcony and spun me around. I laughed, my hair whipping in the wind—a true laugh of joy and relief and thankfulness.

I kissed him as he drew me in. "I love you, Cadean, and I'm never going to stop."

"I didn't know what it was to be complete until I met you," he said as he carried me and laid me down on the bed. "You saved me when you chose me, my beautiful mate. You are my love and my goddess."

I pulled him down on top of me and brushed my lips softly against his, each touch an invitation to discover more. To become one forever. "Tell me, what does it mean to be your goddess?"

The corner of his mouth turned up in that half smile I knew so well.

"Unending service and devotion," he said, swiftly pinning my hands above my head.

My chest rose and fell in anticipation as my body arched against his. "I hope you realize that I will accept nothing less than eternal adoration."

He slowly kissed down my neck. "I'll give you more than adoration. I will worship you in ways you never imagined, and I will love you without end."

46

Frostfall, Cadean's Realm—two weeks later

Samantha

The feasting hall at Frostfall hummed with activity and the chatter of voices. Laughing and shouting werefoxes competed with those trying to sing along with the harper or drum out the beat of his song on the table.

The whole village had nearly returned in the weeks since the wall fell, despite it being midwinter.

"It didn't feel right for us not to be here for the midwinter holidays," Selene had explained.

The werefoxes had un-boarded their houses and made repairs, then burned the dead fae and monsters from the battle on the plain. Too bulky to remove and too wet to burn, they'd left the severed highway of vines for summer, an ominous reminder of how close the queen had come.

Cadean and I had helped them the best we could and brought food and supplies from Shadowstone. The joyous return had, of course, required a feast. And as always, that would mean hangovers for all.

My heart was full as I watched Selene zipping back and forth like a bee. I'd offered her a spot at the high table, but she'd refused, preferring to be in the mix. I'd felt the same once, the old habits of a bartender fading hard, but now my position as the Dark Wolf God's mate required that I play a different role.

We'd only told Auren and our inner circle the truth of what happened in the Well of Life. There were plenty of rampant rumors, and the villagers knew that Cadean and I had defeated the queen, but not about what I had become—though there was no hiding the new power that emanated from me.

Thankfully, no one was brave enough to ask. I wanted to keep my transformation under wraps as long as I could. I wasn't comfortable yet with what it even meant to be a goddess, let alone how I should act. For now, I was happy just to be Sam. To be with my mate and my friends. To be with my people and surrounded by their joy.

Wreathes of antlers had been hung above us, and Cadean and I sat like a king and queen, our council beside us. While I still felt awkward in my role, Cadean held absolute command over the room, a perfect king for this wild place and people. The shadows that flowed to him danced in the warm firelight, and I could see his contentment despite the steely set of his jaw.

Full plates of roots and venison forgotten, Fang was fleecing Wulfric at dice, while I made small talk with Mel, my constant companion.

Auren, half-drunk and lounging in his chair to Cadean's right, bellowed over us all. "No, I am not helping you rebuild that fates-damned fae city. That's your mess. You clean it up."

"Come now, brother," Cadean rumbled. "You have nothing better to do, and you know it."

Auren scoffed and folded his hands behind his head. "I have plenty to do, and it begins with a pair of nymphs and a barrel of wine I've been saving for a special occasion. I've done enough for you already."

I raised my brows and butted in. "Like how you hunted down and practically defeated the queen in single combat? I think I heard something about that."

Some rather *embellished* stories had started circulating around town since his arrival, and I had no doubt of their original source.

Cadean smirked and raised his goblet. "Ah, then let's drink to my brother, the great hunter."

I toasted as well.

Auren's expression knotted in annoyance. "I saved you from being drained by the vines during the battle, didn't I?"

"Wasn't that the other way around?" I asked, then jammed a hunk of succulent venison in my mouth.

Auren put his feet down and leaned forward. "You two would have been lost without me, and you know it. Fates, that's the last time I do anything for free."

"I gave you our father's fucking axe. You can't complain about compensation," Cadean grumbled.

"That was for the girl." Auren gestured at me with his fork like I was a piece of meat. "Anyway, the bloody thing is a nightmare to wield. I'm going to hang it over my mantel just so that I can relish your expression every time you visit. That's about all it's good for."

Cadean gave him a furious and hateful look that only siblings could master.

Auren shoved back from the table and rose. "Anyway, I know when I'm not welcome. One of your maids stole my boots this morning and left a live fish in its place." He raised his eyebrow at me. "You wouldn't know anything about that, would you?"

I shook my head, but it was impossible to keep the hint of a smile from my lips.

"I thought so," he grunted, and finished his drink with a

long, satisfied sigh. "I *will* miss the mead from this place—not to mention the meadmaker."

His gaze drifted across the room to where Selene was pouring wine and laughing brightly, giving her an absolutely lascivious look.

I pointed my knife at him. "Stay away. The people here are not your playthings."

Auren smirked, then sauntered off through the feasting hall in her direction.

"Your brother is an absolute ass," I said to Cadean.

"He's always been that way. Gods never change, you know?"

I took his hand and squeezed it. "I'm glad you did."

He brushed his thumb gently over my knuckles. "For you, little wolf, I would change the stars themselves."

Although he was wrapped in shadows, his presence was sunlight on a winter's day and his voice like cool water running over my skin. My heart was full and glowing like the great hearths at the center of the hall.

He'd fought against death itself for me, even when he thought there was no hope. He'd bought me time to choose my path. To become what I needed to be.

In my heart, I knew that I'd chosen him long before, when I'd first taken the golden thread of our bond from the Fates. We'd always been meant for each other, moonlight and deep shadow.

Cadean slipped his hand from mine and leaned back in his chair, gesturing out across the hall. "Someone has their eye on you."

Sigrun was weaving her way between the tables, long gray hair swaying and a brimming mug of mead held precariously in her raised hand.

"I'm glad you had the sense to sit at the high table this time around," she said as she mounted the dais.

I grinned at the tough old werefox. "I saw your smoke. You stayed through everything—even with the queen's army practically on your doorstep."

"I had faith you'd come through," she said, her single eye twinkling. There was something about the way she said it that was more than praise, a deep belief that warmed my soul. She sniffed, then gestured to Cadean with her mug. "I was a little more worried about that one, but he did all right by you in the end, I suppose."

My brow furrowed. What exactly did she mean? We hadn't told anyone but Auren and Cadean's advisors about what had happened in the Well of Life. She was—reputedly—a seer or something like it, so could she see what I was?

I opened my mouth to ask, but Sigrun waved her hand dismissively and motioned for me to follow. "There'll be plenty of time to chew the fat later. I have an old friend who wants to speak with you. Come along."

Making my excuses to Mel, I rose and followed the old werefox through the main hall and out of the side door. The night was still and cold, and a thousand stars pierced the clear sky.

I stopped in my tracks as my chest tightened.

The Moon stood on the hillside, silhouetted against the horizon, wrapped in a white pearlescent cloak with her ice-blonde hair pulled over her shoulder.

I tensed and took a step away, but Sigrun pressed a hand lightly against my back, pinning me in place. "I think some fences need to be mended. Or made."

I glanced back into the hall at Cadean, sitting at the high table.

"This is between the two of you. It has nothing to do with him," she said, then cleared her throat. "Well, it probably has quite a bit to do with *him*, but it's for the two of *you* to sort out Moon to Moon."

How did she know the Moon? Who the fuck was Sigrun, anyway?

She patted me lightly. "Best of luck, dear."

Then she slammed the door shut, and I was left beneath the dark sky, alone with the stars and Moon.

I took a deep breath of the cold night air, then slowly made my way toward the silent woman in white. I called a trickle of moonlight around me, changing my shoes into snow boots and my shoulder wrap into a heavy white parka. The Moon could be elegant and perfect to her heart's delight in her fancy cloak, but I wanted to be cozy—also, preferably inside by the fire and far away from her, but that didn't seem to be in the cards at the moment.

The crisp snow crunched beneath my boots as I rounded the low wall and headed up the hillside.

The Moon watched me approach with a cold, judging eye. "The Dreamlands has a new moon, I see."

It was impossible to read her emotions. I could almost feel them lurking at the edge of sensation. Fury. Resentment. Sadness.

But nothing showed on her face.

When I didn't answer right away, she sighed and looked out across the snow-covered plain, letting her gaze drift over the trail of dead vines and the burned-out funeral pyres beside them. Her lips tightened with the faintest hint of resentment. "Maybe you will do a better job of watching over this place than I did."

Whatever she felt, she had more control than I'd ever had. But then again, she'd had thousands of years to practice.

Hopefully, she was here to make peace. Maybe, if she forgave me, she'd help me learn.

"How do I watch over them?" I asked. "I'm not sure what it means to be the Moon or a goddess."

Her gaze drifted to the stars above. "It means that when people look up and pray for help, it'll be you they're speaking to, not me."

I swallowed. There were some serious implications to that statement. "Will I hear them?"

"You'll feel it here," she said, touching her chest. "Their beliefs, their hopes and dreams. All of it. But you'll have to learn to listen."

"And do I answer?"

She shook her head, then met my eyes. "Your job isn't to answer prayers. You're a mirror, there to reflect their own strength back to them and to remind them that they aren't alone. That there's someone watching over them." The hard line of her perfect lips bent slightly with the hint of a smile. "It seems I should have kept more of an eye on you."

"Are you mad?"

"I'm furious," she said. Her voice was soft and steady, but the word rammed into me like a knife. All was not forgotten or forgiven.

"The Dark God is your problem now. You released him, and you'll have to deal with the consequences."

"He's not who you think he is. He's the protector of this place. He swore an oath to never threaten the waking world again." I straightened my spine, and without thinking, my foot slipped back into a fighting stance. "I won't let you imprison him."

She sighed with a hint of remorse. "I don't have the power to anymore, or the desire. I never wanted to imprison him in the first place, but I believed he'd never change. I think that was the real prison I made for him."

A hint of her emotions slipped through the cracks. Anger for sure—but at herself as much as me. Regret and guilt. Sadness.

"I understand why you did it. You were trying to protect your people. Your children."

"Did I, in the end?" she asked, though I doubted the question was for me. "I think I may have deprived the world of a voice it needed, that fear of the wild. Maybe things will change now that he's back. You've changed him for the better—we all owe you thanks for that."

She folded her hands in front of her, and despite the flawless mask she wore, I could see that she was tired and emotionally spent. "You've taken on a great burden, whether you know it or not, and I don't envy you. The Dreamlands and its people are yours now. Watch over them. And *him*."

"I will."

The Moon turned and started to walk away through the snow. "Come to me if you ever need counsel. We'll never be sisters, but I will teach you what I can."

A tingle of frost rushed over my cheeks as she slowly faded, leaving the Dreamlands in my hands forever.

It was daunting, but I knew I was ready. This was the path I had chosen, not just because of Cadean, but for me as well. To be a protector. To do what good I could in a ruthless world.

That chance was worth the burden.

The heat of Cadean's gaze warmed my skin as I returned to the feast. Wrapped in wisps of darkness, he was almost impossible to see in the shadows of the great hall, except for the glint of his fierce blue eyes.

"Hiding from someone?" I asked, unable to repress the grin that formed at the thought.

He stepped out, draping the darkness over his shoulders like a cloak.

"Why? Should I be worried?" He chuckled, but I heard the slightest hint of concern.

I scrunched up my nose. "Probably not. But I don't think we'll be invited over for dinner any time soon."

I started back toward the warm light of the open door, but he took my hand. "Come. There's something I want to show you."

We hiked through the snow up to the edge of the woods, to a place where two ridges met. We descended into a small clearing, where a stone archway stood in the center. I ran my fingers over the pattern of chasing wolves that had been carved into the cold, dark basalt and felt the low thrum of its magic. It was a portal.

"Where does it lead?"

"Magic Side."

I raised my eyebrows. "Didn't you say something about leaving the waking world alone?"

The Dark Wolf God released a subtle laugh. "I might recall something like that." Some of the playfulness left his eyes as he took my hand. "I can't undo what I did or bring back the people I killed, but maybe I can give them this."

He gestured to the valley before us and the plains and mountains beyond. "Your people need a place to run, a place to breathe the air as it once was and escape from the concrete prison they've built around themselves. As long as they respect the land, this valley is theirs."

It was pure and beautiful in the starlight. I inhaled, savoring the scents of the pines and brush, of the clear night air and the newly fallen snow. I imagined Jaxson and Savannah and the pack being able to run as far and free as they wanted, with no cars to dodge and nothing to hold them back. To run all the way to the mountains if they wanted and learn to love this place like I did.

I met Cadean's eyes. "It may take time for them to trust, just like the fae."

"They'll trust you. Bring them through when they're ready." He squeezed my hand. "For my sake, please."

"I will."

He turned me to face him and smiled down at me. "The Dreamlands will always be your home, but I will never keep you here. There's another door for you in Shadowstone. Use it to visit this place or Magic Side anytime you wish."

The thought of seeing my pack again made my chest swell with joy. I could be there for the birth of Savy's twins. I could be Auntie Sam and maybe even take them on weekends. I could watch them grow and...

My throat tightened.

I knew I'd lose my friends one day. That was part of the cost. But I'd be able to watch over them and their children for all the generations to come. I could repay the love and trust they'd shown me a thousand times over.

I thanked the Fates for the gift they'd given me.

My vision slightly blurred, and I turned away. "Should we go back to the hall?"

"No. Werefoxes never feast for only a day," Cadean said with an air of amusement. "There'll be time for drinking and dancing and hangovers later. For now, there's nothing I want more than to be with my mate."

"Then where to?"

Cadean slowly pulled me into his arms. "Come run with me, my little wolf. The wall is gone, and there are places I haven't seen in a thousand years. Places I loved, and places that are beyond your dreams." He gently brushed his lips across mine and kissed me. "I want to see all of them again, with you, for the first time."

Shadows pooled around him as the Dark Wolf God took his true form, and moonlight danced as I took mine. Light and shadow, we slipped into the night and into the lands we'd sworn to protect forever.

Thank you so much for sharing Sam and Cadean's journey with us. While they'll live on forever, this is where their series ends—though if the Fates will it, another might begin...

Our next series is a collaborative project with our bestie Linsey Hall. Book 1 is a standalone Cinderella retelling with a vampire prince and an assassin plot!

Grab it now: mybook.to/Cinders-and-Glass

If you want to be the first to know about our books you can sign up for our newsletter here: https://www.veronicadouglas.com/newsletter. We send out writing updates, sneak peeks, and covers reveals, as well as alerts for new releases and giveaways. We also have a Facebook Reader group (Veronica Douglas' Magic Side Insiders) where you can talk about books and interact with fellow readers: https://www.facebook.com/groups/veronicadouglas

And finally, if you want more of Savannah and Jaxson's story, they have their own four-book series (which put in motion all the events leading up to Wolf God). Their journey together begins with a dangerous encounter on a dark abandoned highway...

mybook.to/Wolf-Marked

Thanks again—we adore and appreciate you all!

-Veronica

In a world ruled by immortals, her only hope may lie in the heart of their darkest prince.

Read it now: mybook.to/Cinders-and-Glass

REIGN OF CINDERS AND GLASS
FATED FAIRYTALES: ELLA AND THE DARK PRINCE

When my sister Belle goes missing, I venture deep into the cursed woods to find her. Ruthless vampires rule over our kingdom, and I'm terrified she's been murdered like so many others.

As I'm searching, I'm caught by the worst immortal of them all: Prince Cassius, dark Lord of the Bloodvale. I barely escape with my life, and the memory of his cruel beauty haunts me. So does the thought that Belle might be in his castle.

When I join the mortal resistance, I get the chance to infiltrate his stronghold. I'll find Belle and fight the vampires from within. It's not easy. I'm worked to the bone by a pair of wicked sisters and danger abounds, but the secrets I discover are worth it.

The castle is filled with magic...and so am I.

I'll have to keep my mission and power hidden if I want to survive, but the prince's stormy gaze follows me everywhere. When he chooses me as his personal servant, can I hide the truth? Or will the magnetic pull between us drag me to my doom?

Reign of Cinders and Glass is a standalone Cinderella Romantasy with vampires, a dark prince, and a powerful heroine who will endure any risk to save the people she loves. Prepare for action, danger, and a steamy romance with a HEA.

Read it now: mybook.to/Cinders-and-Glass

ACKNOWLEDGMENTS

Thanks to all our readers for sticking with us on this journey! This book was written in the midst of a chaotic move back to Hawaii with our five cats. Veronica was simultaneously finishing her dissertation—as such it took a little longer to write than we anticipated, but we made it just in time! Veronica actually had to do her PhD defense the same day we uploaded the final manuscript of Forsaken Fate to Amazon, so we are very much looking forward to some sleep at last!

We would like to say a special thanks to Gene and Kyle. We couldn't have managed the move without you. Seriously. All our stuff would have been stranded in Chicago.

Linsey, Ben, Mark, and Carol—we owe you more than we could ever repay for helping us transport our family of kitties 4,000 miles. You have our eternal gratitude.

Thank you to Ash Fitzsimmons and Lexi George for your patience, incredible flexibility, and your amazing editing skills—you both went above and beyond to help us get this out.

Thank you as well to the amazing readers on our advanced review team, especially Amanda and Penny for all your last minute catches! We love your feedback, and your sharp eyes always make our books better.

We owe a huge thanks to Amber Garcia for keeping us rolling on Facebook when we go deep into our writing cave. And thanks to Caethes Faron, for her insightful analysis and support. We'd be lost without you both.

Thank you to JV Arts for designing the awesome double-wolf cover for the book. We want to also give a shoutout to JoY Author Design for creating the gorgeous character art and alternate covers that inspired our writing from the very start!

ABOUT VERONICA DOUGLAS

Veronica Douglas is a duo of professional archaeologists that love writing and digging together. After spending an inordinate amount of time doing painstaking research for academia, they suddenly discovered a passion for letting their imaginations go wild! A cocktail of magic, romance, and ancient mystery (shaken, not stirred), their books are inspired, in part, by their life in Chicago and their archaeological adventures from around the globe.

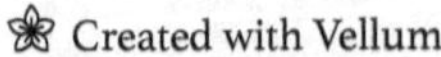 Created with Vellum